THE

PUPPET'S

BLIGHT

Book Two of The Dark Angel series

COURTNEY LILLARD

ISBN: 979-8-9858212-7-7

Cover Design by Etheric Tales & Edits | MC Damon

ACKNOWLEDGEMENTS

This book is dedicated to everyone who contributed some fraction of their time to help shape the person I am today, including my parents, siblings, friends, teachers, and colleagues from across the country. I also must thank my husband, Darren, who not only gave me the push I needed to begin writing seriously and reads all of the drafts but who also listens to my ideas with honest, eager ears.

A NOTE FROM THE AUTHOR

The Dark Angel series has gone through several changes; however, this final version combines The Shadow's Grasp and what used to be the second book titled The Guardian's Deception. Because of this, The Puppet's Blight was originally the third book in the series. This decision was not made lightly considering the amount of effort it takes to rebrand a series, as well as my readers who were familiar with the original first and second books, but each story has been kept the same. Chapter titles have also been added to every book, and the rest of the series will follow a new order, so to speak.

This note serves as a notice for those of you who may see The Guardian's Deception, whether online or a physical copy. That book will now be considered the second half of The Shadow's Grasp, and the rest of the series will be numbered appropriately. Other changes will be mentioned in future notes.

Contents

Nim-Vala
Parnic
Verona
Sindaly
Fester
Western Woods
Umbridge
Twindela
The Vale
Dala
Medina
Marinich
Umbrich

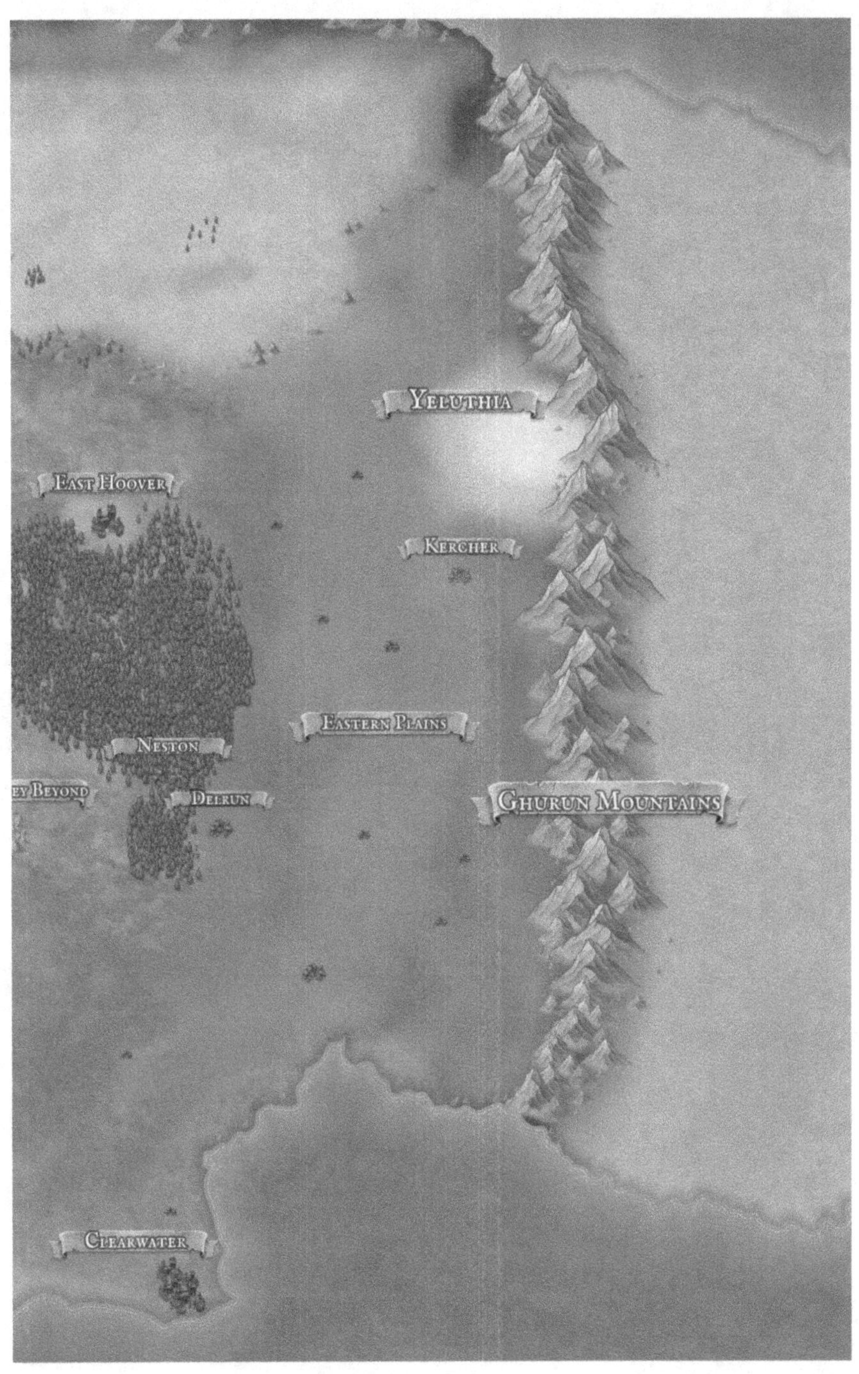

YELUTHIA
EAST HOOVER
KERCHER
NESTON
EASTERN PLAINS
EY BEYOND
DELRUN
GHURUN MOUNTAINS
CLEARWATER

Part One

Questionable Circumstances

The halls of the palace remained silent in the late evening, their stone walls cold to Grace's touch. Her hand grazed one side as she wandered aimlessly and savored the peaceful quiet.

Dinner had been strange. King Hernan and High Priest Hendal, somebody Grace spoke to often, were both absent, leaving her to eat alone, or so she thought. Once the servants brought out the main course, featuring a succulent, roasted boar paired with mouth-watering gravy, the master light mage named Emilea Bayporter joined her. They conversed a handful of times before but had always kept matters strictly professional, so she prepared for a similar discussion. Oddly enough, Lady Emilea asked rather personal questions relating to Grace's home and family before sharing more about her own life. Although the shift in subjects seemed jarring at first, Grace warmed up to the light mage almost immediately and found herself engaged in their talk.

"Is your husband here?" Grace asked while scanning the room. From what the mage shared, the man called Clearshot had an infectious personality, and she wondered what it would be like to meet him.

Emilea shook her head with a sigh, and as she glanced around, her mind went elsewhere. "I'm afraid he's been away on an assignment in Dala."

"Oh!" Grace exclaimed when she recognized the city and remembered Coura, Marcus, and Will. Emilea's following, sidelong look caused her to giggle. "My friends were reassigned to Dala as well."

At that, the master mage's eyebrows lifted in surprise before she asked for their names. After Grace explained, Emilea fell silent for a while.

"They are strong and reliable," Grace added. "I am sure if your husband is as likeable as you say, then everybody will get along well."

"Tell me about the one with the… I mean, Coura. How do you know her?" The woman's tone sounded controlled and neutral.

As Grace recalled how the two met and their shared meals in Marcus' quarters, she found herself becoming more enthusiastic. Meanwhile, she couldn't read Lady Emilea's facial features. When she ran out of things to say, the mage politely thanked her for the conversation before excusing herself. Grace left a few minutes later and went to her own room. For most of the night, she stared out her window and wondered what her friends were doing.

Did I displease Lady Emilea when I brought up those in Dala? she wondered while recalling the woman's change in behavior at the mention of them, specifically Coura. Then, she remembered her first impression of her friend. *I almost forget about the demonic presence I sometimes sense from her. As a light mage, I am sure Emilea notices the power too and dislikes her for it.*

A gentle breeze tickled Grace's face, making her realize just how awake she stayed. After grabbing a shawl to wrap around her shoulders for warmth, she strolled without a purpose, becoming lost in her thoughts. She wondered what Dala was like and when she would see everybody again; however, her mind returned to Emilea's reaction to her friendship with Coura. Over time, Grace began to consider if the master mage was justified in doubting their relationship, and her trust wavered.

Perhaps I had been too impulsive to befriend her because of how lonely I became. Do the others know about the demonic presence? I never heard anyone mention it, even when Coura was not around. But…

A longing tugged at her heart at the memory of when they met. *Everything about Coura has always been genuine. I might not know what she is, and we may have only known each other for a few months, but I truly like her. I want her to be my friend... I want to be her friend too! Could it be a new manipulation spell we are all under?*

Grace felt like striking her head against the nearest wall for having such an idea.

When she reached the opposite end of the palace, she decided to backtrack to her room. In that time, she made up her mind regarding Coura. *I will try reaching out to her tomorrow. Not only will I be able to see how Marcus and Will are doing, but I am going to ask about what she is. I believe her true reaction will reveal if she is lying or not. At least I will get some-*

"Idiot!"

Grace's mind and body froze at the word echoing through the nearest, empty corridor. She held her breath as a stream of curses followed at a much softer volume before a second voice, one she recognized, hissed in frustration.

That voice belongs to the person who sent those mysterious orders a few months ago. I could never forget it!

With as little noise as possible, she turned on her heel, ignored those farther down who paid no attention to the outburst, and followed the hushed voices to a nearby room. Just like before, they led her into the center of the palace. A metal door shined dimly in the light of a single lamp placed just outside with no one nearby. Her heart started beating faster, hammering her chest as she approached and listened to the conversation taking place.

"You had three orders, did you not? Yet here I stand, without a prince and with the base still intact!"

Another voice, much quieter than the first, responded barely loud enough for Grace to understand. "I apologize on our behalf."

"Not only did you manage to disregard my initial orders, but you screwed up the last," the angry man continued.

"I take full responsibility for the demon," a third, richer voice added.

"I don't need a reminder of where the blame should be placed," the first man growled.

"I did not know the blade could not be removed," the third voice replied, as if the first said nothing.

"Of course you didn't. Do you know why? Because you were not the one who was supposed to use the dagger to seal the demon. *You* had your orders, and *you* failed to complete them!"

A heavy pause followed before they mumbled too quietly for Grace to catch the words. She heard three footsteps and a painful-sounding slap after. Another moment of silence and more shuffling made her concerned they were preparing to leave.

Without another thought, she tiptoed to her quarters, never glancing behind even as she closed the door to her room and leaned against it. Then, she sank to the floor and listened with her breath held. She remained that way for a ridiculous amount of time before crawling into bed and pulling the covers over her head. While her body feigned sleep, her mind raced.

Those must have been the angels sent to Dala. Why did it take this long for them to return? The man claimed they failed to take the base and capture Prince Aaron. That is positive news, so why am I frightened? Somebody mentioned a demon... Could he have meant Coura? I cannot wait. I must try reaching out to her!

Grace closed her eyes and stretched her mind as far as it would go, yet she still remained enough away from Dala to prevent her from forging a connection. After another moment, her head began throbbing, which meant she used too much of her power at once.

I cannot do it, she admitted on the verge of tears while reeling in her mind. *How else can I speak with them in time?*

An idea came to her once she relaxed her tense muscles.

Master Emilea is a powerful light mage. I wonder if she would be able to lend me her energy. That would mean revealing some of what I learned though.

She contemplated her next move with growing confidence until the excitement of the evening caught up to her, and she fell into a deep sleep.

*

The first rays of sunlight peeked through the window in Grace's room, a characteristic of the space she initially didn't care for when she moved to the eastern side of the palace. That morning, she felt grateful for the signal to rise. With more enthusiasm than she'd had in days,

4

Grace washed, threw on a lavender gown, and tied her hair into a tight bun before hurrying out the door.

She greeted each person she passed with a polite smile; some were surprised to hear her speak to them and babbled a response while bowing. Grace made it a point to see if she recognized any voice among the people on her way to the mage's quarters.

Since she didn't know where Emilea could be, she stopped several of the younger humans wearing colored robes to ask. Most claimed the master mage never arrived at the palace until mid-morning, and others couldn't tell her where the woman lived in Verona. She prepared to give up hope until she recognized the high priest heading her way.

"Good day," she greeted him with a curtsy and smiled up into his jolly face.

"Why, Lady Grace! It seems like ages since I've seen you," he replied and chuckled in his gentle manner. "I suppose that's what I get for squeezing business in place of meals and gatherings."

She laughed before continuing. "Would you be able to help me find Master Emilea? I only received mixed answers."

High Priest Hendal's eyes widened a bit, and he glanced at the ceiling to consider her request. "No wonder you haven't had any luck. Lady Emilea and her family own a home just outside Verona, to the west. Where exactly, I do not know."

"I see." Her gaze lowered until she stared at the floor.

"If you would like, I can assist," he added and placed a hand on his chest.

She looked into his face again and found his cheeks raised so high by his smile that both eyes were nearly squeezed closed. *Should I tell him? I am not even sure if I will share what I heard with Lady Emilea...*

"Thank you kindly," Grace answered. "I appreciate the offer, but I am afraid it is a matter I think only the master mage can help me with."

"Oh." Hendal paused, as though startled by her answer, then he opened his mouth to say more before rethinking his words.

"Good day, High Priest," she decided to add before slipping past him to hurry toward her room. In the next few minutes, she carried a cloak in one hand and strolled outside the palace and into the streets of Verona.

*

What am I doing? Am I lost?

Despite her concern, Grace continued along the slim path leading her deeper into the woods beyond the capital city. Because of her early departure, she felt confident enough to explore until the sun crept higher in the sky. Besides the beautiful day, which seemed unnaturally warm for the middle of winter, she became reassured in her course by the well-worn trail branching off Verona's main road. She wandered on a while longer, taking pleasure in the peaceful surroundings and the fact that the guards posted at the palace entrance trusted her on her own after months of supervision.

Leafless trees allowed beams of light to break through and shine on the dead grass below. In the distance, she spotted another color besides the grays and browns. It turned out to be a brick-colored maroon, and Grace hurried toward the nearby building. The path opened into a wider space where a two-story home sat adjacent to a shallow pond.

"This must be it," she told herself against a growing anxiousness as she went to what she assumed was the front door and knocked three times as firmly as she could.

No response came, forcing her to swallow her nerves and pound a fist on the thick wood again. Her heart leap when a voice on the opposite side told her to wait a moment, and she saw a shadow beyond the curtain in the nearest window.

"How can I help you?" the master light mage asked while opening the door. A blanket had been wrapped around her shoulders, and at the sight of Grace's awkward smile, her mouth fell open before she raised a hand to cover it.

"Hello, Master Emilea." Grace curtsied, then the woman gestured for her to enter.

"It's an honor, Lady Grace. Please, take a seat. I will fetch you some food and a drink."

Emilea disappeared into the kitchen at Grace's right, so she hung her cloak up before smoothing down her hair and dress.

"Who are you?"

6

She froze and glanced over at the room to her left. Seated on the arms of a leather chair were a boy and girl, who watched the stranger with curious expressions.

"H-Hello," Grace stammered and curtsied, unable to select a proper greeting for the children.

They continued to stare as she entered the room and accepted a spot in another armchair placed across from theirs. Her body sank into the cushions, relieving most of the tension in her body. Moments later, Emilea returned with a cup of steaming tea and a sandwich Grace discovered contained slices of ham and cheese.

"I prepared extras for lunch earlier," the master mage explained and handed the dishes to Grace.

She thanked the woman for her hospitality before sipping the drink. The boy and girl hopped off the chair as their mother took a seat.

"Now, to what do I owe the pleasure of your visit?"

As the voices from the previous night echoed in her mind, Grace lowered her eyes. Emilea did not press for an answer but only waited with a friendly smile.

"I..."

She cast a glance at the children lingering behind the furniture. The light mage seemed to understand the importance of the matter then.

"Mace, will you please bring your sister upstairs while I talk with our guest?" Emilea asked and patted the boy's head.

He pouted yet grabbed the girl's arm and led her away. Once they were gone, the master mage met Grace's hesitant gaze, as if urging her to go on.

"Our talk at dinner last night reminded me of how long it has been since I spoke with my friends in Dala," she began again. "You are well aware of my goddess gift, I presume, but I am unable to reach them from this great of a distance. I am hoping you can lend me your energy."

While she sat holding a controlled expression, her palms grew sweaty.

Emilea assessed Grace, then tilted her head and narrowed her eyes. "You're lying."

"What?" she squeaked, shocked by the accurate accusation. Even as she did so, Grace realized that gave away her innocence.

The mage's smile stretched wider. "I'm a mother. I have plenty of experience from when my children and husband lie. Also, you're not good at it."

"I see." Grace's chin dipped as she contemplated her next move.

Without any sort of prompting, Emilea rose and came over to kneel in front of where she sat. Then, the woman held her hands in a comforting gesture.

"My Lady, I would be honored to work with you so you may speak to your friends; however, I sense there's more to your request. You can be honest with me."

The sincere nature of the light mage and her willingness to help snuffed out any doubt in Grace's mind. She returned Emilea's smile and nodded.

"I will tell you what I know."

***

"It's been three days since we sent a messenger to Verona and still no response!" General Tio pounded a fist on the oval desk in the conference room to emphasize his frustration.

Byron wisely remained silent and let the man vent.

The past few days had been stressful for everybody at the base and the people in Dala. News of the angels' trap and plans to destroy the area spread around the city, causing panic. Since Tio and his outer squad were injured, the remaining groups traded shifts guarding both locations. The fear became so strong Byron thought he could feel it in the crisp air.

Meanwhile, the general, his troops, and Marcus had been treated by the handful of light mages, non-magic healers, and volunteers from the city. Dala never experienced such serious conflicts and didn't expect to host the recruits for another couple months, so requesting additional mages ahead of time hadn't been a necessity, according to Tio. In their current situation, letters and messengers were on their way to Verona and Twindela, the two cities they knew for certain contained trained healers.

With the tunnel's damage, the general deemed it too dangerous to ask for help from the southeast. Four of the injured soldiers teetered on the brink of death while the colder weather brought on the threat of disease and fevers. Fortunately, all except the four could be patched up, though Byron wondered how long the break in action would last.

Not to mention Coura...

A surge of emotion tugged at his heart. How Marcus, Aaron, and Will had noticed her appearance upon their return from the Valley Beyond remained a mystery, yet he became indebted to them for alerting the rest of the squad.

Her condition hadn't changed since they carried her to the base's the medical station. The healers tended to her outward wounds, but Byron sensed something wrong underneath the surface. He detected no magical energy in her, and her pale complexion, which resulted from more than the physical wounds, baffled him.

He closed his eyes and shifted away from where he stood looking absently out the window. "We just need to be patient," he told the general while forcing his mind to deal with the matter at hand.

The man growled in response. Together, they kept to their own business for a few minutes.

Just when Byron picked up a new wave of strength, Tio spoke in a sympathetic tone. "I have yet to tell anyone about your student."

The reminder stung, though Byron tried to remain composed despite his weariness. "That's probably for the best. As I mentioned earlier, there's enough tension and paranoia in Dala. An update about how our strongest fighter is out of commission would bring on more."

"I agree," the general added. He pushed himself to his feet and approached to place his left, and now only, hand on Byron's shoulder in a reassuring manner before moving toward the door.

Although his breathing shortened and eyes itched, Bryon grew determined to act as a leader first and foremost. He followed Tio into the empty hallway, which seemed gloomier than ever. His appetite never returned over the past three days, and he knew if he stayed somewhere alone he would sink into a steady depression.

On the other hand, he wanted to be away from his companions. As soon as they returned to the base, Marcus demanded to be placed where

Coura stayed. The prince refused to leave either of their sides, though the general ordered him to remain inside at all times, Clearshot volunteered to guard the city, and Will locked himself in his room. Byron hadn't spoken to them since exiting the tunnels.

He became so detached as he trailed behind the general that he didn't notice somebody calling his name until Tio stopped and gestured with the stub on his right arm.

"Byron, wait!"

It was Will who shouted and doubled over to catch his breath when he reached them before lifting his head to reveal a bewildered gaze.

Byron leaned forward a bit, fearing the worst. "What is it?"

The young man shook his head and stared at the general.

"Out with it," Tio responded. The man's voice boomed with an authority that told them he wouldn't be left out.

Will's eyes darted back to Byron. "It's Grace. She wants to talk to us."

At first, Byron's mouth worked without sound as he processed the news. Then, he hit his forehead with the heel of his hand once he remembered the ambassador's ability. "That's right! Now how should we..."

Will stepped away and began moving down the hall toward the staircase. "She specifically requested to speak with Coura," he added.

As the two hurried to the medical station, Byron noticed the general following behind. "There's a lot to explain."

"I'll catch up sooner or later," Tio replied, and that was that.

*

Once outside the room Coura and Marcus shared, Byron ordered Will to find Clearshot and bring him there as well. The herbalist scampered off without a word, leaving Byron to internally thank the boy's sense of obedience as he pushed open the door. Two cots rested below a pair of windows with a nightstand in between, and a table stood off to the side. Its wooden surface had been littered with bottles and papers, but the space appeared rather plain otherwise.

In front of the nightstand in his own chair sat Aaron. The prince glanced up, revealing tired, reddening eyes, and stood to greet each of

10

them while Marcus pushed himself into a sitting position from where he lied on the leftmost bed.

"By all the gods, it looks like you two haven't slept in days!" the general rumbled loudly enough to startle everyone and cause the young men to blush.

In order to cover some of his embarrassment, Aaron offered his seat to Byron, who declined and walked to the farthest wall near Marcus' cot. His eyes instinctively avoided his student resting in the second bed. Her pale skin blended in too well with the white sheets, and his gut twisted at the reminder. Tio also moved out of the doorway and crossed his arms.

After a moment, Marcus and Aaron shared a look.

"Pardon my curiosity, but is there a reason you're visiting us?" the assistant general asked Byron in an innocent manner.

"Will didn't tell you?"

The two shook their heads.

Despite their situation, Byron huffed a laugh. "It seems he was in too much of a hurry," he commented before filling them in. At the mention of Grace, they instantly grew alert. He knew they became friends over the months since her arrival and how the prince informed his father of her goddess gift.

All they could do once he finished was wait. Fortunately, it didn't take long before Will and Clearshot burst in. The latter murmured a curse when he noticed Coura, then Byron watched as his friend sat on the end of her bed and analyzed her appearance. If it wasn't for the slight rise and fall of her chest, she could be easily mistaken as dead; the thought threatened to break Byron's resolve. He tore his gaze away while Will slammed the door shut and paced around as much as he could in the remaining space.

"Will, what's going on? Did Grace reach out to you?" Aaron was the first to ask.

"Just hold on," came the impatient response when the young man knit his brows together in concentration.

Byron didn't understand how the Yeluthian's mind-to-mind communication worked and prepared to inquire until an unexpected voice chimed in his head, causing his spine to stiffen.

{*Hello? Are you there?*}

Grace? Byron wondered as he felt a warm, though faint, magical energy fill the room. The sensation reminded him of the instances when a noblewoman wore perfume everybody in the immediate area could smell.

They all stared at one another, and he grew amused at seeing the general's eyes widen with awe. The silence lingered, both internally and externally, before her voice returned.

{*Please, one at a time! I cannot hear you when you send me your thoughts at once. There is a lot I must share with you; some of it I told Coura. Where is she? I cannot reach her mind.*}

No one spoke.

{*Did you hear me? Where is Coura?*}

Tio threw up his arms and shot a frustrated glare at each person present. "You're acting like a hopeless bunch, aren't you? Start focusing on the task at hand! We got a way to reach the capital, and who knows how much time we have. I'll be the spokesperson since we can't coordinate our heads. Tell me what you want me to say."

Byron was so taken back he could only look on dumbly while Clearshot instructed the man to begin by sharing their encounter with the angels and what befell Coura. It took the general a few minutes to do so. Once he finished, Grace's sorrowful voice rang out again.

{*I cannot imagine what you are going through, but what I know might relieve some of the stress from your situation. Last night, I overheard a group discussing their failure to capture a base and the prince. They must have been the Yeluthians I saw leaving the palace those months ago. I did not catch any other orders being issued. Since I would guess it is a four-day flight between Verona and Dala, you should be safe for a couple days, at the very least.*}

"General, can you ask her how she's able to speak with us from this distance?" Marcus requested while his face remained set in an impassive expression. "We were led to believe it would be too far."

As Tio closed his eyes to repeat the question mentally, Aaron echoed what was also on Byron's mind.

"They're in the palace."

Despite their growing concern, Grace's voice sounded more alive.

{Lady Emilea is here lending me her energy. I am filling her in as well. She urges you to stay in Dala until everyone is healed and the base is back to normal. Once Byron returns to the capital, the mages assigned to the southern base will leave and introduce a magical presence there.}

"She would say that," Byron muttered to himself.

Clearshot repeated his wife's name and gazed upward as his lips curled into a loving grin before he requested their spokesman express how greatly he missed her.

"This isn't the time for pleasantries," the general grumbled yet presumably relayed the message.

The Yeluthian must have only spoken to Clearshot then, for the man chuckled and settled down.

{That is all I needed to share at the moment. We can hold the connection if anybody would like to talk with one or both of us.}

Everyone opened their mouths to pounce on the opportunity.

"I'll return to my duties, thank you," Tio interrupted before taking his leave. "Keep me updated on any more news from the palace."

"Who should go first?" Marcus asked after the door closed.

When nobody volunteered, Byron figured he should resume his leadership role. *Grace? Can you hold on for a moment while we sort this out?*

{Of course.}

He cleared his throat to get their attention. "I understand we have a lot on our minds given how much has happened in three days, but it hindered our need for a proper night's rest."

No one denied his words, so Byron continued.

"We'll be safe tonight, so once you speak with Grace, it's off to bed for *each* of us. No arguments." He half-expected at least one person to protest, yet they nodded in agreement. "Who would like to start?"

"I can," Will offered. The herbalist kept his conversation brief and let them know when he finished.

"I'll speak next," Clearshot said, raised his hand, then bent his upper body forward over his hands, as if in prayer.

Will prepared to exit and opened the door only to find a medical workers bearing a tray of mugs standing in the way.

"The general ordered me to deliver sleep medicine for your group," she explained. "He also mentioned he'll slice off your hands to replace the one he lost if he catches any of you awake during the rest of the day."

Byron noticed the younger men grimace upon hearing the ridiculous threat despite the woman's wink when she set the drinks on the table.

Reluctantly, Will picked up a cup, swallowed the contents, and set it down before leaving.

Clearshot savored his time until he stood, stretched, and excused himself.

"I'll go," Marcus threw out next. While he relaxed against the bedframe, Clearshot tiptoed to the door.

"Not so fast," Byron snapped and pointed at the tray.

"I'm technically on duty," his friend joked with a shrug.

When Byron raised an eyebrow to show his doubt, Clearshot snatched a drink, tipped it back right away, then tilted the mug upside down to show it was empty before returning it to the table. "Get some rest," he suggested after.

Byron turned his attention to Marcus and Aaron as soon as the door closed. The former remained deep in thought while the prince fiddled with his fingers anxiously.

"I'm sure if anything is amiss Grace would have told us," he said to ease their nerves.

Aaron's eyes met his. "I know. It's difficult to be away, though. We need to figure out who their leader is or their motives."

"It's too much to ponder over now, let alone carry on your shoulders alone."

Before either of them could continue the conversation, Marcus faced Aaron. "You're up."

The prince grunted in confirmation and bent forward just as Clearshot had done. Byron brought Marcus his medicine so the assistant general could lie down once again.

"I asked Grace and Emilea about the soldiers and mages," the young man began between sips. "Everything is exactly the same. I assume nobody is aware of what happened in Dala yet."

"It *is* a seven-day trip on foot. Besides, the palace is one of the safest places in any situation."

Marcus finished his drink and handed the mug over before wrapping himself in the blankets and shifting to his side. In another minute, he was snoring.

"Good luck thinking clearly with *that* noise," Aaron startled Byron by joking with his eyes still closed. The prince blinked for a few seconds after, rubbed them, then rose to take his mug and exit.

"Not a bad idea," Byron muttered, complimenting the portable method.

{Byron, are you the last?}

She sounded as exhausted as he felt.

Yes, and we are all thankful for you and your gift.

There came a tickling sensation in his mind, as if she were laughing.

He stood, grabbed the lone, untouched mug, and left with a brave glance at his student. On the way back to his room, he realized he didn't have anything pressing to bring up.

Grace, my questions were answered for the time being.

{There is something Lady Emilea wishes you to know regarding Coura.}

An idea popped into his head as he sipped from his drink. *Would she be able to help us learn what's ailing Coura?*

{I believe that is what she intends to try. Can you describe what Coura was like when you found her?}

There's not much to tell, Byron answered. His heart hurt while he recalled her injuries and lack of dark or demonic energy. A pause followed as she clued the master light mage in on the situation.

{Interesting... If you remember, those I overheard yesterday evening mentioned a dagger. Emilea and I both believe they are related.}

I've never heard of a weapon that drains magical energy.

{Me neither, but Emilea says she will do some research.}

Would you two be available tomorrow at the same time?

Another pause.

{There is something you should know. Lady Emilea requests only you, her husband, and General Tio be made aware of it now. She will

be leaving Verona tomorrow morning to head south and meet you in Dala.}

Byron nearly dropped his empty mug when he approached the door to his quarters. *What? Why?*

{She is bringing several healers and dark mages assigned to be stationed there, and she hopes to study Coura's condition.}

What about her children? And the students at the palace?

{Emilea says not to worry. She will have that business taken care of before she goes. If you sent a messenger, then they should be here soon enough, so she may go with a primary reason. I am sorry, but she has not shared the details, and our connection is fading.}

Byron bit off a curse before responding. *Thank you, Grace. Please be safe; do not go looking for trouble anymore.*

The spell disappeared entirely before she could reply, leaving him alone with his thoughts. Then, sleep took over until the next morning. If it wasn't for the medicine, he would have continued to ponder what they discussed for the rest of the day.

*

Tio took it upon himself to inform his soldiers about the news from Verona. At first, they were thrilled because the rogue angels fled so they could rest easier for a couple days; however, the general's commanding fist still demanded guards posted at attention.

Nobody from the capital heard from Grace over the following three days, though the consistent nights' sleep resulted in clearer heads and more energy to spare. Aaron and Will felt active enough to practice and work out in the training ground, leading to Marcus begging to join until one of the healers assisted him to a bench outside. Even then, the assistant general requested a sword in order to demonstrate motions as he sat. Byron also rested better knowing the base steadily returned to normal, if not a more defensive state.

Between himself, Will, Aaron, Marcus, and the medical station staff who checked in once or twice a day, Coura was never left alone, not that her progress changed. She remained unconscious, growing paler and weaker, in Byron's opinion. He would often talk to her about what went on in the base in order to keep her company. He believed the words helped, or at least succeeded in keeping him sane.

16

As he sat in the chair at her bedside six days after speaking with Grace, he began recalling their former lives at the Magical Arts Academy. He chuckled to himself over some incident involving his student's stubborn behavior before noticing several pairs of footsteps echoing down the hallway. Without warning, the door flew open and there stood Master Emilea in her travel pants and vest, sporting a riding cloak and windblown hair.

He rose in preparation to greet her, but she gestured for him to stay seated.

"It's been a while, Master Byron," she said abruptly, entered, then stopped at the foot of Coura's bed. Behind her, Clearshot, Will, Aaron, and Marcus trailed inside to observe the light mage.

"What do you think?" her husband asked after a moment before wrapping his arms around her shoulders.

Emilea shook her head, and a baffled expression replaced the initial concern. "This can't be the same person, can it?"

Hesitantly, she moved to the side opposite Byron and knelt next to Coura before placing a hand on the colorless forehead, lifting the closed eyelids, and checking for a pulse on the wrist. "You claim she appeared out of nowhere?" the woman asked while focusing her attention on her patient.

"Yes," Aaron answered with visible apprehension. "We noticed a flash of light from where we passed in the tunnel system. When we backtracked, we found Coura on the ground just like this."

"Her condition hasn't changed since?"

This time, Byron replied. "Not at all. The wound on her left side and the other cuts and bruises are mending on their own."

Emilea pulled the blanket down to Coura's waist before inspecting the injury. After the squad brought her to the base, the healers torn off the mangled clothing in order to clean up the blood and bandage her body. They then dressed her in a loose shirt and pants meant to limit discomfort.

Everybody besides Emilea politely turned away when she lifted the clothing covering Coura's midsection. Byron sensed magical energy flowing and chanced a glance. The woman's palms hovered over the wound as a faint glow emitted from underneath. Within another minute, she removed her hands to reveal only unmarred skin. The master mage repeated her healing about a dozen more times, each lasting shorter durations, until there were no more visible scratches or bruising. It might have been his imagination, but Byron swore a bit of color returned to his student's face.

Emilea covered Coura again and wiped her forehead. "That takes care of her outward condition. Byron, have you been able to sense any energy from her?"

He shook his head. "It's the same for me. Nothing except a kind of mute sensation, as though her center of power cut off."

The light mage dipped her chin while everybody else continued staring.

"What should we do now?" Clearshot asked from where he stood next to his wife.

"I don't know," she admitted. "I have never seen a case this complicated. Besides, no one really has experience with demonic energy and possession. The likeliest cause is the demon gave up its hold on her body, resulting in a physical stasis and mental isolation."

"That can't be!" Will exclaimed. His voice reflected his emotional pain.

"It's some of what I *think*."

"What else?" Byron pressed, catching on that she withheld more.

"It's what Grace told us, about the angels who attacked you discussing their failures. One mistake happened to be how they stabbed *somebody* with a special dagger, but it wasn't supposed to be removed. I never heard of a weapon with such a restriction. Have any of you?"

No one answered.

"I assumed as much," Emilea finished. "I brought a few texts along that might reveal relevant information. We can skim through them later. For now, there are other serious injuries I must attend to."

Clearshot helped his wife to her feet, and they left. With a grunt, Marcus rose, gestured to his two friends, and the three were gone soon after. For hours, Byron considered Emilea's diagnosis, racking his brain for a way to wake his student.

Recovery

A sea of white surrounded Coura. No ground, no sky, no wind or water; only an empty void.

She knew nothing of this place nor how she came to be there and had no energy to spend on thinking. Whether she faced upward or not, she wasn't certain. Her entire body felt numb, though her eyes could stay open for a short period of time.

How did I get here?

Her thoughts seemed to swirl around her head, as if she spoke aloud, yet her mouth wouldn't move.

What is this place?

The weak questions rang out and disappeared into the abyss until her world faded in between lapses of darkness. Every so often, she heard muffled voices. They sounded far away and too distorted to understand, but she grew to like listening to them.

Who are you?

She asked this without contemplating what she expected. Soon, another wave of darkness swept over her for a long time.

Suddenly, a warm touch jumped to various parts of her body. Coura noticed patches of light on her skin, each giving off a gentle tingling: the first real sensation she had since waking up. She gasped in amazement and shifted to glance down at herself. When the spots vanished, the numbness returned.

No, come back!

The voices began then, and she found she could understand a few words.

"What…"

"…don't know…"

"…can't be!"

She recognized they belonged to different people, not just a single person. With what strength she possessed, Coura forced her mouth to work.

"Hello?" she whispered before repeating the plea, projecting it each time until she was practically screaming.

"Hello!"

The final call echoed farther than any of her thoughts, but the voices disappeared. Her hopes dwindled before everything went dark.

*

When Coura came to, she took advantage of her speech to shout nonsense that eventually formed into sentences.

"Where are you? Where am I?"

Still, the only sounds were those she made.

"Perhaps I should try exploring," she mumbled to herself.

The wave of darkness and fatigue she understood as sleep threatened, but Coura forced her mind to stay awake.

"Move," she ordered her limbs.

Nothing happened.

She attempted to curl her fingers and saw them twitch while the numbness receded. The corners of her mouth turned upward without her control in response.

Smile.

The word became the last thing she remembered as she fell asleep.

When she woke again, a pain lingered in her throat, though she could speak for periods of time before losing her voice. Her entire body dully ached as well. With the numbness all but gone, Coura had an urge to move around.

She stretched each arm and leg, then their fingers and toes, until the muscles warmed up. By then, she expected the regular, looming weariness, yet none came.

After wondering what she could do next, she stared out into the white world. *Where am I?*

She extended her legs below, as if reaching for the ground, and something firm pressed against her feet. In order to settle herself, Coura imagined an invisible floor until her body cooperated to shift into a standing position.

"What is this?"

Soul space.

The two words surprised her, mainly because they were so unlike the muffled voices from beyond; these sounded clear, bright, and somewhat familiar.

"Why am I here?" Coura asked into the openness.

You are damaged, in body, mind, and spirit. You must rest here until you recover.

"How? What happened to me?"

No more answers came from the new presence, so she decided to sleep while she could.

*

Upon waking, she felt better than earlier because the numbness almost completely receded into her chest. She stood before taking one step, then another with each arm extended to help her balance. In no time, Coura could walk without effort.

As she wandered without a purpose, the voice returned.

Run.

It wasn't an instruction but a sort of question.

"What do you mean?"

Around her, the whiteness shimmered into images taking shape out of thin air. Coura studied the nearest one of a girl no older than eight or nine moving in a free manner across an open field. The others displayed similar scenes of the same, dark-haired girl.

"Are these all of me?"

Yes. They are your memories. Many have been repressed for years, but now you can summon them at any time.

Her mouth hung open as more of the images appeared and vanished.

"Let me try," Coura said while walking again. She strained her legs into going faster as her hands balled into fists until she ran exactly how she did in the memories. Only when she found herself panting did she need to stop, and once she relaxed a bit, a tightness in her chest began to suffocate her.

"What's…going on?" she demanded between breaths and clutched her chest, noticing a faint heartbeat in the process.

The connection to your physical form is returning as the one with your mind strengthens. Your body experienced serious damage from some sort of spell. When it happened, your spirit retreated here, to your soul space, while your mind coped with the recovered memories. The pieces were unaligned, but your body healed. Your mind is active too, so your soul should fit itself into place, allowing you to properly awaken.

"Properly awaken? How can I do that?"

Her question was met with silence.

Coura brushed the notion aside and instead chose to become enraptured by the various memories continuing to manifest. As she strolled along the endless path, more scenes of times and places once forgotten decorated the area.

At first, they showed her childhood. She observed a conversation between her and a woman she knew as her mother, and her breath caught.

"It's been so long," she whispered while one of her hands reached out toward the figure. The woman's caramel-colored hair rested above her shoulders; her matching eyes shined bright enough to stand out against everything else. She proved naturally thin, boasting no attractive curves, though her expressions and mannerisms drew people's attention.

For a while, Coura remembered her past in the eastern town of Neston. She lived a simple life, as far as she could tell. Most people practiced a trade or craft, and despite being the only child in her family, she saw few memories of herself alone. Her mother remained present in almost every instance, but several displayed Coura with a man she recognized as her father. She shared his eyes and lean build, but not the blond hair or cheek-to-cheek smile on such a chiseled face. Most of the memories remained pleasant, except right after he left.

With nobody to talk to, she thought about the voice and spoke to it, as if it belonged to a person nearby.

"Mother told me he went away one day," she began before touching her cheek where a tear had fallen. "She promised he would return so we could be a family again. I'm assuming I was eight or nine when it happened, so around ten years ago."

The voice didn't reply, though Coura really wasn't expecting it to. She moved on from her earlier childhood and halted when she reached images of a blazing fire.

"This was the night I met the demon, Soirée."

She bonded with your soul.

Coura stood blinking for a moment until recalling what took place. "I let her because we made a deal. If I accepted her demands, then she would spare Neston. I expected to become her servant or a play-thing, but Soirée…"

And you agreed?

"Of course I did. She put a hand on my shoulder and used her magic on me. I don't think she intended it to be a possession spell, yet somehow it ended up connecting us, trapping her presence within my body. Because it wasn't the result she wanted, she grew enraged and tried taking out her anger on Neston despite my end of the deal. Byron mentioned how he saw no one, living or dead, when he found me. Something must have caused them to flee beforehand. I wonder why my mother never contacted the academy after they visited the town again."

Coura turned away from the memory and continued through the past. Glimpses of her years at the MAA and Verona flashed by, including how she met Byron, Will, Marcus, Aaron, Grace, and others along the way. Even beyond her childhood, she had to appreciate how the majority sparked positive emotions. Whether she sparred with soldiers, practiced magic, or traveled alongside her friends, she usually wore a smile. Her feet stopped at the images of the Harvest Festival and its lively environment.

"My life isn't bad at all. People ignored, disliked, and cast me away, but I had friends at my side when it mattered."

The scenes began taking place in Dala's base soon after. The farther she walked, the less clear they became until she spotted the last filled with wicked laughs, splashes of red, a glint of gold, then nothing.

We reached your most recent memory.

"Now what?"

You can wake up.

"What will I find when I do?" Coura asked, growing unreasonably tense at the question. The tone of the voice kept steady until that point where it sounded concerned.

I can't say. I am a deeper part of your conscience, only seeing, hearing, and feeling what you experience. You might be the same person or somebody entirely different.

Coura closed her eyes and remembered the faces of the people closest to her. "I think I need to go and find out," she admitted with no small amount of reluctance.

I agree.

"Besides, if I don't, who will protect them? From what I experienced, I'm the only one who possesses the power to stop those angels."

That may have been so, but I must warn you, the demonic presence which lingered here is no longer part of you. The final memory is fractured, as you noticed, meaning the challenges will be more burdensome once you return. Do you still wish to leave?

Coura paused to process what the voice explained. Despite her anxiousness for the future, in the end, she understood her spirit did not belong sealed within her soul space; she said as much after.

I'm glad you had a chance to be here. The demon repressed your memories for years, and I feared they would fade out of existence. Although I believe you will come here again, please take care of yourself.

She considered those final words before her thoughts slipped away and her body relaxed. Instead of floating or lying on the invisible ground, she felt herself falling until there was nothing except the darkness of sleep.

*

This time, Coura opened her eyes outside the inner world then squeezed them shut as sunlight flooded the room from a window above her head. After, she noticed how weak she had grown. With trembling fingers, she instantly reached for her left side.

I...remember a little...

Because of her foggy mind, she couldn't fully comprehend her situation. Pieces of various memories returned far too fast and incoherent for her to understand.

Dala... Is the city still in danger?

Her first instinct was to hurry outside and see. Nothing revealed what exactly threatened Dala, yet Coura believed an enemy lurked somewhere. She squinted to gaze around the room and found no one else in the space, though it didn't belong to her. Because of her physical state, she needed to move with caution, so she slowly pushed herself into a sitting position and pulled off the covers. Somebody had dressed her in looser clothing and cleaned off the blood.

Where can I find a cloak?

Her legs wobbled terribly, forcing her to grab on to the bed for balance as she staggered to the closet. Inside hung three, heavy cloaks. Coura snatched one, wrapped it around her shoulders, and raised the hood over her head. Though it provided warmth, her body seemed numb rather than cold. She scanned the halls beyond the room and snuck out once it cleared before closing the door after.

Her mind went blank as she leaned against the wall with one hand and walked. The grayness blended together through the winding corridor, making her forget what she intended to do.

Where am I going?

A break in the wall piqued her interest. Beyond a wooden door that took all her strength to open was a world of white. Snow blanketed the ground and dropped from the sky in fat flakes while a harsh breeze pierced through her cloak, causing her body to shiver.

I know this place, she thought, remembering the emptiness of her soul space. Each step away from the building sent chills along the parts she could feel, and she became so lost in herself that she forgot to close the door behind her.

***

"What do you mean she's *gone*?"

Byron stormed through the hall after Will, Marcus, and Aaron. Each babbled something else, but the message came across clearly: Coura's body was missing.

"Did you see her get up?" he asked with frustration, which grew equaled his concern.

"No," Will answered as they approached the medical station. Outside her room, a pair of middle-aged women argued about who should have been there that morning and when their shifts switched.

"We stopped by to visit her after our session," Marcus explained between breaths. The assistant general had not completely recovered yet still exerted himself.

Byron prepared to order them to calm down until he opened the door and stood dumbfounded in the empty space. "Where could she be?"

"We don't know," Aaron commented, showing a hint of his irritation.

"Do you think someone kidnapped her?" Marcus asked next in a deathly serious tone.

Byron went to her bed and observed the sheets before noticing the closet door cracked a bit. He moved back into the hallway to share his conclusion with the three. "She's definitely awake."

"How can you tell?" the assistant general countered.

"The blankets are thrown aside, as they are when somebody gets out of bed, and the closet door is partly open. I'll bet you one of the cloaks is missing too. Coura's never been the type to lie in bed or stay inside after being kept in confinement." He cast a glance down each side of the hall. "Let's split up."

"I'll search the training ground," Aaron offered before sprinting in that direction.

"I can ask if anybody found her on the north side," Will offered. "Maybe she returned to her room."

Byron commended the idea as the herbalist followed in the prince's wake. "Marcus, I would like you to find Emilea for me in case we still need her healing magic. I believe the light mages are researching in the meeting chamber. I'll check the southern entrance."

The assistant general bobbed his head then hurried toward the south side of the base with Byron on his heels. When a staircase appeared to their right, Marcus leapt up two steps at a time. Although envious of the soldier's physical energy, Byron held his pace until he spotted a man standing alone farther ahead.

"Hello," he called while slowing to a halt.

The man raised a hand in a friendly gesture and, after noticing the urgency on Byron's face, walked over to meet him. "What's the matter?"

"Have you seen a young woman around here? She's pretty pale, has black hair, and might be wearing a cloak." Byron waited while the man scratched his head before staring upward at the ceiling.

"I saw *someone* wrapped in a cloak and barefoot heading in this direction. I didn't get a good look, though. They were pressed against the wall, so I asked for their name or if they needed help. Well, they ignored me and kept going. I planned on reporting it at the end of my shift until I thought better of it and came back."

Byron sighed with relief. "Where can I find her?"

"Sorry, but I didn't run into her again. One of the doors leading outside was left open, so she could have gotten out. I shut it on my way over since the storm's growing nasty."

He thanked the man and slipped past him to continue forward.

If she is outside, she'll freeze in no time.

A wooden door against the outermost wall caught his eye. He approached to shove it open even as the wind howled on the opposite side. The snow prevented him from peering too far ahead while a gust cut through his clothes. Without hesitating, Byron hugged himself and trudged outside while regretting not grabbing cover for himself.

He shouted Coura's name and glanced around until a dark shape caught his eye. The slick ground prevented him from hurrying, but soon he stood near the figure.

"Coura, it's Byron!" he shouted above the howling.

The only color visible in the snowstorm came from the cloak around her body and her hair, which whipped in the air. He assumed the hood blew off at some point and muttered a curse as he forced himself to her side, then he said her name once more. No expression crossed her face, though her eyes shined brighter than ever and stared ahead without truly seeing anything.

A piercing gale cut through his shirt to send shivers down his spine. Byron swore again before wrapping an arm around her. "Come on," he grumbled and spun them both around.

She did not resist as he guided her back to the building, though he did notice her clutching the cloak.

No shoes, no thick clothing, and she's barely able to walk... We'll be lucky if she isn't ill from this excursion of hers.

When he left the base, Byron kept the door wide open in order to find his way, prompting them to rush inside. Coura leaned against the nearest wall while he pulled the door shut and bent over to catch his breath. In the next instant, he saw her body sliding to the floor and lunged to catch her. Without a word, he scooped her into his arms, choking down a cry at how delicate she had become in the process, then returned her to bed wrapped in her own blankets and those on the other cot soon after.

"Marcus should be well enough to stay in his own quarters," Byron commented, more to himself than to Coura, before taking a seat in the chair at her bedside.

Her blue eyes appeared glossed over when she stared at the ceiling with eyelids half closed. His first instinct was to lecture her, but he thought better of it given how unresponsive she acted. Instead, he tucked his hands into his armpits for warmth and waited for Marcus and Emilea.

Minutes ticked by until he prepared to find the master light mage himself. When he rose and muttered about the circumstances, the door opened. Both the assistant general and master mage slipped inside with Clearshot behind them. Marcus said his friend's name first as the trio went to the opposite side of the bed, and Byron noticed his student had fallen asleep.

Emilea knelt next to the younger soldier, placed a hand on Coura's cheek and forehead, and flinched. "She's freezing! I already sense a fever approaching."

While the light mage started a brief healing spell, Byron waited for her to finish before responding.

"She found her way to the hill overlooking Dala."

"There's a snowstorm outside!" Clearshot exclaimed in disbelief.

"Do you think I didn't know that? I dragged her in and carried her here before she could faint. Honestly, I have no clue what's wrong with her."

The room fell silent as Byron rubbed his running nose and sniffed. Then, Emilea moved to her feet.

"We may have discovered something important pertaining to Coura's case," she shared. "I would like to hear your input, if you're willing to do so now."

He immediately agreed, and the pair left together after he ordered Marcus and Clearshot to stand guard.

***

Coura's mind seemed far more active when she woke for the second time. She became confused upon learning she was in bed again since she remembered exiting into the hallway, though nothing else.

Is this one of the medical stations?

As she blinked and let her eyes adjust to the dim lighting, her stomach growled. There came a laugh to the right, drawing her attention.

"It's been a few days since you ate. How about I fetch you dinner?"

Coura turned her head to where Marcus and Clearshot sat on the other cot with playing cards in hand and on the sheets. She didn't seem ready to speak yet, so she just watched them until Clearshot rose and left the room.

Marcus switched to the chair at her bedside after and leaned forward on his hands. "Are you feeling better?" he asked in a soothing tone.

Still, she stared while her mind caught up to the present. When she didn't respond, he talked about his own recovery from an injury she had been unaware of. As he spoke, she sensed how stiff her body had grown and hoped to move more freely. She tried pushing herself into a sitting position but found her arms too weak to manage the basic task.

"Here, let me help you." Marcus jumped to his feet, put his arms around her chest, and lifted her to lean her torso against the headboard.

She intended to refuse his assistance, but no sound came out of her mouth because her throat had been unused for so long.

Once Coura settled down, he released a breath in a hiss. "You're still freezing."

Her friend adjusted the covers to wrap a couple around her shoulders, making her feel tiny in the bundle of blankets. He didn't appear satisfied, though, and seemed to be contemplating doing more.

Before she understood what was happening, Marcus sat beside her on the bed, tucked himself under the sheets around her shoulders so their bodies touched, and hugged her to his chest. The action surprised Coura, but she leaned into the warmth he provided and noticed how his heartbeat picked up. She grew so comfortable she didn't notice Clearshot's return until he spoke.

"Oh my! I leave you two alone for five minutes and-"

"Don't even finish that sentence," Marcus growled before helping her sit up.

Coura glanced between the two without comprehending their behavior as Clearshot set a tray on her lap.

"The cook says to go slow so you don't become sick. She also recommends this." The man reached into his pocket and fished out a bottle that he set on the table. "It's a common potion used around here to make sure you sleep soundly."

She lowered her eyes to stare at the bowl of broth and chunk of bread.

"Do you need help eating?" her friend added.

The thought of food didn't seem appealing, yet her stomach tightened with hunger. Coura ignored the steaming liquid, picked up the bread, and chanced a bite.

Fresh from the kitchen...

Various tastes and smells returned to her, and comforting memories associated with them followed. After swallowing the initial amount, she took another mouthful less fearfully before remembering the broth and dipping the bread into the bowl. Although hot, it cooled enough to enjoy. Coura ate every crumb before diving into the broth and finishing that too.

Marcus and Clearshot conversed about people in the dining hall as she did so, but she paid them no attention until the latter removed the empty tray and left the room. She reminisced about the newly rediscovered memories and felt more like herself with a full stomach. Marcus let her lean into him again as they sat in silence until there came a knock at the door. Her friend called for the guest to enter, and she saw the familiar face of Prince Aaron. He moved inside, stood by the door, then crossed his arms. For some reason, he appeared grumpy.

"Clearshot ordered me to relieve you so you can get dinner," he announced before jerking his chin toward the opening.

Marcus rose and assisted Coura to lie down before asking if she needed anything else. On the way out, she heard the prince's fierce whispering while Marcus' voice stayed at a quieter volume. The door closed behind him, and Aaron occupied the chair next to her bed.

"How are you feeling?" he asked without the bitterness she heard nor the upset attitude she witnessed.

Even though the broth eased the dryness in her throat, Coura didn't respond. Her mind wandered onto random topics instead. The prince fidgeted under her gaze until he started talking. None of the words made sense to her, but they lulled her into near sleep. Just as she could slip away at any moment, a soft touch grazed her cheek. Her eyes opened to meet Aaron's sapphire pair. He must not have intended for her to be awake since he gasped and recoiled his outstretched hand.

She didn't understand why, but seeing a royal figure get startled amused her, and her lips curved upward as a result. Although he blushed, Aaron offered a genuine smile too, then Coura fell asleep.

***

Byron read and reread the pages Emilea pointed out in the two texts until his eyes hurt. When he couldn't take it anymore, he tore them away to spare his mind for a few seconds.

"What do you make of this?" he inquired, unable to comprehend the purpose of the material.

The master light mage stood with both hands on the table and leaned forward over another book. "I'm not sure. That's why I brought you here, remember?"

He folded his hands in front of his face and pressed his forehead against them in an effort to concentrate. The text on his left contained the history of Asteom and included a section dated nearly two-hundred years ago. He scanned a chapter dedicated to the alliance forged between their country and Yeluthia, specifically four pages explaining their meeting.

Let me get this straight. The king of Yeluthia gifted the royal family six weapons to protect against demons: two swords, two bows, and two daggers. Each had been crafted using gold and embedded with a sealing spell. That is all the author knew for certain.

The book on his right initially made Byron wary because it proved to be a record of patients categorized under demonic possession, which the line of master light mages living in the palace passed down to their successors. In order to learn more about the creatures and how to proceed with a recovery, if possible, each person in the position noted their experiences, healings, and executions.

This particular page contains the most extreme case, according to Emilea. A man in his fifties could move and talk as the demon inside him commanded. The master mage used something called a prism sealing spell on the victim's body to forcibly extract the demonic energy. As a result, the man died from the experience, and the power dispersed into the planet without revealing the source.

"We read through each section several times, yet these two pieces of information relate to our situation the most," Emilea explained, interrupting his reflection.

"Why are these important to us?"

She closed the book in front of her and sighed. "First, Coura is, or was, a host for demonic energy. In the possession archives, a sealing spell placed on a host will pull out the unnatural power, leaving the human in a near-death state. Second, her stab wound definitely came from a dagger; I've healed plenty to know. Once I realized this, I tried to find records of weapons with the sealing ability, or a characteristic like it. That's all there is."

Byron glanced at the book to his left. After a moment, he shot a smirk at Emilea. "It seems you figured it out."

She must have assumed he was being sarcastic since she responded with a glare before realizing what she put together. "You're saying my guess is correct? I merely summarized our research."

"Yes, but sometimes the answers reveal themselves in the right moment. Perhaps we needed to break it down to the bare minimum in order to understand."

Emilea lowered her eyes to the pages and bit her lip. "We are assuming one of the angels stabbed her using an ancestral weapon, one of the daggers, and the sealing spell removed the demonic energy."

"You don't sound too sure." Byron raised an eyebrow when she shook her head.

"With sealing spells, their nature is to contain. The reasoning behind the result of the case in front of you is that the spell had been activated as a confined space, which left nowhere for the power to escape. The original author goes on about it for a while in the next section. I would guess an ancestral weapon wouldn't have such an issue. In addition, neither of us are able to sense anything from Coura, meaning the energy has been released or slumbers within her center."

"Not to mention what Grace heard," he added, recalling the rogue angels' leader's words on misusing the dagger.

The two kept to themselves and reviewed the information until the lower part of Byron's back started to ache, and he rose to stretch.

"What we discussed so far makes the most sense to me. My true questions lie with the enemy. Where are they from? Who is in charge, and how did they come to possess such a powerful weapon belonging to the rulers of Asteom? However, it's too late to dig deeper. Besides, we read enough for one day."

"Perhaps you're right. A night's rest should provide us with more motivation."

Out the window, the white snow became shaded by the evening's darkness. As he left for his own room, he wondered if speaking to Coura would reveal the missing pieces.

The Enemy's Return

In the midst of their dilemma, Byron and Emilea were still responsible for organizing the mages who traveled from the capital, which put their personal work on hold. General Tio and Calin left that business to Byron instead of joining the installation process, but it didn't matter too much since the preparations had already been arranged.

King Hernan intended to send four groups containing a dozen mages each week for the next month, according to the master light mage. Because Aaron met with Tio beforehand, he remained well aware of what needed to be done. Together with the prince and Emilea, Byron spent the following days implementing details identical to those established when the mages from the MAA moved to Verona, only on a smaller scale. They assigned rooms, organized training and guard duty schedules between the mages and soldiers, and adjusted the squad positions.

By the time all four of the groups traveled to Dala and settled into their positions, spring crept up on the base. Byron had been too busy to notice until he supervised the newcomers as they practiced their spells in the training ground. One concern early in the planning process had been how magic would impact the earth and surrounding trees and building. Emilia suggested the mages could work on shielding too, so they arranged shifts between the groups in order to keep up their endurance. With the shimmering walls in place to prevent damage, everything ran smoothly.

Byron glanced up from where he stood under the outline of a tree and caught buds forming at the tips of the branches. The realization of the passing time shocked him as he vividly remembered the days of snow and wind, allowing him to savor the rising temperature.

How can it be spring already? It seems like we just arrived here.

"How about that," a deep voice began from behind before someone slapped his back in a welcoming gesture Byron became familiar with.

"General," he greeted the man without looking away.

Tio stepped beside him and traced his gaze. "Spring already?"

Byron smiled to himself. "I thought the same. I guess the world is moving too fast for us to follow the changing seasons."

"Aye."

They turned their attention to the mages inside the glittering, silver shield for a while until the general spoke again in a casual tone.

"It seems your student's acting more alive these days."

Byron noticed the direction of Tio's stare and mirrored it. From the opposite side of the courtyard, Coura sat alone on one of the stone benches to observe the training. Even with somebody around her at all times, she rarely ever spoke, and it would be a few words at that. Whenever he stayed nearby, she never seemed to be thinking about much in particular.

She's lost. I didn't believe it related to her mind at first, but now I wonder if a part of her has been mentally damaged by the wound.

"My soldiers aren't comfortable around her. It's hard to get used to someone hovering over you. You know what I mean?"

"I do," Byron admitted.

The general never inquired about what the light mages found in the texts, claiming it's their business, yet he made it clear he had open ears if anybody wanted to talk. At the moment, Byron felt it was necessary to share.

Without a prompt, he told Tio about the ancestral weapons, their sealing ability, the lack of energy coming from Coura, their assumptions, and whatever else popped into his head. The general listened and remained silent when Byron finished, only clearing his throat and tugging on his lengthy, brown beard after.

"There's news you should know," he muttered so Byron had to lean a bit closer to catch the words. "When we returned from the Valley Beyond with my injured soldiers and your student, I sent a messenger with a letter every day that week requesting for information and aid from the king. None of them returned except for the first, who reported his letter had been taken without further instructions. If it wasn't for the Yeluthian in the palace, we would never have received aid from Lady Emilea. Next, I asked if she spoke directly to King Hernan. She did indeed meet with him, and he responded by sending the mages here."

"You mean to say someone is intercepting messages between Dala and the capital?"

Tio nodded grimly. "We're pretty independent from the north, but I always receive communications. Remember the addition of these mages? Most of the work had been done through letters and messengers until you arrived. All of a sudden, nothing."

Although he tried not to show his emotions, Byron grew nervous. "I fear there's more to it."

"What do you mean?"

"Before this assignment, suspicions of interference between Yeluthia and Asteom floated around the palace." He informed the general of the letter containing information about Grace's unique ability and the formal greeting from Yeluthia's ruler.

Tio spat a curse then shook his head.

"I'm no strategist, but I strongly advise you to remain independent and as uninvolved with Verona as possible," he continued.

A grin stretched across the general's face before he walked away. "Thank you for you input, Master Byron."

He watched Tio return inside and wondered about the man's scheming before concerning himself with the mages' training once more. From across the area, he spotted Coura staring at him while wearing a neutral expression.

I've put off questioning her. Perhaps Emilea and I should free up enough time tonight to pay her a visit.

*

His fellow master mage hid in the meeting space to review paperwork regarding the newest additions to the base. Since the positions for magic users had never been in place, every detail needed to be recorded, from their schedules down to each pillow placed in their rooms. The Dalan base requested a copy in order to prepare future previsions while the palace asked for two; one would be kept in the archives and another used as the foundation for the readjustments and assignments in various cities and towns over the upcoming months.

Initially, she declined Byron's offer to speak with Coura that night, but the woman caved in when he pushed a little more. Although she probably didn't acknowledge it, he had a growing suspicion the light mage was warming up to her patient.

It helps that she can't sense the demonic energy, he thought with some amusement as the pair made their way to the medical station.

Once they reached their destination, he knocked on the door before entering. No one felt entirely confident leaving Coura on her own yet, and she didn't seem too inclined to be alone either. At the moment, Clearshot and Will discussed herbal potions the latter worked on at the table while Coura listened from her bed.

"We weren't expecting you," Will was the first to say, glancing up from the items as he did so. "Is something wrong?"

Meanwhile, Clearshot waved and plopped down on the empty cot.

"You worry too much," Byron responded with a chuckle. "We're here to see Coura. Why don't you clean up and enjoy the rest of your day."

The herbalist showed his relief and hurried to sort his bottles and ingredients as Byron turned to Clearshot.

"You too."

"Maybe I'll go when you and Emilea finish," his friend replied then sent a knowing wink.

Byron rolled his eyes. He understood how often Clearshot and his wife spoke, so his friend must have figured out what they planned to do. Will didn't question them, though, and soon exited the room.

"How are you feeling?" Emilea asked Coura as soon as they were alone before accepting a seat on the other bed beside her husband.

"Fine," came the softly spoken reply while she stared at the closed door.

Byron took the chair next to her bed and cleared his throat. All afternoon he rehearsed what he planned to say and hoped for her cooperation.

"We want to help your recovery, so please be honest," he began and waited for her reaction. When none came, he continued. "There's information regarding the Valley Beyond we need to discuss. A lot is going on, and I'm afraid we can't afford to wait any longer."

"I know," she startled him by responding with a sad smile.

Byron raised an eyebrow at Emilea, who appeared just as uneasy.

Coura turned her head to look between them. "I've been dreading this for a while."

"What do you mean?" he asked. His nerves rose even as he questioned why he became so apprehensive.

She returned her eyes forward before elaborating. "I meant to tell you about a few things too. My old memories returned when I woke up, but it's taken me weeks to sort them out and remember what happened."

Coura inhaled a shaky breath while Byron held his and prepared for her to explain.

She's never been this vulnerable with me. What could possibly be influencing her behavior this way?

"When you found me in Neston, I didn't know anything about myself. Truthfully, I had no interest in my hometown or family once you confirmed nobody was there and I would be staying at the academy for training. Before our reassignment to Dala, a few parts of my childhood started returning. They were painful, but I saw faces and locations I forgot about. When we entered the valley and I fought those angels, something happened, but I can't recall it too well. Then, the rest of my memories came back when I lost consciousness."

The room went still as they waited for Coura to continue. Just when Byron opened his mouth to urge her to go on, she closed her eyes and picked up speaking, seemingly unphased by their worry.

"You discovered me and thought my magic had awakened, causing the damage to Neston. In actuality, I met a demon when I wandered through the woods just before sundown. Her name is Soirée, and she's the most beautiful, evil being I've ever known. I immediately recognized what she is and that my life was in danger, so I tried distracting her after she claimed she would attack my home. I offered to make a deal with her if she spared Neston because I heard demons like to play around. They're tricksters who offer no sympathy toward humans unless they find them entertaining. Soirée apparently believed a child was worth enough to bother with. She offered protection and power if I agreed to test a new spell. I have no idea why she wanted that, but I accepted. For a brief amount of time, she manipulated my body and went to destroy Neston anyway because her spell failed. We found no one, though, and I got control again. She repressed my memories afterward to prevent me from telling anybody about her or threatening to kill myself.

I don't know what her intentions became once I lived at the academy, but she saved my life and Will's when I challenged the two angels outside Fester. I would have died if she didn't release her power then or during the second encounter in East Hoover. Her presence stayed with me after that. We communicated mentally, just like how Grace can speak to us through her goddess gift. I needed to learn how to use her demonic energy, so we practiced in secret. She threatened me every step of the way about revealing our secret; now, I believe those were hollow lies.

So, that's how it went until the Valley Beyond. I vaguely remember what happened because I exhausted myself. One of the angels stabbed me with a dagger, and I felt that pain. It also cut off my connection to Soirée. It's hard to explain, but she was gone, my memories returned, and I wound up alone and too weak to understand it all. I waited to mention this until I knew for sure she wouldn't be here and the details were straight in my head."

Byron watched Coura with his mouth hanging open, appalled by what she revealed. A mixture of anger and his sense of responsibility brought on thoughts of the cult leaders executed for seeking out the creatures and making sacrifices in exchange for their power.

She should be executed for this. We assumed her case involved possession, resulting in her ability to wield that energy. What she explained falls under allying with an enemy. What was she even thinking? Trusting an actual demon is beyond idiotic! What if it still has a hold over her?

On the other hand, he felt sympathetic, and his heart ached for her. *She's been fighting this on her own. Not to mention, she used the demon's energy to protect so many people. I don't know what to say...*

Byron became so internally conflicted that he desired nothing more than to be away from her. Emilea must have felt the same since she rose and departed without a word nor a glance at Coura, who remained unmoving and kept her eyes lowered in a shamed manner.

A touch on his shoulder startled him into glancing around. He saw Clearshot tip his head toward the door then followed his friend out of the room.

"Will she be safe?" Byron asked as they turned down another hallway on the south side of the base.

"Sure." The short answer revealed how upset Clearshot became.

He had no idea where his friend planned on bringing him until they passed out of the structure, down the main road, and through the city toward the centermost building: The Stinger's Tavern. The only time Byron visited the place had been on the day their group from the capital first arrived in Dala.

Life seemed simpler then, he reflected with dejection while a waitress fetched the pair two, tall mugs of ale. Clearshot didn't hesitate to guzzle the entire beverage and order more before Byron even touched his.

"Drink," the soldier ordered, then he shoved the mug closer to Byron.

"What am I supposed to do?"

"I already told you."

For the first time in years, Byron lacked a thirst for alcohol. He stared at the ale with a heavy heart, rubbed his forehead, and starting to contemplate Coura again.

A few seconds later, Clearshot slammed his empty mug down on the table, creating a loud thud. "Master Byron Rinod, I've known you for over a decade, trained and fought side by side with you during most of that time, and never once have I seen you this reluctant to share a drink with me."

"What do you want me to say?" Byron snapped, verbalizing his frustration. "My student, my Coura, not only broke the law and formed a bond with a demon but also lost her magical abilities and nearly died! How can I be sure the girl I raised and taught was even her? What if the person lying in there is someone I never met, and all I've come to know has been a demon pretending to be her?"

Clearshot snickered into his next mug. "You know how ridiculous you sound?"

The remark pushed Byron's hysterics to their limit, and he stood to exit. Where he would stay, he had no idea, but he wished to be far away from everyone.

"Where are you going?" his friend demanded and hopped up.

The bar remained busy enough to cover their words, yet some eyed the two because of their abrupt movements.

Byron didn't answer. Instead, he turned to leave until Clearshot grabbed the collar of his shirt and yanked.

"Get off me!"

When Clearshot didn't let go, Byron twisted to shove the man backward with both arms. His friend stumbled in a dramatic fashion, practically falling over a chair, and glared before recovering and swinging a fist. It slammed into Byron's cheek forcefully enough to rattle his teeth.

By that point, their half of the bar watched in preparation for making bets, cheering, and jeering, as was custom during fights.

However, Byron's emotions fled after the blow. He reached up to brush a finger along the puffy cheek. It hurt, and he glanced at his hand to see a smear of blood. Somehow, the punch jolted him awake enough to think more clearly.

"Just for that, you're buying," he said at last as he returned to his seat and took a swig of the ale.

Although Clearshot sat down, he still scowled. Those in the area picked up their conversations again with obvious disappointment while the pair drank in silence.

***

Despite the results, revealing her background to Byron, Emilea, and Clearshot breathed new life into Coura. For weeks, she closed herself off from the world, unable to come to terms with the past and reluctant to admit the truth. It wasn't until she began to feel a faint power that she developed the confidence to face her problems.

While she occupied a bench outside to observe the soldiers' training and enjoy the sunshine, she considered the internal energy and how familiar it seemed. Her mind worked normally, yet she hoped to be more active. Practicing magic made her nervous, if she could do so at all, as did physical combat. Worse still, she required supervision everywhere she went until recently. The people who interacted with her emanated pity and often commented on what they assumed could benefit her the most, whether it be sitting in the garden space, resting, conversing, eating, or another option. In any case, Coura understood she had a ways to go toward being whole again.

Her hand brushed against her left side where she remembered the dagger wound. *Ever since that moment, Soirée disappeared; it seems as though a piece of me left with her. A hole rests in my center, and nothing has been able to heal it.*

As if in response to the notion, a cold, invisible grip seized her chest, causing her to gasp in alarm and jump to her feet. She glanced across the clearing to where the reach stemmed from. Without realizing what it could be, she began walking toward it.

People shouted at her once she moved into range of the combat before somebody grabbed her arm. She stared down at it then up into Aaron's face as he held her in place. Behind him, Marcus held two swords and Will one.

"What's wrong?" he asked with a worried expression.

Coura prepared to answer when a surge of demonic power erupted from the same spot she was moving toward. Her head swung around, and others in the area who could sense it did the same as warning cries filled the air.

"Get back!"

"What is that?"

"Watch out!"

They began shouting at the soldiers, who couldn't detect magic, and urging everybody to the opposite end of the clearing. Meanwhile,

Aaron shook her arm and repeated his question more urgently, but she froze once she recognized the energy.

It's Soirée's power! I would know it anywhere. Is she coming here? That doesn't look like her at all.

Nothing appeared in the area for a moment, then a thin wisp of fog swirled by, circling until more tendrils appeared and joined together. The cloud grew thicker, and a shadow began forming underneath. Within seconds, the shape of a deformed demonic creature stood analyzing those around with the signature violet eyes. It reminded Coura of the beasts outside Verona she defeated in order to rescue Mace and Lexie; however, this one loomed taller and possessed pointed ears and stripes of grayer fur against the black, sleek body.

It stepped forward, baring sharp canines and releasing a low growl reminiscent of thunder. As it moved its head from side to side to scope them out, Coura noticed its eyes fall on her and linger. She had no time to wonder about it, though, because Aaron jerked her arm to pull her behind him, almost knocking her over in the process.

"Shield!" someone to the left ordered.

She sensed the patterns of light and dark energy spread into two walls in front of the creature, sealing it against the outer side of the space.

It snarled, almost as if grinning at the spells, and roared, a deafening sound that made everybody wince and some cover their ears. Then, it leapt straight into the first shield built from light magic, bringing its head down to slam using all its weight. The wall cracked with a sickening noise before shattering altogether.

Gasps and murmurs surrounded Coura, but she became too captivated to be concerned.

What is this monster?

Instead of repeating its previous motion, the creature approached the next shield made up of dark energy, rose to stand on its hind legs, and pressed its front paws onto the spell. The sharp claws screeched as it rocked, scratching the surface repeatedly.

"Get ready!" Marcus called from Coura's right loudly enough for those nearby to hear.

A few of the soldiers yelled challenges and raised their swords in response. He handed Aaron the second sword, so both prepared themselves while she lingered uncomfortably. The demonic creature's bellow drowned out the shouts when it struck one more time to bring down the second shield.

A whistle flew past Coura at that moment. In the blink of an eye, an arrow found its way into the beast's throat before its paws touched the ground. She glanced to her left where Clearshot came forward to continue shooting arrows. By then, mages and archers from all over the area began launching other projectiles, such as more arrows, lightning bolts, icicles, and flames. The creature snapped at the air when they found their marks on some part of the unnatural body.

Still, it accepted the attacks without attempting to dodge or flee until no more arrows flew and less elemental spells hit with any impact. The result displayed a frightening sight. The beast stretched its limbs to appear taller and shook itself, releasing the arrows embedded in its skin.

"That didn't do anything," Will commented nervously from Coura's right.

As the demonic creature prepared to creep closer again, they caught a flash from nearby as a bolt of lightning shot out and struck it. The force of the blast sent it to its side, and the beast remained unmoving on the ground. The resulting clap of thunder hurt Coura's ears but faded with a lingering haunting sensation.

"Get inside!" a rough voice barked in the silence.

She recognized Byron's magic and Tio's voice before they emerged from one of the leftmost entrances into the courtyard. By that point, the creature began to rise.

As it turned its attention to the newcomers, a glimmering shield formed around it, one so thick it became difficult to make out what waited on the other side. Emilea lined up with the two men, and her light energy projecting a flood of warmth, like a summer breeze.

This magic... I felt a similar presence...

Coura had no time to consider the sensation further as Clearshot took her arm and led her backward with him while everybody in the clearing hurried inside through the nearest doorway. The farther away they moved, the tighter the hold on her chest became until she found herself struggling to breathe.

What do you want? Do you belong to Soirée?

Despite being pulled ahead, she darted her eyes to where the beast started clawing at Emilea's shield without success. Coura imagined the mental conversations between her and the demon and internally screamed her next thought, utilizing what remained of their connection.

I'm here!

She didn't understand what the cry did, or if she wanted to interact with Soirée again, but dread weighed on her shoulders when the creature stopped attempting to damage the shield. After tugging her arm free from Clearshot's grasp as they approached the crowded exit, she spun around to face the opposite end. Even without seeing its shape clearly, Coura expected the beast became drawn to her. She squinted to try and make out the shadowy figure before it vanished from the other side of the shield. The energy dispersed, along with the pressure on her chest.

"Come on," Clearshot ordered before grabbing her arm and resorting to dragging her along.

"Stop it," she complained while attempting to free herself. When the man didn't listen and everyone continued to flee, she raised her voice. "The creature's gone!"

Those who heard her, including Marcus and Will, paused to wait for confirmation.

"She's right." An older mage raised his hands in the air to attract their attention. "I don't sense its energy now."

Additional magic users supported their companion's remark. Upon hearing the reassurance, the people's panic shifted to curiosity over where the beast had been moments ago, which Tio, Byron, and Emilea inspected. Clearshot released his hold, and Coura chose to sneak inside instead of joining the investigation or remaining near her friends.

*

The demonic creature returned twice that week. Coura sat outside during each instance and sensed its arrival, though trying to explain her connection to it proved useless. Once its energy spiked, the mages alerted everybody in the clearing, and the situation repeated itself.

Byron and Emilea could contain the beast until it disappeared because they were present right away on both occasions. Neither had spoken to her since she revealed her secret to them.

After the third incident, the general issued an order for his troops to stay inside the base unless they asked for the general's permission. This meant Will, Marcus, and Aaron had nothing better to do than spend their time chatting, working, or playing games in the medical station. Coura appreciated her closest friends and the effort they put into keeping her company, yet something bothered her over the past week as she considered how Clearshot treated her.

Am I lying to them by hiding who, or what, I am? I can't imagine Byron and Emilea will keep quiet about it for much longer, especially if the beast continues showing up.

The guilt of hiding her past soon outweighed their likely responses once they knew the truth.

They deserve it. Besides, that creature is my responsibility, she concluded with a heavy heart while watching the three play a card game. When Will claimed victory over the other two, and they began complaining about it, she decided to act.

"I'm glad you're having fun, but can I ask a favor?" she interrupted from where she sat on the edge of her bed.

They glanced at her with smiles and eager eyes. Ever since her awareness strengthened, she noted their enthusiasm to help whenever possible. *Such chivalry for a weak girl. How amusing. I'm going to take advantage of it now.*

She held a hand to her forehead and relished their blindly sympathetic looks. "I would like to get some rest, if you don't mind."

"Do you need medicine?" Will offered.

Coura shook her head, shifted to lie down, and pretended to be tired. As the three collected their playing cards and rose to exit, she swallowed and found a lump in her throat.

"I have one other request," she continued. It became difficult to hide the pain behind the words, which piqued their interest. "Tell Byron to share what I informed him of a week ago."

"About what?" Marcus pressed.

She closed her eyes, hoping they would take the bait. "I'm sorry. My voice is too weak for the lengthy explanation. It's important for you to hear, though."

"We'll find him right away," Aaron replied.

As Coura heard the door close, a surge of emotion welled, and she could barely suppress it. Despite her control, a single tear slid down her cheek when she considered how each of her friends treated her throughout their relationships. Memories of Will's avoidance and disgust after she used the demonic power, Aaron's reluctance to be her friend, and Marcus' caution and unintentional betrayal came to mind too. That was all the persuasion she needed to begin accepting they would soon treat her as dismissively as Byron, Emilea, and Clearshot did.

*

When the light outside grew dim, Coura released a sigh and sat up. "I should be going," she muttered to herself.

Earlier, she dressed in a comfortable set of clothing suitable for travel. Most of her belongings had been brought over to the medical station since she was meant to stay there until she fully recovered. She prepared a single bag with camping tools and shoved in a couple outfits and a blanket. The only item she hesitated to grab had been the sleeping potion collecting dust on the nightstand, but she decided to leave it behind. With a cloak on her shoulders, a hunting knife at her waist, and the hefty-sized pouch of coins she saved up during her time in Dala, Coura shouldered her pack before exiting just as the sun began to set.

Plenty of people roamed the halls because of Tio's order to remain inside the base, making it difficult for her to sneak out toward the city. Her plan involved resting at the inn in town for a night or two then heading south to Clearwater through the tunnel system.

The farther I am from Dala and Verona, the safer everybody will be until I can sort this out.

Instead of cowering behind her cloak, she smiled at the people who passed her. If she acted suspicious, they were more likely to stop and question her business. Many people returned the gesture and went on their way while a few she recognized inquired about her health. While she offered a polite answer, she internally despised the questions regarding her condition.

When anyone brought up the pack, she lied by saying she had been permitted to stay in her own room instead of the medical station and proceeded to move her belongings. As soon as she reached one of the southernmost doors, she paused and lingered for a few minutes until nobody came near enough to notice her slip outside.

The evening breeze smelled delicious, and Coura paused to inhale a deep breath, savoring the freedom of being on her own, before heading toward the city. The trail to Dala consisted of a simple, worn path, which proved to be empty because people used the main road farther west to bypass the base altogether. It amazed her to see no guards posted on the bridge; however, she understood how much the troops, including the new mages, respected Tio as their leader. Going against his orders would put them out of his favor, probably resulting in a reassignment and a public lecture.

A pity I won't be coming back, she remembered with a hint of amusement at the idea of being reprimanded by the general.

Around the city, though, guards patrolled their routes along the roads. She already concocted a ploy to enter from the south as a traveler searching for work. It would take extra time to circle around the perimeter, yet it felt necessary for her to avoid triggering misgivings from the soldiers.

The lights of street lamps began to shine against the growing darkness despite a full moon steadily glowing brighter in the sky. All seemed calm for the moment.

Then, that peacefulness vanished.

The gripping sensation plaguing her body tugged at Coura's chest, and she swore as her breathing sped up.

Not now!

She traced Soirée's energy off to her left and glanced between Dala and the distant woods on that side. *If I go into the city, I might lure the creature there; then, more people will be in danger. I could flee in the opposite direction, but it's unfamiliar wilderness.*

Coura instinctively stepped backward before getting a hold of herself. *I'm not returning to the base. If I do, I won't find another chance soon enough. I need to see what she wants if this game is to ever end.*

Walking toward the demonic presence gave her time to think. Naturally, she considered a weapon and winced when she realized she only brought the hunting knife. It was too late to reconsider her decision since the distance shortened until she reached the woods. In fact, as she neared the tree line, Coura could see relatively well between the light from the city and that of the moon.

No creature became visible when she stopped a safe distance away from the trees, not even the always-alert, violet eyes. She clenched her hands into fists to prevent them from shaking and directly addressed the presence.

"I never believed you would hide in the shadows," she accused with mock confidence. "What's the ugly form you've taken this time?"

She expected the same, wolf-like creature to stalk out and braced for an escape into the woods. If it chose to attack, her best option for survival involved embracing the environment. All her muscles grew tense in anticipation, yet nothing happened.

"Well?" she snapped impatiently after a minute passed.

The leaves within rustled in response, and she continually blinked in order to adjust her eyes when a darker shadow approached. She became wary when, instead of a beast, a grayish, human figure emerged, then she gasped as she recognized the angel standing in front of the brush.

"Look what we found," the leader she remembered as Drake boasted. He wore an all-white outfit while his cropped hair seemed to glow in the night.

More shocking still, Coura sensed the demonic energy behind him.

He must be able to sense this, right?

"What's going on?" she demanded and glared at him, spurring an amused reaction.

"I am not sure how, but you managed to escape my companions and I last we met. We were sent to find you again. I guess we just needed bait."

What is he talking about?

Drake took a step closer, so she began backing up.

"Do not fret," he continued in a smooth voice. "It will be painless if you can-"

Someone shouted her name from nearby, interrupting his words. They both turned and spotted a group running over; soon she recognized Byron and Clearshot leading Emilea, Marcus, Will, and Aaron, each with weapons drawn. Coura didn't know what to say, so she called for them to stop. Instead, Byron went straight to her side while the others stood behind.

"What a pleasure," Drake greeted them sarcastically and rubbed his chin. "I was only ordered to handle one nuisance."

"Why are you here?" Byron demanded.

The angel's frown deepened as he looked the group over before shrugging. "Our leader requested we learn what became of the base and its defenses. I can also spare you a warning."

The resulting silence grew unbearable, yet they waited.

Meanwhile, Drake savored their rising aggravation. "I must say, losing has made you humans much more patient."

Coura bit her tongue and held her breath, mostly due to her curiosity stemming from the demonic energy farther in the woods.

"Fine. I will give you that warning for being so obedient," Drake continued and shifted his expression into a serious gaze. "Stay in Dala, unless you do not care about the lives you left in Verona."

Emilea stepped up to Coura's other side. "What do you mean, snake?"

The angel laughed at her question before crossing his arms and staring directly at Coura. "I almost forgot. Somebody came along to see you."

Not a leaf rustled as she glanced into the trees with growing anxiousness. *It can't be... She's not really...*

"Hello again, Dear One."

From behind Drake, the silhouette of a woman appeared and slid beside him. The figure's violet eyes shone like an animal's as her raven hair bounced with each step. When she stopped, she licked her lips, put a hand on her cheek, then grinned, revealing pointed canines.

Coura stood petrified and remained at a loss for words upon meeting the demon. *It's exactly like our first encounter.*

Soirée wore no clothes. The demon had no use for them since a slick, black substance covered every part of her body except her face, hands, and feet; Coura didn't know whether it was fur or just her skin. Her hair flowed in waves left unbound and, accompanied by her physique, made her look similar to a human woman.

Those around Coura mumbled in frightened voices to each other. Byron leaned closer to ask something but lost the rest of the question after the first couple words.

She told her mind to focus, forcing herself to be in control. "That's the demon," she replied loudly enough for everyone to hear.

"What an informal greeting," Soirée replied and feigned an offended pout. "I'm truly hurt by such a poor way to introduce a creature as stunning as myself. Have you already forgotten? You *were* injured before I departed, so maybe that's the case."

She sauntered forward, intent on reaching Coura until Byron raised his sword. Upon noticing his movement, she paused to cast an annoyed look at him and his companions. "Your friends, I remember. A shame we couldn't have more fun before-"

"Let us depart," Drake cut in. "We do not have time for games." With that, he spun around and disappeared into the trees.

The demon let out a disappointed sigh while narrowing her eyes. "What a disgusting being he is."

She turned her back on Coura to follow until a wall of light energy manifested in her way. There came the whistle of an arrow, and Byron's free palm glowed red as he prepared to launch his own magic.

The arrow buried into Soirée's shoulder where she stopped in front of the shield before facing their group once more. Without a word, the demon lifted a hand to stretch her energy around the area. Coura's body stiffened, and her arms and legs snapped to her sides, becoming bound by an unseen spell. She dropped onto her side after and heard the thuds of her companions falling as well.

"What is this?" Marcus demanded through gritted teeth.

They struggled to no avail and growled in frustration. Soirée flashed a pleased smile and continued to head for the woods.

"No, wait!" Coura cried out.

I need answers!

From her center, a band of energy lashed out like a whip to crack against the demonic power. Some part of the spell seemed to break at her legs and wrists, allowing her to move, though off balance. Soirée observed with a raised eyebrow and expressionless gaze.

Coura panted from the effort of pushing herself to her feet before stumbling toward the demon. Everyone else yelled at her, but she didn't care.

What is she doing with the rogue angels? What happened to separate us? This may be my only chance…

Soon, she stood toe to toe with Soirée. The demon was about a head taller, forcing Coura to look up into the creature's face. She opened her mouth, unsure of what she planned to say yet taking comfort in her newly found courage.

Before she could make a sound, Soirée's hand darted to seize her by the throat, cutting off her breathing. As she flung both hands on top of the demon's in an attempt to pry herself free, Soirée lifted her onto the tips of her toes until their eyes were at an even level. The horrified shouting became muffled as the two stared at each other.

She began kicking the air and dug her nails into Soirée's arm, yet the creature remained unfazed. Just when Coura began to see stars, Soirée brought her head close enough to talk into her ear. The demon's breath tickled her skin, but she kept her attention on every word.

"I decided to follow a new human for a while. He is the one you are searching for in the palace. Go there, and I can show you how you can get our power back. As a bit more incentive, you should know this man had his pets slay this country's king. They will not send word to you or the base, and you cannot stay here, even though they offer empty threats."

Colorful spots blotted Coura's sight by that point, making her aware of just how close she came to losing consciousness. Soirée released her then, letting her collapse straight to her knees while gasping for air. When she glanced up after, the demon was gone.

Change in the Wind

yron, Emilea, and the others remained where they fell for a few minutes because Soirée's magic took time to wear off. Meanwhile, Coura stayed hunched over on the ground, coughing and wheezing until her vision cleared and her head stopped pounding. Shuffling noises behind her signaled when her companions could move, and they rose, stretched, and brushed away the dirt and grass.

The light mage spoke first in a low, trembling voice. "I never experienced a binding spell so strong before."

"Neither have I," Byron replied in a similarly perturbed manner.

Coura could hear the fear beneath their words as they conferred with one another after. Her mind tired and body grew heavy while she considered what to do next and thought about Soirée's message again.

She said we need to return to Verona, yet Drake told us to stay here. How are they working together when they want opposite results? Soirée called someone her "new human" too, someone who...had the king killed? A wave of dread overshadowed her disbelief once she realized what had happened. *That person is using Soirée and those angels to take over Asteom, and we're a threat to his plans!*

It became too much to consider at the moment. The sound of nearing footsteps made her sit straighter anyway.

"Get up," she heard Byron say, though he offered no assistance or immediate reassurance.

Coura shook her head to clear it and struggled to her feet, remembering how they were aware of her relationship to Soirée and how poorly they must view her after her recent actions. Despite growing lightheaded, she managed to stand on her own with wobbling legs and follow him to where the rest of their group waited while keeping her eyes down to avoid theirs.

"Well, what now?" Clearshot asked Byron as he cradled his wife in his arms.

"If all they hoped to accomplish was to warn us, I suppose we shouldn't need to worry about more tonight. Let's return to the base and recover. I'll find General Tio and share what took place. Perhaps tomorrow we can discuss our next course of action."

There came nods and mumbles of agreement in response before they began walking away.

Coura didn't move. She stared at them until foolishly realizing no one else heard what Soirée whispered to her and called for them to wait. Everybody halted with mixed expressions of worry and annoyance.

"What is it?" Byron demanded impatiently.

She understood their mistrust; oddly enough, it motivated her to try and prove she was separate from the demon, regardless of her past decisions. The returning warmth in her center supported the notion.

"Soirée told me something important before leaving. She's working with the same person in the palace who is controlling the angels and interfering with communications outside Verona."

"How do you know the creature spoke the truth?" he countered.

Coura considered what else Soirée revealed and chose to address Byron directly instead of projecting to everybody. "I know how she is. She's one for toying around with people, but she's never lied to me. Drake warned us not to go to the capital; Soirée said the opposite. The man they're helping is who we need to find, and…" She recalled the news about Hernan and hesitated.

"And what?"

This time, she let her own temper show by matching his glare. *We need to hurry to Verona. I won't tell them about meeting Soirée again or her comment on getting my magic back, but they deserve to hear the rest.*

"She claimed they killed the king."

Byron's eyebrows rose while his face dropped, and he glanced over his shoulders to the others, who also crept closer to catch her words. Coura anticipated Aaron's reaction and closed her eyes. Despite her resolve, her heart felt like it cracked upon hearing his devastated response.

"What did you say about my father?"

When no one replied, she heard hurried footsteps and opened her eyes to catch the prince sprinting toward the base. Marcus shouted Aaron's name before chasing after him.

***

The moon floated high in the night sky when everybody returned inside. Byron's eyes burned, and his head throbbed from the rising concerns. In spite of what Coura believed, he wasn't certain if he trusted what she or the angel mentioned. An anger boiled in his chest throughout the past few days, and it threatened to overflow that night.

He rushed down the hallway in an attempt to find Marcus and Aaron, who would presumably depart for the capital, and swore to himself when neither came into view. Clearshot called to him from farther behind with Emilea still wrapped in his arms. Her face had paled into a grayish color, which looked worse under the lamps' light. A surge of sympathy hit Byron once he realized the impact the demonic energy must have had on her.

"Go," he ordered while gesturing for the pair to leave, knowing nothing else would get done that evening. "I'll find you in the morning."

Clearshot sent him a grateful nod before leading his fellow master mage away. The only person remaining in the corridor after was Will, who also blanched and became useless for the moment.

"Will, you can return to your room too."

The herbalist bobbed his head once in confirmation and passed Byron, who rubbed his temples. Containing so many emotions drove him crazy.

At least I've had previous encounters with demonic creatures. Those three will most likely have nightmares after hearing about Coura.

He had finished sharing what she revealed to the young men, apparently at her request, when he picked up the familiar energy surge

55

from outside the base. Emilea did too and met Byron, Marcus, Aaron, and Will in the field beyond with her husband.

Seeing one of the angels again had been startling; an actual demon terrified him. His power flared in response to the unnatural presence, becoming a distraction and tensing his muscles. Still, Coura's behavior around the creature had truly frightened him.

She's never acted in such a way before, he thought after abandoning his chase for the prince and assistant general. *She seemed afraid too, but she longed for the demon's attention. That monster also wanted her, or else it would have killed her.*

He paused to put a hand on his warm forehead.

I need rest...

"Byron?"

He glanced farther ahead and saw Coura staring at him. The confusion, frustration, sympathy, and other emotions began to stir.

"We need to talk," he began while ignoring his gruff voice and moving closer.

"Wait until tomorrow. We're both tired." With that, she turned to start walking in the opposite direction.

Coura's careless attitude chipped away the last of his patience. He stomped over to catch up and snatch her wrist, which she didn't expect. She gasped in response before twisting to face him while he stormed by, dragging her behind.

"Byron, stop it!"

Afraid his tongue would betray him more than his actions, he remained silent and pulled her through the halls to her room in the medical center. Those who noticed them recognized the pair and kept to their business, rightfully so in his opinion. During the entire trek, she attempted to free her arm, swore at him, and stumbled when she would plant her feet.

"Let me go!" she cried. "Why won't you listen to me?"

Once they reached his destination, Byron opened the door, shoved Coura inside while releasing his hold, and slammed it shut. With arms crossed, he blocked her escape; however, he didn't realize how much force he used to throw her into the room until he watched her hit the end of the first bed's frame and fall backward.

For half a second, he suppressed a laugh at her baffled expression as she sat stunned on the floor. Then, her face filled with a rage he hadn't seen for quite some time, and she climbed to her feet, marched over, and glared at him.

"Do you care to explain what *that* was about?" she demanded, sweeping an arm in a wide gesture toward the door.

Byron finally let his control slip. "Why can't you behave?" he shouted instead of answering her question. "Why is there always trouble surrounding you? What made you believe running off would be a smart idea? There's also an appropriate time for discussing what took place. Now, everyone's shaken up. Who knows what Aaron and Marcus will do!"

"I'll tell you what they'll do," Coura raised her voice without skipping a beat. "They'll go to the palace and find what I said is true!"

Byron inhaled through his nostrils before matching her volume. "What are they going to find? A murderer? Their lives are in danger, not to mention other people's. Even though you assume you're invincible because you don't have attachments doesn't mean you can throw away all caution! What if they go after Clearshot and Emilea's children next? What about the rest of the mages under my authority?"

Her eyes widened then narrowed into daggers. "So, that's what this is about. You think I don't care about anybody except myself. Is it because I had a demon with me? Does that scare you? Do you even remember why I agreed to her deal? I wanted to save my home and my family. None of that matters to you now, though, because you won't trust me."

Byron opened his mouth to disagree, but the words wouldn't come out. She took advantage of the moment to throw more in his face.

"What makes me any different than before I could use demonic energy? Sure, Soirée appeared, but I always stayed in control. *I* fought to save people you so easily claim I don't care about. Meanwhile, I had a crazed demon in my head trying to convince me of how awful I am for fighting to keep you all safe."

As Coura's words started to sink in, Byron's anger dwindled until he felt guilty for sparking their yelling match. Worse yet, she mirrored his stance to continue the bout.

"Do you know what the worst part is? I can tolerate the prissy mages who don't want to associate with me, and I can understand why nobody likes to be involved with someone using demonic power. When Hernan said I'm nothing and I belong to him and his council, I was livid. Through all of it, as long as I knew people were fighting for the same things I am, I vowed to protect them. I assumed you would dismiss me when I told you about Soirée, and I accepted the fact that I'll never be treated the same because at least I can admit everything has been *my* choice. You can blame and hate me, but don't you dare pity me for how my life played out."

Byron's mind went blank while he felt his face flushing with embarrassment. "I don't hate you."

She turned her back to him and, to his surprise, went on in a subdued manner.

"Do you remember the first day I left East Hoover and you forced me to make a fire without magic? According to you, it served as a lesson in obedience. You said I need to follow my leader's command in order to earn their loyalty."

Although he vaguely recalled having the discussion, Byron remembered her bitterness at his request regarding obeying orders more than the actual conversation.

"What I shared then is still how I live each day," she explained. "I follow what I believe is right and earn others' trust through my actions and decisions. Even when I fail, I can never go back on my word or I'll lose sight of who I am."

His worry about the demon replacing Coura and his concern over his pupil's real identity were snuffed out by her reasoning, leaving Byron to stare at the young, vulnerable woman in front of him.

What have I done? he thought and buried his face in his hands while regretting ever bringing her there. In the resulting silence, he wondered if he should go, yet it felt wrong to abandon matters as they were.

"Coura," he offered and took a tentative step toward her.

"You sound exhausted," she replied without glancing at him. "I'll come find you tomorrow."

He couldn't have asked for a more deliberate excuse to leave.

*

58

The next morning, Byron slept in as late as his body would allow before going to see Tio. The general and his assistant planned to discuss business with Emilea in the meeting chamber and let out a huff at Byron's unpunctual arrival.

"It's about time!" came their leader's harsh welcome.

Byron apologized, bowed slightly, and accepted a seat.

"You look well rested," Emilea leaned over to whisper with a smile.

"I feel well rested too," he commented before focusing his attention on the map of Asteom spread across the table.

The master light mage filled him in on what they already covered. "Prince Aaron and Assistant General Marcus left for Verona last night on horseback. General Tio and Calin are both aware of what took place outside the base. We're trying to figure out our next steps. If we're not careful, we could-"

A knock on the door interrupted her summary, and the knob twisted.

"This is a private meeting!" Tio boomed and stood, like a predator preparing to attack.

"We know. Why do you think we're here?" came a muffled response.

Coura entered first, surprising the trio, with a timid Will and displeased Clearshot trailing behind. She wore a plain, brown dress, and her braided hair hung over a shoulder, making her appear as ordinary as ever. The three joined those seated at the table, yet Tio decided not to argue.

"You're not in a position to be deciding where you should and shouldn't be," was all the man muttered to warn Coura.

She merely shrugged. "Marcus and Aaron are our friends, and everyone present, besides you and Calin, went out of the base last night. We don't keep secrets between us."

"Not anymore," Byron couldn't help but grumble.

She shot him an annoyed look then focused solely on Emilea.

Despite how they ended their argument the previous evening, he felt in better spirits with her. *Her mannerisms seem to be normal, along with that attitude. I suppose we have nothing more to linger on for now.*

"Go ahead," Byron urged his fellow master mage, who appeared unsure about the additional members.

"As I was saying, if we're not careful how we utilize the information Grace shared and what the rogue angel presented, the panic resulting from your battle in the valley will return twofold."

Byron scratched his chin and contemplated the subject before answering. "Nobody knew about the prince's arrival besides those in the base, but word has most likely spread to the citizens of Dala."

General Tio dipped his head in confirmation.

"From my understanding, there are several issues," Calin picked up. "First, the five rogue angels are a looming threat, and they serve a powerful man in the palace. There's also the demon you mentioned working with that group. We need to remain in a defensive position in case they appear again since their plan involved capturing Prince Aaron and eliminating our base. We can't rely on Coura's abilities for protection either."

Their eyes fell on her while she analyzed the map with an unreadable expression. Emilea continued when Calin didn't go on.

"The second part of our dilemma is something we cannot be certain about since the information came from the demon."

Byron expected Coura to interrupt and claim the authenticity of the message, yet she remained silent, letting Emilea finish.

"King Hernan might be dead. With a lack of communication between Dala and Verona, there's no way for us to hear what happened."

The room quieted as everyone kept their ideas and considerations to themselves.

Although it proved difficult, Byron forced himself to put aside his personal feelings for those in the capital in favor of fulfilling his duties at the base. He plotted stations for the soldiers and mages in Dala in his head and a rotation cycle in case they were attacked. When he completed the basic layout, he cleared his throat and prepared to explain. The others' eyes shifted to him before he launched into the time-consuming process of assignments and preparation. All the while thoughts of the palace stirred in the back of his mind.

Once he finished speaking, he glanced from face to face, waiting for somebody to add their input. Each person, except Calin and Tio, wore a distracted expression, and he understood deep down how they longed to be on the road returning home.

I feel the same way, but we can't give up when this city and base need us too.

Movement out of the corner of his eye caught his attention. Byron noticed the general and his assistant exchange a glance before nodding to each other.

"I believe it's about time I dismiss you lot," Tio stated while knitting his brow in a menacing fashion.

"What?" Byron, Clearshot, and Coura responded at once with varying degrees of alarm.

"You heard me!" The general slammed his hand on the table and pushed himself up to tower over those seated. "Ever since you arrived, you've been nothing but trouble. Dala hasn't seen angels or demons in generations, and now I got both to concern myself with! Never before have my soldiers fought this hard to protect our city. In fact, most were never wounded in battle until recently."

As he spoke, Tio strolled over to the window and stared at the afternoon sky. His face became set in a mask of calm, but the gruff voice sounded exasperated.

Byron stared, confused and unsure of what to do or say next. *I guess I didn't consider how the general would react to uncontrollable circumstances. Perhaps we were never destined to stay in the southern base.*

Without turning around, Tio went on. "I want you gone by sundown, unless you'd like to be imprisoned here for the rest of your lives."

Emilea and Clearshot instantly rose from the table, bowed, then hurried out. Byron's chin dropped to his chest as a wave of disappointment enveloped him. More shuffling took place to signal the departure of everyone besides Calin.

Once he raised his eyes, he found the assistant general grinning, as though the soldier was trying not to laugh. A wink from him after revealed their intentions, and Byron gently slammed the heel of his hand against his forehead.

He's not actually mad! Tio removed the burden of our assignment so we can leave without issue.

He released a sigh of relief, stood from his chair, and bowed. "Thank you."

While Calin snickered, Tio flashed a wide smile in their direction. "I should be thanking you, Master Byron. I'm lucky I let you speak before or else we'd need to fumble together some sort of strategy to fortify the area. Now, it's time you lead that unusual group of yours to the capital before the place falls apart."

Byron returned the gesture, feeling freer than ever at the moment. "I will, and I promise to send word as soon as we make it back."

After rushing to pack and eat enough to hold him over, he met Emilea and Clearshot outside the main entrance while a handful of men led five horses to them. The former shared the general's orders to take the horses she and the other light mages brought when they first arrived at the base. By the time the three of them saddled up, Coura and Will ran out and followed suit.

"Are we ready?" Clearshot asked once the preparations were complete.

Each rider expressed their confirmation before Emilea assumed the lead.

"Shout if you need to stop; otherwise, we'll go until I decide when to rest," she explained before edging her horse forward into a trot, then a full gallop. Her husband kept close behind, followed by Coura and Will. Byron chanced a final glimpse at the formidable structure with an oddly nostalgic sensation and hurried away.

*

Their group covered an impressive amount of ground during their trek to Verona. On foot at a leisurely pace took Byron and their initial party nine days; he could see the top of the palace in the afternoon on the fourth. Of course, no one seemed willing to request a break until Emilea could no longer ride because they were all determined to continue. Their animals galloped most of the time, and they only paused during brief moments for meals, to feed and water the horses, or to sleep. They also didn't hold conversations since the journey wore them down at a steady rate as the days passed. Everybody managed to pack some sort of food, or at least no one complained about being hungry, though Byron's anxiousness deterred him from eating too much despite his appetite.

The towns we moved through appeared too inactive for my liking. Perhaps it's my nerves, but I don't feel confident about returning, he thought solemnly.

Emilea slowed once the main road became crowded before dismounting, directing the others to do the same. While they walked into the city, Byron scratched his horse's neck with pity for the panting animals.

Poor creatures. Given how soon Emilea and the light mages arrived in Dala, I would bet they procured rides specifically bred for such grueling travel. Even so, I promise you'll be brushed and given fresh water along with a treat by my order for the effort.

Will and Coura spoke with one another in hushed voices, as did Emilea and Clearshot, and many strained faces accompanied their group into Verona.

It seems nothing changed dramatically.

He glanced around and relaxed. The extravagant homes along the western main road always brightened in late spring from a variety of colored plants, and gardeners could be seen tending the flowers, trimming bushes, or preoccupying themselves by doing other outdoor tasks. A sweet, floral scent wafted through the air, mixing with the doughy aroma of baked breads and treats from farther in the city.

From up ahead, Clearshot halted his steps to reach over and give his wife his animal's reins and a kiss on the cheek before addressing Byron. "This is where I leave you. My children have been in the care of a friend for too long. I'm sure I'll hear what I need to eventually."

He approached one of the estates on their left and, after speaking to a gardener, was let in through the polished, silver gates. Emilea went on toward the palace, leaving Byron, Coura, and Will to catch up.

All around, he noticed friendly waves or smiles in their direction, as if the people recognized and became comfortable with mages and soldiers wandering through the city. Emilea and Byron did their best to act confident, though he assumed Emilea grew as concerned as him. Meanwhile, Coura averted her eyes, and Will glanced around to show his nerves.

They stayed on the main road leading straight to the palace where one of the guards posted at the entrance approached them. Emilea requested servants to relieve them of their horses, and soon the four entered, looking and smelling of a four-day ride.

"Where should we go?" Will asked from behind when Emilea moved forward with Coura.

The distress the young man projected did nothing for Byron's own mentality, yet he put a reassuring hand on Will's shoulder and led them on. "If you would like, you may return to your room, clean up, eat, and sleep."

He intended for the words to remove the burden of their journey, but Will's eyes widened, reflecting how the comment offended him.

"Why would I? I can't just abandon everybody! I have to know where Aaron and Marcus are and make sure they're safe."

Byron apologized and berated himself for considering pushing Will away. Together, they followed Emilea and Coura up the staircase and through the winding maze of the palace's hallways. As soon as they entered the rear side of the second floor, it became noticeable that something was wrong. Servants of varying ages and heights scurried past or excused themselves while sneaking around from behind to jog ahead.

"What is going on?" Byron heard Emilea mutter. He sensed her beginning to search for a person of importance near the council's meeting room, which proved to be a fair assumption given the business of the area.

A few minutes later, they reached the chamber only to find both doors propped open and six guards posted instead of the usual two. Several, male voices conversed at once inside, and Byron saw Generals Casner, Dillon, and Tont huddled over the wide table littered with papers while High Priest Hendal paced closest to the door. Each man abandoned their sentences as soon as they noticed the four.

"Why, it can't be!" Hendal exclaimed and faced the newcomers while opening his arms to them.

"Finally, some positive news," General Dillon said by way of greeting and gave the master mages a weak smile.

The high priest stepped closer to Emilea. "My lady, we were not expecting your return, nor Master Byron's."

"I wish we didn't come with such ill tidings," she replied. Her expression softened, and she looked around the room.

Like a single mind recalling a disaster, the mood of the space sunk enough to worry Byron. Then, General Casner gestured for the group to enter.

"Let them in," he ordered the guards. "Close the doors. Let us have some privacy."

Emilea, Byron, Coura, and Will accepted seats around the wide table before the chamber doors slammed shut. The generals glanced at one another while they considered who would speak and how to begin. At last, Casner continued to act as the leader in that moment.

"Much has befallen us this week, and I'm afraid none of it is anything other than terrible."

"We heard rumors," Byron admitted and rubbed his eyes. "No details reached the Dalan base."

"Well, let me put those to rest for you," the general began in a grief-stricken tone. "Six nights ago, King Hernan and Queen Freya were found dead in their private quarters, His Highness face down on the floor and the queen in bed. Both received stab wounds straight through the heart. The guards assigned to patrol their wing had been unconscious, claiming they last remembered spotting a pair of cloaked figures. None wound up with worse than minor head trauma, though, proving the murderers' targets had specifically been the royal family.

We're horrified and baffled by how somebody could enter and exit the palace without the patrols noticing. Our suspicion is the murders have a source on the inside, one possessing the knowledge and power to sneak them in. Prince Aaron had been on his routes, as I'm sure you knew, so we were unable to contact him. In this sort of situation, the king's council takes up command until a new ruler is appointed."

The strain caught up with Casner then. He coughed and reached for the pitcher of water and an empty glass sitting across the table, leaving Dillon to continue the briefing.

"We began following protocol for such an occasion. Each of us accepted separate responsibilities and consulted together, according to

His Highness' wish if such an emergency arose. Our first task was to alert the soldiers, mages, and citizens of Verona and urge them to remain on guard until the murderers are captured. I have been handling the messages in and out of the palace to the nearby towns and cities. Also, I spoke to the supervising mages appointed by you, Masters Emilea and Byron. Courses and training are suspended until further notice. Next, we assigned our best healers, guards, and agents to the murder scene. Preston spearheaded the investigation, but…"

He paused to put a hand over his eyes. Everybody waited patiently for him to compose himself before he could go on.

"Two days after the murder of the king and queen, General Preston's body turned up in the outer hallway on the third floor. Why he had been there, no one can say. No witnesses had been present this time, but the killing wound appeared exactly the same: a precise stab through the heart."

"What?" Byron breathed when his mind went blank.

Dillon nodded. "It's true. Three murders within three days."

Another moment of silence resulted from those around the table recollecting themselves before Casner cleared his throat. "The situation has changed. The palace isn't safe anymore. Guards are posted at just about every corner, though most are willing to do so without a proper assignment, and we requested the mages stay on alert in case magic is involved."

"Where is Prince Aaron?" Emilea asked next. "He stayed in Dala with us nearly a week ago. Did he inform you of what took place in the Valley Beyond?"

The generals and high priest looked at one another before shaking their heads, and Hendal spoke from where he sat to the light mage's left.

"The prince hasn't spoken a word since hearing the news about his parents. He wished to visit them, then he shut himself in his quarters."

Byron turned toward Tont. "What about Assistant General Marcus? He returned with Prince Aaron and surely would have explained the southern base's issues to you already."

"I was unaware anything went amiss in Dala," the man answered, scrunching his face into a displeased expression.

"In that case, there's much we need to share."

Tont dropped his head into his hands with a groan. "I ordered my son to return to my wife, daughter, and her family. My intention had been to keep him safe from this mess, but I ignored his outbursts."

"A father who cares for his family deserves not to be chastised for protecting them but praised," Hendal added.

"Allow us to recount our experience, and possibly patch some holes," Byron began and prepared to recap the longest weeks of his life.

First, he told them about Grace's cryptic message before skipping to the alleged threat in the Valley Beyond. He omitted no details when he described the angels they encountered, including their names and reasons for luring General Tio and his outer squad to the secluded location.

Despite his reluctance to complicate matters further, Byron informed them of Coura's sacrifice and how she lost her magical power in the process followed by the appearance of the giant creature, the lead angel, and a demon. The only piece he purposefully refrained from revealing was Coura's connection to the demon since he hoped to remove all suspicion from her. Even without looking in her direction he noticed her physically attempting to make herself smaller in the presence of those in charge by dipping her head and sliding lower in her seat.

They had no way of telling how much time passed, but everyone appeared stiff and more worn out than earlier when he concluded the report.

Casner frowned deeper and swallowed another drink of water before standing. "We cannot thank you enough for your work in Dala and for watching over Prince Aaron. I believe it is appropriate for us to take a brief respite from this meeting. If you could spare the extra energy, Master Byron, Master Emilea, we would appreciate your opinions on where matters lie now."

Byron glanced at Emilea, who nodded slightly to him, then responded. "You needn't ask, though I should bathe and find new clothes and something decent to eat before rejoining."

A wave of relief passed over the generals' and high priest's faces, and they agreed.

"Take as long as you need," Hendal urged and clapped his hands together while everybody rose to exit. "We will resume when you two return."

Byron placed a hand on Coura and Will's shoulders and waited for the space to empty before addressing the pair. Both of their expressions reflected a weariness that had him concerned they would fall over from exhaustion, yet a buried drive to assist burned beneath. When the three were alone, he smiled at them while avoiding the urge to wince at the despair shining in their eyes when they met his.

They're not only hungry, dirty, and tired from the ruthless journey, but hearing such news, especially concerning their friends, puts an extra blanket of sorrow on their backs.

"I want to thank you for all you've done these past few months. As of this moment, I'm dismissing you from business related to Dala, Prince Aaron, the rogue angels, and the demonic creatures," he said sternly, though he expected backlash.

To his amazement, it wasn't his temperamental student who protested, though he noticed more color decorate her pale cheeks, and her eyes danced with disapproval.

Will's face fell to project his disappointment. "What do you mean we're dismissed? I thought we're involved in this together?"

"I said 'as of this moment.' There's too much going on and matters that need settling for me to keep an eye on you two and tell you what to do. I'm sorry, but murders in the palace are a serious matter, and special protocol takes place involving the council members."

The young man's eyes lowered to the floor. "What should we do then?" he asked in a defeated tone.

"I know it seems difficult right now, but all we can do is begin to pick ourselves up again. Focus on taking care of yourself first, then others. With your hearts and minds as a strong foundation, those who need your support will be glad to lean on them, including myself."

Byron gave them a gentle shove toward the door after offering the advice. He desperately desired food, a hot bath, then to return and mentally prepare himself for the night, in that order.

At the gesture, Coura spun away and left without saying a word. Will watched her until he decided to trudge out too.

Picking Up the Pieces

Three days passed since Coura returned to Verona and despair lurked around every corner of the palace. She rarely stayed anywhere besides her room because of an overwhelming depression draining the energy from her body. Meanwhile, her mind wandered for solutions to their problems, ultimately making her feel worse about her uselessness.

A lone benefit emerged from her lack of malicious power, which related to how the mages treated her. In a way, they didn't seem to recognize her when she wandered through the halls. This allowed her to listen in on their conversations during meals. She sat alone at dinner one evening and overheard a gray-bearded solder explain what had been taking place in the city to a group of light mages.

"It's customary for passing members of the royal family to be cremated in a private ceremony," he shared. "Their remains are then given to the heir, who has the responsibility to do as they see fit."

He went on to share how most living relatives spent a few days traveling to a special location to bury or scatter the ashes while others keep them in order to be closer to their lost loved ones. At some point, the generals, master mages, and high priest decided it was time to move forward with the private ceremony. Coura returned to her room after, letting the news seep in.

*

More time flew by, and she heard nothing from her friends, which she half-expected once they became aware of her connection to a demon. She did notice the servants and kitchen staff begin preparations for some sort of event. Multiple pairs of shuffling feet scurried by in the corridor outside her room, piquing her curiosity.

I wonder what's happening now, she absentmindedly thought before lying on her bed to stare up at the ceiling. *I didn't think assignments or training resumed yet, so why are so many people moving at such a hurried pace?*

Ever since Soirée disappeared from her mind, Coura still expected to hear the familiar voice chime in. She paused and waited for the words before sighing with both embarrassment and frustration as she hugged a pillow over her face.

"What's wrong with me?" she shouted, though the bundle of cloth and feathers muffled her voice.

No matter what I believe might help, I can't motivate myself to try. My direction and support are gone too. I don't know what I should do.

A strong surge of self-pity threatened to overtake Coura, as it had several times since she lost her magic and Soirée. For hours, she remained in that position, too awake to nap yet physically lethargic. The noise outside her room lessened, reminding her of how lonely she had grown, and the unhappiness returned with it.

No... I refuse to cry again. I'm so sick of this!

Remembering the incidents that took place over the past weeks and the humiliation, isolation, and ire she experienced raised her temper. She sat up and threw her pillow against the far wall with a grunt in response. It flopped against a spot to the left of her window then slid to the floor while she glared.

Instead of lying back down, she decided to go and grab the pillow before staring at the field below where the last sunlight of the day shined across the area. She pushed the window open and welcomed the gentle breeze. The fresh air picked up the scent of cut grass, which settled her emotions. Coura closed her eyes and let it flow over her skin and through her unbound, messy hair.

This reminds me of the freedom when I could...

A pang of anguish immediately followed her memories of flying after the reminder of her lost abilities, specifically the wings she would never be able to manifest again. She shut her eyes and expected the next breeze to increase the internal pain and desire for the unobtainable; however, a new feeling arose.

From her hollow center, a brush of energy startled her. A hand lifted to rest on her chest, and she opened her eyes as the sun disappeared beneath the line of trees from the forest far beyond the southern clearing.

What did I just sense?

The presence of a faint power acted like a shadow of her former energy, reminding her of what she used to be. Coura remembered the familiar sensation of casting a spell, of holding the power in her hand, and worst of all, of the wings weighing on her shoulder blades. Again, she winced, expecting to be struck by negative emotions.

Nothing responded except the distant memory of what she had once possessed.

She observed the night outside for a while before beginning to understand how she currently felt. *Whatever that was, it blocked my...no, not blocked... It stopped me from allowing the past to hinder my present mindset. I swear I've experienced it another time as well. What does this mean?*

Coura straightened, shut the window, then decided to address her physical condition, another item on the list of things she'd grown despondent over. She couldn't train after her injury, though she showed no enthusiasm toward participating in any sort of activity at the Dalan base, and it had been a while since she finished a decent meal. The lack of attention to her body caused her muscles to weaken and build to become the shell of a combatant. In response to the recognition, her limbs grew stiff with a desire to move and stretch, as they once did daily.

"Maybe Byron's right," she mumbled to herself. "What's done is done. I need to focus on moving forward in order to fix what problems I can control. I suppose I can start with my training."

She skimmed over her wardrobe until she spotted the appropriate clothes and worn boots. As she dressed, she felt more like her old self and grew eager to push her body through an exercise session. Finally, she combed her fingers through her hair and took a deep breath. In retrospect, she probably looked terrible, but she ignored the restless doubts before exiting the room.

With a curfew in place from the generals, the hallways emptied as Coura descended to the first floor, then she walked outside into the training ground. The guards on duty eyed her suspiciously, yet no one interrupted or questioned where she planned to go.

The only light in the area came from the widest stable housing several dummies used for practicing and the majority of their wooden and steel weapons. She strolled in, nodded at the two soldiers chatting farther away, and rummaged through the bins. After procuring a wooden sword, she stood opposite her chosen target consisting of bundled straw and leather padding. For a minute, she gripped the hilt so tightly her arms trembled.

What am I doing here alone? What if I don't remember how to fight?

As if on cue, the spark in her center brushed the fears aside until she charged and struck the dummy in the area considered its neck. A thud echoed when her blade bounced off the outer layer, and she suppressed a groan.

I'm in worse shape than I thought.

Despite her damaged pride, Coura decided returning to the basics would benefit her the most; from then on, she forgot her problems and emotions to instead focus on the task at hand.

One of the guards checked in on the stable later that evening. He scolded her for still being there, which she apologized for before continuing. Then, he tried sweet talking her into going inside the palace. In reply, she claimed if he felt so concerned then he could stand watch at the entrance. That flustered the man, and he left her after vowing to report such disobedience to his superior.

*

The fatigue set in just before dawn. Coura slouched to the ground, panting and smiling while reflecting on the session. *I'm not nearly as efficient as I used to be, but I haven't lost too much skill. A few more days' worth of work, and I'll be back into my normal routine.*

Sunrise crept over the eastern horizon, so she pushed herself to her feet and hurried to catch breakfast before the mess hall became crowded. After grabbing a bite to eat, she returned to her room and promptly fell asleep.

That afternoon, she woke and dragged her body out of bed despite its soreness and the lack of a proper night's rest. She repeated motivational phrases more than once in order to support herself through the second half of her day, opting to be positive rather than let the pessimism set in.

Perhaps it was her rising confidence, but Coura noticed how downcast everyone else looked. Soldiers, mages, servants, and those she couldn't identify appeared glum while they went about their business, which reminded her of Byron's words in the meeting chamber.

'With strong hearts and minds as a foundation, those who need your support will be glad to lean on it.' They have nobody to turn to since the generals, Byron, and Emilea are supporting Aaron and trying to catch the murderers. They're acting similar to how I behaved: without direction and afraid of the unknown. Perhaps what they need, and what I could have used all along, is someone to show them how to take command of their life when the world is bleak.

She pushed open the door to the training ground and found herself temporarily blinded by the sunlight. As she blinked to help her eyes to adjust, she noticed the area was empty except for the regular guards and a handful of younger men conversing in the shade of the stone structure.

"I know the sessions have all been canceled, but *no one* is bothering to train?" she wondered aloud while nearing the main stable.

During the previous evening, it seemed easier to work under a lamp inside the walled and roofed space because onlookers couldn't scrutinize her. Now, Coura forced her mind to set aside the rising sense of loneliness in order to scan the racks and bins of armor and weaponry. She settled on a sword before deciding to drag one of the dummies into the dried grass while ignoring the rising heat of early summer.

By late afternoon, sweat dripped off her forehead, and she felt certain her face, neck, and arms had burned under the sun. Still, she sucked up her insistent thirst and hunger and went through the steps of another, offensive maneuver. Once she executed it cleanly at a slower pace, she sat on the ground to catch her breath.

A door opened and closed from the direction of the palace followed by hushed voices. A brief glance toward the building showed three boys about her age approaching. They seemed interested in why she practiced alone, but Coura didn't mind the attention. In fact, she had noticed several faces peeking down from windows and the upper floors' outer hallways all afternoon. A couple dozen people came outside as well, though nobody seemed to be in a serious mindset to work on their combat skills.

"What's wrong?" she startled the trio by calling and waving.

The tallest boy took the lead when they walked over. "We assumed the training ground had been closed because the sessions aren't taking place," he answered with more courage than he showed.

Coura wondered if they recognized her at all because of how nervous they acted but soon thought otherwise and chuckled. "Just because you're not in your scheduled groups doesn't mean you can't come here and practice."

"We were ordered to stay inside under the generals' authority," snapped the shortest one, as if he challenged her laid-back view.

She shrugged it off, stood, and faced the dummy again. "So what? Being soft and weak are ideal qualities for a soldier of Asteom now?"

"Never," two responded at the same time, though all three straightened.

Coura took the opportunity to run her offensive attack at full speed, swinging her blade around the dummy in a distracting fashion, then striking its side with a loud thwack. She grinned when she caught the boys watching; their faces held the same desire to be active that she had felt the previous night.

"Well, what are you waiting for?" She used the tip of her sword to point at the main stable.

"Yes ma'am," the one in front responded and saluted, much to her embarrassment.

The three jogged away after, and Coura rolled her eyes as her stomach growled.

I guess I can't go eat just yet.

*

Having people in the area stay to train must have made it more inviting. Otherwise, she underestimated how many soldiers longed to be working outside again. Before she retired for the day, a couple boys familiar with the first three joined them to pair up, an older man asked Coura to practice, beating her almost as badly as Byron used to, and a pair of middle-aged men found space to spar.

Once she begged her partner to excuse her for dinner, he laughed and followed her into the palace. Together, they merged with a group seated in the mess hall, and she got to know them a little. Their enthusiasm led her to convince them to spend time in the training ground with her the next morning. When she returned to her room, Coura collapsed onto her bed and fell into the best night of sleep she earned in months.

The following day, she began working again before anybody else; however, it didn't take long for soldiers to file out. Even a group of mages awkwardly holding weapons sparred among themselves off to the side. As she studied them, the foreign hint of energy in her center stirred, and Coura abandoned her dummy to approach.

They started at her friendly wave. She could tell they recognized her but were uncertain about returning the gesture, most likely due to the lack of demonic power she used to possess.

"You're holding your sword wrong," she said by way of greeting while gesturing to a young woman gripping the hilt too far down.

"W-What?" the mage stuttered before readjusting her hands. "I knew that."

Coura shrugged before turning her back to them and deciding to pursue lunch.

"Wait!"

She looked over her shoulder to spot one of the young women with short, golden hair and bright green eyes jog toward her. With a raised eyebrow, she hesitated long enough for the girl to speak again.

"I'm not sure if you remember me, but I was in your weapons class at the Magical Arts Academy. My name is Jamie Sullivan-Briar."

The shy nature of her smile prompted Coura to ease up. "I'm sorry, I'm not good at recalling names or faces."

"I remember you, Coura," Jamie continued. "You excelled in every combat and spellcasting class. Of course, you did study under Master Byron, so nobody was ever surprised."

Coura chuckled and rubbed her neck as the mage's positive memory touched her. All she could think to do next was offer her thanks.

"I'm wondering if you would help us with our sword work," Jamie asked after while her friends stared down at their feet.

The request took Coura back. "What about your training sessions?"

"We just arrived from the academy about a week ago. Our schedules were supposed to begin already, but given what's happened…"

It's been over a year since the Mage Service Law was established? This must be the first graduating bunch since it passed. Coura shook her head to avoid drifting too far into the past. Then, an idea came to mind.

"I'll work with you under one condition," she began and held up a finger to emphasis the statement.

"What is it?"

"The soldiers assigned to your training are either busy or out of the palace at the moment. I need you to tell as many new mages as you can that early work is available to prepare them for the real stuff."

Jamie nodded. "We'll try our best."

"Believe me, what they do here is no joke," Coura added with a wry smile. "Without warming up, your bodies will become exhausted, and you'll regret not starting sooner. Repeat my warning to anybody who is unsure."

Throughout the afternoon, she assisted Jamie and her friends while considering when their training would resume. *I haven't spoken to Marcus since we were together in Dala. The generals and Byron are probably too preoccupied to worry about what goes on out here. Perhaps I can organize a routine to kick-start the mages' exercises for the time being.*

When her pupils appeared ready to drop, she released them. At that point in the day, twenty soldiers practiced against dummies and each other in the area. She felt grateful for their efforts to do more than sit around sulking as she hurried inside for dinner.

The three mage recruits joined a group who already finished eating. Meanwhile, Coura grabbed a couple plates and prepared to head up to her floor, though not without overhearing them discussing her training regimen.

Maybe I am better off now, she wondered, yet the notion hadn't fully set in.

Since both hands held the meals, she approached her goal and kicked the door twice. As usual, it took Will a minute of shuffling to crack open the door to his room; once he caught a glimpse of who waited, it extended wide enough for her to enter.

"Coura, I'm glad to see you!" he exclaimed while ushering her inside. "Is that second plate for me?"

If the space had been cleaned at all during their time in Dala, she couldn't tell. "Your room is a disaster."

He shoved books, papers, and various items off the bed and hopped onto it. "Are you really surprised anymore?"

He laughed when Coura rolled her eyes and grinned before accepting a seat by his side. Then, the two dug into their meals. Will entertained her with insight on his readings, which she assumed was what he accomplished since returning to Verona. Meanwhile, the sky turned shades of purple and scarlet to signal the setting sun. She put her plate aside, went to the windows, and pushed them open, allowing fresh, clean air to blow through the room and replace the mustiness.

She sighed contently as she leaned on the sill. "That's better."

"You haven't said much," Will noted. He balanced his empty plate on the desk's contents in order to stand beside her and watch the approaching night.

"It's difficult to sneak more than a word in between your many," she commented and shook her head, causing him to blush.

They remained quiet for a moment before he picked up the conversation in a neutral tone. "I haven't seen anyone since we returned."

Coura nodded as she sensed the gloom hovering over her shoulders. "Me neither," she admitted and turned her attention to the task at hand. "Actually, I'm hoping you can assist me with a project."

"Project? What is it?"

She informed him of her resumed training and the soldiers who participated for their own goals after realizing it was acceptable to be outside, ending with her idea for the new mages.

"I'm wondering if you talked to Marcus because he can help me organize some sort of warm-up sessions for the recruits since nothing will be starting soon. In fact, now that I think about it, you've become pretty adapt at the basics of combat."

"I only learned as much as they did at the academy, maybe a bit more," he hurried to explain. "There's absolutely no way I could train somebody to fight. I'll search for Marcus, though. That's something I can do."

When she didn't respond, Will ran a hand through his hair before slipping off his glasses to polish them on his shirt. She raised an eyebrow while waiting for him to budge. It became obvious from his nervous behavior that he continued to consider the position and weigh his personal feelings on the matter. After he began pacing and stepping over the items on the floor, Coura hurried to light some candles.

"I suppose we could start where I did, but they're beginning at varying levels," she heard him mutter and smiled to herself.

"You won't be alone, Will. For starters, I'll be there, and I'm sure I can persuade some experienced soldiers to assist us. I trust you with the trainees who aren't familiar with wielding a sword or who lack confidence. We'll do this together."

He groaned to show his reluctance but agreed anyway.

"Besides, it's not as if the program should last more than a week or two," Coura offered as she moved to the door.

"You're leaving already?"

"There's one other person I'd like to visit tonight."

Once their goodbyes concluded, she proceeded to the corner of the fourth floor where Grace's quarters were located. Before the reassignment to Dala, she brought up the poor position of the Yeluthian's previous room to Aaron, who wholeheartedly agreed to move their friend to a more comfortable space. She hadn't been there since they met for their regular, friendly dinners.

That seems so long ago.

She knocked on the chosen door even as she doubted her memory of the correct location. Thankfully, the girl's face appeared, and the colorful eyes widened to reflect a startled joy. Grace cried her name and wrapped both arms around her, so Coura returned the embrace. They broke apart and opened their mouths at the same time to greet the other until a woman's voice came from behind her friend.

"Please, come in you two."

Coura craned her neck to peer around Grace. "I didn't see you had company," she began and prepared to apologize until the Yeluthian pulled her forward.

The room appeared completely new compared to what she remembered. A white banner with bronze wings embroidered on it hung next to a sketched portrait of her friend. Both waved gently in the slight breeze entering from a pair of open windows. The desk held decorative boxes, gems, and jewelry while a gray rug covered most of the floor space. Sitting in a chair beside the farthest window was Emilea, dressed in a professional-looking robe and gazing at them with a bored expression.

"This is nice," Coura admitted while joining Grace on the edge of the bed.

The girl bounced up and down excitedly, her striking, blonde hair moving with her. "Thank you! I have to tell you about so much when we get the chance."

At the reminder, Coura looked between Grace and Emilea. "I'm sorry if I'm interrupting."

The light mage shook her head in a helpless manner and, to Coura's utter surprise, directed a kind smile at her. "It's quite all right. Actually, it's better you arrived when you did. There's news that concerns you and information I'm seeking from Grace."

"Emilea just began recounting the incident in the Valley Beyond and the four strangers you fought," the Yeluthian added as she shifted her expression into one projecting a sense of seriousness before turning to the master mage.

"That's correct. Where were we?"

During the retelling, Coura avoided wincing at numerous parts while keeping quiet. By that point, she expected the negative reactions, which softened the reveal of Soirée and their previous connection. Being close to Grace made her nervous, though, and she wondered what her friend thought of the situation. Soon after, she found herself invested in the conversation when Emilea explained details she hadn't heard before.

"Byron, the mages I brought along to Dala, and I researched the books you recommended on Asteom's relationship with Yeluthia. That's when we learned about the ancestral weapons."

"What are the ancestral weapons?" Grace asked.

"That's not a good sign," Emilea muttered before continuing at a normal volume. "According to the texts, your people gifted the king of Asteom two swords, bows, and daggers embedded with a sealing spell. On another subject, my notes mentioned a demonic possession broken by the prism sealing spell, which is a high-level ability used by light mages to forcibly remove the demon from its host's body."

"What do those have to do with me?" Coura interjected.

"The ancestral weapons are made of gold," Emilea continued in a patient tone. "You mentioned seeing a glint of it before losing consciousness and had a dagger wound in your side."

"You are saying the sealing spell went into effect when she was stabbed, but because the dagger had been removed, the demon's energy released instead," Grace summarized while Coura tried to process what this meant.

"That's correct. The breaking of the spell also snapped whatever hold had been established. At least, it seems that way."

Soirée is free, Coura realized. Her heart beat faster when she considered the consequences. *She's no longer bound to my soul, yet I know what I felt when I came in contact with her demonic energy in Dala. Is there still a connection between us? She also urged me to return to the palace, claiming she could get our power back. What could she mean by-*

"Coura?"

She glanced at Emilea, then Grace. "What did you say?"

"Do you understand what this means?" the Yeluthian asked with an eager grin.

Coura shook her head, prompting her friend to hold her hands in a supportive manner.

"It means you are free. You are back to normal!"

Despite the warmth her friend projected, her spine stiffened, and she shot Emilea a look to reflect her uncertainty. The discomfort grew worse when the master mage smiled again.

"She's right. I can't sense demonic energy from you anymore. Unless, of course, you're hiding it."

This is wrong...

Once Grace let go of her hands, Coura stood and moved to exit, causing the Yeluthian to make a startled sound.

"Where are you-"

"I need to go," she interrupted.

Both Grace and Emilea rose as she opened the door and thanked them for the visit before slipping into the hallway. Her friend's voice chimed in her mind immediately after.

{Coura, what is the matter? Why did you leave?}

She opened her mouth to respond before remembering to use her thoughts. *What else did Emilea say? Was that why she came to talk with you?*

{Lady Emilea said nothing else, I promise. She hoped to learn about the ancestral weapons because I believe she is concerned they fell into the wrong hands. Will you please come back?}

Coura didn't answer until she returned to her own room and dropped into bed. By that point, her riled emotions settled enough to where she could notice how exhausted her body became. *I'm sorry. I'll visit tomorrow once I finish training. If you want, you can stop by in the afternoon. We can see Will too.*

The resulting reply hadn't been vocalized, but she felt Grace's presence fade away just as sleep took her.

The Funeral Procession

Even with their progress, the mages and soldiers had a difficult time focusing on their practice sessions when the day brought more apprehension and sorrow. A servant hurried into the training ground to share an update, shifting from one group to the next while repeating the same message.

"News from the king's council and Prince Aaron," he announced as he reached Coura, Will, and their selected partners. By that point, he sounded out of breath.

Coura held up a hand, signaling for him to wait until everybody gathered around.

Once they were set, the boy in his late teens cleared his throat. "News from the king's council and Prince Aaron," he repeated. "First, the murderers responsible for the deaths of the king, queen, and general have yet to be captured. Despite this, the issue for soldiers and mages to stay indoors, especially after dark, has been lifted."

There came sighs of relief from the audience along with murmurs about the lack of justice.

"Second, the private cremation ceremony for the royal family is complete, and the general's body has been returned to his family. The thirty-day mourning period began at sunrise, so a public honoring will take place this afternoon as Prince Aaron and his selected representatives move through Verona toward the western coast where the ashes of King Hernan and Queen Freya shall be buried. All soldiers, mages, and servants of the palace are expected to be present in the grand hall by three o'clock."

With that, the messenger spun on his heel and sprinted inside, leaving those who heard the information to their own business.

Aaron...

For all she dealt with in Dala and upon the group's return, Coura never bothered to consider the prince and what he was going through after losing his parents. Will reached over to touch her arm in a sympathetic gesture, and she noticed he appeared concerned as well.

If Aaron must stay strong, then so will I, she resolved and forced a smile before dismissing the lingering recruits.

They sounded appreciative, which she assumed had to be a result of how hard she worked them, and everyone began heading into the palace. Coura and Will followed at the rear until they noticed a figure in white exiting the building at the same time. Those moving in the opposite direction shuffled out of the way with bows and respectful greetings, revealing Emilea as she crossed over to approach them. In her shadow strolled Grace, much to their surprise.

"What are you two doing here?" Coura inquired.

"Grace said I could find you in the training ground," the master mage began with a gesture for them to follow her toward the door. "Come along. I've been instructed to prepare you for the procession."

The four hurried inside and through the grand hall to go into the city. During their passing, servants polished the floors and dusted the busts and paintings, cleaning as much as they could. Shopkeepers in Verona and their employees closed their establishments, swept the streets, and cleared away their belongings near the road.

It grew eerily quiet as they walked along the western main road, and at least one Asteom banner hung on each gate. Coura didn't anticipate the drastic change and raised her eyebrows when Emilea approached the same gates Clearshot had disappeared through when they returned to the capital. She lingered farther behind until a servant appeared, recognized the light mage, and opened the gate.

"Where are we?"

"This is Lord Donovan Neneme's home, and his wife, Lady Katrina, is a close friend of mine," Emilea explained. "She offered to host us for the procession."

The servant led them through the garden, which ranged in color from yellows and oranges to purple lilacs along the two-story house. Once they stepped through the doorway, Coura stood awestricken in front of a line of portraits placed around the walls. They didn't stay there for long, instead entering a sitting room adjacent to the foyer. Several chairs positioned in a circle overlooked the backyard, which seemed just as elaborate as the front with flowers, plants, and lawn decorations.

"Lady Katrina will be with you in a moment," their escort said before bowing and exiting.

Coura couldn't suppress a grin as she inspected each item on display. "You keep wealthy friends," she commented and bent over to admire the floral pattern engraved on a vase holding trimmed lilacs. The fragrant scent made her nose itch.

"Please be on your best behavior," Emilea replied while seating herself in one of the chairs. Will and Grace did the same while Coura continued roaming nearby.

Soon, the clicking of heeled shoes echoed closer until a woman emerged wearing a lacy, black gown with the scarlet crest of Asteom sewn onto the left breast. Her chestnut hair had been twisted and pinned under a matching hat bearing yellow lilies. Coura's face twitched at the amount of makeup adorning her face but overall found the lady attractive.

The master mage rose, and they greeted each other with a hug.

"Emilea, lovely! I see you brought guests, as you mentioned."

"I cannot thank you enough for allowing us in your home, especially during these troubling times."

Katrina, visibly flattered by the words, allowed Emilea to lead her over to the three others.

"Here we have Will Shairp, one of the researchers in the palace."

He squirmed under the woman's gaze yet managed a deep bow.

"Oh my, how polite! You seem to be around the size my son Bernard was a few years ago." She snapped twice, and the male servant arrived to wait at her side. "Leo, make a list for our guests. Check Bernard's belongings for a suit fitting this boy."

The way Katrina spoke, with her high-pitched exclamations and dramatic tone, irritated Coura.

Next, they moved to Grace, who curtsied before greeting their host. "It is an honor to meet you and be welcomed into your home, Lady Katrina."

"Who is this pretty girl possessing such excellent manners?" the woman asked with a blush and glanced at Emilea.

"That would be our Yeluthian ambassador, Grace Zelnar."

At the mention of Yeluthia, Katrina's expression filled with pride. "Such an important guest in my humble home! Truly this is an honor for *me*, Lady Zelnar," she added as she began inspecting Grace.

It took a few moments for her to decide on an outfit, then she shook her head before pouting.

"Leo, see if you can dig out one of the dresses from my younger days. They should be packed in the attic with my other possessions from years ago. My apologies Lady Zelnar, but we will do our best."

Grace curtsied again while the woman sidestepped to stand in front of her next target. From the closed distance, Coura could smell the other's perfume and nearly gagged. The master mage began introducing her until Katrina interrupted.

"What stunning eyes," the lady commented and glanced between her, Grace, and Emilea. "You three share similar shades of blue. Did you know that?"

Coura frowned while her friend giggled, and the master mage cleared her throat to respond.

"I hadn't noticed."

"Goodness, forgive me. I am so easily distracted!" The woman swatted a hand in front of her nose and laughed, allowing Emilea to continue.

"Actually, Coura is one of Byron Rinod's students from the Magical Arts Academy."

At the mention of the other master mage, the lady's eyes widened, and she grinned bashfully. "Byron Rinod. Now, that's a name I haven't heard in a while. I remember the grand times we spent together when he was stationed at the palace, before I married, of course."

Coura felt her face beginning to flush because of what the woman hinted at.

Katrina leaned closer and cupped a hand around her mouth to whisper after. "Tell me, how is he doing? Is he keeping active?"

"W-What?"

"Surely you've known him long enough."

Coura gasped at the accusation and stumbled backward, nearly tripping over herself in the process. "You're crazy!"

Although Emilea glared at her for the outburst, the lady straightened and winked without taking any offense. Then, she continued as though nothing transpired between them. "Leo, my raven gown from the Harvest Festival five years ago should be in the attic as well. Fetch our guests their outfits."

While the servant rummaged around, the master mage and Katrina gossiped, mostly about the king and queen's deaths and who thought what about it. Coura kept as far away from the woman as possible, which left her standing by the window to gaze outside. Meanwhile, Will and Grace snuck up behind her.

"What did the lady say to you?" the former asked at a hushed volume.

"Nothing," she snapped without hiding her annoyance, though not before her face heated up once more.

*

It took a while for Leo to return with the two gowns and a suit for Will. He explained where they could dress as he proceeded down the corridor to usher them into separate areas. Coura spent a brief amount of time squeezing into the dress, which she found comfortable enough if she didn't move around too much. To her displeasure, the skirt spread wide, a characteristic she had never been a fan of.

Once she emerged after wrestling the clothing through the door, she found Leo waiting with a pair of heeled shoes and a hat identical to the lady's, except with roses instead of lilies. When Coura refused the additions, he followed her into the sitting room where Katrina insisted she wear them. She rolled her eyes and let the man change her boots for the snug shoes before he left her with the hat to tend to either Grace or Will. While she attempted to fit it on, she found it contained numerous pins, further complicating the process.

"Let me help!" Katrina squealed from her seat and hurried over, to Coura's dismay.

She bit her tongue as the woman tugged her hair and stabbed the pointy bits into her skull. When her patience prepared to run out, the torture ended. The lady stood back to examine her while appearing satisfied.

"Now, all we need is some jewelry," Katrina added before slipping away despite Coura's attempt to convince her otherwise.

"She sure has taken a liking to you," Emilea commented from where she sat.

When Coura groaned, the master mage offered a sympathetic smile. Will appeared moments later in the all-black suit.

"I feel depressing," he concluded while Leo combed his hair neatly into place by using a special gel.

"It will be an emotional day," Emilea agreed.

Katrina returned then to drape an emerald necklace around Coura's neck accompanied by a gold bracelet for her arm.

"They're yours to keep," the woman shared before returning to her seat.

Before anybody could start a conversation, a knock at the door caused them to jump.

"Who could that be?" Will asked as the women stood.

In another minute, Mace and Lexie jogged down the hallway in their own dress clothes and bowed in front of their host. "It's nice to see you again, Lady Katrina," they said in unison, to the woman's utter delight.

"My favorite children! You're adorable in these outfits!"

She fawned over them until Clearshot entered, wearing the soldier's uniform. The sight of it brought a wave of emotion over Coura since she remembered her own, special clothes being shredded and tossed away, though the crimson coat still hung in her room thanks to Will, who held onto the item after she abandoned it in the Valley Beyond.

"My Lady," Clearshot greeted Katrina and kissed her on the cheek.

The woman acted coy and shooed him away before noticing Grace lingering behind him. The dress she had on was too large, as evidenced by how she held the upper half uncomfortably with both arms.

"No, no, no. This simply won't do!" Katrina cried, scurried over, then dragged Grace into another room.

This left the space silent until Mace and Lexie noticed Coura and started showering her with compliments on her appearance.

"You look like a real noblewoman, like Lady Katrina," Lexie mentioned.

I sure hope I'm nothing like her, Coura thought while laughing.

Emilea led her children into the backyard where they explored under their mother's watch. Will decided to get some fresh air as well and wandered around the garden in a carefree manner. This left Coura and Clearshot alone to observe through the window.

"So, how's it been since we arrived?" he asked in a casual manner.

"I'd be glad to never come back."

The soldier snickered, then he leaned closer to be discreet. "Why do you think we live in the middle of nowhere?"

He chuckled at the rhetorical question, prompting her to do the same.

Time passed until the two grew restless. Soon, Emilea, her children, and Will returned inside to search for Katrina and Grace.

"Where could they be?" the master mage wondered aloud.

Coura shrugged when Emilea glanced her way and dropped into a chair, wincing when the dress pinched her midsection. They heard the clicking shoes shortly after and stood when the lady appeared with Grace. The gown the girl donned now sported two straps tied behind her neck to hold the outfit up, giving the illusion that it fit the Yeluthian's petite frame.

"You would not believe the work we needed to do for this," Katrina started.

Emilea looped an arm around her friend's elbow. "I think I would, but you can explain along the way."

Coura couldn't see the western main road from the sitting room because of the foliage and gates. By the time they positioned themselves in front of the estate, the street had grown crowded with people heading toward the center of the city or lining the edges. Most were noblemen or ladies dolled up as much as their group in shades of gray and black.

Since the procession led to the south before winding west, they could remain in front of Katrina's home as it provided plenty of space. Still, summer had nearly arrived, which became apparent when everyone began sweating in their heavy clothing.

"How long does this last?" Coura asked Clearshot in order to keep her mind off the sun beating down on them. She could tell he desired to remove his stifling coat yet knew it would be disrespectful to do so.

"Not very," he replied. "The prince rides in a carriage accompanied by the high priest and surrounded by his escorts. Once he's out of sight, that's it for us. Shops must remain closed for the day, so the majority of citizens spend the extra hours with their families or host their own mourning ceremonies."

"What do you and Emilea do?"

"The way we both see it, the afternoon should be for supporting loved ones. We never plan on doing anything except cooking a meal together and sharing stories with Mace and Lexie. That way, they'll be able to hear about the better moments in the world during difficult times like this."

"That is rather sad," Grace commented from Clearshot's other side.

He dipped his head a bit while flashing an encouraging smile. "Today marks the end of King Hernan's reign. We should honor and remember him and his wife, as well as General Preston. Tomorrow is when the world changes. Preparations for a new king start taking place, and life will go on."

"What about the mourning period?"

"It's used as a sort of excuse to organize the palace and plan the next ruler's coronation."

"It seems so rushed," Grace mumbled loudly enough for them to hear.

"Would you wish for us to spend thirty days not working and crying over your death?"

"I suppose not," the Yeluthian answered, visibly stricken by Clearshot's blunt question.

"If we focus on those who have passed, we stop ourselves from continuing toward our futures. Never forget those closest to you, but don't let a natural process like death hinder you from enjoying the rest of your life. In a month, Prince Aaron will inherit his father's position. Until then, you'll notice more excitement as the event draws closer. It's a celebration, kind of like the Harvest Festival, and one to anticipate after grieving."

While he spoke, a hush fell over the road until Coura could faintly hear the sound of bells and hoofbeats. She peered toward the city and saw the aforementioned carriage turning in their direction; everybody waited in silence as it approached.

"I don't like this, Mother," Lexie whispered inconspicuously.

Emilea pulled her daughter closer and hugged the girl in a comforting manner.

White horses rode in front, in back, and to the sides of the wagon and carried the generals and Byron, who wore his formal, midnight-blue robe. Although their faces were set in calm masks, Coura noticed how their eyes darted around to show they remained on constant alert. The bells she heard adorned each animal's bridle and jingled as they continued at a steady pace.

Atop the roofless carriage sat Aaron with the high priest behind in a golden outfit and bearing a silver staff. She studied her friend as they passed by, and an odd sensation struck her because of how unfamiliar he appeared. He wore a colorless suit embellished with gold buttons and embroidery on the chest. His hair had been combed so a slim band could rest upon his head, and he held a crimson vase on his lap.

His face was what bothered her. The rich, sapphire eyes always stared ahead, he held his clean-shaven chin high, and his mouth straightened into an even line.

When the procession rode by Katrina's home, each person bowed or curtsied as low as they could until the prince and his escorts moved farther away. A chill ran through Coura, and she recognized the ill sentiment she had earlier upon observing her friend.

The first time Byron, Will, and I met Hernan, he glanced over us with a similar projection of his authority. I knew I disliked him ever since that moment. I wonder if Aaron will turn out to be like his father after all.

The streets began clearing when the carriage moved out of sight. Katrina invited her guests in for dinner where she proceeded to chat their ears off about a variety of pointless topics. Coura pushed the food on her plate around and thought about Aaron the whole time.

I've been to see Will and caught up with Grace. Perhaps it's time I find Marcus too so we can all visit Aaron. I hope he's not too busy for his friends.

***

The prince's passing through Verona went well, and Byron felt better once they reached the coast the following evening. A guard station monitored the path just outside the Western Woods, a wild space where the foreign Sie-Kie people dwelled, and the group spent the night with Aaron, Hendal, and Byron resting in the shelter and the generals taking shifts on guard duty. Although he offered to stay up as well, he had been ordered to remain close to the heir and only stared at the structure's ceiling for hours.

He had never visited the coast because he didn't find a reason to do so in the past. Still, stories of others' experiences circled frequently, meaning it appeared as he imagined. Open grassland led to a cliff overlooking the sea, which sparkled beneath while they admired the vast horizon. Its beautiful shades of blue enraptured him, and he wished the journey's purpose didn't have to arise from such grim circumstances.

"We'll start monitoring the perimeter," Casner stated before the generals left Byron with Hendal and Aaron.

"Will you be needing anything?" he asked the prince while being careful to use a gentle yet respectful tone.

"No, thank you. I wish to be alone," Aaron replied without a waver in his voice.

Together, Byron and the high priest retraced their steps in the grassy area to join Tont, who stood unaffected against the powerful wind from the coast.

"I've been here once," the man started while the three waited.

Hendal nodded. "As have I."

"It's quite an amazing view," Byron added. "I'm not certain I would ever go close to the water."

The general picked up the conversation then, though he seemed interested in talking more to himself. "I always thought about bringing my family here. The grandkids would play in the field, Marcus and I would wrestle, and my wife and daughter would laugh at us men for our horseplay. I can't remember the last time we went on a vacation, you know?"

As Byron listened, he recalled his travels with the assistant general. *Marcus is an admirable soldier, that's for sure. He's dedicated to his duties as a leader and honored to follow in the footsteps of his notable father. I wonder how much the two interact outside their assignments.*

Hendal cleared his throat before recommending the general indulge his family with the trip.

"There's no time for luxuries," Tont responded and focused his gaze on the lone figure nearby.

"Ah, yes."

"His father inherited the throne at twenty-five, three years older than Prince Aaron. When I began my work in the palace, Queen Lilla lived for many years after, providing the guidance necessary for King Hernan to rule. I assume we'll be the ones he'll lean on."

The notion rolled around in Byron's mind when he considered his and Emilea's positions as master mages and new members of the king's council.

The general turned to face him and drew a dull flask from one pocket. "Got any children?"

"With my work, it's impossible to settle down anywhere, let alone to find a woman willing to travel or not see me for days or weeks at a time. Besides, my students filled that vacancy over the years."

"I've been meaning to ask you a question," Hendal joined at a lower volume. "How has your student been faring? Is she staying sane?"

Byron understood what the high priest hinted at, though he didn't appreciate discussing the topic at such an inappropriate time. "Coura's fine," he answered curtly and accepted the flask from Tont.

Technically, I'm not lying. I haven't seen Coura since we arrived at the palace. As long as I don't sense demonic energy and she stays out of trouble, she's fine. On the other hand, hearing nothing from or about her usually isn't normal.

The three continued their small talk until Aaron returned much later with the empty vase and puffy, reddish eyes.

*

They returned to Verona along the same trail they exited on, though the change in the citizens was apparent. Instead of gloomy, sympathetic expressions, the people greeted their group with smiles and bows. Byron's spirits lifted from the shadow of their business; however, when he glanced at Aaron, the prince's face set into the same impassive mask he'd worn since Byron met him in the meeting chamber.

The young man's repressing his emotions, he reflected with dismay before focusing his attention on the gorgeous stallion beneath him. He reached down and scratched it behind the ear, which resulted in a satisfied neigh from the animal. *There's too much for him to do without the council's assistance, yet I doubt he feels much better when he's alone. Perhaps we should begin preparations for the coronation ceremony. Considering his future might make him nervous or eager enough to put part of his grief aside.*

As they approached the palace, Byron watched a handful of children kicking a ball in an alleyway, prompting another idea.

How could I forget about his friends? Sometimes I'm amazed I can function properly given how my mind works! I'll need to find Marcus, Will, Grace, and Coura and request they visit him. I'm not sure when, but the negative emotions should die down enough for a gathering to happen soon.

The guards and servants were expecting their return and handled the horses and carriage while Aaron entered, trailed by Hendal, Byron, and the generals. Everybody in the palace appeared relieved by the group's return as they paid their respects. Hendal assumed the lead when they strolled through the grand hall and straight to the meeting chamber as planned.

Once inside, an arrangement of food trays and pitchers of water and juices awaited them, and they dug in after taking their seats. Emilea requested to join at a later time, so her chair remained unoccupied, and until Aaron officially became king, the throne would stay empty.

"Now then," Casner began while reclining in his chair and inspecting a sheet of paper. "According to the agenda we laid out before the procession, we have three priority items to address. The rest of the country has been notified and a letter sent to Yeluthia about the change of power from King Hernan to Prince Aaron. The paperwork is complete for the ceremonies, wills, and who knows what else. We still have the murderers to locate and apprehend, the palace schedules to adjust, and the coronation ceremony to organize."

The prince kept silent as the council threw out ideas of what to accomplish when and who would assign responsibility for what. Byron noticed how uninterested their new leader seemed and cleared his throat, recognizing his own desire to return to his personal business.

"Your Highness," he started while keeping the heir as the ultimate decision-maker. "I would like to suggest delegating the work between us council members. Emilea and I, along with our underlings, are more than capable of supervising the mage recruits and setting up their schedules. I believe General Tont, his son, and the other assistant generals have been in charge of the training. We should resume our duties for the mages and soldiers."

He paused to wait for his cohorts' approval. Both heads nodded without hesitation, so Byron went on.

"If I may ask it of you, General Dillon and General Casner, please continue investigating the murders."

"There's so little to go on," the former grumbled in frustration and shuffled through a pile of documents. "You know we haven't found more. No leads, no accusations, nothing! The mages assigned to help investigate didn't sense a magical trail either. How do you suppose we approach this?"

Casner voiced his agreement, then they waited for Byron's response.

They're right. The bodies were thoroughly inspected and are no longer available. We discussed the rogue angels and demon, but without any energy left behind, we can't be certain if they were involved or not.

While he struggled to piece together a response, Hendal spoke from the opposite side of the table.

"Perhaps, and it is merely a suggestion, what if we close the case for now?" Before the others in the room could protest, he held his hands up in a gesture for them to wait. "Please, listen! We should not waste time and effort on a dead end. We can be doing more with less."

"I will not abandon the murder of my parents," Aaron replied in a calm voice, though Byron saw a fire burning beneath his cool exterior.

So did Hendal, who actually flinched and became flustered. "I think you misunderstand me, Prince Aaron. Would it be more beneficial to have a secret search group investigate while the matter is announced complete publicly?"

"You're making no sense," Tont barked.

"I catch what you're trying to explain," Dillon interjected and straightened in his seat. "The culprits might become sloppy if they believe no one is looking for them anymore."

"Yes, exactly!" Hendal exclaimed, clapped his hands together, then sighed with relief.

Byron pondered the idea before voicing his support. "I can see it working. Besides, we shouldn't meet every day to go over the same details and questions. This is our major concern at the moment and requires special attention."

The generals agreed, and though he appeared displeased, Aaron ultimately caved in.

"Let us take care of this," Dillon offered while pointing a thumb at Casner. "We'll put together a team."

Byron stretched his shoulders when the matter resolved. The council had been in their meeting for hours, and lunch had worn thin.

"What is your final idea, Master Byron?" Hendal asked next without hiding his own weariness.

"We covered the first two items, so all that's left is the coronation. Your Highness, I believe it would benefit you to organize this with the high priest because he's familiar with some of the traditions. You should add whatever you please to the event since it's unique to the crowned ruler."

"What a wonderful idea," Hendal added and beamed at Aaron, who raised an eyebrow in Byron's direction.

"Isn't the coronation weeks away? I could be doing more with the time."

"It would be appropriate to plan this far in advance, especially when we need to notify the servants, kitchen staff, and vendors in Verona and across Asteom. The sooner, the better essentially."

The generals shared a few comments on the coronation before the topic concluded. To everybody's irritation, Byron decided to continue speaking after.

"I have one last request. I'd like a guard or two accompanying you at all times, Your Highness." He didn't elaborate. The idea of the heir being alone made him nervous, and not only for the young man's physical safety.

"I'll find somebody," was all the prince said before he rose as a clear dismissal for the members.

*

Byron made his way to his quarters after a brief visit to the dining hall. Throughout the weeks, he considered the recruits sent from the academy and spent whatever time he could spare verifying their paperwork and arranging their schedules.

I should stop by the training ground to confirm the stable holds the appropriate equipment or set some aside for the mages in order to avoid possessive conflicts with the soldiers. I've been away long enough to need a reminder.

With how late in afternoon it grew, he assumed those in the palace would be heading to dinner, giving him an opportunity to check. He redirected his route away from the staircase to cross the first floor and exit into the northern field. For a moment, Byron paused to soak up the heat from the dipping, summer sun, then he walked forward until two men nearly barreled into him.

"Pardon us," they apologized and hurried inside.

He recognized how populated the area was in that moment.

At least a hundred people of varying ages practiced weapons work with those closest to the stable appearing experienced enough to keep to themselves. A group of less skilled, younger men and women paired up and steadily moved through sparring motions. Byron recognized the exercises and found himself smiling when he spotted the overseers wandering around to correct postures, grips, or attack directions.

Will noticed him first and waved from closer to the front. The newcomers followed his attention, then lost their focus to approach their former instructor.

"Master Byron, is it really you?"

"We're so glad to see you, Master Byron!"

Because he just reviewed their paperwork, he had been reminded of students he trained in the past, causing his smile to broaden while he properly greeted the dozens at once. He caught Coura's eye before she glanced away to say something to Will.

I never would have imagined they could be capable of leading an organized group like this, he thought with pride and recalled when the two each began their combat lessons. He kept that in mind while the mages began returning their practice weapons to the stable bins and hurrying inside to eat.

"I see I don't need to worry about there being enough equipment for the additional recruits," Byron began when Coura and Will came over. Both faces were shaded crimson from their sunburns, but any trace of exhaustion or bitterness from when they returned to Verona had disappeared.

His student put her hands on her hips. "Is *that* why you're here?"

"It's been a few months since I last explored the training ground," Byron answered as he studied the outdoor area.

When he considered the wooden weapons the two held, an idea formed without too much prompting. He extended a hand toward Will and gestured for practice blade. Although the young man raised an eyebrow, he said nothing as he handed over the sword, which Byron weighed and twirled to warm up his wrist.

"That's how long it's been since we sparred, hasn't it, Coura?" he continued, intending to use the precious free time available to him to loosen his muscles from the stress-inducing meetings, as well as gauge where he stood physically with her.

In the next, brief moment, a mixture of alarm and shame passed over her face before she covered it by chuckling. "Of course you wait until the end of the day to jump in when we're hungry and tired," she commented before passing her wooden weapon to Will and strolling toward the building in a confident manner.

Will called for her to wait and glanced down at the blade.

"Don't worry," Byron reassured him. "I would never expect you to spar with me on a whim. Here, I'll return the weapons."

He procured the swords, to Will's relief, and studied his pupil as she lingered near the entrance.

"What's wrong with Coura?" he ventured to ask when he understood something seemed off with her.

"I understand what you mean," the herbalist startled him by admitting. "Whenever a recruit or soldier requests she spar or demonstrate a maneuver with serious intent, that same expression appears, then she laughs at the question instead of answering."

"Why is she behaving like that?"

"If I had to guess, I would say she's embarrassed by how much speed, strength, and skill she lost while recovering."

Byron remembered her attachment to the demon and grunted. *I don't believe it was completely due to her injury.*

Before they could discuss the issue further, Coura spun around to jog back to them.

"What is it?" Byron asked when she paused to catch her breath.

"I tried to find you sooner," she began, straightened, and shot him a determined look. "Will, Grace, and I would like to visit Marcus and Aaron."

"That's right!" Will blurted and ran a hand through his messy curls. "I forgot too."

Their request surprised Byron, even more so because of his earlier plan to surround the prince with familiar faces. His heart desired to reunite their circle because it would help them all mentally, yet his conscience encouraged him to wait.

Marcus hasn't returned to the palace, but he will as soon as the training schedules are set. As for Aaron, he has plenty to handle that requires his complete attention. I'd hate to meddle in their lives by forcing him to socialize when he isn't ready.

"Perhaps in a few days," he decided. "Marcus should be resuming his responsibilities tomorrow or the morning after, so you can reconnect with him then."

"What about Aaron?" Will continued in a hopeful tone.

Byron shook his head. "The prince is busy. Once the palace is in order, I'll mention your request."

"Nobody should be left alone after what he's been through," Coura protested and crossed her arms in a displeased manner. "Why can't we just speak with him?"

"I think you underestimate the severity of what it takes to rule a country. The royal family must always make sacrifices in order to keep their kingdom functioning smoothly. Their emotions and feelings come second to the betterment of Asteom, especially during unpredictable times."

"At least let us see him once," the young man pleaded.

Again, Byron considered the request. "I can ask him what he wants to do, but we must respect his decision. If he's not prepared, you need to be patient until he is."

When the two didn't press the subject a second time, he left to deposit the wooden blades in the stable. They still lingered after he returned, hinting that they needed more from him.

"What else?"

"So, the training schedules resume tomorrow?" Will inquired in a completely different, less passionate tone than a minute ago.

"Yes, and thank you both for your leadership. It seems the mage recruits are settling in well here." He prepared to move closer to the palace until their time in Dala came to mind, causing him to halt and assess the duo. "I forgot neither of you have a schedule since we were in the southern base. What do you plan on doing now?"

Will eagerly shared his intentions first. "I'd like to join the mages' combat training session in the morning. I found I fit in best with their group, and it's basic enough not to scare me away."

"I suppose you can spend the rest of the day researching?"

"Either studying indoors or conducting research outside the city's limits. The healers in the medical station would like some input on their supplies and potions since it's consistently being updated."

Byron eyed his now-former student, who refused to meet his gaze. "What about you, Coura?"

She shrugged, avoiding the question.

Without her previous skill, not to mention the loss of her magic, I worry she feels she's not adequate enough to do much. I need to snuff out those concerns before she strays too far.

He gestured for her to follow him, bid Will a pleasant evening, and started back across the field. For a second, he didn't think she would come until he heard footsteps and craned his head around to catch her trailing behind.

She knows what this is about then.

He brought them to the stone wall outlining the training ground and leaned against it. Meanwhile, Coura climbed onto the structure to sit above him and wore an unamused expression, which made him smile. They watched the remaining soldiers for a while until Byron felt ready for the conversation.

"What are you actually planning on doing with your time?"

"I don't know," she answered as she stared off into the distance.

My heart hurts for her. I can see the longing in her eyes, though I wonder if her physicality is that poor compared to when she possessed demonic power.

"Any ideas?" she startled him by asking after.

"Just because you don't have magical energy anymore doesn't mean you can't become a soldier. You're capable of matching their movements and are as knowledgeable as those I know."

"You really believe so?"

Although she expressed her doubt, Byron projected his honesty. "Of course I do. After all, I was your instructor. It might be worthwhile to speak with Marcus about working alongside him too. I observed how you and Will directed the mages. You're a natural leader when it comes to combat training. The assistant generals rely on people willing to step up in certain situations."

"That's interesting," she mused.

Byron still sensed her uncertainty about the future and devoted the rest of the day to her. At some point, their conversation reminded him of their years at the academy, and a warmth filled his chest when he reminisced on his simpler life there.

***

Marcus returned to his duties the next day, as Byron had mentioned. Coura found her friend that afternoon in his room unpacking bags of shirts and pants, and she stared at them when he invited her inside.

"What is all this?"

"My mother thought I might need more training clothes since I apparently outgrew my old ones." He fell onto his bed with a huff, giving her the impression this must be an annual event.

"At least somebody cares about you. You should be grateful for her consideration," Coura couldn't help herself from commenting before taking a seat in one of the desk chairs.

Marcus watched her for a moment but didn't say anything else about the gifts. "To what do I owe the pleasure of this visit?"

"I was wondering," she started before losing her nerve.

Her hesitation proved enough to have him sitting up while wearing a concerned expression. "What's wrong?"

Coura stared down at her hands and felt her cheeks flush as she braved the subject. "Ever since I lost my power, I've become weaker."

"Oh."

A shadow crept over Marcus' face to remind her of the distance forged between herself and her friends after they found out where her dark energy originated from.

If Soirée was here, she would scold me for pitying myself and order me to be productive. It's Marcus' and anybody else's decision if they don't want to be around me. I'm tired of being useless.

Her cheeks still burned from admitting the problem, yet Coura forced her chin to raise so she could meet his eyes. "Can you train me?"

"Seriously?"

"I know you're busy, but you're the only person besides Byron I'm completely comfortable sparring with."

This time, Marcus' face turned a shade of pink before he glanced away and scratched his neck. He muttered bits and pieces of sentences until he reached a decision.

"Fine, I'll do it. I don't know who advised you to come to me, though. We were near equals in Dala, so I can't imagine you've gotten that much worse."

Coura released a sigh of relief as she reflected on the practice sessions she participated in over the past few days. *My speed and strength decreased once Soirée's energy disappeared. No matter how many times I repeat the same routine or strike in the same spot, I'm not the same fighter. Not to mention, without my magic the best I can hope for is a position as an ordinary foot soldier...*

"It's not a big deal," he reassured her. "Don't get so worked up."

When she realized she began moping, she thanked him before rising to leaf through the clothes his family sent along. He got up too, and together they managed to put every item away. By then, the sun shined in through his western-facing window.

"Those shirts were nice," she commented after they sat down again.

"The women in my family have a knack for locating fine materials."

They chatted for a bit longer as the light dropped into a colorful sunset. A somber sensation weighed on Coura when she recalled the memories made with their friends in that room.

Marcus apparently felt the same. "It's been a while since we ate meals in here," he said in a melancholy tone.

She nodded. "Will's doing much better than when he first arrived. I'm jealous of the friends he managed to make, both mages and soldiers. I convinced him to help me train the new recruits from the MAA. I've also been to see Grace twice now, and she's bonding with Emilea more. I'm sure they would be glad to see you."

"I'd like that. Maybe the four of us can dine together again, in here or the mess hall."

"What about Aaron?" she ventured to ask. If anybody was close enough to visit the prince, it would be his best friend.

Unfortunately, only sorrow etched into Marcus' expression. "I haven't seen him since we returned to the palace. He rushed away to go to the king and queen, and my father ordered me home. I knew something went wrong, yet it's not my place to question either of them. I didn't know what happened until my father escorted me home and informed my family."

"Are you doing better?"

"After hearing about General Preston, I became worried for my father and wanted to protect my family and stay out of his way. He's one of the strongest soldiers I know, physically, mentally, and emotionally. I had faith he'd be safe and the situation would be taken care of, but..."

"You're worried about Aaron," she finished for him.

"He didn't speak to me on the ride from Dala. When I tried to find him after he ran off, and even yesterday, the guards under the council's command urged me to leave him alone until he requests visitors. I asked my father about him in order to hear how he's doing and learned Aaron is in his mother's garden outside the meetings. There's no telling how he's handling the loss. He's going to become king in less than a month, and I want to be there for him!"

"We all do," Coura replied in a soothing manner while sorting through her own emotions.

She didn't return to her room until well into the night yet felt thankful for the opportunity to work with Marcus and reunite with another friend.

A Willing Ear

Ten days passed since Coura and Marcus spoke. They began training early in the morning before his scheduled groups came outside, but Byron, Emilea, and their appointed assistants practiced magic together at dawn too. It pained her to confront the fact that she would never experience casting a spell again, so she ignored the others in the field as best as she could.

Despite her attempts to brush aside the encounter with Soirée, she considered the demon's parting words whenever she was reminded of her lost power, which occurred multiple times a day. *She claimed if I returned to the palace, she would help me get my power back. I suppose I have no other option except to trust her, even if the idea makes me wary. Still, I haven't seen or heard any sign of demonic activity around the capital.*

Working with Marcus proved easier than her experience with Byron because he didn't push her as hard, either due to their friendship or her lower skill level. She swallowed her pride each instance he repeatedly bested her, using the defeat to solidify her resolve to become better. Marcus picked up on her fortified attitude and never offended her by simplifying his instructions or holding back his actions.

Grace and Will joined them for lunch and dinner in the mess hall, which became a regular event. Even Byron and Emilea stopped by to check in every once in a while. Steadily, their lives were tying together again. In the meantime, she concocted ideas for reaching out to Aaron, the one person she believed needed the most support; however, she chose to keep them to herself.

Marcus said Aaron is always in the private garden. I snuck in before, but would it be wise to do so a second time?

Coura, Grace, and Will usually studied in the Yeluthian's room when they were free during the afternoon. On that particular day, she chose to make her move when the sky filled with clouds, allowing sunlight to peek in often enough to create a comfortable temperature. After lunch, she excused herself and promised to meet them for dinner before hurrying toward the western side of the palace.

She paid no attention to the servants rushing to complete their errands. Laundresses used an exit near the cleaning rooms to hang clothes, towels, sheets, and other items to dry in the summer heat. They made no attempt to stop her as she moved outside and shifted north to stroll along the palace's outer wall. She paused once to lean against the building and soak up the sun for about a minute. Once she noticed the majority of women head inside, she took off at a sprint toward the northern corner and snuck around to press her back against the added section protecting the garden. A thrill shot through Coura as she recalled her initial experience sneaking into the private area.

I was young and reckless then; now, I'm just a bit older, she thought with a grin and climbed over the bricks.

The first time she slipped into the queen's garden, the flowers were blooming, the grass had been a bright green, and a sense of freedom and life drifted through, like a gentle breeze. As she hid and searched for guards, a heaviness hung in the air thickly enough to lower her spirits as she snuck farther away from the wall.

A handful of guards chatted with one another nearer to the entrance, and Coura found she could avoid them altogether if she kept off the paths. The fountains ran, yet in the shade of the afternoon, the water didn't glisten, and each statue's face appeared gloomy, even those carved to smile. She sat in the grass for a moment while a solider patrolled nearby and found the blades prickly and dry, along with most of the bushes. As for the colorful flowers, they drooped in the heat, deflating the mood.

It's almost as though the entire garden is withering in grief, she realized in the silence of the afternoon.

Coura peeked into each area to confirm they were free from roaming guards, though nothing she heard nor saw indicated somebody else might be around.

Maybe Aaron's not here, she thought and tried to plot the layout from her previous visit. By that point, she reached as far back as she dared to go, which happened to be a vine-covered wall with only a single opening leading toward another section.

Last time I found the end, I heard voices beyond. Could they have belonged to Aaron and his mother? When we met, he startled me after I had been through every spot, except in here.

She swallowed her concern before tiptoeing through the hole cut into the stone blocking most of the view from either side. Her breath caught once she glimpsed the brick wall ahead and learned it was the end of the garden. Along the ground, various flower beds lined up so no two petals of the same color were next to each other, vines crawled up and down the walls surrounding the space to create an emerald backdrop bearing violet and gold flowers throughout, and four trees stood with fruits beginning to grow and blossoms still fluttering down.

Coura meandered on a worn path cutting through the plants until she saw where it ended. A white bench had been arranged in the middle, and sitting alone with his head bowed was Aaron.

She dismissed her initial instinct to call out and hurry over because somehow she knew it wouldn't be the correct course of action in her position. Instead, she remained in place, studying the flora. Every plant and vine sagged in the shade of the fruit trees. She turned away from the prince, clasped her hands behind her back, and inhaled the aroma surrounding her. Before long, she closed her eyes and enjoyed existing in such a special place.

Minutes later, Aaron discovered her standing nearby.

"You shouldn't be here." His voice sounded like a grumble, almost to the point where Coura missed his words.

All she could think to respond with was, "Is that right?"

Silence followed, then gentle footsteps approached. She still kept her back to him, even when he began speaking, and dared not interrupt.

"I was just an infant when my mother begged for this place. She had been the child of nobility, so upholding an image remained a priority.

Whenever I would join her here, I assumed the garden was used for status, a token only the royal family had the honor to appreciate. Every day it seemed she spent at least an hour in this area alone. One afternoon, I asked her why she loved it so much."

He paused, but Coura kept quiet.

"I'll never forget her answer. She turned to me with a wide smile and explained how it acted as a sort of escape from reality. Whenever she went in her garden, she didn't have to worry about anything. Then, she requested I accompany her when I could because she hoped I would become part of the best moment of her day. Sometimes my father would come too. He never discussed politics or business when the three of us were together in here." His voice wavered faintly at the end.

Coura's eyes widened when she made the connection. *This place is an escape for him now. He shoves his problems aside to forget what happened and remember the happier days with his parents.*

Again, she desired to reach out and tell him it would be all right.

What would Byron do if he were here? I've never been gifted at comforting people, except Mace and Lexie. When they were in distress after the creatures' attack, I opened my arms to allow them a safe space to weep. Is that all some people need, a chance to free themselves from their fears and burdens without judgment?

This time, her heart agreed she was heading in the correct direction. It motivated her enough to face the prince and grab his arm. He allowed her to bring him to the bench and sat next to her with his head dipped.

"Tell me about them," she said in a gentle manner.

A huff escaped him. "They were both amazing in their own way."

"What was your mother like?"

"Stunning. Absolutely one of the most beautiful women I've ever known. She was kind-hearted toward the people she cared about, but she had no interest in my father's work."

"And him?"

"He was the most talented speaker, and an honest and just man. I respect him for those characteristics, even in death," Aaron concluded in a whisper.

Although it became difficult for Coura to picture any reputable characteristics about Hernan, she listened while the prince continued.

He shared memories and experiences involving both his parents from throughout his life until he abruptly stopped. She had been watching the environment as he spoke but glanced over to catch his shoulders shaking.

Just as she somehow sensed what Mace and Lexie needed in that particular moment, she extended an arm around her friend's back and leaned on him in a partial hug. She didn't expect him to shift his posture and bury his face into her shoulder, yet Coura wrapped both arms around him in a full embrace when he did. They sat in the peacefulness of the cloudy afternoon broken only by several of the prince's sobs.

*

When her body began cramping from the unnatural twisting at the waist, Aaron straightened, reached into his pocket for a piece of cloth, and blew his nose before wiping his eyes. She gave him some privacy by pointedly admiring the flowers until he seemed composed.

"I'm sorry," he apologized in a frail voice to reflect his embarrassment. "It's not proper for a king to break down like that."

Coura shook her head before staring at him. Without the pink eyes, red nose, and pale face, her friend looked just about the same as he always had. "A king should understand they're not invulnerable. At least, any honorable king should."

She offered a smile, which broadened when he returned it with a timid one of his own. After, she stood, stretched, and began leisurely moving along the trail. Aaron scrambled to his feet and walked behind.

"This garden looks so sad," she noted and crouched to touch a bunch of white, star-shaped flowers she had never seen before.

"Those were my mother's favorite."

An idea prompted by his comment came to mind as Coura rose. *He needs to open up. This garden shouldn't be a prison reminding him of those lost times but a celebration of what it meant to his mother, and means to him.*

"What a unique place this is," she began again. "It would be a shame to let it lose its life. I heard your coronation ceremony will be soon. Do you want to know what I would do if I were you?"

Aaron shook his head.

108

"I'd throw a huge celebration. There would be dancing, musicians, food, and everybody could dress up. Then, I'd open this garden to the public. Couldn't you picture the soldiers and mages using it to relax from their training and paperwork? Why keep it to yourself? Unless…"

"Unless, what?" she heard him ask.

"It doesn't seem right to let this beauty go to waste or allow it to remind you of your mourning. Maybe, just this area you can keep for yourself, as a memorial to honor your parents." Coura laughed at her rambling. "Listen to me! I don't know the first thing about caring for plants. Will would call me a fool, and you probably think I'm crazy."

She looked over to find Aaron observing her with an odd, blank expression.

"Do you want to talk more?" she pressed when he still didn't speak.

He shook his head slightly.

"What *do* you want?"

For a while, he didn't respond. Then, the prince bowed his head. "I want everything to go back to the way it used to be."

The words and hurt in his voice reflected Coura's own, personal struggle. *My energy, strength, confidence… What I developed in Dala is gone. Even so, I can recognize the past, but that doesn't mean it hinders my future unless I let it.*

"I do too," she replied solemnly.

His attention focused on her for the first time since she entered the space.

"I wish I could redo parts of my life to erase the mistakes or change it so none of this happened," she continued while feeling Byron's numerous lectures worming their way to the forefront of her mind. "There's nothing we can do besides accept the past and move on. If we aren't able to do that, we're not really living the best lives we can. Honor your parents, Aaron. Don't ever forget them or the memories you shared. Never be ashamed to mourn their loss, but you'll go mad if you keep cooping yourself up."

More light returned to his eyes as he processed her plea.

"Besides, the others will throttle me if I can't convince you to join us for meals again," she added with a wink.

"The others?"

"Marcus is practically hysterical. He's been attempting to reach out and hear how you're doing. Will and Grace are worried too."

"I didn't mean to…" Aaron's voice faded away, concerning Coura since she believed he would give into sorrow if his emotions remained unchecked.

In response, she reached out, took one of his hands in both of hers, and shook it slightly to get his attention again. The touch startled him enough to jump, yet his hand squeezed hers with the same gentleness.

"You're not alone. You have friends who want to help you recover and succeed. It's not just our group; Byron, Emilea, the priest and generals, the soldiers and mages, and everybody in Verona and Asteom support their new king. We're here for you, so there's no excuse to fall into self-doubt."

Their eyes locked while she spoke, allowing Coura to stress each word in an attempt to make him believe her. They stared at each other until a male voice shouted for Aaron at a distance too close for comfort. She released his hand before blushing and glancing toward the opening.

"Don't worry. They wouldn't dare enter without my permission unless they wish to be punished," Aaron reassured her in a strange, calm tone.

The vulnerable friend in front of her moments ago slid into the royal persona he had always hated pretending to be, though his eyes seemed livelier. He moved to pass her, and she let him go.

"Coura," she heard him say and turned to find him smiling as naturally as he had in the past.

"Will you ever learn to use the garden's entrance before climbing over, or should I keep somebody inside to watch for you?"

She couldn't stop herself from grinning and shrugged before he left her alone. Once she became certain they were gone, she crept into one of the more spacious sections and hurried over the wall just as the bells from Verona chimed for the dinner hour.

***

The newer mage recruits adjusted to Byron's training regimen easily, though he had to recognize how well Coura and Will prepared them in the week prior. He expected to spend the rest of his day relaxing since he completed all the documentation and his subordinates grew comfortable enough with their schedules to leave on their own business. Unfortunately, fate did not plan a break for him.

As soon as he sat on his bed after stuffing himself at lunch there came a knock at the door. With a groan, he rose to open it and found the high priest waiting.

"Master Byron, you're here! I'm so glad."

"To what do I owe your visit, High Priest Hendal?"

"Please, there's no need for formalities," the bald man chided in jest and made a shooing motion with his hands. He then gestured for Byron to join him before walking down the hallway.

"Am I needed for something?" Byron asked while hurrying to catch up.

"The prince requested your presence for the coronation ceremony discussion."

He sensed the high priest's nerves but didn't press the subject. They made their way to the meeting chamber, passing several noblemen wandering from that direction, and found Aaron sitting alone in the room, except for the guards keeping watch until Hendal and Byron's arrival. Once they entered, the soldiers resumed their positions in front of the door. The young man stood to greet Byron with a much more relaxed expression.

I wonder what happened between our last meeting. He appears to be in better spirits.

"Good afternoon, Your Highness. I hear you began planning your coronation ceremony," he said to initiate the conversation before accepting a seat.

"We have some ideas, but Hendal thought it might be worthwhile to get your input before making the final decisions." His words carried more confidence than they had during any of their previous discussions, which amazed Byron.

It's not just my imagination. Perhaps the other topics occupying his mind allowed him to set those negative emotions aside.

"Let's hear them," he offered.

"I would like the ceremony to be a public affair in the grand hall. Just as we welcomed Grace to Asteom, the soldiers and mages will be present as witnesses during the coronation, and whoever else wishes to may do so. Afterward, we will lead a procession into Verona toward the eastern side of the city where scheduled performances and music can start."

"Like a festival?"

The prince nodded and become enthusiastic with his descriptions. Meanwhile, Hendal fidgeted in his seat and frowned.

I bet the high priest hoped for a safer, traditional ceremony. I'm also guessing he suggested my presence as a voice of reason against Aaron's extravagant ideas.

When the prince finished outlining the event, which sounded like a replica of the Harvest Festival, Byron closed his eyes to ponder what direction he believed to be best. *What he described might take a lot of work to organize in the two weeks left of the mourning period, but it's not impossible. Besides, it could be a relief to the people living in the capital who are concerned about the murders.*

"I like it," he ventured to comment.

Aaron's smile widened while Hendal's frown deepened.

"Do you think it is wise to put on such a display while criminals are on the loose?" the high priest countered. "We would need guards assigned to the prince, generals, and Yeluthian ambassador, not to mention the limited amount of time left to inform the palace servants, soldiers, and citizens across the country." After a minute, his ramblings spiraled into mutters.

When the chamber fell silent, Byron raised an eyebrow at Aaron, who observed the two in a passive manner. "If I may ask, where did you come up with this? Pardon me for saying it, but the last time I saw you, I thought you might prefer a private event."

The young man's smile faded. A trace of despair lingered, yet his eyes remained fearlessly steady. His nod reaffirmed his suggestion against Byron's concern.

"I've come to realize my suffering will not stop this kingdom from moving forward. The people will continue to live, and the longer I wait to assume my duty as heir to the throne, the more struggles will land on others' shoulders. By creating a public ceremony and encouraging these festivities, I'll show them how dedicated I am to future prosperity. Many merchants and business owners can choose to take advantage of the day, the entertainers share their talents, and our troops learn how much I appreciate their loyalty and service."

Well spoken, like his father, Byron thought with swelling pride.

Hendal kept quiet but seemed more convinced when their leader addressed the topic seriously.

Byron cleared his throat before responding. "If that's what your heart is set on, then who are we to stand in your way. We will need to send a schedule and related items to the kitchen, citizens, mages, soldiers, and servants as soon as possible."

"I believe we have records of such details from the festivals throughout the year," Hendal added. "I will see they are taken care of."

"There's one, final part I would like to address," Aaron mentioned while shifting his features into a controlled, neutral expression.

"Yes, Your Highness?"

"I wish for my mother's garden to be open to the public beginning immediately after my coronation."

At that, Hendal started all over again. "The garden areas were created for the royal family! Why would you want anybody wandering around? Are you not concerned about theft or vandalism?"

"There's a space I would prefer to remain private. Otherwise, the garden had been a request from my mother. Since she is no longer among the living, I see no reason to let it wither."

Byron appreciated the suggestion and was about to say so when the high priest continued listing his concerns.

"I must stress my doubts about the space remaining a beautiful reserve. There are many precious fountains, statues, plants, and relics. It will be impossible to monitor everyone and be certain they behave. The garden belongs to the royal family, and-"

"Am I not part of the royal family?" Aaron startled them by snapping at the high priest. His annoyed glare and tone reminded Byron of the late King Hernan's other, aggressive side.

"I-I didn't mean… Of course, but I-I-"

"I find no reason why my request should be denied aside from your vague worries. We have enough guards to spare on protecting the area and servants to tend to the floral life. It would be a waste of space and an insult to my parents' memory if it remained unused."

Both Aaron and Hendal looked to Byron for his opinion. Instead of arguing, he crossed his arms, leaned back in his chair, and decided to oblige the prince's wish.

"You're fairly adamant about this, so what I say won't sway your mind. I'm in support of opening the garden, though it will be necessary to organize the guards and gardeners beforehand. Also, I would consider crafting a policy for those who enter. For example, if anybody steals or damages the property, they could be fined and banned from visiting again. With rules in place, I believe assigning positions will flow easier."

The three of them spent the remainder of the afternoon planning the festivities, ceremony, and garden's policy until Byron grew comfortable with, and even excited for, the day when Asteom would welcome their next king.

***

When Coura heard about the upcoming coronation and what Aaron's plans were for the celebration, she became elated. Not only did he take her advice to heart, but he also stole Marcus away after his morning training sessions with her and the soldiers. From then on, she ate meals with Will and Grace until the private dinners resumed and the Yeluthian ambassador's presence was requested. At first, Grace became conflicted over whether or not to abandon Coura and Will, yet they convinced her to attend and inform them of Aaron's status. When they did see her again, her report reassured them.

Their friend acted mature while continuing to be himself around her and Marcus, who always stayed by the prince's side. The Yeluthian acted as a messenger between the pairs and passed along news to keep them in contact with each other. Coura found it amusing, if not a bit arduous, and forced herself to be patient until the ceremony.

Similar to the days prior to the Harvest Festival, servants and kitchen staff busied themselves preparing for the event. Banners hung in the grand hall, and the crimson carpet leading from the entrance to the staircase had been rolled out. The preparation reminded her of both the annual festivals as well as the welcome held for Grace's arrival. She ventured into Verona with Will a couple times and noticed the sense of pride in the citizens' faces. Decorations in scarlet and gold were all over the city too.

Circumstances had lined up for Coura recently, including her physique, friendships, and future role in the army, leading her to feel as though her life should be complete; however, she never truly liked the person she was becoming. As she waited outside in the blazing sun two days before the ceremony, she raised a hand to shade her eyes and considered Soirée's words, or rather, what she desired most.

I tried desperately to fill this hole in my center. I thought maybe it was a result of my physical weakness until Marcus helped me. Then, I wondered if it's because I'm alone without Soirée, but my friends accepted my past so we can be together again. Without the demonic power, I'm able to live a normal life. I expected that to be enough. If my energy has nothing to do with it, why don't feel complete?

She locked the question away and waved to Marcus as he approached, stretched his arms straight up in the air, and yawned.

"Good morning," she exclaimed to demonstrate her activeness before tossing him a practice sword.

He caught the wooden weapon and scratched his head. "You know, we don't have to do this today."

"Are you being lazy?"

"No, it's just that everyone else has taken today and tomorrow off to prepare for the ceremony. I've been guarding Aaron too, so don't call me lazy."

"Fine, I'll quit teasing you," she said with no shortage of reluctance.

Once he warmed up, Marcus raised his blade to initiate their spar. Coura's movements became swifter in time as her confidence rose, but her strikes were never precise. He overpowered her each match, though she managed to hold her own across a greater duration.

The assistant general knocked the sword out of her hand twice that morning, resulting in a welt she rubbed down. The third time, he shoved her onto her backside where she remained panting.

"Had enough yet?" he asked before laughing and plopping down beside her.

She chuckled in response. They were both drenched in sweat while the sun continued sucking their energy away.

"Again," she demanded and pushed herself to her feet. For a moment, a wave of dizziness passed over her from rising too suddenly, causing her to waver.

Marcus rose in a heartbeat and reached out to steady her. "We're done for today."

She shook her head to clear it. "One more time."

"I said that's it, Coura." He crossed his arms to emphasize the order.

After working with him for as long as she had, she understood when he was being serious. She caved in and dropped onto the dry grass. "If that's your excuse for quitting, then I won't argue with you."

He shrugged off her joke before walking toward the palace. "I'll bring us some water, and we'll see how you feel after that."

She thanked him before wiping her forehead and lying on her back. With one hand over her eyes, she caught the sound of the door closing. A passing breeze cooled her body momentarily as she remained on the ground, too physically exhausted and comfortable to move.

What's taking Marcus so long? she wondered after a few minutes flew by.

It was then Coura realized a familiar power growing in her center, a stifling sensation against the sun's heat. She sat up, utterly confused, and gasped when it became overshadowed by a suffocating presence.

Demonic energy? Where is it coming from?

Again, dizziness threatened to bring her to her knees when she scrambled to her feet and scanned the open field. None of the guards near the stable seemed to notice the issue, yet the tightness became so unbearable that she struggled to breathe. As if a path stretched from the pool of power, the energy narrowed so Coura could sense the direction of the source. She glanced at the palace then to the woods beyond the stone wall farther away.

She's in there…beckoning me…

With as much strength as she could muster, she stumbled to the wall, climbed over, and continued into the trees beyond.

*

The closer Coura went to the source, the less pressure gripped her chest, allowing her to control her breathing under the cover of the canopy. Despite the ease, her heart beat frantically enough to hurt, and she searched while remaining attentive in case an enemy jumped out.

Last time, Soirée appeared behind Drake. Before that, we encountered the demonic creature three times. If she wants me to get this power back, she wouldn't attack me. It was never like her to lie either. The notion helped to settle her nerves, and she halted her steps.

"Come out, Soirée," she shouted into the woods.

Somehow, she knew the source could comprehend the words and began creeping closer. From the bushes to her right, a shadow approached.

Coura's eyes widened when, instead of Soirée, another demonic creature emerged, though this one took the form of a stag. The head raised above hers, and on it branched huge antlers covered with a sickly, green slime. Its violet eyes observed her before it stepped forward until it stood within an arms' length away. The stench from its oily fur made her gag.

"What do you want?" The question sounded muffled because of the hand over her nose.

What power had been swirling in her center stirred.

In a single, smooth motion, the creature lowered its head so they stood at eye-level with each other, leaving her no other place to look except into the hypnotic voids. In the process, one of the antlers' tips brushed against her cheek. The venom dripped onto her skin and spurred a burning sensation, though she became too distracted to care. After, her eyelids grew heavy and closed.

*

{*You haven't figured out who the traitor is yet, have you?*}
Soirée?

Coura's eyes flew open, and she peered in each direction for the demon whose wicked laughter chimed all around. The stag-like creature remained still with its head bowed to watch her body, which stood motionless apart from where she found herself at the moment. The sensation reminded her of when she woke in her soul space months ago. Unlike that first experience, the world around her darkened, as if it became the middle of the night.

"Where am I?" she asked aloud.

117

{I reached out to you, so your mind crafted this scene based on your most recent memory.}

"Why did you do that? *How* did you do that?"

{We share a soul, Dear One. I can call upon you, and you can answer, willingly or not. Now, as to why I did so, I would like to discuss our lost power.}

Coura almost scoffed at the demon's offer until she considered the prospect of possessing magic once more.

{I'm glad you're eager to accept. When you were stabbed by that vile dagger, all the demonic energy inside you, including myself, should have been sealed into you. It could have left us useless, unable to act until your human body aged and died. Even after death, with my soul in you, I'm not sure I ever would have been freed.}

"The dagger was removed," Coura responded and realized what the oversight meant.

{Yes, so the sealing spell shattered. The result drained you of your power. Since it belonged to me, instead of being released into the planet, as a human mage's does, it searched for new lifeforms to feed off of.}

"You once told me demons possess creatures to steal their energy in order to become stronger."

{My, how attentive you are! This is why you're so important. In order to return my power to you, these creatures will need to be tracked down and killed.}

Coura sensed more the demon kept hidden. "Why don't you command your traitor find them? Why keep me involved in this at all?"

Soirée's answer came after a lengthy pause.

{I have plans in motion regarding the other human. As for you, we are connected. Any living being with my energy will forfeit the power once they die. Only a body, soul, and mind shaped to contain such energy can attract and recapture it before it finds another host. Otherwise, the cycle continues.}

"You want me to defeat the creatures carrying your power and take the demonic energy into my body so you can add it to your collection. Is that right?"

{Exactly.}

Even without being in her physical form, a shiver slid down Coura's spine. *I've been longing for the ability to use magic again, but I won't if it means strengthening a demon. I would never risk the danger she can bring to the kingdom!*

Soirée picked up on the impending rejection.

{I should add that those creatures are roaming the country, causing chaos and slaughtering innocent beings to increase their power. You alone possess the ability to absorb the energy because of our bond. Without you, Coura, who knows when they will reach a human town.}

The shadows in the forest crawled out to cover the ground and sky until nothing remained visible.

I can't possibly accept. If I do, Soirée will take advantage of me. But if I don't, who knows what could happen with those creatures running wild, especially if they're similar to the beast from the Dalan base.

Half of her grew repulsed by the offer and knew better than to accept, yet a lesser part swelled to fill the hole in her center through a satisfying desire for power.

{Excellent. Since you are aware of what's happening, I'll leave it to you.}

"Wait!"

The sudden pressure from earlier slammed down on her body then, forcing her to her knees gasping for air. Her eyes watered until everything went still and she lost consciousness.

***

How did I get myself roped into this? Byron wondered while carrying a pail of soapy water in each hand.

A man with dirt-stained clothing waited to take the buckets where they would be used to scrub the hallway leading to the queen's garden. He expressed his thanks in a chipper mood while smiling as Byron rolled his shoulders and offered his own gratitude for the assistance.

Under Aaron's orders, the garden would open the following afternoon when the coronation ceremony was complete via an announcement before the procession into the eastern square. For the past week, volunteers watered plants, cleaned the fountains, and trimmed bushes. Although Byron had never been in the area until that time, he supervised some of the tasks alongside Hendal and realized the striking changes.

It will be wonderful to have a meditative space for those in the palace to escape to. What a brilliant legacy for the late king and queen.

As he continued toward the laundry area to fetch more pails, he caught Marcus striding toward him from the opposite direction and offered a greeting. Then, he noticed the lines of concern etched into the young man's face.

What is it now? He's been by Aaron's side ever since the prince allowed it. If he's upset, it could mean something is wrong with the upcoming event.

"Good afternoon, Master Byron." The assistant general gave a hasty bow.

"What's the matter? You seem worried."

Marcus chewed on his lip before replying. "It's Coura. I haven't seen her since yesterday morning."

"What do you mean?" Byron asked with growing apprehension. His mind recounted similar instances in the past where his former student would disappear without notice.

"We finished our training, I went to fetch a couple waterskins, and she was gone when I returned. I figured she'd moved inside for lunch, but I didn't find her in the mess hall. That evening, I visited Will to see if she mentioned an issue with our session. She never met him for dinner."

"Have you checked her room?"

"I knocked several times at various points today. Nothing."

Only after Marcus' thorough evaluation did Byron become troubled. *I haven't spoken to her in days, though she didn't hint at any problems. Then again, I never know with her.*

"I'll keep an eye out and question those who would recognize her as well," he said to reassure the soldier.

"I appreciate it." Marcus dipped his head before passing to march toward the garden.

Byron went on, pondering why Coura would abandon her friend without warning and when he should start searching for her.

***

Coura first felt a soreness on her face when she came to, followed by the stiffness of her body. She found herself lying flat on her stomach in the cool grass surrounded by woods with a cheek against the ground.

Where am I? The hazy thought reflected how muddled her mind had grown.

In another minute, she readjusted herself into a sitting position, wincing at the aching joints and tender muscles. Birds and insects chirped in a natural manner, and the treetops swayed from the wind above. The more Coura glanced around, the sooner she realized she had no idea where she was.

A hand brushed the spot bothering her cheek, which proved to be an open sore no wider than a fingernail, as she tried to recall what happened. Her right arm throbbed worse than any other part of her body, so she prepared to analyze the pain but froze when she stared at it. Along her entire forearm, a pattern traced in black and blue, like a spontaneous bruise lacing into an unfamiliar design. It stretched across the front and back sides of her arm and appeared so stark anyone who noticed it would recognize it hadn't been caused by a normal accident.

I remember now! Soirée told me about the creatures carrying her missing power and the danger they pose to the rest of Asteom. Am I really the only person who can successfully recapture the demonic energy?

Coura hugged her knees while allowing her flustered mind to calm down and consider the demon's explanation. *The stag-like creature must have been one of those I'm supposed to find.*

In response, a spark from the energy inside her center flared slightly to answer her question.

With nothing else to accomplish and in need of a proper night's rest, she decided to find her way back to the palace. By using what peeks she could get of the sun and relying on the distant sounds of the city and training ground, Coura managed to reach the stone perimeter and climbed over it before hurrying inside to her quarters. Immediately, she snatched some bandages from her travel pack and covered her right forearm. This led her to contemplate who should know about the demon's bargain, or if she should reveal it at all.

If I mention the interaction to Byron, Marcus, or Aaron, they'll order me to stay in the palace at worst or send me away with guards at best. I should leave the capital, that's for certain, but I refuse to drag others into this. It stems from my mistakes. Where can I go, though? I've never traveled on my own before...

A knock at the door interrupted her planning, startling her into gasping and jolting up to open it. On the other side stood her former mentor.

"Byron?"

A relieved expression crossed his face. "You're here."

"Of course I am. Do you need me?"

He shook his head and chuckled. "Marcus hasn't seen you since yesterday morning, so I promised I would look."

"Well, I've been in my room," she lied while covering her astonishment that an entire day and a half had passed since she last spoke to the assistant general. She prepared to end the conversation there when Byron continued.

"You were in here for nearly two days? Last I remember, you hate staying in one spot inside the palace for too long. Are you sure nothing's bothering you?"

For a heartbeat, Coura prepared to share her dilemma, if only to hear his advice; however, her doubts returned to remind her of the risks posed to anyone involved with demonic energy. She held her tongue and shook her head while silently vowing to avoid letting those she cared about worry over her.

"Will you be at the coronation tomorrow?" she asked to switch subjects.

"Prince Aaron requested Emilea and I accompany him for the entire day, along with the generals and high priest. I probably won't see you then, but it should be an entertaining event."

She forced a smile as they conversed for a few minutes. After Byron left, she watched the sun sink in the late afternoon and decided what she would do next.

A New Journey Awaits

In order to ensure he felt adequately prepared for the ceremony, Byron rose at dawn to bathe and dress. He was becoming accustomed to his formal robe since he wore it more in the past few months than in recent years. After combing his hair, he double checked his appearance to make sure he looked presentable before departing. Many people had the same idea and crowded the mess hall for breakfast in their uniforms. In addition, servants hustled in all directions while transporting trays, flower bouquets, and decorations.

The coronation would last about an hour due to various traditional speeches, then the rest of the day would be spent in merriment. He found Emilea on her way to the prince's chamber, and they greeted one another.

"Is Clearshot up as well?" he inquired.

"I doubt it. I spent the evening here just so I could be on time."

"Shall we wager if he will be punctual?" Byron joked after noting his friend's laidback attitude. When he noticed Emilea's neutral expression, he worried he offended her somehow until she responded.

"Two, silver coins say he and the children sneak in halfway through."

"Make it five, and as soon as Hendal finishes his prayer."

They shook hands on it as they reached their destination. The high priest arrived a minute later in his gold-embroidered clothing and carrying his staff, and the generals in their uniforms after. Finally, Grace and her guards stood farther down the corridor. The Yeluthian donned a pearl-colored gown and matching jewelry, appearing much older with makeup on.

"Isn't the prince ready yet?" Casner asked while fidgeting under his coat.

"The ceremony won't begin until we enter," Byron started to remind the man but abandoned his next sentence when the door's latch unlocked and the knob twisted.

Everybody snapped to attention as Aaron emerged, and Byron's eyebrows rose at his appearance. The men of the royal family possessed their own set of uniforms similar to what the generals were wearing, except with more shine. Like King Hernan, Aaron's coat had been meticulously crafted and adorned using golden thread to reflect the light; only a king of Asteom had the right to wear a crimson outfit with that much decoration. The rest of his attire wasn't much different, though he didn't possess any sort of headwear.

"Your Highness," General Tont addressed the prince and bowed, leaving the rest of them to mimic his words and respectful gesture. Life shone in the young man's eyes, but Byron sensed much tension in him as well.

"Thank you all for your service," Aaron said while scanning the faces surrounding him. The generals led the way toward the grand hall, keeping their new ruler in the middle. Meanwhile, Marcus had slipped out of the room after his friend and walked beside Byron.

"How nervous is he?" Byron leaned over to whisper.

The assistant general appeared visibly anxious, and his gaze never left Aaron. "Very. We were awake for half the night just talking."

Although he knew he shouldn't pry, Byron couldn't help himself from lagging back to get Marcus alone for a moment. The assistant general understood the intent and slowed his pace.

"Tell me, will Aaron be all right today?"

"Yes," Marcus answered with a weak smile. "He's come to accept his responsibility as king. The loss of his parents is still a burden, but our conversations over the past couple weeks reassured him. Besides, he often mentions how many people are supporting him."

"That's positive news. I just needed to confirm it in case there's anything we should keep an eye on."

Marcus's lips stretched into a grin as he glanced sheepishly at Byron. "Perhaps it might be worthwhile to stress how late we were up last night. If you see him drifting off, give him a shake."

Byron chuckled at the comment, feeling much more comfortable with what was to come.

The group entered from the doors at the top of the staircase in the grand hall. Besides the crimson carpet cutting a path through the center, every inch of the space had been packed with people. Along the back wall stood soldiers in uniform, then the light and dark mages in their robes, and finally the noblemen and ladies dressed in various colors up front. A line of hand-picked guards monitored the carpet where the procession would begin. After a moment, Byron and the rest of the prince's escorts settled into position. Aaron stood next to Hendal, who welcomed everyone before proceeding with the ceremony. The master mages remained on their right and the three generals to his left; Marcus joined the soldiers at attention near the door.

The high priest began saying various prayers and chants, inviting Aaron to kneel in front of him for blessings. These were traditional, time-honored customs apart of the ritual to wish the best for the new king and prosperity for the country.

Byron's eyes wandered around the hall while he half-listened. He spotted many familiar faces in the crowd, but he searched for Will and Coura in particular. When Hendal reached the conclusion of his speech, he spotted the two near the bottom of the stairs. Will wore his outfit with the green vest and Coura a lavender dress. Her hair had been pinned up into a bun while someone painted her face to redden her lips and cheeks and highlight her eyes. It seemed uncharacteristic of her to put that much consideration into her appearance, but it did make her look rather pretty.

A soft nudge in the side brought his mind back to the ceremony. He tilted his head a bit at Emilea, somewhat surprised by her behavior. Her sapphire eyes shifted from him to a location across the hall, and when Byron mirrored her gaze, he caught movement farther along the left wall. It became a struggle for him to keep a straight face when he recognized Clearshot and his children weaving through the crowd to join the line of soldiers.

Is Hendal almost finished speaking? I should have kept the bet to two coins.

The high priest paused then while a servant ascended the staircase to pass off a neatly wrapped bundle of scarlet cloth. He pulled the corners aside in dramatic fashion, revealing the gold crown, to awe-influenced noises from those below. With a final blessing, Hendal placed the crown on the young man's head before instructing their new king to rise.

Cheers and applause greeted Aaron as he stood tall and wore a controlled yet proud smile. The hall's celebratory noise rang for at least a full minute, which proved long enough to cause him to blush and raise a hand for silence.

"People of Asteom," he began once the sound died down. "I am honored to be welcomed with such support as you have shown me." His voice boomed to reach the entire space, just like Byron recalled King Hernan's always had, and he offered a rehearsed message of well wishes.

After, it was Grace's turn to step forward and give a blessing to reaffirm her country's affiliation with Asteom. Initially, this caused some controversy in the council because of Yeluthia's silence on the murders and coronation notice. Byron had been the one to remind the members of their missing culprits, as well as the rogue angels who were interrupting communications between the nations.

Hendal used the closing section of the ceremony to explain Aaron's request to open the queen's garden. Byron appreciated how well the high priest crafted the announcement, wording it as though it were more of a gift from the royal family than anything else. He presented the rules, and Aaron signed the document in front of the entire hall. That way, all who entered would be aware of the penalty of defying their new king's wishes to respect the area. Many onlookers chatted in excited voices, then the crowd applauded the news.

With the main event complete, Hendal stepped forward once again to officially close the ceremony, mention the reception in the eastern square, and begin the procession. The resulting, joyful cheers drowned out all other sounds.

Byron offered an elbow to Emilea and followed in line behind the generals. Their group descended the stairs, strolled across the hall, and left through the main entrance where their carriages awaited. It was no surprise to see the roads packed with civilians lining the streets to catch a glimpse of their new ruler. Aaron kept his chin high amid their noisy approval and congratulations. The guards surrounding the king made sure nobody came too close, though Byron expected the people were also aware they would be facing the wrath of three generals and the master mages if they interfered.

He held his breath until they reached the platform overlooking the eastern square. Although it was a tight space, enough seats had been prepared for the generals, Aaron, Hendal, Byron, and Emilea. Marcus stood behind his friend, and the other assistant generals rotated positions at the bottom of the stairs leading up to the private viewing space.

The first minstrels to perform waited for the group to settle in before beginning with an introduction honoring Aaron and wishing the kingdom prosperity. By that point, an eager crowd filled the area below. The king nodded as a cue for them to play, then Byron relaxed.

The worst of it is over. He should be able to enjoy the festivities and recover over the next few hours. Everyone else can unwind as well since we're out of the spotlight too.

Trays of specially prepared food and drinks were offered, so Byron stuffed himself and drank his share without becoming incoherent. As night approached, six musicians and their instruments replaced the final group of actors on stage.

"I suppose it's time for the dancing," he mused to Emilea. The light mage spoke with him throughout their time above the square, revealing more of her true colors as a compassionate woman, teacher, and guide for those under her supervision.

"There's no need to stay up here any longer," she replied and rose from her seat. "I better check on my children."

"I'd like a break too," Dillon added.

As the two descended to the ground area, Tont gestured for Marcus and put a hand on his son's arm. "I'll take over for tonight."

"I can continue," Marcus protested until his father shoved him toward the doorway.

"Go on! Get down there and practice your dancing."

With one, last glance at Aaron, whose eyes didn't seem to leave the stage for most of the afternoon, the assistant general hurried away.

"What a day, Your Highness," Byron offered to comfort the new king.

"It wound up being less exhausting than I imagined."

Those remaining in the upper platform sat in silence, spectating the musicians and dancing. Emilea returned and chatted with Byron about her family, including how she briefly berated Clearshot for sneaking into the ceremony late, and they laughed at her husband's expense. Tont pointed out the women Marcus danced with, including Coura and Grace, in a proud, paternal manner. The assistant general eventually returned to relieve his father despite the latter's wishes.

Byron closed his eyes in the peace of the evening and let his mind clear in a meditation adapting to the noise. When he began to drift toward sleep, a nudge from Emilea had him alert at once. She didn't speak but pointed to her eye with one finger then to Aaron. Although he raised an eyebrow at the unusual signal, he turned his attention to the young man.

Their new king rested an elbow on the arm of his seat and his chin on that hand in a casual posture. His face still held the mask of calm, though his eyes danced under the glow of the nearest lanterns. They remained fixated on a particular spot below, which Byron figured had been why Emilea involved him. After following Aaron's stare across the square, he recognized the group who situated themselves nearby and eased up. In an open space, Grace and Will danced together while Mace and Lexie each held one of Coura's hands and twirled her around. Clearshot clapped in time with the music before being dragged out by his children.

I'm sure he would rather be among friends than stuck here throughout the evening, especially when they appear to be relishing the festivities.

Byron's initial conclusion altered during the next song when Clearshot, Grace, and Will moved to sit on one of the benches at the edge. This time, Mace and Lexie held each other's hands and spun around while Coura smiled and clapped for them. Byron had noticed her at various points throughout the day; each time he did, he noted how happy she appeared. It warmed his heart to see her adjusting to a life in Verona and reminded him of the seemingly scarce moments when she could truly appreciate the positive moments in her life.

He savored the sight before returning his attention to Aaron again. With eyelids half closed, the young man continued studying that spot, just as Byron had been doing, except with a slight smile that softened his face. Emilea had been waiting for Byron to make the connection and giggled at his flustered expression when he turned to her again.

"He's been like this ever since I returned to my seat," she leaned closer to whisper, her voice teeming with humor. "You honestly haven't noticed his reserved behavior until now?"

"You don't believe he's actually…"

"Don't worry. Infatuation is far more common than love at their age."

"That's what I'm worried about," he replied in a grumble. An odd nagging poked at him before he dismissed the idea of somebody being romantically involved with the student he partially raised.

Why am I fussing over her? Coura is an adult, free to decide what she wants in life. I'm not her father or in any way responsible for her choices. Recognizing their ended mentorship due to the loss of her magic made him feel discouraged instead of better.

Emilea placed a hand on his shoulder, as though she sensed his internal strife. "I meant no harm by bringing it up and am only assuming. It's been a long day. Perhaps he's too exhausted to care about focusing on anything else, and she might not even be the target of his gaze."

Although he agreed aloud, Byron kept an eye on the royal figure. Two songs began and ended, but nothing changed. The musicians on stage switched to a new group, who started a ballad intended for a paired, slower dance. Many people chose to line the square or seat themselves instead of finding a partner.

Coura ushered the children toward their father and stood next to Will. As she looked around the square, her pleasant expression settled into one projecting sorrow. When her gaze rose to the upper platform, Byron caught Aaron jerk his head to face the stage and avert his eyes. Whether she noticed it or not, her attention moved to and stayed on the performers after.

Byron heard Emilea giggle, revealing she too had been continuing to observe the young man's behavior. He rolled his eyes and decided to drop the subject, but not before catching their king's faint blush.

*

It became earlier in the morning than later into the evening when they decided to retire from the event. The generals and their assistants escorted Aaron and Hendal to the palace while Emilea returned below where Clearshot carried their exhausted daughter on his back and led his family away. Byron figured they arranged to stay in the city instead of attempting to return to their home.

The music went on even without the prime audience present, lulling him into a meditative state once more. When sleep threatened to overcome his mind, he ventured back to his quarters alone.

What a remarkable day, he thought with a yawn. *Asteom crowned a new ruler, and we can start falling into a routine for the future. It's about time I fill General Tio and the Dalan base in on what's happened since I don't plan on traveling too much, at least not for some time. Besides, I must support Aaron and continue to look after Will and Marcus too. There's no telling when we might hear from Yeluthia either, so Grace will need to be given attention by the council. Then I have Coura to worry about, though maybe not so much after tonight. Without the demonic energy forced upon her, she can move on from her past. She's free to do what she wants. I better talk with her tomorrow and ask if she's reached a final decision on a position in the army.*

Despite his active thoughts, once Byron dropped into bed, he slept soundly throughout the rest of the night and most of the next morning.

***

The light of dawn shaded the sky gray outside the window in Coura's room. She hadn't been able to sleep since returning from the square, which provided time to pack her few belongings and dress herself in proper traveling clothes. Then, she slipped into the mess hall

130

to grab breakfast and stuff her bag with whatever would last for a few days.

Her final goal ended up going much easier than expected, considering the previous evening's celebration. The training ground looked empty except for the soldiers on duty, who merely waved and rested against the stable's outer wall. She didn't think they realized she dug into one of the bins to procure a sword, hide it under her clothing, and return inside to buckle the weapon on her waist.

Throughout the weeks, she had been saving up her pay and counted it once more to ensure it would cover supplies for the next couple months. With a final glance around the space, she nodded to herself and willed her beating heart to a steadier pace. She wore the cloak she kept from Dala, wrapped it around her shoulders, and drew the hood to cover her face.

"Time to go," she mumbled before shouldering her bag and departing.

The halls were abnormally quiet. Coura only saw a couple servants here and there sporting droopy eyelids. From her experience with public events, nobody became active the following morning until around noon, giving her the perfect opportunity to leave without being noticed.

Her footsteps echoed as she strode to one of the doors leading into the grand hall and shoved it open, wincing when the metal hinges creaked. A pair of guards talked to each other from their positions by the front gate and noticed her right away, yet it was obvious the two lacked a proper night's rest by their shifting feet and yawning as she approached the exit.

"It's a little early to be out and about," the older guard with peppered hair said in a neutral tone.

"You won't find much happening in the city for at least another hour or so," the other continued, smiled, then raised a hand to cover his yawn.

Coura didn't respond. She noticed them shrug while she moved outside, and they closed the gate behind her.

A glance at the horizon hinted at fair weather, which proved ideal for the journey ahead. *I don't plan on stopping until I'm out of Verona. In the cover of the woods, I should be-*

"Who's there?"

She had been keeping her face down as she began crossing over the bridge, so she hadn't seen the approaching group of men. Several in uniform, still from the festival it appeared, jostled each other using loud voices in the sluggish morning. One of them pointed her out, and though most ignored her altogether, a trio slowed to assess the stranger exiting the palace. Among them was Marcus.

"State your business," the leftmost man demanded with a boisterous attitude and crossed arms.

His companion scolded him for the harsh order while Marcus leaned forward to peer closer.

"Coura, is that you?"

She straightened and attempted a greeting once there became no conceivable way to deny the accusation without acting suspicious. "I didn't think I would see you around today. You're the liveliest bunch awake."

The soldiers by Marcus quieted when she addressed him before hurrying to catch up to their group after figuring she wasn't worth bothering with. Meanwhile, her friend didn't budge.

"What's going on?"

"I planned to head into town for the day," she lied and attempted to sidestep him.

"For what?"

"Nothing in particular."

He blocked her path. "Why?"

She didn't answer.

"Why do you have a pack and your cloak?"

"Don't worry about it," she snapped while preparing to push him aside.

He reached out to grab her arm and held it tight. "It's almost as if you're leaving the city," he commented in an ominous tone.

"I told you. I'll be out for a while, so don't-"

Marcus shook her arm forcefully enough to jolt her upper body and startle her into meeting his narrowed, hazel eyes.

"Tell me the truth. What's wrong?"

Coura attempted to pull her arm away, but the movement proved useless. She knew she shouldn't underestimate Marcus' strength, both in body and willpower, and stopped fighting him. "I need to leave Verona."

"Why?"

"I can't tell you," she answered after remembering how much of a risk the creature in Dala had posed.

"Why not?"

Despite his annoyance, Coura didn't reply.

He stared at her a moment longer before releasing his grip. "Fine, then I'm going along."

"You can't," she argued, leading him to cross his arms.

"It's far too dangerous for you to handle. If I've been able to beat you in every fight we've had, what makes you think you're capable enough to keep yourself alive outside the city? Have you forgotten about the demonic creatures wandering around lately?"

His words hurt, but that didn't make them any less true. "Marcus, I need to do this. I'm the only person who can stop them from causing more destruction."

"How will you do it by yourself?" he countered as his frustration raised the volume of his voice.

Coura pursed her lips, unsure whether or not to reveal Soirée's confrontation before deciding against it. "I can't tell you, but if I don't try, there will be terrible results across the country. Ask Byron and Emilea about it; they should understand."

"We can talk to them together, perhaps even organize a team to go instead."

She shook her head. "You're needed here. You have responsibilities, a family, and a duty to protect Aaron. Getting a group set up would waste time. I don't have a purpose here anymore."

"That's not true."

"Yes, it is. Without my magic, I'm living a completely different life. At least this will give me a reason to learn about the world and explore what I can do."

Marcus looked away as sunlight poured over the city. His next words carried enough distress to make her heart ache. "I can't just let you go."

"There's someone in the palace who's responsible for the murders. Figure out who it is, then stop him. I'll be back as soon as I can."

With that, she walked into Verona without a glance behind.

***

Three days after the coronation ceremony, Byron grew concerned about Coura. He tried to locate her the following afternoon but figured everybody was still recuperating. Then, he asked around. Will went on at length about how she hadn't been to any meals with him in the mess hall, and Grace had said the same.

In the meantime, Byron wrote a full report of the past month for the Dalan base and scheduled a meeting with Aaron and the council to review the information.

After his training sessions the next morning, he spotted Marcus working with a group across the area, prompting him to inquire about his former student. He had been aware the two were actively practiced together, so he assumed if anyone had seen her, it would be the assistant general.

"Marcus," Byron called and waved when the young man noticed him.

"Master Byron, what can I do for you?"

"You know it's just Byron," he chided with a chuckle before putting a hand above his eyes to scan the field. "I'm hoping you can tell me where Coura is. I'd like to discuss a few things with her, but it seems she disappeared again."

He intended the joke to lighten the conversation, yet the soldier's bothered expression resulted in the opposite reaction.

"She's not here."

Byron smile faltered. "What do you mean?"

Marcus shook his head, requested a moment, then jogged over to the soldier in charge of the session to briefly converse. When he returned, Byron pressed for answers.

"Where is she?"

"I don't know."

"She couldn't have vanished. You said this happened before the coronation ceremony too, remember? I visited her in her room that afternoon."

Marcus didn't respond, though he appearing to consider if he should or not, so Byron figured they could try her quarters again. The assistant general trailed him to the third floor and stood behind as he knocked on the door. When no one answered, he twisted the knob and was shocked to find it unlocked. Inside, the bed was made, the window was shut, and her belongings had been neatly arranged, as if it hadn't been occupied for a while.

She left the palace? Why?

He inspected the room in search of clues regarding her whereabouts until Marcus' uncharacteristically timid voice said his name.

"What is it?" he grumbled.

"There's something I need to ask you about."

"Well then?" Byron urged. His patience wore thin when the soldier paused, and he glanced at the doorway to see Marcus fidgeting in place. "What is it?"

"I caught her heading into Verona the day after Aaron's coronation. She claimed she intends to stop the demonic creatures showing up across Asteom and that you and Emilea would know more about it."

Byron stared at Marcus, allowing his bemusement to show. He believed the young man hid additional details given the continued shifting but realized they were preparing to dive into a serious matter.

If I'm going to approach the topic of the demon and its creatures, in addition to what Coura might be doing, I don't want to repeat myself. I've been considering it ever since we were stationed in Dala; it's time we begin figuring out the issue.

He left Coura's room and gestured for Marcus to remain with him as he selected a path.

"Where are we going?"

"We must prepare for an overdue meeting of sorts."

*

By mid-afternoon, Byron gathered Marcus, Will, Clearshot, and Grace in his room. They looked bewildered by his request and, in his opinion, agreed because of the lack of an immediate explanation accompanied by his grave expression.

"I should apologize for dragging you here so suddenly," he began while pacing as much as he could in the cramped space.

"Not a problem," Clearshot replied on their behalf. "It's not like we have anything better to do."

"This concerns the demon we encountered in Dala. I fear the kingdom is putting off this problem instead of tackling it before it spirals out of control."

At the mention of the terrifying encounter, their faces fell.

Will was the first to venture a comment. "I thought it was left for the council to discuss. Shouldn't Coura be here too?"

"That's part of our problem…"

A knock on the door saved him from explaining, and he called for his final guest to enter. The master light mage held herself as polished as any noblewoman until she recognized those around her, including her husband.

"Emilea?" Clearshot sat straighter before glancing at Byron.

His wife did the same. "What is this about?" she demanded with more distress than annoyance.

Byron rubbed the bridge of his nose and sensed a headache approaching. "Please, come join us."

Without another word, she closed the door before sitting beside her husband on the bed. Then, all eyes darted to Byron.

I hope this produces worthwhile results.

"Thank you for being patient. The reason I requested for you to meet me is because we're no closer to finding the murderers responsible for the three deaths in the palace; however, I'm certain they're connected to the demon and rogue angels from Dala. This afternoon, I will send a letter to General Tio containing details of what took place here and where we are at now. No news has come from the base, which I'm assuming means they haven't had any major encounters since ours. I'd like to see if we can piece this together on our own."

"Excuse me, Master Byron," Grace chimed in her softer voice. "I did not stay in Dala, so why did you ask me to come here?"

"I'm glad you reminded me. If you're willing to use your goddess gift to assist us, I would like you to reach out to Yeluthia about our situation. If the angels who attacked the base are allying with dangerous sources of power, especially the demon, we'll need their help."

"I will need to practice extending my mind since my home remains too far out of reach."

Byron nodded then paused, uncertain of how to bring up his former student's absence.

"Is there another purpose?" she asked, likely sensing his apprehension.

"It's Coura. I'm afraid she left Verona to try and solve this problem herself."

"Are you sure?" Emilea pressed. Her perturbed expression matched everybody else's. "Where would she go?"

Byron looked to Marcus. "Am I wrong?"

The assistant general scowled. "Why are you asking me?" he began defensively but let out a defeated sigh into the resulting silence. "She told me she intends to stop the demonic creatures and confirmed there *is* a traitor in the palace."

"She didn't mention where she planned to go?" Clearshot commented while frowning at the circumstances. "How foolish."

"Even so, we have our own business to handle before pursuing her," Byron admitted. Deep down, he desired nothing more than to hurry after Coura because of her headstrong behavior and vulnerability without magic.

At the moment, none of us are worth sparing, he repeated to himself before Will spoke up.

"I still don't understand. If we're letting her go, what are we supposed to be doing?"

"Allow me to summarize. Somebody possessing power in the palace has control of the five angels we faced outside Dala, as well as the demon who warned Coura. There's been an increase in demonic creatures over the years, but recent reports show frightening numbers. I believe these points are correlated, especially since one appeared inside the Dalan base. Lastly, we haven't heard any updates from Yeluthia, which reminds me of how Asteom's past efforts to communicate were intercepted. Does that make sense so far?"

Everybody nodded.

"I have a hunch Coura knows more about the demon and those creatures than she let on, which is why she chose to act on her own. Also, I don't want Aaron to hear of our suspicions regarding the traitor just yet."

"You believe it's someone on the council," Emilea concluded for him.

"It makes the most sense to me and is why I organized a group with various affiliations. If you're all willing to contribute what you see or hear, we have a chance to begin unraveling this mystery."

Byron took a moment to meet each set of eyes. When he arranged for them to gather in private, it was with the understanding he would not throw them in harm's way unless they expressed their willingness to commit to the cause. Nobody voiced any disagreements, so he continued with the initial steps of his plan to utilize their strengths.

"Grace, I have two favors to ask of you in addition to contacting Yeluthia. Are you trained in wielding light magic?"

"I only know how to use my goddess gift," she admitted and dipped her head a bit in shame.

"In that case, I'd like for you to work with Emilea in secret, if it's all right with her." Byron glanced at his fellow master mage.

"I support the suggestion," Emilea offered with a sharp nod. "This way, we won't raise suspicion, and you'll be safer if there is another attack in the palace."

"As for the second favor, can you locate Coura with your ability?"

Grace raised her eyes to the ceiling in thought before answering. "I will try. I have spoken to her before, so her mind is familiar to me. It will probably take time, if it is possible at such a distance."

"That's fine. We need a way to give and get information if she intends to stay away from the capital. I'll send my letter to Dala today and attempt one to Yeluthia as well. The rest of you, keep an eye out around here for any unusual activity. When I learn more, we can plot our next course of action."

Part Two

Secrets in the Western Woods

The ordinary sounds of chirping birds and leaves rustling in the treetops above hushed as Coura groaned in frustration and dropped to sit cross-legged in the grass.

"Why did my sense of direction have to lead me west?" she mumbled while watching other people pass on the nearby road she had been using.

Three days of traveling southwest helped her avoid the towns outside Verona, but after glancing at the map of Asteom she snuck with her, there seemed to be nothing except woods ahead.

"Maybe I read it wrong." She reluctantly slipped off her pack to dig out the parchment.

Coura had no indication of where the demonic creatures would appear and figured trailing along the country's perimeter would lure them away from the populated areas. The original idea she came up with was to begin moving until she reached the coast; however, no single path went there.

Here... If I continue on this road, it should branch at a station in front of the Western Woods. Then, I can go north and survey the area before returning south.

With a huff, she stood again while keeping the map in hand and returning to the path.

Unlike her previous travels through forested areas, this dry time of year meant less bugs and plenty of shade to shield her from the sun. Although most of her provisions remained available, they would need to last for another week or so when she could purchase more.

By mid-afternoon, the road opened into a grassland. The wind picked up without cover from the trees and swept all around her, causing her hair to whip in black wisps until she threw up her hood. Many others venturing in that direction did the same.

Despite being alone with only her thoughts, Coura found herself savoring the freedom. *For the first time in my life, I don't need to rely on Byron for a destination or follow anybody else's pace. If it means tolerating the solitude, I can manage.*

When the branching trail appeared, no one else joined her to head west, opting to shift directly south instead. As tempting as it became to spend the night in the open field, she knew she would be safer after reaching the station on the map and not wasting sunlight. As she continued, a shadow stretched to Coura's left, prompting her to pause and inspect the map again.

That must be the Western Woods, she realized with no shortage of awe at their expansive width.

While she did so, a faint but familiar presence tugged at the limited energy in her center. She placed a hand on her chest, recalling the previous pressure from Soirée's power, and her contentment lessened.

I guess I picked the right direction to start with.

As she drew nearer to the trees, Coura marveled at their enormous size. Each rose to the height of, if not taller than, the palace, and their emerald, summer leaves shrouded the inside to add to their mystery.

The path she occupied led to the entrance of the woods before splitting north and south. The sight of a brick house at the fork with a cheery stream of smoke puffing from its chimney intrigued her enough to approach the front window, which hung open. A middle-aged man in a soldier's uniform startled her by poking his head out when she moved closer.

"Who's there?" he barked before spotting her.

"Hello," she began and raised an eyebrow. "Who are you?"

"What does it look like?" he retorted while leaning on the windowsill and scratching his scruffy, brown hair. "I'm the station's guard on duty. What are you doing here?"

Coura expected to run into a few people, either on the road or in town, who would be curious enough to question her business. At first, she considered borrowing Will's title as a researcher but soon decided against it. If somebody were to dig deeper into her self-proclaimed studies, she didn't possess the knowledge to carry on with the lie. Then, she remembered Aaron's purpose for traveling to Dala earlier in the year.

"I'm conducting a survey of the soldiers and mages assigned to the towns out west."

"What for?" the man asked in a rough yet not unkind tone. It became more and more obvious he wasn't used to interacting with people often.

"The generals in the capital wish to restructure how many of their troops need to be positioned in what areas."

"Well, there aren't any places to the west in need of more soldiers or magic. Send that back to the capital."

Coura stopped herself from outright glaring at him for his ignorant view. *Perhaps there's an issue feeding his stubbornness.*

"Have you seen a lot of people moving along this path?" she brought up next.

His expression softened. "No."

"Is there a reason?"

The guard's eyes widened before narrowing. "What's your name, surveyor?"

"Paulina," she lied.

"Which direction are you heading in?" The man swung a finger back and forth between the north and south routes.

Coura remembered the tug on her center and the demonic presence, so she instinctively glanced toward the woods.

"No," the man snapped upon noticing her gaze. "That path is off limits!"

"Why?" she countered.

He pointed out the window at the trees to emphasize his warning. "Those forest dwellers like their privacy. Besides, they got their own problems. I've been hearing far too many unnatural noises and seen enough dangerous-looking shadows to allow travelers on the road, especially alone."

Initially, Coura felt insulted by the guard's assumption that she was a frail, young woman with no training. When she further reflected on his explanation, she realized his intentions were to protect those wandering in the area. It seemed noble given the energy emanating from the woods likely meant a demonic creature lurked within.

"I suppose I should follow the trail north then," she resigned and started walking. "Thank you for your assistance."

"Wait a moment, Miss Paulina. How about staying the night inside the station? The sun's about ready to drop. You'll only be about halfway to the nearest coastal town by midnight."

Coura kept moving until his calls faded and ceased, then she rested off the path. She returned to the station after darkness fell, snuck around the building, and ventured into the trees beyond.

*

The Western Woods were unlike any place Coura had ventured through during her previous travels. With branches reaching up to brush the sky, their leaves blocked the moonlight. She stumbled over several rocks and sticks on the road, even losing the dirt trail twice and catching herself when she felt grass beneath her feet instead. The wildlife seemed more active as well, filling the area around her with unidentifiable noises, many close enough to give her shivers. Fortunately, she remained wide awake and alert.

Soon, the demonic energy became worse to handle than the environment. As she continued forward, the pressure on her chest grew until she prepared to scream at the unseen creature she sensed stalking her.

A howl in the distance pierced the night, and the wildlife hushed into a deafening silence for a while. Coura halted to listen for hints of danger but couldn't make potential threats out beneath the sound of her panting. When the effort became fruitless, she told herself to keep moving. It disturbed her even minutes after, and her stress rose as the woods stayed quiet. She grasped the hilt of her sword in case of an ambush.

Minutes later, she noticed a red glow through the trees to her left. *Is it dawn already? Have I been wandering all night?*

The thought amazed her, but she breathed easier, expecting the sun to eliminate some of the shadows among the brush; however, when the light flickered in the distance but didn't increase, she understood it was a fire nearby, not the sun, and debated whether or not to pursue the light.

Before she could make a decision, a shout reached her from that direction.

Coura froze to wait. When the cry came again, she recognized it as a man's voice and instantly sprinted toward the source. She tripped over herself and her surroundings too many times to count, causing her to swear under her breath after each instance as she rose. The memory of finding Mace and Lexie fending off two demonic creatures came to mind. She tightened her grip on the sword in response, and the stranger stopped yelling, which also became concerning.

At last, she burst into a clearing and noticed a bonfire at its center. Her blade slid from its sheath with a soft hiss while she prepared to call out to the unseen man.

"Run! Flee!"

She started at the voice then found herself gasping for air when what felt like a giant hand held her body and squeezed.

What…is this? It's definitely here!

She dug her fingernails into her palm in order to distract from the immense pressure before staggering to the fire.

"Stop!" The weak cry came from the opposite direction.

Coura placed her back to the flames and glanced around warily. "Who are you?" she asked into the emptiness.

A low rumble, like a deep whisper, answered.

The bushes to her right rustled next. She pointed her sword there but restrained herself when a young man emerged and limped over to join her.

At first, she hesitated to trust him because of his odd appearance. He wore darkly colored, loose pants, bore markings across his exposed chest, arms, and face, and his hair trailed past his shoulders. That was all she could glimpse in the moment. When he reached the fire, the stranger threw himself in front of her and extended a hand to gesture for the sword.

A shadow dashed toward them from where the young man had been with frightening speed and slid to a stop. Coura tensed once she recognized the energy. This demonic creature appeared like a giant lizard on all fours standing at half her height. Its smooth head tilted from side to side, gazing at its prey with each eye while the tail, which equaled the length of its body, waved vertically to show its impatience. Every second or so, a forked tongue flicked to taste the air.

Coura didn't look away from the enemy, yet the stranger still held his hand out for her weapon. When she stared at him, she noticed fresh blood and some sort of thick, inky substance along his upper thigh.

"Stand back," she ordered as she adjusted herself in front of him while raising the blade at the creature. It bared dozens of tiny, pointed teeth at her, but she sensed it behaved in an intrigued manner rather than aggressively.

"Stop!" The young man's voice sounded raspy, and he put a hand on her shoulder. "We must hide until morning."

She rolled her shoulder to remove the added weight. "I'll hold its attention," she began at a lower volume and without removing her eyes from the creature. "You're in no condition to fight, so either stay by the fire and call for backup or go into the bushes for cover. I don't care which you choose; just don't be in my way."

He remained quiet while she stepped away to stand in front of the lizard. *The previous demonic creature willingly gave me its energy, but it seems I need to convince this one. I don't possess my healing ability anymore, so I can't let it injure me.*

With a grunt, Coura charged. It moved swifter than any being she fought before, crawling forward to slide along her left side and swing its tail like a club. She lowered her blade to effectively block the strike before spinning around and stabbing. In response, the creature leapt backward to bring itself nearer to the stranger and the bonfire. The young man had picked up a flaming branch to wave at the lizard, causing it to hiss at the new threat.

Its head darted between the two humans while Coura stepped closer until she could lunge with a downward slice when it became distracted. She targeted the neck, but the creature spotted her intent and attempted to dodge. By the time her blade connected with its body, the head moved out of range, resulting in a slice halfway through its tail instead. The lizard spasmed and let out a painful wail. In a second strike during that moment, the tail came clean off to wriggle on the ground.

She gasped at the limb's unexpected jerks before the creature shrieked at an ear-piercing volume. Black blood sprayed all over the grass and onto her legs and boots, prompting her to stumble away and inadvertently draw its attention again. Before she could recover, it leapt with its mouth open to sink the tiny teeth into her left shoulder.

This time, she inhaled sharply in response to the pain before pushing against the creature with the flat side of her blade until it released its hold. The teeth were short enough to puncture flesh but not shred or tear, yet her skin burned, as though it caught fire.

The lizard made a gargling sound then scurried into the brush before more voices came from behind. Although she planned to face the newcomers, a surge of pain caused her body to tremble and vision to blur. With a hand on the afflicted shoulder, Coura dropped to one knee.

A minute or two passed until somebody stood beside her. The surrounding noise consisted of male voices and spoke in a language she couldn't understand. After squeezing her eyes shut to fend off a wave of dizziness, she focused on steadying her breathing as the exhilaration from the fight wore off.

It got away...

"Remove your hand," a baritone voice commanded from her left.

She opened her eyes to spot three men, who appeared the same as the wounded stranger, kneeling beside her. Without a word, she obeyed and prepared herself when one unwrapped a bitter-smelling salve. It wasn't the first experience she had with the medicinal treatment, though it happened years ago.

The man massaged some of the paste onto the bite marks, which stung worse than the burning until the area numbed. The strangers stood after, then the one in the middle offered her a hand. She accepted and found his skin completely callused. As he pulled her to her feet, she swayed from lightheadedness before passing out.

*

When Coura woke, she noticed a dull ache in her shoulder where the demonic creature bit her. She tried to relax yet found her body stiff from sleeping on the hard floor. With a groan, she cracked each eye open, pushed herself into a sitting position, and studied her surroundings.

The structure of the furniture-less room appeared to be made of wood, and her pack and a wicker basket rested against one side. Sunlight poured in around a heavy curtain on the wall used to darken the space during the daytime. Then, she inspected herself and discovered she still wore her blood-covered traveling clothes. The top of her shirt where the lizard struck had been sliced so the wound could be wrapped, but somebody removed the bandages on her right arm, revealing the bruise-like markings. After stretching her tense muscles, she rose from the thin bedroll they placed her on.

Where am I?

The movements caused her head to spin and shoulder to begin burning again. In the next instant, she threw up a hand to cover her eyes as someone drew the curtain, allowing blinding light into the room.

"I see you are awake," a high-pitched, female voice exclaimed in surprise.

Coura stepped forward to meet the woman while offering a greeting and found her throat dry, leading her to cough instead. The newest stranger hurried to her side then held Coura against her slim torso, as if in an invitation to lean over for support. Though the woman lacked muscles, she proved fit enough to show how well she took care of herself. A leather headband restrained the short, brown hair threatening to drape over her hazel eyes.

"How are you feeling?" she asked.

"I'm fine," Coura unconvincingly croaked.

"We better find you medicine for your throat," the stranger responded while guiding her to the bedroll.

They probably don't trust me and hope to leave me in a room without possessions or furniture, she thought when the woman left.

Soon after, the stranger returned, knelt beside Coura, and poured her a cup of steaming liquid from a clay teapot. "Drink as much as you'd like. I'll fetch more once this is gone," she explained before smiling, dipping her head in a bow, and exiting.

Coura polished off the medicinal tea before it could cool. Then, her stomach began growling. Just when she prepared to explore outside, her caretaker returned carrying a wooden plank topped with unique finger foods.

"Finished already? We aren't sure what your people eat, so we kept the meal mild for your tongue."

Coura examined the tray and chose what appeared to be jam on a dried piece of bread. Its tart favor paired well with the additional herbs to give it a warm, earthy undertone; the other items tasted similarly. Her hunger ebbed when she consumed the last piece, leaving her refreshed and more alert.

Meanwhile, the woman introduced herself as Shina Tenderheart, an unusual name in Coura's opinion, and retrieved the healing paste from the basket. With a reluctant sigh, Coura willed her shoulders to remain still while her caretaker unwound the bandages to rub the mixture over the wound. The expected numbness resulted as a consolation before Shina wrapped the skin again.

"Your injury is much better than it was two nights ago."

"*Two* nights ago?"

"That's correct," the woman continued despite Coura's shock. "Our scouting party found you with one of their own. He claims you saved..."

Footsteps approached from beyond the entrance, and someone pulled the curtain aside. A man sculpted by years of physical activity walked inside. He wore loose, tan pants and showcased inked markings, which Coura studied as he addressed Shina in their own language. When he would glance at her, she made sure to return the stares.

"What did he want?" she asked after the man left.

"He inquired about your recovery. Our chief and witch wish to see you as soon as possible."

Chief and witch? Who are these people?

When she began to stand, her caretaker gestured for her to remain on the floor.

"Please, do not strain yourself."

"I'll be fine," Coura said while attempting to sound reassuring. "I've been resting for too long."

When it became apparent she desired to exit the confines of the room, Shina led her outside where her breath caught. What she assumed had been a shed or building on someone's property was actually its own hut suspended on branches at least three stories off the ground. More structures varying in width were spread among the trees with bridges consisting of planks and rope connecting them. A line stretched at waist height on the edge of each path, supposedly as a means of protection against falling.

Out of instinct, Coura recoiled to press her back against the hut's outer wall. This amused her caretaker, who offered a hand.

"Nobody has dropped out of the canopy since I've been alive. That's thirty-nine years, if you are wondering."

Coura accepted the assistance and clutched Shina's arm once the woman began moving over the nearest bridge, which proved to be sturdier than she gave it credit for. They passed into a busier area with leveled platforms instead of bridges, and her confidence grew. More strangers stood around chatting or emerged with baskets in hand; they mumbled and observed the pair as they went on.

Above the structures, the blue sky peeked out from behind layers of leaves in various shades of green while birds and mammals adept at traveling through the treetop filled the air with their chirps and squeaks. The surrounding environment reflected the most natural aspects of life itself.

"What is this place?" Coura muttered, disbelief hushing her voice.

"We call this…" Shina used an unfamiliar word before clarifying. "In your tongue, I believe you say 'Sie-Kie.' We thrive in harmony with these woods. They are our home."

It took Coura a moment to recall the name, then her jaw dropped. The people of the Western Woods were considered a mystery to the rest of Asteom because they preferred to live in isolation. Not even Will could share much, except how little they involved themselves with the world outside the trees.

She felt eyes on them and glanced around to catch the villagers following behind while whispering to each other. Shina noticed too but didn't comment. They entered a circular space consisting of a platform appearing nearly as spacious as the eastern square in Verona, a detail that left her awestruck. It had been smoothed and stabilized to hold the many people filing into the area.

A handful of huts surrounded the perimeter too; Shina stopped in front of the centermost one. Those who joined the walk lowered themselves to sit in a casual manner and wait in silence.

Two people emerged from the nearest structure: a man and an elderly woman. Coura figured the first had to be the chief. He appeared the same as the other men, though possessing far more markings than any person she encountered so far, and he wore a headband adorned with half a dozen hanging feathers. The older woman hunched forward, relying on an intricately carved stick bearing designs similar to those on the chief for support. White hair draped behind to hover just above the floor, but otherwise she wore a tan dress like all the other women. The pair approached Coura, who stood alone when Shina slid down to sit beside her people.

The chief studied her, leaned over to whisper to the elder, then returned his gaze. "State your name, stranger."

"Coura Galdwin," she replied after deciding honesty would help her situation instead of lies.

"Where are you from?" His voice wasn't as deep as she imagined, though his tone teemed with suspicion and distrust.

"The capital city, Verona."

"We do not often have contact with those outside these woods, Coura Galdwin of Verona; however, you rescued one of our own, and for that I'm grateful. What drives you into our woods? You carry no trading goods, as most do when they move through."

"I came here to find and defeat the creature who gave me this wound." She appreciated how directly the Sie-Kie voiced their questions because it lessened the pressure of admitting such unpleasant information.

The chief raised his voice to speak to the group around the platform in their own language. Several villagers responded, including the man who originally applied the medicine to her shoulder. Their conversation continued for a few minutes with neither party sounding jovial. Then, the elder at the chief's side tapped her staff on the ground twice, quieting the crowd. Her next words as she spoke to the leader were barely audible over the sounds of the wildlife.

The man turned to Coura again. "Do you know what that creature is? Our witch claims it's made of energy belonging to the planet."

She frowned while trying to recall Byron's lessons on the history of Asteom, demons, Yeluthians, and light and dark energy. *Who would have thought they'd come in handy at such an unpredictable moment?* she reflected sardonically as she composed an explanation.

"We refer to it, and those like it, as demonic creatures. They prey on the energy within living beings. I'm able to keep it from continuing to hunt in these woods."

"Why you?"

The chief's sharp retort made her grow tense. She was saved from crafting an excuse by their witch, who stamped her staff and nodded. That seemed to be the end of the questioning, to their leader's obvious disapproval.

"Our *shalma* wishes to speak with you in private," he went on and raised his right hand. A dozen men, some of which stood earlier in the discussion, rose to exit the area as a single unit.

"Where are they going?" Coura asked.

"They shall track down the beast who harmed you and threatens our village."

"I'm going with them." As she prepared to follow, Shina suddenly grabbed her ankle.

"You cannot!" the woman exclaimed, visibly appalled by the notion.

Coura tugged her leg free and glared at her caretaker, then the chief. "Why? I told you, I'm the only person capable of preventing it from becoming more powerful."

"It's against our custom for a woman or a wounded soldier to leave on a hunt," Shina replied in a frantic whisper. "You are both."

Coura ignored the remark to direct her words at the chief. "That creature feeds off others by stealing their natural energy. If I'm present, I can manipulate the-"

A thud interrupted her sentence. All eyes darted to the elder as she knocked her staff on the ground twice more. Her slim yet knowing smile caught Coura off guard.

Did she stop me from sharing my ability to wield dark magic?

The witch spoke in their language without removing her attention from Coura. Despite the gentle tone, the chief's eyes widened. He began grumbling a plea to the older woman until it evidently proved useless.

"What did she say?" Coura ventured when neither clarified.

"Our *shalma* would like for you to accompany the hunting party, if you are recovered."

"Really?" She eyed the witch but didn't argue.

The woman's strange, that's for sure.

"You'll join them there," the chief explained while pointing toward a path off to the right where the men went. "My son, Barnelus, will fit you with a weapon and armor and direct you through your position."

There came startled murmurs in their people's language all around as Coura nodded before weaving to hurry after the party with growing nerves.

If anybody gets in the way, who can say how the creature will react. Besides, I'm not even sure what should happen to the demonic power when we defeat it or how I absorb the energy.

These worries and more raced through her mind. She spotted the men ahead, forced the negativity aside, and held her chin higher before they took notice. A lone Sie-Kie hunter, the one she recognized from earlier in the day who visited to inquire about her condition, met her as she neared the supplies.

The soldiers in Verona, both male and female, were modest with their clothing, never revealing much besides their arms in sleeveless tunics. These warriors matched in tan pants made of the same material as the women's dresses, muddy brown shoes with noticeable padding on the bottom, and inked markings in various places along their exposed arms, chest, and back. Some used leather breastplates to add protection for their vulnerable spots, but all carried a spear or dagger lengthy enough to be mistaken as a short sword. Eleven hunters waited at attention for their leader's orders.

"You're coming," the man said as a statement rather than a question.

She nodded, ready to stand her ground.

His eyes moved to her torn shirt and the bandages beneath, yet he didn't comment, except to offer her a weapon and armor. Although the extra padding sounded beneficial, the idea of fitting into something that risked being more uncomfortable than necessary had her refusing the latter. The man seemed to understand. After rummaging through the supplies, he returned with a sheathed sword. She strapped it across her back and mimicked the others' stance.

"I am Barnelus Dagger-Diver, the leader of this hunting party," he shared after. "Stay close to me, and don't act without alerting me either."

When he turned away to move to the front of the group, Coura rolled her eyes. *I'll behave, 'Dagger-Diver.' What does that mean anyway?*

Before she could spend time wondering, Barnelus nudged something on the ground with his foot, causing a clattering noise, and dropped off the edge of the platform in a single, fluid motion. Each hunter followed just as efficiently until she was left staring at a ladder hanging from the ledge. After a deep breath to muster her resolve, she descended with much less finesse.

On the Hunt

By the time Coura's feet touched grass, the party had gathered farther through the woods ahead. She bit off a curse and caught up as they prepared to move out.

She never trained for running over periods of time and especially struggled without her previously enhanced speed. Barnelus halted them often to analyze various trails she didn't possess the skill to discern, which allowed for sufficient breaks. She remained at the rear in order to merge in without drawing too much attention to herself.

As the day crept by, those around her began panting and sweating from the heat, and she expected the sunset to approach when the shade deepened. This led her to worry about spending another night wandering in an unknown area, so she opened her mouth to voice her concern until another man at the front spoke first. Of course, whenever any of them talked, it was in their own language, alienating her. Barnelus grumbled a response, then they started bickering.

Everyone else took the opportunity to rest, leaning against trees or drinking from waterskins. She decided to backtrack while assessing the trunks' various bark. The trees, bushes, and plants appeared the same to her no matter the direction, though they crossed an enormous distance.

I haven't noticed a connection to the demonic creature, which means it's not near here. What if it left over the past two days while I was unconscious?

"Hey, girl!" Barnelus called. "Stay with the group!"

In response, Coura jogged over to rejoin the others as they readied to set out.

The party crossed a shallow stream and a clearing where they paused once more. When they left the space, a tug at her center of power froze her in place. She spun around to squint into the foliage as the demonic energy beckoned her the way they came.

The tendril is close. How did I not sense it when we passed through? Could it be on our trail?

Without consideration for the hunters, she started returning toward their previous resting point. Her suspicions solidified when the presence grew.

"Girl! Come back here!" somebody shouted.

Coura controlled herself enough to halt while continuing to scan the foliage. The sound of footsteps and rustling from behind were followed by a firm hand landing on her unharmed shoulder.

"Did you not hear me, girl?" Barnelus demanded as he pulled her away to face him and the rest of the party. None of them looked pleased with her behavior.

"Call me that again and I'll slap you. My name is Coura, and we're going the wrong way."

He narrowed his eyes while the other men glared at her for the disrespectful words. "What do you mean?"

She pointed behind in the direction of the energy, choosing to go against secrecy. *It would take too long to come up with a believable excuse.*

"I'm able to sense the creature's magical power. It seems like it's been following us from farther away, hiding at a safe distance. I wager it's waiting until we rest again or travel far from your village."

Instead of the doubtful or angry backlash she expected, Barnelus' expression shifted to one projecting surprise and awe, which made her curious about what they thought of her. Everybody else whispered to one another at the change.

Their leader shot a glance for them to be quiet before returning his attention to her. "Lead us to it."

"Are you sure that's smart?" she asked after considering her previous, head-on encounter. "It's too fast to fight using close-combat. Unless it stays in a wide enough space, I doubt we can attack together."

"Lead us to it," he repeated in the same, unphased tone.

She sighed and shrugged, opting to face disaster with the demonic creature rather than just the hunting party.

*

Although visibly tired, the group didn't complain or stop until Coura did. By that point, the immense pressure squeezing her chest became too heavy to jog against, and she leaned on a tree for support as she struggled to breathe.

Fortunately, Barnelus showed more patience and concern than earlier. "What's wrong?"

"I believe it sensed our return. We might as well wait in the last clearing until it reveals itself," she suggested, deeming it the best option with enough space for combat.

He spoke to his men in a low voice for a while before they broke off into pairs and moved as a coordinated pack. Six hunters used knife-like, hooked tools to climb one of the trees with ease before fanning out, hopping from branch to branch as they did so. Coura watched until they were gone, amazed by their skill and balance. Meanwhile, the remaining four on the ground sprinted underneath their comrades, leaving Barnelus and another member with her. Their leader said something to the man, then he clarified for her.

"They will be set by the time we reach the area. If you intend to continue, you must remain with myself and my second-in-command, Craulder. We'll deliver orders while everybody surrounds the creature."

She agreed, pushed off the tree, and began composing herself for the expected fight. As she inhaled, forcing the tightness of her muscles to relax, she faced Barnelus and nodded; however, instead of leading the way, he stepped closer, bent forward, and scooped her up in his arms so suddenly she had no time to react. The two hunters started jogging through the woods together after.

"W-What are you doing?" she stammered as her face flushed. "Put me down!"

"Not yet," Barnelus answered. "You mustn't exhaust yourself before meeting this creature."

She desired to argue, if only for her pride, but didn't. She felt like a child in the man's enormous arms and bounced with every step until he slowed. Once they were within sight of the open area, he set her down gently, like a fragile vase.

"Wait for your opening," he ordered before slipping away to hide among the brush.

"Whatever," Coura muttered to show she was still upset from being handled in such a degrading manner. She brushed the feeling aside to focus on the task at hand as she scanned the clearing. It required a keen eye to spot the hunters because of their ability to blend into the surrounding greenery.

I can imagine how much I must stand out, she thought with a wry smile before addressing the demonic creature's energy. It lessened but not enough to suggest it fled. A glance at the sky after revealed several stars in the dusk hour. To remain after nightfall would mean building a fire in order to have visibility; the notion influenced her next course of action.

Without consulting Barnelus, Coura strolled into the open area, being sure to create plenty of noise as she did so. She sensed the party's negative reactions while avoiding looking at their locations. Once she stood in place at the center, she drew her sword and sat in the grass. Acting as the bait proved nerve-wracking, yet she kept her legs strung in order to spring up at a moment's notice.

You might as well slither out, she attempted to call using her mind. *I won't wait for you forever.*

To her surprise, the constant weight on her chest eased as the bushes across from her position rustled. The lizard-like creature crawled forward cautiously a minute later, halting just beyond the foliage. Somehow, it appeared wider than before, and to Coura's disgust, its tail had regrown. The tongue flicked in the pause, then its head swayed to look around.

I wonder if the party covered their scent, she realized as she climbed to her feet.

Before she could raise her sword, a glimmer of metal passed through the air. The creature dodged the projectile without much effort by charging ahead, scurrying for the trees behind Coura. She prepared to pursue until the hunting party carried out their own plan more fluidly than any strategy she had ever seen.

Two of the grounded men burst from their hiding spots in opposite directions with the lizard forced to the middle, lifting their spears and releasing a unified cry but not striking. Instead, the pair stepped around to circle it and keep to the sides while preventing it from escaping. That was when she noticed something she hadn't during the previous encounter: The creature couldn't move sideways because its legs jutted out on either side and not beneath its elongated body. This forced it to move forward or backward only.

The hunters distracted it enough for several daggers to noiselessly rain down from above. Each landed on their target in various spots yet did nothing to slow it. The lizard opened its mouth wide, baring the dozens of sharp teeth, and hissed. Its violet eyes narrowed to display its rage before it attempted to flee into the bushes again.

Coura stepped toward them, determined to join in the assault until the final men on the ground sprang from their spots to hurry in front of the creature. At the same time, Barnelus and his second-in-command darted over from behind her to focus on its backside. She couldn't decide what to do because of the amount of movement.

Despite the additions, the creature continued wiggling around in search of an escape route. The hunters on the ground stabbed with spears, except for Barnelus, and those above pelted it with branches, rocks, and other debris. The lizard shrieked in response to the overwhelming barrage.

I have a feeling it might become desperate if it isn't killed soon, she thought. The idea prompted her to hurry and join Barnelus, but her concern proved justified.

One of the men on the creature's left shouted to their leader, removing his eyes from their target in the process. His lack of complete attention provided enough of an opportunity for the creature to leap over the spears, lacerating its underside during the attempt, and sink its teeth into the Sie-Kie's shoulder, just as it had done to Coura. Its victim wailed in horror, dropped his spear, and attempted to shove the creature away.

While his comrades yelled and gestured wildly, as if urging him to stay still, she winced at the reminder of the venom that had burned her skin before realizing their advantage. *If it remains in one spot, this may be our best chance!*

Brushing aside the danger, both for her and the injured hunter, Coura charged with her sword poised to strike. Barnelus seemed to understand her intention and ran at her heels.

The lizard still latched onto its victim, which posed a problem, but a dagger flew from behind to land in the creature's neck, causing dark blood to splash in the air and its hold to release. Another, louder shriek resulted as it shook its head until the weapon dropped to the ground. By then, Coura had slipped into its blind spot.

She gripped the hilt of her weapon with both hands, raised the blade upward, and plunged it into the creature's thick skull. The tip pierced through flesh and bone to emerge on the other side as more liquid oozed from the blow. Its body froze then relaxed to drop into the grass after a few seconds.

Despite its twitching limbs, the hunters confirmed the kill. Coura's knees trembled as the exhilaration wore off, and she sank to the ground.

Did I overdo it? What happens to the demonic energy now?

The hunting party remained where they were, observing warily, until Barnelus gave instructions in their language to dismiss the formation. Those in the trees began climbing down while everyone on the ground, except their leader, rushed over to their injured comrade. The man had curled up to hug the shoulder and let out pained groans once somebody began cleaning the wound.

Meanwhile, Barnelus came to stand beside Coura. "Is it truly dead?" he asked without hiding his disgust for the creature.

"I don't know."

He accepted her honesty and left to retrieve his dagger before kneeling and cleaning it off.

How could I be so careless? I'll never get that power back. What will happen to it? Soirée claimed her energy finds and feeds off living beings. Is it only a matter of time until another one is born?

The questions spiraled in her mind as she watched the lizard cease twitching. Its whole body seemed to droop, giving the appearance of a shadow like those filling the space near the end of the twilight hour.

Barnelus rose, stared up at the darkening sky, then turned to his party. She prepared to join them, assuming their discussion involved what to do next because it grew late. Whether she made it to her feet or not, she wasn't certain, for an unseen force struck her in that moment, causing her to lose consciousness.

*

When Coura could open her eyes again, the clearing appeared empty. Time froze during a colorful sunset spreading throughout the woods, and no sounds acknowledged any animals beyond her line of sight. She prepared to call out but found her voice gone. The thoughts that came to her fled before developing fully, leaving her to stand alone in silence.

Then, a set of hands gripped her shoulders from behind, holding her in place.

{*Such a weak creature.*}

The voice sent shivers down her spine. It gasped for breath in an inhale and hissed as it exhaled; the raspy words created the image of a sick being who begged for death.

No matter how desperately she tried, Coura couldn't speak. She opened and closed her mouth, but nothing happened. When she tried to communicate through her mind, she only heard the sentences echo.

{*It cannot hide. Nothing comes from it except fear.*}

A glimmer below caught her attention, and she gazed down to find a puddle forming at her feet. The inky liquid clung to her boots to prevent her from escaping, increasing her urge to panic.

{*It wants too much now.*}

While she still stared at the ground, something dripped from her shoulder into the puddle with a plop. She gasped when she saw what she mistook for hands. Globs of the black slime shone in the sunlight and trailed over her chest. This time, when she opened her mouth, she was able to scream. The substance stuck her to that spot, like gluing paste, and continued to spread all over her body until only her hands and head were free.

163

{Doesn't it want this?}

Coura's mind filled with uncontrollable terror as she imagined suffocating, unable to find help. The lone sensation she felt became the beating of her heart until a surge of sharp pain shot across her left arm. It grew to be so intense she could do nothing except whimper and wiggle under the slime.

{Too loud! It is being noisy.}

As if the substance acted like a living creature, it crawled up her neck and onto her face, forcing its way into her mouth. She coughed and attempted to spit it out, throwing her head from side to side. Steadily, it choked her. Bright stars spotted her vision, then she could do nothing except cave into the darkness' embrace.

*

Coura woke and jolted upright, gulping in air. The room spun enough to make her dizzy until she could catch her breath. Her frantic heartbeat slowed, yet her body continued shaking.

Was that really a dream? It felt too real…

After some time passed with no changes, she opened and closed her hands before pushing herself to her feet, wincing at the new aches. She still wore her traveling clothes stained from the demonic creature's blood and a mixture of old and fresh sweat.

The brief survey showed not only her filth but also new markings on her arms. Previously, just her right forearm bore the unidentifiable pattern in black, purple, and blue, like an elaborate bruise. Now, each arm displayed the markings, winding and curving from wrist to shoulder in an array of intertwining designs. They were beautiful, in an odd sort of way, if not on her body. She reflected on her encounter with Soirée outside Verona's training ground and the result then.

Does this mean I absorbed the creature's energy after its death? I doubt anything else caused this, and that dream… Her entire body shuddered, forcing her to push the recent memory away.

The person who recovered her after the attack left her in the room she had stayed in upon her arrival at the village, though no one stopped to check on her as she paced anxiously. At last, Coura figured she could clean up and seek out answers regarding the hunt. A dim light peeked around the doorway's curtain, and upon exiting, she figured it was either dawn or dusk judging from the grayness of the sky.

A dozen or so Sie-Kie men and women wandered with pots or trays in hand. She waved to the nearest person before attempting to cross over to where the chosen woman waited on a slim path. The stranger's eyes widened in alarm before she dropped to her knees, startling Coura.

"Excuse me," she hesitated, unsure if the Sie-Kie villager could even understand her. "Where can I find water to wash with?"

At the question, the woman jumped to her feet and pointed farther ahead. "Beyond this path you will find a ladder leading to the bathing pools. Would you like me to fetch you new clothing?"

"Yes, thank you. Would you also bring some bandages?"

"Are you hurt?"

The woman grew tense, but Coura assured her she was unharmed before hurrying on. As she turned away, she noticed an unreadable expression pass over the Sie-Kie woman's face when the stranger studied the markings on her arms.

I need to be more careful, she realized and hugged them to her body. *If anyone connects the demonic creature's death or its energy to these, I could be in a lot of trouble.*

The bathing area consisted of several pools both dug into springs and routed from a nearby stream. They were spread over a wide area organized to coincide with the foliage, trees, and bushes as well, and Coura found she wasn't alone. Men, women, and children leisurely bathed or splashed in their own spaces, some hidden in private while others had been intended to fit many people.

She did her best to sneak around until she found a pool tucked away behind the cover of blackberry bushes. Then, she stripped off her disgusting clothes and let out a content sigh as she lowered her body into the warm water, sliding deeper until only the top of her head, eyes, and nose stuck out.

How has this spot not been chosen? It's perfect for relaxing in peace. Not to mention it comes with its own treats.

After her muscles sufficiently loosened, she scrubbed herself clean as best as she could without soap before nibbling on a handful of the berries. A rustle in the bushes had her dipping herself deeper into the water again.

"Hello?" The woman from earlier emerged while raising her eyebrows once she noticed Coura. "I bring new clothing and the bandages you requested, *shalma*. Is there anything else you require?"

"Thank you, and no," she answered while projecting her sincerity and wondering what word the woman just used.

"Our chief and witch request you to pay them a visit when you're prepared." She gave simple directions to the main square before departing.

Once alone, Coura dried herself with a towel the woman brought and donned a tan dress identical to every other woman's in the village. Using her fingers, she combed through her hair before leaving it unbound to dry and wrapped her arms with the bandages to cover the markings. Since the demonic creature would no longer stalk the Western Woods, she had no reason to stay and hoped to avoid drawing attention to herself more than she already had.

The sounds from the pools lessened as she returned to the ladder, climbed up, then began searching for the chief's hut. Many people roamed the platforms as she passed through and either gave her curious glances or acted similarly to the helpful woman from earlier by bowing their heads or muttering in their language with timid smiles. Coura said nothing to any of them along the way.

The square where she initially met the chief and witch didn't appear as populated, though neither figure was in sight. She paused to examine the huts and consider what their people viewed as a polite replacement for knocking when a middle-aged man noticed her dilemma. He cleared his throat, pointed to the second structure on the right, and winked before continuing without a word.

Since she received no other assistance, she approached the opening before stating her name. When she didn't get a response, she reluctantly drew back the sheet and was astonished to find an elaborate room compared to the one she slept in.

Instead of plain walls, these were decorated with paintings on cloth, feather-adorned masks and glass beads, and various pieces seemingly crafted by an amateur artist. Items likely found in nature, but *unnatural*, hung from the ceiling. An eagle's foot that developed an extra talon caught her eye first, then a heart-shaped pinecone with a fat top and thinner bottom. The most disturbing turned out to be the deformed skull of a rodent possessing giant front teeth and two bones at the top, giving the impression of misplaced eyebrows. On the floor, a woven rug containing red circles, yellow stars, and green leaves covered every spot from corner to corner. Despite a low window at the opposite side, the amount of stuff cluttering the space shaded it darker.

While she admired the room, she noticed its owner sitting in front of the open window. The man who hinted she enter this particular hut had sent her to the witch, and the older woman sporting the uncut, white hair studied her before speaking.

"Quite a collection, isn't it?"

Although her tone sounded unbothered by the unexpected entrance, Coura hated the thought of intruding. She didn't answer or move in farther until the Sie-Kie elder patted the ground as an invitation.

"Was it you who requested me or the chief?" she asked while accepting the offer to approach and sit cross-legged in front of the witch. A band of braided vines rested on the woman's head, and a wooden staff remained in her hands.

"I did," came the response.

For a while, they relaxed together, soaking in the heat and listening to the birds' chirping. The elder opened her eyes wider to reveal their emerald color, to Coura's surprise, and spoke again.

"I've been wondering where I should begin with questioning you, young lady of Verona. It's been months since an outsider has had contact with us for more than a day or shared more than a few words." She paused, allowing that key piece of information to settle. "Our *shimla,* or our chief in the common language, asked me to interrogate you about the creature and the energy you carry. I have my own ideas and questions as well; however, they would confuse you or raise suspicion about our intentions. So, I decided to reveal a summary of our history with you."

Coura's interest piqued at the opportunity to learn about the Sie-Kie, though a history lesson didn't sound too appealing. It must have shown on her face, for the older woman chuckled.

"Now, don't frown! I'm certain this will be more fascinating than you think. Where to start? The Sie-Kie originated as a group of naturalists who preferred simple ways over the growing age of farming, herding, and tool-working. Over three-hundred years ago, the first *shimla*, Claudius Village-Builder, met with the king of Asteom and begged for his people to be granted permission to live in these woods. I'm not knowledgeable on the history of Asteom, but the world knew peace, so the ruler saw no reason to deny his plea. The Sie-Kie were officially founded after and began building homes above the ground and forming their own language because too many curious eyes and ears, both human and non-human, put pressure on their simple life."

Her lips turned upward into a sly smile. "Here's the fascinating part. Only the *shalmas*, or witches in the common tongue, learn about magic and energy. Everything I am about to tell you has been passed down since the beginning and will be shared with the next in line when my time is at an end. Claudius and most of the Sie-Kie never possessed the potential to use magic, nor were they interested in such matters since it complicated life and reminded them of what they purposefully left behind. The funny part is, as I'm sure you are aware, magical energy is inherited from generation to generation. The *shimla* married and produced a son and a daughter, each with the potential to use magic. When their mother discovered this, for she could control basic spells and sense the power, she told the *shimla* and asked for it to remain a secret."

A thoughtful pause followed and stretched until Coura pushed for her to continue.

"This is the confusing branch of the story. At the same time that the children were growing and their mother learned of their slumbering abilities, two events came to pass. A sickness spread throughout the forest, leading to weakness and death for an infected being. Plants, animals, and villagers contracted this sickness, plaguing our people with fear and paranoia. During this occasion, a wave of creatures like the one you and the hunting party defeated a couple days ago attacked the woods. Their venom was as devastating as their claws, bringing harm to the many men who defended the village until the *shimla* ordered everyone to stay off the ground. That became the lowest point in our history."

"What happened next?" Coura asked when the woman stopped again.

"Change," the witch replied with a sincere smile. "When the *shimla's* children entered their decade years, the son trained to become a hunter, as most males do when they come of age. His daughter shadowed her mother in the ways of becoming a wife and housekeeper. When the sickness grew worse, the mother feared for the children, so she taught her daughter what spells she could. When the *shimla* found out, he grew upset until the remaining villagers cried for aid. At last, Claudius sent his second-in-command into the city to find a cure for the illness and permitted his wife and daughter to wield their magic, keeping the creatures at bay while healing what they could. In the end, the messenger returned with knowledge on how to produce medicine to treat the sick, and the creatures fled when the mother, her daughter, and the hunters drove them away. The people then burned any plant or creature carrying the plague, cleansing the area. Peace returned to the woods and to the Sie-Kie."

"Then, the chief's wife became the first witch," Coura concluded.

The elder shook her head. "Many years passed before the sickness had been completely wiped away. The *shimla* and his wife were too old and worn by then and didn't know what to do for their children. Claudius spoke to each of them, beginning with his son. The young man showed no intention of learning to wield magic because he already developed into a skilled warrior and had a wife and child of his own. Claudius decided then to pass on his title as *shimla* to his son, thus creating the line of succession. When he and his wife addressed their daughter, her views were quite the opposite.

She became headstrong after her experience fighting the creatures and healing the afflicted and refused to deny her magic since it saved the village and forest. Claudius and his wife grew distressed by this, especially since their daughter wed no husband, bore no children, and the people felt unsure about her. At first, the *shimla* intended to banish his daughter but loved her too much to turn her away. He also understood her thoughts on magic, though admitting it would merge something new into their tradition, which had been what the Sie-Kie hoped to leave behind upon their founding. Eventually, he concocted an idea. If the village could contain one magic user, one woman to possess the knowledge and skills for protecting their people in case history repeated itself, she would hold a special position among the Sie-Kie and be respected.

You see, it wasn't the *shimla's* wife who became the first *shalma* but his daughter. After being granted such an honorable title, she found a husband and produced her own children. Of the four, three possessed magical potential she could sense. This became a problem because there could only be one *shalma*. As a solution, she established a role inherited by a single daughter, just as the chief's son becomes the *shimla*. Whichever daughter is chosen is bestowed the title and customs while the others are not trained in magic."

Even though she remembered to be respectful and keep her judgements to herself, Coura couldn't stop herself from gaping at the notion. *How could anybody not desire to use their magical abilities? I would be furious if my mother rejected my training in favor of someone else's, even my own sister.*

Still, her main concern hadn't been addressed. "Your customs and history are interesting, but you didn't mention what they have to do with me?"

"Aha! You understand why I'm having trouble recounting this tale. I suppose you fit in two places, each side weighing as heavily as the other. So I ask, which do you prefer? Would you care for my questions or those of our *shimla*?"

The gravity of her expression and the offer to choose took Coura by surprise. *Hers are probably going to be personal and relate to magic, whereas the chief's might focus on the hunt and demonic creature. I would rather face whatever will benefit their people the most.*

After a moment to mentally prepare, she replied. "I will answer whatever questions are most pressing."

"I see." The woman dipped her chin and kept her face expressionless. "Our *shimla* desires to hear about the creature who attacked you and several of the hunters because it killed many animals living in these woods. You hinted at your knowledge of it, claiming you were the only one who could stop it. I'm also curious about the markings on your arms."

Coura instinctively crossed them as she contemplated what she should tell the *shalma. These people are secluded from the rest of Asteom. To share what I learned about the demons and the Yeluthians would break their rules, and I don't want to be responsible for changing their customs. Perhaps that's why she's asking me in private. What was passed down to her isn't common knowledge to the rest of the Sie-Kie. Because of her limited involvement, I think I can trust her.*

After leaning back on her hands to gaze through the window, she rubbed her neck. A headache arose when she recalled her lessons from the academy on the basics of magic, one of the first topics she had been taught upon arriving.

"I'll tell you about magic to enlighten you on the subject. There are opposite types of magical energies: dark and light…" She started with the demons and angels, a mage's light and dark spellcasting, and what the demonic creatures were before sharing some of her own past. She didn't tell the *shalma* about Soirée, only that she made contact with a demon and developed the ability to absorb its power to keep the stray energy from possessing other beings and repeating the cycle.

Once she finished, Coura felt parched. The afternoon wore on, and voices and other noises came from outside the hut.

"You give me much to think about," the witch said as she laced her fingers together and knit her brow. "You answered my questions, and I appreciate you sharing such relevant information. It seems as though this is the first time you've been asked to recount it."

Coura chuckled before agreeing. "You can thank my mentor. He never let me forget a lesson."

"He is a wise man, for I find the country's history important. I don't just mean for our village either."

The *shalma* reached over to take one of Coura's wrists. She didn't stop the woman from removing the bandages to trace the pattern with a finger.

"Once I saw these markings, I figured you had some sort of connection to the demonic creature. If this isn't proof enough, I sense the same energy inside you. I was able to ever since the hunting party brought you into the village, though it had been fainter than it is now."

Coura raised an eyebrow. "You knew this whole time? Was that why you sent me with them?"

The *shalma* nodded and re-wrapped her arm. "I did so mostly out of curiosity. You're fit and young, so I knew you could keep up with them, but I'm afraid I regret my actions."

"Why?"

"I must share my observations. These are the beginning of what is to come if you continue to pursue those creatures. I sensed the strife behind your eyes and felt your pain when you recounted your tale. Not only will they grow worse, but I predict physical changes will occur overtime as well. For the moment, you bare markings. Who's to say what else could take place? If you value your life, it is not wise to continue seeking the unnatural beings and taking in their power."

Coura found herself entranced by the words and held her breath at the warning. The woman gave her much to ponder; all of it made her afraid. *How many creatures are left? How much damage could they do to my body, or my center?*

The elder's unexpected laughter broke the tension and her concentration.

"Like I said, you answered most of my questions. The rest can wait until after the celebration."

"Celebration?"

With a groan and the support of the staff, the *shalma* rose, shooing Coura away when she tried to assist. "After a successful hunt, our people enjoy a feast and dance to pay respect to our ancestors for watching over us."

"That must be what all the noise is outside," she muttered to herself before her host went to the entrance and exited the hut without waiting. She hesitated while her mind still recovered before following.

A Sie-Kie Celebration

The main platform didn't physically transform, yet they stepped into a decorated version of the public space that made it seem new. Candles in clay bowls acted as lamps along the outer edges and paths to cast the area in a golden glow. Villagers mingled with one another, either standing or sitting on flat pillows spread all over. An eager energy projected by the grins of the Sie-Kie filled the air.

The *shalma* ushered Coura to her side and pointed at a row of cushions in front of the centermost hut. "You will be next to me, and I next to the *shimla*," she explained.

They walked over to take their seats as everyone else began doing the same. Footsteps sounded from behind, causing Coura to glance over a shoulder at the newcomers. The chief and a woman carrying a baby while holding the hand of a toddler joined them in the line. After, a pair of younger men filed to stand behind. The first was the stranger whose leg had been injured during her initial interaction with the demonic creature; the second was Barnelus.

With a nod from the *shimla*, the woman Coura presumed to be his wife and the children took their spots on the opposite side of the witch, leaving a single seat open for the chief, who remained standing, opened his arms, and began addressing those gathered.

"I shall translate for you," the *shalma* leaned closer to say at a lower volume. "'My people! It's been many days and nights since we could celebrate a successful hunt. What say you to those in my son's party?'"

The audience erupted into hoots and cheering. Barnelus straightened as he accept the praise and faced his father when the *shimla* continued.

"At this point, the party and their leader are excused to receive honor markings," the witch shared with less enthusiasm.

"Honor markings?" Coura asked as she watched Barnelus and the other eleven members be led away.

"They are prized among our people as a means of displaying accomplishments. The more patterns bestowed on a man, the more pride he brings to the village. It also makes him more appealing when he's seeking a bride."

Several questions popped in her mind, but somebody presented their food on individual serving trays, suspending her curiosity. While everyone else enjoyed the food and socialized, she tasted each item offered. Most were edible to her while some with roasted insects nearly caused her to gag. Nobody spoke to her or the witch during the meal, which she found odd.

"*Shalma,* what's your real name?" she decided to ask.

The elder offered a crooked, confused smile. "My real name? What do you mean?"

"What should I call you?"

"*Shalma.*"

Coura frowned. "You have no name aside from your title?"

"We cast away our former selves once we're chosen as the *shalma.* It's a position requiring little individuality, as is the *shimla.*"

She glanced past the older woman to where the chief, his wife, and their younger children ate while considering if Byron, Emilea, Grace, Marcus, or Aaron ever had a similar issue.

"You've been quiet throughout the feasting," the witch continued. "Tell me what you wish to know about the Sie-Kie."

With the woman's permission, Coura dove into a series of questions steering away from their history and toward their culture. She heard plenty during the discussion and made a mental note to summarize for Will whenever they could meet again.

Sie-Kie men assume the laborious roles, such as hunters, builders, and surveyors, while the women were responsible for gardening, harvesting herbs and crops, tending to the pools, watching the children, and creating or mending clothing. Depending on what promising skills a person shows as a child, they are assigned to a single job out of those offered. Activities like games, arts, crafting, music, and other pastimes were available to everybody. Life in the treetops seemed similar to the rest of Asteom except for one fact that amazed her: The honor markings a man collects throughout his life are used to woo a woman into choosing them as a husband.

"You mean, it isn't a mutual agreement?"

"No, nothing of the sort," the *shalma* confirmed as a woman removed the remains of their meal. "Everybody here is familiar with one another, as least casually, so women often have an idea of who they would like to take. It's more personal than you might think and can happen at any time."

When Coura inquired about her status, the older woman mentioned a husband in a solemn tone. Whatever she prepared to say after was interrupted by the pounding of drums in the distance. The people cheered as six men and two women paraded onto the platform playing percussive instruments of varying sizes to an enchanting, unified beat. The group positioned themselves in a section of the square as the remaining villagers moved their pillows and other belongings to the farthest edges. This opened the area up for dancing.

Compared to the intricate or intimate movements in Verona, the Sie-Kie behaved wildly. They raised and waved their arms, stomped their feet in time with the drums, and shouted chants together at certain points, lacking any sort of hesitation. She couldn't imagine participating but found herself either clapping or smacking the ground along with those still seated. Her worries about standing out or looking foolish fled once she joined in.

Three songs later and the chief's younger sons pulled the *shalma* away for a dance, leaving Coura alone. The *shimla* and his wife held each other in the mass while chatting with a different pair. She gazed around the square lazily to savor the atmosphere.

Wait until everyone in Verona hears about this. They won't believe me! After all, who else has encountered the Sie-Kie in such a way before? I wonder if their people will remain secretive as long as there are demonic creatures around. Surely the shalma *can't be expected to stop them by using magic. Perhaps I should-*

A set of hands fell on Coura's shoulders, startling her enough to jump. Hers shot up to grab the other's wrists a second later, and she prepared to dig her nails into their skin or yank them away until a smooth, relaxed voice spoke.

"How are you enjoying the celebration?"

She glanced upward to where Barnelus stood behind her, bending over to rest his hands on her shoulders and stare at the dancers. She released her grip before offering a polite response as he moved to sit beside her.

"I must express my gratitude for a couple instances," he began after a moment.

She raised an eyebrow.

"You helped chase away the creature who wounded my younger brother, then you volunteered to join the hunt for it and landed the finishing blow. You truly deserve the honor markings gifted to you."

Coura found herself taken back by his kinder demeanor and noticed the new design etched onto his right forearm with some sort of ink. The skin appeared red and swollen, yet the pattern's lines came across clearly. Barnelus caught her staring before startling her again by smiling.

"My men and I were given these before the feast."

"I saw," she commented, letting her eyes wander over the various images weaved around his upper body. That seemed to open the conversation for the Sie-Kie man, who took it upon himself to explain the most recent additions to his collection.

"What's this one for?" Coura inquired afterward and pointed to the left side of his chest where the design of an abstract knife had been carved.

"It's my first marking, what earned me my title. We're able to start receiving honor markings after the tenth year of our lives; however, the original is most important and goes above the heart. It also assigns you the name associated with yourself."

"What do you mean?"

"My full title is Barnelus Dagger-Diver. This honor marking came from my first hunt. I'm skilled with a dagger and prefer leaping among the trees to strike at prey. Few Sie-Kie are ever able to successfully do so. On that particular day, I brought down three deer and a stag, which normally takes at least four men to do so on the ground."

The use of titles makes sense, Coura thought as she remembered the *shalma's* story of the Sie-Kie village's founder and when Barnelus introduced himself.

"In the rest of Asteom, the second name is given to you by your parents," she added as the musicians transitioned into the next song. "Some prefer to have their name attached to their children while others use a common one for their lineage."

"I'd like to learn more about your people," Barnelus mumbled without looking at her, making her wonder if he meant for her to hear the comment.

An idea came to mind after she recalled the witch's history lesson. "Why don't you leave?"

His head snapped to her, and his eyes widened in alarm. "Our people don't leave these woods."

"Why must you stay? From what your *shalma* told me, there are those itching to explore the country. Besides, I can't imagine what could happen if another one of those creatures shows up, or a war took place and your people had no idea..." Coura caught herself from continuing when her mind wandered down a pessimistic road.

Barnelus' eyes narrowed as she spoke, and he studied her face. When she didn't go on, he released a sigh.

"I'm sorry," she offered, assuming her words had offended him. "It's none of my business to say what you should or shouldn't do."

"No, I'm sure you didn't mean any harm. After all, I believe you're correct."

This time, it was her turn to assess him.

"For many months, some of us, especially the hunters, voiced our concerns about remaining secluded in these woods. My father respects tradition and thus refuses to discuss the subject. Still, since those unnatural creatures are threatening our home, the number of people expressing their desire to seek outside help is increasing."

"Shouldn't your *shalma* be able to use her magic?" Coura wondered. The thought had been on her mind ever since she met the witch, yet it didn't feel appropriate to bring up with the old woman.

"I can't speak for her," Barnelus replied. Then, he tried and failed to hide a smirk. "Based on her recent behavior, I believe she's pretending to lack the strength in order to support the wish to send some of the Sie-Kie out of these woods."

"What?"

Coura hurried to locate the witch and caught the older woman watching her and Barnelus from the opposite end. Her mouth hung open when the *shalma* winked with a knowing smile. The Sie-Kie man laughed at her resulting scowl.

"It makes sense," he attempted to reassure her. "A stranger possessing the ability to defeat the immediate problem and end its power permanently would encourage anybody who opposes the idea to at least consider learning about outside help."

"There have been other creatures like what we faced in these woods, haven't there?" Coura asked when the pieces Barnelus and the *shalma* revealed merged together.

His voice lowered, as though he became afraid what they were discussing would ruin the mood. "None as sizable nor as fierce as the one the party defeated but enough to harm some of our people and raise defenses."

Even with such off-putting talk, she closed her eyes and lightened her spirits by listening to the drumming. She lost herself for a while, imagining the dancing and music in Verona and what the citizens there would think. When the song ended and clapping ensued, she rose.

"These woods will be safer with the aid of Asteom's new king and the mages in Verona. They would appreciate your culture too. I won't push anymore, but if I were you, I'd suggest sending one or two of your hunters to the capital to speak to the king's council."

Barnelus accepted the advice before wishing her a pleasant evening as she took her leave of the event.

*

The lack of windows in Coura's hut made it difficult to gauge the time when she woke the next morning, though she contemplated if the limited light helped her sleep better, for she had a sound rest and felt refreshed. She was also confident about moving on from the Western Woods after defeating the demonic creature and staying with the Sie-Kie.

After dressing in her travel clothes, which happened to be washed and mended by someone, presumably Shina, she dug out the map of Asteom from her pack. The woman entered the tent as she shouldered her bag and kept the parchment in hand.

"Come with me." Her caretaker gestured toward the exit, seemingly expecting her to be prepared to depart.

Once outside, Coura repressed a groan once she gazed at the sky and saw heavy rainclouds blocking the sun. Her escort guided her through the village and along a path in the opposite direction until they reached a dead end where a ladder hung down to the ground. Shina, like the rest of the Sie-Kie, proved adept at descending, but Coura took her time in order to avoid slipping.

"Where are we going?" she asked once her boots touched grass.

"The *shimla* requested I bring you to the main road. Travelers use it often, and you should be able to reach the woods' end by nightfall."

Above them, leaves rustled from a strong breeze higher up, signaling the approach of rain. Coura's stomach growled at the same time, and she wished she had requested breakfast before heading out. They jogged until their bodies broke through a line of bushes onto a wide, dirt path. Waiting for them were the chief, witch, Barnelus, and his second-in-command, Craulder.

"Good morning," the *shimla* greeted her with a bow. He then dismissed Shina, and his son stepped forward to hand over a satchel. "Here is a gift. This should last as you travel to the town south of here."

"Thank you. That's very kind," Coura replied as she slung the additional bag over her head.

"It's not merely through generosity that we wish you a safe journey. Without your assistance, according to both my son and our *shalma*, the creature haunting our village would be causing more harm."

Her insides tightened when she recalled her discussion with Barnelus; the feeling led her to offer a warning at the risk of upsetting the man. "I wish it were that simple. What we faced is the beginning of something worse taking place all across Asteom. Although my goal is to stop them, I cannot honestly say another won't find its way into your woods."

The *shimla's* straight face darkened. "Your concern isn't necessary. We are more than capable of defending our home and protecting our people, though we will never forget how you fought alongside the hunting party. We give you lesser items than you deserve. If you should ever return, we'll repay you in full."

"Make it up to me by ensuring the safety of the Sie-Kie. Send men to Verona to speak with the master mages there. They'll know what to do to help without interfering in your traditions. That's all I ask."

Coura used a gentler tone in order to convey the request as a plea. From the chief's narrowed eyes and tight lips, she understood she overstepped her boundary. Still, she couldn't regret encouraging him to seek outside help.

The *shimla* said no more. With a brief nod to Barnelus, he turned to his right and walked away down the road. She stared after him before noticing the three remaining in front of her.

"Is there anything else?"

The *shalma* used her staff to point to Coura's right. "This direction leads south. I don't know what you'll find there, but remember my words. If you choose this path, be smart about that power."

It became obvious how Barnelus and Craulder were curious about the ominous warning by their expressions alone, yet the pair didn't comment on the subject. Coura shared her gratitude before moving along. Soon, she heard footsteps approaching from behind.

"Are you my second escort for the day?" she joked with a glance over her shoulder, assuming Barnelus would be the likeliest of the three to follow.

Indeed, the chief's son caught up to walk beside her, eyeing the trees above in a casual manner. "Craulder and I are supposed to make sure you find the end safely; however, I think one of us is enough."

Together, they continued in silence except for the wildlife surrounding them. Coura's peaceful mindset wandered back to her days at the palace and how long she'd been away. She prepared to mention it, yet Barnelus spoke before she could.

"Should my father wish to send me to speak with your king, what can I offer to prove our intentions are true?"

The question was unexpected given the *shimla's* displeased behavior, but she considered what Aaron and his council's response would be to meeting the Sie-Kie. *I have no doubt they'll be welcoming, though I worry for these people, especially with the drama surrounding the murders. It could be dangerous to involve them at all. Still, I gave Barnelus and his father the opportunity to request assistance from the capital.*

After her reflection, an idea came to mind. "If you meet the king or master mages, tell them Coura Galdwin sends you with friendly tidings."

I don't want anybody coming after me, but by hearing what took place in the Western Woods because of the demonic creature, they should be able to understand why I left.

Barnelus shot her a doubtful glance. Then, he chuckled when he realized she was being serious. "I don't distrust you. I'm just wondering how much influence you hold over such powerful leaders, and how that came to happen. Whether it's my business or not, I will comply, Coura..." He paused, weighed something in his mind, and smirked.

"What is it?" she pressed at his uncharacteristic behavior.

"I believe you deserve a title."

"You're joking."

"Why not? You possess the markings and skill worthy of a Sie-Kie hunter."

She laughed in disbelief yet waited to hear what he chose. Around them, the environment shaded even further.

Barnelus rubbed his chin for a moment as he considered some options. "My younger brother, Tigute, suggested a few for himself during his recovery. Even though he already earned his, I believe he hoped to be recognized again for surviving against the creature. As you know, that's not how honor works."

"Well, let's hear them anyway."

"Let me think. Fire-Bearer and Fire-Herder, which I rather liked. Night-Cleaver was another, or Shadow-Destroyer."

"Night-Cleaver," she mused. Something about the name felt appropriate.

"You like that one?"

She nodded, so the pair repeated the name sinisterly in jest.

Throughout the afternoon, she nibbled on the gifted fruits and nuts, lightening the satchel. More pieces of the sky became visible when the trees distanced themselves from one another to signal the outer edge of the Western Woods. The stagnant air smelled like rain.

"I can find my way now," Coura admitted and halted.

Barnelus tightened his lips. "Your trip south should be uneventful. The town is a day's worth of walking away, though I doubt the weather will hold off until then."

"I'm afraid you're right." She glanced at the sky and avoided wincing at the thought of sleeping outside, but it became far too late for her to begin pitying herself.

He gave her a reassuring smile and bowed, just as his father had done. "Thank you, Coura Night-Cleaver. Don't be a stranger in these woods. I wish you a safe and rewarding journey, wherever you go."

Without waiting for a response, the Sie-Kie man hurried back down the road and disappeared into the trees. She waved until she lost sight of him before facing the open plains beyond. After inhaling and releasing the deep breath, she mentally prepared for the lonely journey ahead then unrolled the map to study her position. The Western Woods expanded over most of the coast, which curved east to where she now found herself.

"All I can do is take this road south I suppose," she mumbled while tracing the line with a finger.

A raindrop plopped onto the center of the map, and a growl of thunder startled her enough to look up. In answer, fat droplets fell from the sky. Coura scrambled to roll up the map and return it to her bag before she jogged ahead just as the storm started.

Medina

Twelve days after Byron sent his letter to Dala, he received a response from General Tio. The brief time to wait was jarring, but he felt fortunate to have the man as an ally. After reading it through by himself, he brought the message to the council's meeting the next morning. They were conveniently overdue for a regular business session, so once the usual matters had been discussed, he cleared his throat and retrieved the paper.

"General Tio's correspondence arrived yesterday from the Dalan base. He mentions some important items I suggest we give our attention to."

"Who? Oh right, the exuberant character unable to keep up with life in the capital," Tont joked harshly.

"Nonetheless, I updated him on what's been taking place in the palace," Byron continued. A laugh escaped Dillon from his right.

"Really? Dala and all the other cities are informed about the current affairs. Besides, news tends to spread like the wind around this country. Why directly involve him at all?"

Byron held his patience. "We spent time together when I was stationed there, that's why."

"So?" Tont countered. "What does your friendship have to do with us?"

Although it became obvious the rest of the table grew eager to dismiss their meeting, Aaron caught Byron's eye and nodded. "Please, go on. What does the general know?"

He read the letter word for word to emphasize the developing problem he deemed crucial enough to bring up. Ever since their previous meeting about a week and a half ago, messages from cities and towns across Asteom arrived requesting aid against a rise in the number of demonic creatures. Many claimed the lives of innocent farmers and travelers already, and more injured people every day. General Tio echoed Byron's concern.

"This is becoming a pressing issue that cannot be ignored," he concluded after.

The table fell silent in thought until the high priest grumbled.

Casner raised an eyebrow. "What did you say, Hendal?"

"I fear I agree with Master Bryon about this. Creatures are appearing around the country, and there's no telling what threat they may pose if we don't eliminate them now."

"What do you suggest we do about it?" Tont asked while scratching his head.

"I don't know," the high priest admitted before staring upward to contemplate the question. "To my knowledge, the only person who encountered and defeated any has been Byron's pupil, Coura. They attacked Lady Emilea's children, correct?"

The master light mage laced her fingers together and straightened. "You're right. I can't recall anybody else who fought a demonic creature in recent memory."

"She lost her magic," Byron cut in, hoping to avoid involving his former student.

"That doesn't mean her experience won't be invaluable when assessing an approach," Dillon added.

"Emilea and I can instruct you on what to do as well. We've dealt with demonic creatures over the years."

Casner picked up the conversation when his fellow general didn't. "I assume you used magic. What about ordinary soldiers?"

Tont slammed his fist on the table. "Each location in Asteom has access to our troops, including at least one mage. King Hernan began the reassignments and stationed new guards for such a purpose. I don't see what else we can do besides send teams to dispose of them."

"Calm yourself," Dillon ordered, showing his own impatience. "I second your recommendation. There's no telling where these creatures are coming from or how they're multiplying. On top of that, if we send troops south, we leave ourselves open to an attack from Nim-Vala."

Tont rolled his eyes. "The northern country hasn't moved in months."

"Ever since their people began lining the border, our spies have kept an eye on them. Who's to say they're waiting for the chance to strike when we're at our weakest?"

The discussion dropped into mumbles, then the room fell silent. Hendal addressed Aaron after.

"Your Highness, do you deem these creatures enough of a problem to organize the troops?"

Aaron closed his eyes in the resulting pause until he felt prepared to reply. "I trust Byron's judgement. Some sort of action must be done now to prevent additional citizens from being harmed or killed; however, I don't believe we're desperate enough to risk the people we have here. General Tont is correct; our troops are placed around the country to protect their nearest civilians. Because of this, I'm in favor of sending a specialized team trained to eliminate the demonic creatures. Byron, Emilea, would you be willing to choose the participants for this group? We can agree mages, especially healers, are going to be necessary, along with the selected soldiers."

"Of course," both master mages answered in unison.

"I'm personally against it, but I also believe Coura should go along too, or at least assist with the training. She's experienced enough to do either."

While Byron attempted to make up an excuse in order to avoid including her, he caught Emilea glance at him, and the two shared a look.

"What is it?" the king pressed when neither of them responded.

Byron swore to himself for being so careless. "Coura's not in Verona."

"What? Where'd she go?"

"She left for Dala a couple days ago," he lied, making a mental note to inform the base's general of it. "She had personal business to take care of and planned to stay for a while."

Aaron's expression softened. "I see."

They ended the meeting there. Byron rose and stretched as the generals, Emilea, Hendal, and Aaron began exiting the chamber. From his right, Casner tapped on his arm.

"One moment, Master Byron."

"Yes?"

The general waited until they stood alone before elaborating, lowering the volume of his voice in the process. "I would like to speak to you about our search for the murderers, if you have the time."

"Did you discover a lead?" Byron asked. Although the topic hadn't been forgotten by the council members, no new evidence meant there wasn't a reason for them to pester those involved with the investigation.

Casner shook his head. "No, nothing really. I actually need to mention a piece of information to you and request you pass it along to Master Emilea."

"Why not speak with her too?"

"I don't want to raise more suspicion than necessary. I've been working with General Dillon, and I'm concerned about his behavior relating to the case."

Byron noticed his muscles grow tense. "What do you mean?"

"Dillon is a kind-hearted man, yet he's letting his morals get the better of him. We've been interviewing the guards who rotate shifts at night around the palace for days and going over the autopsy records. Yesterday, he mentioned we should close the case, and before you ask, he didn't say why. I demanded a reason multiple times. The man only claims we're diving into a mystery containing too many risks and not enough answers."

"He's afraid to move forward? I suppose I don't entirely blame him. After all, General Preston was murdered as well. No one is safe here."

"That's not it," Casner responded, showing a repressed frustration. "He spoke as if he knows hidden details about the murders! He wore a haunted expression when we met and kept trying to convince me how he would propose closing the case once King Aaron is doing well enough. Of course, I disagree with him."

Byron observed the man for a while, unsure of what to think. *Could Dillon really be pushing the case away for the betterment of the palace? I doubt that's why, and none of the generals are the type to get spooked. Then again, I don't know Casner well either. Could he be trying to get me on his side of this mess?*

"Why tell me this in private?" he asked next. "Why not bring it up during the session? Surely there would be valuable opinions in a council discussion."

"It's for your safety, and Lady Emilea's. We generals know each other, but you two, the high priest, and His Highness probably don't see when people are not behaving as they should around here." The general's final words came in a whisper as he laid a hand on Byron's shoulder before exiting.

Byron made another mental note to find Emilea that evening to hear her thoughts on the matter.

***

It seemed far too late for Hendal to be awake, yet he stood shivering in the outdoor balcony on the fourth floor.

"Where is the general?" he muttered to himself and pulled his cloak tighter. Even in the middle of summer, the top floor in the windowless halls carried winds brisk enough to keep people inside.

He tapped a foot as he gazed into the wide-open training ground below. The warm afternoon turned into a beautiful night, though he wished he were lying in bed and not having to dirty his hands.

"It's about time," he snapped in a harsh whisper when a shadow crept out from the door nearby.

"I'm sorry I'm late." Dillon approached, clutching his own cloak around his toned body.

"Why did you need to meet here and at such an hour? Have you found a lead?"

The general stared down the corridor, listening despite the lack of noise or guards. Hendal figured the latter was due to the man's reorganization of the soldiers normally patrolling at that time in order to give them some privacy. Despite the coolness of the area, he grew uncomfortably hot while waiting. Finally, Dillon leaned forward and gestured for him to do the same.

"I'm going to dismiss the case tomorrow when I speak with King Aaron."

"What?" Hendal's eyes went wide. "Why would you do such a thing? Have you lost your dignity as an officer?"

"Watch your mouth, High Priest."

"F-Forgive me. I just don't understand. What could motivate you to abandon a job this important? It would be disgraceful to the former king and queen!"

"I decided to inform you first since you're closest to the new king. Please, speak with him about it tomorrow so he can accept the change. I wrote letters for the other council members as well to explain my concerns and will send them in the morning."

Hendal's patience strained as he glared at the general. "Tell me why you are deciding this without consulting the council or your partner, General Casner."

"There's more going on than we initially realized. The multiplying demonic creatures, having both a demon and angels not associating with Yeluthia in Asteom, and finding no clues as to who murdered the king, queen, and General Preston are all suspicious. I fear if we continue digging into this specifically, we'll discover what we shouldn't too soon."

"What does that mean?"

"Don't you get it?" Dillon barked before spinning around to trudge away. "It's all connected! Somebody in the palace is manipulating us into falling in step with their plan."

"W-Wait!" Hendal extended an arm in a feeble attempt to stop the man once he reached the door at the opposite end.

"If we quit now, we can focus on other matters and build our defenses," the general continued and rested a hand on the knob. "I can feel a wrongness in the palace. I beg you, tell His Highn-"

From the glassless window behind the man leapt a figure dressed in clothes so dark Hendal barely had a moment to process the person was there. A glint flashed in their hand from the dagger they carried, and in the next instant, they wrapped their arms around Dillon to cover his mouth before stabbing the man straight through the heart in a single motion.

Hendal's hands flew to his mouth as he turned away. Although he didn't see any blood, the image made him queasy. When he faced forward again, the general lied face first on the ground while the figure approached while wiping the dagger clean on their shirt. Then, they tugged the black collar hiding most of their face down, letting a white braid slip out in the process.

"Why did you do that?" Hendal growled and struggled to control his volume.

"He figured us out," the newcomer, one of the angels named Urvin, replied and leaned against the wall. "Besides, the plan had been to kill him anyway."

"You were to strike on *my* order. I cannot trust your kind to do anything right!"

Hendal sensed a headache rising and spun around to hurry away without giving the fresh corpse his attention; however, a gasp escaped him when he stood face to face with the demon, Soirée. His cheeks flushed at the sight of her presence so near, then at the sound of her giggling.

"What a clever human," she chimed before stepping out of the way to mirror Urvin's position against the wall. The dim lighting accentuated every curve from her contrasting pale skin and fur-like covering hiding most of her body.

By that point, Hendal felt on edge from being so close to the murder scene. He took a few breaths, brushed down his robe underneath the cloak, then held his chin high as he walked over to the door on that end.

"Urvin, tell the others to prepare to head south toward Dala."

"Why are we going there again? I thought we were done with-"

"They've been comfortable for far too long," Hendal interrupted before resuming his calmer composure. He nearly lost it again when Soirée strolled beside him and spoke.

"You know, there's a saying among your kind: Those who stress too much during their younger lives won't make it to their later years."

"Shut up," he responded, which amused her more.

I just need to tolerate these nuisances.

He paused to give the angel, who crouched on one of the windowsills, a sidelong glance. "Before I forget, inform Jaspire of this incident and have him visit the general's room to remove those letters tonight. He can dispose of them as he wishes."

With that, Hendal resumed his façade and left the outdoor hallway for the comfort of his own quarters while thunder rolled in the distance.

***

The rain lasted throughout night and into the following afternoon, putting Coura in a sour mood as she approached the guard station outside the next town called Medina. The open plains beyond the Western Woods steadily became another forest area, though not as thick as the Sie-Kie's home. Trees old enough to create wide trunks and branches provided shelter from the rain under their canopies and blocked the wind that picked up overnight. In the morning, she finished her rations and moved into the downpour once again.

She pounded on the station's door, hoping for a dry space to rest, if only for a moment. "Is anybody in here?" she called and knocked even louder.

No one answered.

Coura peered around each side, studying the two-part structure. Guard stations served as a location for travelers to ask for information or aid if necessary, which meant they had to be stocked with supplies. The soldiers assigned to them were also charged with stopping suspicious activity, so they often kept shields and various, simple weapons available. The back section held the provisions while the front contained paperwork and materials to occupy the guards during their shift.

With a groan, she glanced down the dirt road leading into what appeared to be a decently sized town. Twenty buildings clustered together to show off some of the shops lining the main path, and fields sprouting green crops surrounded Medina.

I suppose nobody's on duty, she thought when she stood around for a few minutes. The rain thinned into a sprinkle, but she still shivered.

An eerie silence followed the lack of rain, and nothing else. Her eyes drifted over the crops, and without the rain to hinder her sight, she noticed several spots on the ground displaying inconsistent patches of torn up earth.

This doesn't seem right. It's the middle of the afternoon, yet no farmers are tending the fields or livestock. No people are wandering on the road either, or even walking in town from what I can see.

After deciding to wait for any sign of activity, a sensation of dread gripped Coura.

"Open up!" she cried while banging on the door before trying the knob.

She found it unlocked.

Inside, the only light came from what entered through the doorway. Scattered documents rested on a table, along with a mug and plate of untouched food. She ignored the first section and hurried into the back room. Three swords, a mace, two clubs, and a bow with a quiver of arrows hung on the walls. During her initial fight against the lizard-like demonic creature, her original weapon had not been returned to her, if the hunting party recovered it at all; she assumed they kept the second one she used the kill their target since it belonged to their people. She selected the best sword to strap at her waist and swung the bow and quiver over a shoulder. The additional, long-distance weapon gave her more confidence as she ventured into town after.

No civilians or animals occupied the road while Coura crept forward and ducked behind the nearest brick building. The rain lessened into a drizzle, signaling the end of the storm, but there had been enough over the past couple days to create a muddy mess of the dirt path. Without the downpour, a rotting scent became noticeable in the air, one that would have made her sick if she ate recently.

What happened here?

She drew her new sword and winced when it hissed out of its sheath before continuing ahead. After passing a trio of similar buildings, she reached the center of Medina. A horrified gasp escaped her then as she studied the scarlet blood staining the ground and nearby walls. Coura lowered her blade and used her other, trembling hand to cover her mouth.

At least a dozen bodies, most with missing limbs, lied on the road; the rest of the area contained unidentifiable remains. Meanwhile, doors were thrown open, battered down in fragments, or missing altogether. Glass littered the ground from shattered windows and crunched under her boots while she forced herself to search the buildings for survivors, or answers.

She found neither and couldn't do much for a while after stumbling upon a dismantled family. A space in their home, presumably a child's bedroom, remained untouched, so she let her control slip as she knelt beside the bed to weep and scream into the pillows until her throat felt raw.

I can't... I can't stay here anymore... With choked sobs, she spent time breathing until her mind could process the situation.

Coura departed from the home and avoided taking her eyes off the path until something on one of the bodies caught her attention. She went over while attempting to ignore the shredded torso and froze when she recognized the slick, slimy substance coating the wound.

This is the same venom from the demonic creatures. Based on the claw markings, it's a huge beast, and I bet it holds Soirée's energy.

A shudder ran through her body when she considered the danger of possessing a demon's power, causing her limbs to shake no matter how much she willed them not to. *What if when I met Soirée in Neston and lost consciousness... This could have been... No, Byron never mentioned an outcome like this. I need to calm down and go warn the next town.*

Getting away from Medina became her first priority before figuring out what direction to head in. The reminder of camping so close to the massacre unnerved her, yet a sudden realization steadied her mind.

I've been able to sense Soirée's energy in the demonic creatures before they appeared. There's nothing around now, so I should be safe for the time being.

As expected, she had no appetite and fell asleep easily despite what took place.

More rain threatened the following day as gray clouds hovered low. Coura woke stiff and hungry, grimacing as she stretched and sat up to contemplate her next move. Although she anticipated restocking her food in town, both the idea of stealing from the victims and her concern for the other inhabited areas encouraged her to leave as soon as possible.

She retrieved the map from her bag and stared at the southern half of Asteom. The closest towns were all days away, which became a bit of a relief, yet she didn't know if they possessed soldiers or mages capable of fending off an attack. A handful of villages lined the coast without marked paths, requiring her to wander without a clear direction. The second option involved taking the road east where it connected to more populated cities and eventually reached Clearwater or Fester through the Valley Beyond. Reluctantly, Coura's finger slid over the line and stopped above Dala.

I didn't realize how far west the base is. Going there would risk involving the soldiers and mages, not to mention the citizens. Still, I'm worried the demonic creatures are targeting busier places containing the easiest prey.

For a while, she pondered the idea of cutting through the country. It annoyed her to acknowledge how inconvenient avoiding Dala altogether would be. When her hunger pangs drove her to stand, she chose to decide after eating and warning the nearest town called Marinich.

*

If she could have seen Medina before the destruction, Coura imagined it would be similar to Marinich. She grew far too exhausted to spend time analyzing the space, but at a glance, it contained thirty or forty buildings with cattle and sheep farms instead of crops. It was well into the night, yet the area appeared lit by dozens of lamps and torches surrounding the perimeter, hanging from doorposts, and brightening the homes from inside.

She approached the guard station posted along the road and released a sigh of relief as she knocked. *Somebody alerted them already.*

"Who's there?" a man on the opposite side asked.

"My name is Paulina. I'm traveling from Medina," Coura answered in an authentically weary manner.

The door clicked as its locks unfastened before it swung open to reveal a middle-aged, rough-looking guard. He wore leather padding

193

and a metal helmet to hide most of his face, and she noted the sword strapped to his waist.

"Medina you say," he repeated in an astonished tone while ushering her in. "I assumed there weren't any more folks staying out east."

"There aren't."

Coura dropped into one of three seats at the table. She'd grown hungry and tired, though beneath those, she had been frightened throughout the day alone on the road.

Fortunately, the guard didn't seem to mind her lack of manners. He removed the helmet to shake out rustled, black hair and set it aside. "Would you like something to eat? I can arrange for a bed too."

"I'll accept both." She rubbed her eyes before adding, "Thank you."

The guard disappeared into the back room and returned a minute later with two sacks that he placed in front of her. They held dried meats, berries, and oats.

"Help yourself," he said and leaned against the wall where he watched her.

Coura ate until her stomach relaxed, not feeling quite up to gorging herself. "When did it happen?" she asked once she felt satisfied.

The man scratched his head as his expression became grim. "About three days ago. A woman carrying her youngsters reached us first. She acted hysterical, rambling about a monster as tall as a house. Before we knew what to do, another person showed up spouting the same story. Well, we'd always had issues with the beasts every so often. That's when we lit up the town, seeing as they only come out at night. Anyway, more people from Medina arrived. None today, except for you. We figured the rest…" He cleared his throat and pushed himself off the wall instead of completing the sentence. "I can see you nodding off, so why don't we head into town and find you a place to rest."

Without the ache in her stomach to keep her awake, Coura began drifting to sleep and smiled sheepishly as she followed the guard outside. They walked through the town to a barn behind one house where a haven had been established. A pair of lamps hung at the front and rear ends, providing enough light for comfort, and twenty or so stalls had been built along the sides for the owner's animals. As the man handed her a blanket from the pile on top of a haystack, snores and soft breathing sounded just over the snorts and gentle stamping surrounding the room.

"The inn doesn't have enough space for more than a few people," he shared. "We settled on this in the meantime since it's warm and safe. Don't worry about tomorrow; just find a spot for tonight."

With that, the guard left her alone. Coura didn't care where she went, so she sprawled out in an empty space farther away from the other people and threw the blanket over herself.

Unraveling Ties

The news of General Dillon's death spread far sooner than Byron would have preferred. Verona buzzed with rumors about the murderers who managed to kill the former king, queen, and now two generals.

He and Emilea were called to the scene immediately after the guards found the general's body in the outer hallway while patrolling early that morning. It rested in a pool of his own blood from a stab through the heart. While they examined the evidence and surrounding area, others questioned every soldier stationed around the palace during the previous night. The lone piece of noteworthy information from those posted on the fourth floor had been an odd, brief reassignment from Dillon. When their schedules were lined up, the master mages learned of a half-hour window where the hallway hadn't been monitored. Casner inspected the victim's room for any signs as to why this could be but found it in a normal condition.

After thoroughly examining the corpse, the master mages joined the emergency council meeting. It became obvious when they entered the chamber that the incident rekindled the flame in their king.

"Anything to report?" Aaron demanded as soon as the door closed behind them.

Byron waited to respond until he and Emilea seated themselves across from the remaining generals. The high priest had yet to show up. "No magical energy was present at the scene of the murder."

Tont growled a curse while his hands clenched into fists. "How could he be so careless? Wandering around alone in the middle of the night! If only we could find some sort of clue as to who would commit such a crime again."

"Peace," Casner replied in a melancholy manner. "I believe nothing could have been done to prevent this, even if we had known he planned to be there."

"What do you mean?" Aaron pressed.

The general glanced at Byron before straightening. "Your Highness, I'll admit he seemed off before his death. Master Byron is aware since we spoke about it yesterday. Dillon wished to close the investigation into the previous murders against the council's orders."

"What? Why?"

"He only mentioned some sort of danger waited beneath the surface, and that our involvement would lead us deeper into it."

"I don't understand," Tont began with a scowl. A knock at the door interrupted whatever else he planned to say, silencing the room.

Hendal entered then, appearing pale against the lamps' light. He seemed to cower with each step and refused to meet anyone's eyes.

Aaron frowned at the high priest. "You're late."

"Forgive me," Hendal apologized in a soft voice and bowed before sitting next to Emilea.

The light mage placed a hand on his shoulder. "Are you ill? You look like you haven't slept."

The high priest realized their attention was directed at him then. His eyes flickered around the table, and he hunched over before letting his head drop into his hands. "I wish I had stayed! General Dillon... What a good-natured man!"

"What are you talking about?" Emilea asked while everybody else leaned forward at the emotional outburst.

"Forgive me! Forgive me," Hendal repeated as he removed a handkerchief from his pocket to wipe away the beads of sweat collecting on his forehead. Once he settled down, he pulled out a crumpled sheet of paper from his pocket.

"I received a letter from the general requesting I meet him in the outdoor hallway at midnight. I doubted his mindset, but I went anyway. The space had been empty, so I waited until the chill brought me inside, and I decided to return to my quarters. I thought nothing of it! I told

myself I would find the general in the morning to speak with him..."
The high priest's next words faded into silence.

After, Emilea voiced the question on their minds with wide eyes. "What does this mean?"

"Are we sure this note was written by Dillon?" Byron countered.

To his dismay, the remaining generals confirmed its authenticity by comparing the handwriting to older documents.

"I don't understand," Hendal mumbled once the room quieted again.

The council seemed at a loss. Aaron folded his hands together on his lap and stared at the table. Tont did the same, except while wearing a more frustrated expression, and Casner leaned back in his chair to gaze up at the ceiling. Meanwhile, Byron caught Emilea turning to him.

Could the murderers not have wanted us to give up on the investigation? Is that why they targeted Dillon? On the other side of the problem, why did the general schedule a meeting with Hendal so late? Why would he arrange for the guards to leave the area unsupervised? I have too many questions, ones I would rather not voice here.

The light mage nodded, supposedly sensing the direction of his thoughts. Because they knew of a traitor in the palace, he wasn't willing to ignore his suspicion of the other council members, or the various threats posed outside Verona.

"If I may," Byron began as he pieced together the outline of a plan. "It would be best for all of us to take precautions."

Aaron raised an eyebrow. "What do you suggest?"

"We simply cannot accept another murder. It's obvious they're targeting members of this council. It could be for power, revenge, treachery, or any number of motives, but there are a few assumptions we can make. The most prominent is that I doubt they're working alone."

"You don't mean..."

"I do." Byron met each set of eyes around the table. "I have a feeling the rogue angels and demon we encountered in Dala found their way here."

While the generals mumbled their agreement, he hesitated to mention Coura's interaction with the demon. Emilea had no such hinderance.

"That's right," she added. "The demon told Coura their master is in Verona."

"*That's* where you heard it?" Tont yelled in disbelief. "Have we forgotten what kind of untrustworthy creatures demons are? Besides, your student is nowhere around here. Who's to say she isn't involved either?"

Byron caught Aaron open his mouth to protest before closing it and narrowing his eyes at the general.

"I've already been down that trail," Byron found himself admitting as the argument with his former pupil echoed in his mind. "Coura's abilities may have been caused by the being, but she remained in control for years. Besides, she no longer has any contact with it, thus removing her from the situation."

Emilea cast him a sympathetic look. Meanwhile, their king agreed before picking up the discussion.

"That leaves us with two options from what I can tell, assuming the search for the murderers will continue. I understand if anybody prefers to leave the palace, and possibly Verona, for the time being. Some of you have families. I don't want them getting caught in our mess."

Aaron paused to wait for any opposition and went on when no one objected.

"I order everybody who remains to have at least two guards accompanying them, and none of you are allowed out of your rooms after sundown. If the murderers, and possibly their cohorts, are in the palace, they may be lured out from hiding; however, I won't risk anyone's life to do so. By staying in Verona and the palace, you are allowing yourself to become a potential target. Is that clear?"

Each member confirmed their dedication to their position.

Aaron turned to Casner next. "General, I would like you to continue heading the investigation."

"It would be an honor to fulfill my duties," the man responded while placing a fist over his heart.

"The rest of you can resume your responsibilities until we discover new information."

Although Byron marveled at the young man's growth as a leader, he couldn't help but notice the new king lick his lips in a nervous manner.

"Is there more?" he urged.

Aaron cleared his throat. "It's about time we find Coura and have her return. Reports are coming in every day with descriptions of demonic creatures. I'm afraid if we don't assemble a group to eliminate them soon it could be disastrous for the secluded towns."

Out of everybody seated at the table, Hendal showed the most enthusiasm toward the idea.

"I agree, Your Highness. The increase in their numbers is threatening the country, and who else to send but Master Byron. If anyone can locate Coura and return her to the palace, it would be her mentor. You're also quite acquainted with General Tio already, correct?"

Byron knit his in response. *I don't actually know where Coura is, though. Should I tell them the truth about her disappearance? This excuse to leave the palace might provide the opportunity to learn what's happening from the outside rather than by being kept in the middle. Who knows what help the Dalan base could offer as well.*

With something of a strategy forming, he agreed to the proposal.

*

Byron made his arrangements over the next, few days and planned to leave during the following week. He made no rush to go, especially after General Dillon's funeral. The mood in the capital grew solemn while those in the palace remained anxious. It wasn't until a trio of unexpected guests requested an audience with the king that people forgot about the looming threat for a bit.

He and another dark mage named Lydia met in the queen's garden to rearrange his schedule. When he had been in Dala, she assumed his position and the work involved, which she appeared eager to do again. Still, whenever he found himself delegating to a subordinate, he couldn't help but recall the moments where he hoped to one day do the same with Coura.

200

She had so much potential to be my successor, he reflected before shoving the thought aside and focusing on the woman sitting beside him.

Just as they concluded their business and started chatting about unrelated matters, a guard approached Byron to inform him the council had been summoned for an emergency meeting. Naturally, he excused himself and worried about the reason until he moved inside.

The halls surrounding the meeting chamber appeared packed with soldiers, mages, and servants, as well as several noblemen and ladies hovering close by. Their voices hushed as they gossiped and parted for him, and he slipped in with many eyes attempting to peer past the doorway.

What in the world has everyone so riled up? he wondered as he moved to his seat. Then, he noticed three, male strangers on the opposite end of the table, and his mouth parted in shock.

Each figure stood tall, holding their heads high, wearing no shirt, just loose pants, and displaying an envious amount of honed muscle. On their exposed skin, patterns had been painted using black ink that flowed together into individual images. The stranger in the middle had a headpiece adorned with feathers, leaves, and beads fanning outward. Byron also couldn't help himself from taking note of the daggers sheathed at their waists.

Who are these people?

He looked to the other council members and found them just as surprised by the sight. Aaron cleared his throat a moment later and stood.

"Thank you for your patience," the king began. "Normally, we would be more punctual, but I'm afraid you've drawn attention because of your entrance through the city. I invite you to repeat your original message for everybody present."

He gestured to the table and sat again, opening the floor to the exotic strangers. The decorated man in the middle stepped forward to address the council without a hint of nervousness.

"Greetings. I am Barnelus Dagger-Diver, firstborn son of the *shimla,* or chief in your tongue. We have been sent as representatives of the Sie-Kie to seek a reestablishment of our village's place in Asteom."

By that point, Byron's mouth hung open while he tried to remember what he could about their people. *They're from the Western Woods, but I can't recall the details, other than their love for the forest and secrecy.*

"Sie-Kie?" Tont muttered while rubbing his chin and offering a perplexed expression. "I don't believe I've ever heard of you before."

"I'm not surprised. Centuries ago, our ancestors abandoned the advancing world for the safety and simplicity of the Western Woods. There, we've kept our traditions and avoided conflict, including involvement with magic, at least for the most part. We do possess a *shalma*, or witch in your tongue."

The general appeared satisfied enough with the answer. In fact, underneath the amazement and curiosity, Byron noticed his companions relaxing.

This should be beneficial to everyone if it's a basic pledge in exchange for goods or services. Although, I wonder what drew them from their home? Could they be struggling with a new threat? Is it possible they heard about the royal family's shifting rulership and arrived because of that?

Emilea evidently considered the same question. "I'm sure we are all relieved to hear from your people after so long, yet I must ask what prompted you to seek an audience with King Aaron and our council."

Ever so slightly, the corners of the man's mouth twitched. "A visitor from Verona aided my hunters and I in defeating a creature plaguing our home and causing injuries and death."

As the Sie-Kie leader named Barnelus described the experience, it became apparent they were attacked by a demonic creature. The image of their village and the towns around the country fending off such beasts without his and Emilea's level of power frightened Byron.

"So, what is it you're seeking from us?" Casner asked after the explanation, apparently unaware of the danger afflicting the man's home.

"Magic," Barnelus replied immediately. "The creature in our woods hasn't returned since its defeat, but we have seen others possessing the potential to be just as harmful. This swayed my people to request outside help. In return for wielders living in or surrounding the Sie-Kie, we offer you our warriors."

At his nod, each of the three unsheathed a dagger from their belts, knelt, and offered the weapons to the throne. The swift, unexpected motion startled those at the table, causing them to jump to their feet in order to prevent the guests from striking Aaron. Their king didn't flinch. Instead, he raised an eyebrow at the proposal before turning his glance to the council. They eased into their chairs as he addressed them.

"I see no reason to deny a request from fellow citizens of Asteom. What are your opinions?"

The initial concern presented was the experience and level of mages necessary to kill a demonic creature. Barnelus eased some of the stress by detailing how their hunting party cornered it without too much trouble.

"Your wielders will not work alone but together with us and our *shalma* to protect the woods," he said as encouragement.

Once the council members had been convinced, they discussed the skills, strengths, and numbers of the Sie-Kie warriors to be exchanged. Barnelus went so far as to offer himself, his personal group, and a dozen more.

"That's all we can spare at the moment. Whatever our worth is in mages, we will accept, even if it equals only one," he concluded.

Do their people value magic users that much? Byron wondered before waiting to hear Aaron's decision.

The king's eyes reflected his compassion. "I understand how great of a threat this is upon your home and your people and would never leave them undefended by your standards. We accept your bargain; however, there is no way for us to equally predict the worth of one life for another. I suggest we discuss the necessary numbers needed in the Western Woods and go from there."

The Sie-Kie leader bowed low, visibly flabbergasted by Aaron's generosity, and Byron smiled at the sight.

Well done! Although their hunters aren't necessarily needed here, it would've been rude to turn away their offer and could have offended their people since we don't actually know their abilities. He also reestablished their place in Asteom by offering aid as an expectation for an ally, not one group above another.

They discussed the mages and let Byron and Emilea provide the final say in who would be assigned to fill the position. After, Casner wrote the proposal in a formal document offering the services of the Sie-Kie. When every detail seemed wrapped up, including stations and housing, Aaron welcomed the three formally as citizens before releasing them to return the news to the Western Woods.

Barnelus led the other two toward the door yet hesitated to exit.

"Is there anything else?" the king inquired when the trio spoke to each other in their own language.

The conversation ended as Barnelus turned around. "I don't believe it's necessary now, but the person who fought the demonic creature with us offered a message to support our cause. Her name is Coura Galdwin, and she sent us with friendly tidings."

Byron's face fell.

"Coura?" Emilea exclaimed, expressing the bafflement reflected around the table.

The man tilted his head, as if confused by their reaction. "She expressed interest in us requesting aid from the mages in the palace and claimed using her message would act as a means of earning your council's trust."

Hendal glanced at the thrown with a frown. "I don't understand."

"Thank you for relaying her words," Aaron added before nodding to the men as a clear dismissal.

The three bowed once more before passing into the still-crowded hallway beyond where they would be escorted through the palace and Verona. Even after the door closed, the room stayed unnervingly quiet, and Byron fumed beneath his mask of calm.

How did she end up so far west? There's no way around my original statement that she's staying in Dala, or that she has no connection to the demonic creatures. I feel as though her agenda isn't simply to stop them, which is more concerning. What are you up to, Coura?

Despite the success of reestablishing a relationship with the Sie-Kie moments ago, his heart plummeted at the idea of his former student fighting on her own. He released a sigh while rubbing the back of his neck, catching the others' attention.

"It seems she's taken a detour on her way to Dala," Byron admitted after realizing how foolish it would be to dance around the subject.

"Are we even sure that's where she's heading?" Casner grumbled.

"In any case, I'll still go to the southern base first to search for her."

"If I may voice my concern, I don't believe we should waste our most skilled dark mage by sending you off on a wild-goose chase," Hendal interjected without hiding his disgust with the situation. "Who's to say she would be worth the effort in the end?"

"I thought you were in favor of sending Byron to Dala," Tont added while sliding his eyes from Byron to the high priest.

"It seemed reasonable before when we knew where she *would* be. I also wonder what drew her to an area containing a demonic creature."

Whatever fears prompted him to speak poorly of Coura didn't sit well with Byron.

"She's not somebody who's ever been straight about her decisions," he responded firmly enough to shake the high priest. "Despite what you might assume, she helped the Sie-Kie and encouraged them to visit us. Without her being there at the right time, the demonic creature could still be roaming around the Western Woods or have done worse to the hunting party. A few days passed since then too. She hasn't returned to Verona, which means she's most likely moving southeast, bringing her to Dala."

Hendal opened his mouth and closed it twice while wearing a bitter expression. Byron met the look with a hardened stare, refusing to believe the high priest's argument.

I'm curious, though. Why should Hendal have any reason to distrust her?

In the next moment, the man realized the scene he caused and shifted his expression into one of distress. "Forgive me, Master Byron. The lack of a proper night's sleep and many hours of paranoia push me to express caution at every turn. Coura's knowledge and expertise are still useful to prevent further chaos associated with the creatures. I shudder to imagine facing such monsters without the proper defenses in place."

"I understand," Byron replied. He prepared to snuff out the doubt remaining at the table until Hendal interrupted him.

"Your Highness, don't let a fool like me keep us here to fiddle over what's already been settled."

Tont rose and bowed to Aaron. "I agree. If we've nothing else to discuss, I will begin the preparations for the recruits from the Sie-Kie. I'm sure every person in the capital is intrigued by our new friends."

Nobody objected to closing their meeting after. The generals walked out together before Aaron, his guards, and Hendal, who refused to look in Byron's direction. Emilea seemed to be the only one to notice his sour attitude when they were alone in the chamber.

"What's wrong?" she asked. "Is it about Coura?"

Byron shook his head. "It's the high priest's outburst. How could he encourage me to leave then completely change his mind after suspecting her once we learned her whereabouts? His behavior is strange."

The light mage gave him a quizzical look before shaking her head. "With what he went through regarding General Dillon, I can believe he's extra cautious around anything and anyone involved with the demonic creatures. Also, none of us know Coura as well as you do. Wouldn't you be suspicious of a soldier weathered by a troubled past abandoning their position without providing a clear direction?"

"I suppose," he muttered.

She patted his back and smiled. "Don't be so grouchy. While you're away, I'll be sure to keep an eye on the council. Grace's goddess gift will allow me to share what I can with you."

They moved into the corridor together just as it cleared. Emilea continued to speak comforting words, yet by the end of the day, Byron wished he felt more confident in his faith in both the high priest and Coura.

Companions on the Road

As the days crawled by, no other survivors found their way to Marinich from Medina. Those who did began accepting their losses and embracing the town that would likely become their new home. Fortunately, plenty of farmers in need of assistants were willing to offer work in exchange for food and shelter. They continued lighting lamps, torches, and bonfires as the sun set, even though no reported sightings of demonic creatures came from around the perimeter.

Coura remained there because she wasn't certain what road to follow since they all either led north or through Dala. Secretly, she wished for another tug from Soirée's energy to confirm a direction, but nothing happened. When she became the only self-proclaimed citizen from Medina without a position in Marinich, she decided she should go before they assigned her one.

Nobody noticed when she hid underneath her hood, shouldered her pack, and strode across the town in the morning light.

*

In southern Asteom, farmland or fields for livestock replaced forests and plains. Throughout the afternoon, the blistering sun beat down, causing Coura to sweat beneath the cloak until she threw it off, wrapped it up, and stuffed the bundle into her bag.

"Why is it so hot?" she mumbled while seeking some sort of shade; however, the flat land before her stretched without reprieve.

She dug out a piece of fruit tucked underneath her clothes and salivated at the idea of enjoying a refreshingly sweet treat. The people in Marinich provided plenty of the fruit and dried rations for those staying in the barn, even when she became the last. She took advantage of their charity by filling her bag and stopping by their well to do the same with her waterskin.

I wonder what their reaction would have been if I mentioned I'm a soldier from Verona, she thought while raising a hand above her eyes to glance farther down the road. In the distance, a horse-drawn cart rolled in her direction.

After finishing the snack, Coura proceeded to lick her fingers clean, savoring the satisfied mentality. A breeze carrying the scent of dust blew by as the sun began to sink. She continued moving and kept her eyes forward as the cart approached.

"Ho there!"

With a huff, the worn, dirty mare halted and proceeded to dig a dull hoof into the dirt. On top of the rickety, wooden structure sat an old man hunching so his unkempt, gray hair and beard covered his face. His clothes were nothing but rags tattered by age, and he wore no shoes.

"Ho there," he repeated and waved in a casual manner while parting his hair so one eye could study her. "I've traveled on this road many days before, yet I haven't seen a young woman like yourself wandering alone. Where are you off to in such troubling times?"

Coura tilted her head. "Troubling times?"

The man laughed, which sounded more akin to coughing, and pet his mare on the rump. "I assume you're not from the area if you haven't noticed the creatures hiding in the trees, haunting the fields with their silence. Once you spot a shadow, you miss walls and a roof over your head!"

He chuckled again and leaned back.

Despite his genuinely carefree behavior, she grew suspicious of his reasoning the more he talked. "You better hurry to Marinich then. It'll be dark in about an hour."

She readjusted her bag before taking a step to go on. With more agility than she expected, the disheveled stranger swooped down and reached for her arm.

"Wait! There's no safe town within three days from here. How about you hop in so I can bring you to where there's light and a place to stay?"

"No thanks." She avoided his touch while casting an annoyed glare his way, then she lingered next to the cart.

What is this about? she thought and warily studied the man.

His emerald eye darted to the wooden structure.

A trap?

She felt more than saw a second figure moving in the corner of her eye and ducked as something neared her head. Once she was clear of the object, she leapt away while placing a hand on the hilt of her sword.

A woman possessing wavy, raven-colored hair and eyes matching the older man's knelt in the cart. She clenched a log in both hands, revealing her intent to knock Coura unconscious. The pair gawked at her then at one another in shock.

I bet they don't encounter experienced fighters on these mugging sprees.

The woman climbed out to point a dagger at Coura next. Her companion nervously called for her to stop, yet she ignored his warning and charged with a cry.

Two factors became obvious by that point. First, how the stranger held the weapon, as well as the decision to attack without assessing her target, showed her lack of training. Second, and worse at the moment, the two were poor. The woman's yellow dress seemed nice for a lady at one time but now barely clung to her bony body. Dirt and scratches covered every inch of exposed skin on both.

Coura felt conflicted at the idea of hurting people who weren't able to defend themselves. Still, the strangers had challenged her. She dodged the wide side-to-side swipes until she noticed the other's eyes glance at the money pouch she kept at her waist. It became difficult to dismiss her instincts and not knock the dagger away.

What should I do?

She decided sacrificing a portion of her coins would be best, which didn't seem like a major loss because she had the foresight to keep the majority in her pack at the start of her journey. When her attacker swung again, she retreated to put space between them, untied the pouch, and tossed it over at the stranger's feet.

The woman flashed a greedy expression, though she didn't lower her weapon.

With their prize in reach, Coura removed the hand from her sword and began walking east, as if the encounter never happened.

A minute passed after she left the two before they called for her to wait, and she glanced over a shoulder to spot the woman, dagger in one hand and pouch in the other, hurrying over while the man limped behind. When they stood together in front of Coura, the former extended her hand to offer the money back, frowning as she did so.

"Why did you do that?" the stranger asked in a gentler voice than Coura expected. "You're skilled enough to overtake us. Instead, you allow a couple thieves to steal from you?"

"You look like you could use a decent meal and new clothes. I suggest you hurry to Marinich and use that money wisely. There's enough for you both."

Their blank stares reflected their utter shock at such generosity, but they said no more. Coura turned her back to them and continued on, wearing a proud smile at her kind deed until she heard footsteps coming closer.

Are they actually thinking to try another attack?

She braced herself and spun around only to find the woman remaining at a comfortable distance.

"Please, we wish to join your company."

The words startled Coura. "Join my company?"

Despite her reaction, the woman nodded before flashing a smile. "My name is Marcy, and that's Aimes. We're not welcome in most of the places around here because of what we've been doing. When somebody recognizes us, we need to leave before the guards find out. I know it's too dangerous to be in the open like this, especially when we can't even protect ourselves."

The more the woman spoke, the greater her humiliation became until as much as Coura hoped to deny their request, she simply couldn't. She shifted under the pitiful gaze while the older man scratched the thin horse nearby.

I'm supposed to be alone on this trip. How will I ever explain demonic energy, or my markings? I shouldn't accept them. This is far too complicated...

Ultimately, the memories of the people in Medina who were too helpless to fend off the creature tipped Coura in their favor. "I'll escort you to the next town and no farther."

"That's wonderful! What's your name?"

"Paulina," she managed to grumble.

Marcy spun around to jog back to her partner she called Aimes, who also appeared relieved. As they gathered their belongings, Coura contemplated the chance of another trap. She thought better of it when the pair brought only the mare, freed from its burden and behaving tolerably well with its owners in better spirits.

*

The trio made camp shortly after setting out. A trip to the abandoned cart provided enough scraps of wood to build a couple fires on each side of where they slept. Night arrived, decorating the sky with twinkling stars shining around a crescent moon. Coura shared her provisions with the strangers, who accepted them graciously before settling down.

"I'll keep watch tonight," she announced and set her sword on her lap.

I'll sense if demonic power is nearby, which is better than relying on their eyes or ears.

It did worry her how much trust they placed in her, though, for they slept soundly through the whole evening while Coura passed in and out of sleep.

With three people to feed instead of one, they finished what was left in her pack for breakfast before heading out. The sun seemed as relentless that day as it had been the previous afternoon, yet Marcy and Aimes remained cheerful, removing what remaining suspicion Coura had.

By mid-morning, she was grateful the pair accompanied her instead of acting alone, not just for their positive attitudes. They caught glimpses of torn up earth and the remains of deer, rabbits, or other, unidentifiable creatures on several occasions. Like the victims she saw in Medina, their limbs had been scattered and covered with a slick substance. Aimes suggested they use the meat, but she warned him against it, bringing up the demonic creatures for the first time.

"So, those are what's been causing so much trouble," the older man commented while scratching his head before shaking it. "Such a shame to waste life."

"Those beasts aren't capable of empathy," she agreed before urging them onward.

Sometime later, the trio took a break and polished off the rest of the waterskin, giving most to the aged mare named Iris. Coura scouted the area for any sort of living creature while drawing the previously unused bow and knocking an arrow.

It's been years since I practiced archery. I'm thankful Clearshot isn't here to poke fun at my attempts.

Marcy moved to stand at her side. "I don't see anything," the woman whispered after a minute.

Coura nodded and replaced the arrow in its quiver. "Me neither. If we don't find food soon, we'll be forced to rest with empty stomachs."

"Nonsense," Aimes added from where he sat on the ground to rub his bare feet. "Marcy and I have been digging up roots and mushrooms along this road for weeks. We were just over here, though. I'm not sure what could be left."

She raised an eyebrow but didn't respond.

"I suppose we should get going," he continued and rose with Iris's reins in hand.

Before Coura could swing the bow over her shoulder, Marcy said her name and extended a hand for the weapon.

"Allow me to carry it and the quiver. I did archery before. I'm sure after some practice I'll be able to hunt for us."

The offer, as innocent as it sounded, reminded Coura of their original intentions. She gripped the limb tighter and made it a point to pull the bow away from Marcy.

"Did you forget you were prepared to hurt me for money not too long ago? Why would I offer my would-be robber a means to kill me? I'll take care of the weapons myself." Even as she spoke, she knew her words were more insulting than true.

Marcy's eyes went wide and brimmed with tears within seconds. She apologized, clasped her fingers together, and walked down the road alone.

I'm so stupid, Coura berated herself and bit her tongue in frustration. *Why did I say that when I know they mean well?*

Aimes joined her when she followed Marcy, leading Iris on his other side. Instead of acting offended by the accusation, he seemed embarrassed. They slowed their pace to keep a distance behind the woman, who paid them no attention.

"I suppose we owe you an explanation for yesterday," he began before clearing his throat. "You see, neither of us have anybody except each other. I lived in Clearwater once, working as a sailor docking ships and all that. Well, you might've noticed this beauty..." He brushed away the gray hair hiding the right side of his face.

Coura had noticed faint scarring throughout the day and during their initial encounter but couldn't discern how awful it truly was until that moment. The entire area surrounding that eye looked mangled, as if someone hacked away the skin and it didn't heal properly.

"What happened?" she asked when he covered it again.

"It's my own fault. The men and I were drinking, and I decided to challenge a soldier, a young, handsome lad new to the docks. Turns out he was pretty handy with a knife. My men jumped in, his scrambled to protect him, and next thing you know, the place is in an uproar. I woke up in a ditch with my face disfigured."

In the resulting pause, Coura sensed him repressing more pain than he showed. "I'm sorry."

"Me too." He scratched Iris's neck, much to her pleasure. "I lost my job, nobody would hire a man who harasses the guards, and I didn't possess much to my name. I decided to try my luck in the northern cities, but fortune wasn't in my favor there either, so I begged on the streets until Marcy came along. She told me she planned to travel west and we'd stick together if I could keep up."

"What's her story?"

Aimes groaned before hushing his voice. "She never shared, but I put the pieces together. When she found me, she wore that same dress, though much cleaner, carried a bag, and dragged Iris along. Her arms were bruised and eyes swollen and red. I don't care to pry. All I know for certain is, even as broke and hungry as we are, she's been livelier with each passing day."

"You've been robbing and scavenging ever since?"

"What success we had has been on the road. With Marcy's charm, many a man let down their defenses. Even so, this is not the kind of life either of us should be living."

Coura studied the woman up ahead, reflecting on their histories until the group stopped for the night.

*

Iris was the only one content with her dinner that evening when they settled near a field containing patches of fresh grass. Marcy and Aimes showed Coura how to locate and harvest various roots and edible mushrooms, a task she felt certain Will would enjoy demonstrating. In the end, the trio gathered a mere handful of items. She refused her share by encouraging the two to eat what they could and rest while she volunteered to keep watch.

"Aren't you hungry or tired?" Marcy asked when she and Aimes positioned themselves side by side.

"Not really," Coura admitted, which surprised her. "Besides, we're open for a blind attack without a fire."

"Perhaps it would be better to stay on the road tonight," Aimes suggested.

"If anything plans to attack us, moving our location a bit won't help."

After a short pause, Marcy shuffled around. "You're talking about those demonic creatures, aren't you."

When Coura didn't respond, the woman's slim figure rose into a sitting position.

"You heard about Aimes and me, so now it's your turn," Marcy went on. "Who are you? Where did you come from, and where are you going?"

"I've known you for barely a day and you attacked me. What right do you have to demand answers?"

"It's common courtesy. Perhaps you didn't grow up with it."

"And you did? Tell me, who gave you those bruises Aimes mentioned when you met? Why did you decide to run away from home?"

Coura didn't expect a reply to the purposefully cold questions, so the resulting silence amused her enough to chuckle.

"There's no reason for us to share details about ourselves after just meeting. All you need to know about me is that I'm heading east on my own business. I can use my sword and skills to protect you; be grateful I didn't kill you when you pointed your dagger at me."

Again, she bit her tongue when no one spoke afterward. Her hands balled into fists and shook with frustration at her habit of pushing people away. For a while, she considered her behavior and worried that something was wrong with her as she gazed up at the sky.

Marcy's voice interrupted her thoughts.

"I lived in Dala before leaving my husband three months ago. My parents created a wealthy fishing company in Clearwater and often traded with my husband's family. Since I'm their third daughter, they married me off when I turned fourteen in order to bring the families together. My husband was twenty at the time. He assigned me the job of keeping numbers like he did, which I could never understand. I'm not talented or skilled at doing much. Whenever I messed up, he... I messed up a lot over those fifteen years.

The day I quit, something snapped in my head. He became upset over whatever had happened in the city and went to meet with a partner about it. I took what I could, including his favorite mare, and left. When I saw Aimes, he reminded me of home, even before he shared where he traveled from. I guess that just about answers every question you had about me, right?"

Coura sat dumbfounded. Her face flushed from indirectly forcing the information, and her mouth attempted to form words she didn't feel were appropriate for the situation. Never had she cared to think about the problems of an ordinary civilian's life or wanted to be involved.

How many days did I fly over Dala when I was stationed there? Not once did I bother to begin a conversation with anybody outside the base. Do Tio or Calin go into the city to help their people? I became so caught up in my own struggles and the bigger issues that I didn't notice those I could have stopped or prevented. What about when I get my magic back? What should I do then?

A growing stir of emotions welled inside Coura, riling her enough to ward off the weariness. As soon as the sky shaded gray, she hopped to her feet and scanned the area until a dead, lanky tree caught her attention. There, she practiced archery before Marcy and Aimes found her when the sun rose. Most of the arrows missed their mark, forcing her to search for them, but eventually the familiar motions returned.

*

"We should reach Umbrich by this evening," Aimes said between his panting from the afternoon heat and pointed east.

"Have you seen many people on this road?" Coura inquired while glancing farther up and back behind them. They passed a couple moving in the opposite direction during the morning and no one else.

Marcy shook her head from where she strolled a few steps ahead and looked over a shoulder. "Hardly anybody uses it lately. We heard rumors about the creatures you mentioned but didn't understand what a threat they posed."

"She's right," Aimes added. "We caught word here and there yet don't stay in one place long enough to learn more."

Their ignorance didn't reassure or please Coura, though she didn't scold them. After last night, the pair acted soft spoken, sweeping a dreariness across her heart.

Maybe I stand out. Do people usually share details about their life when they meet under these circumstances? There's no reason to tell them about my experiences involving demons, magic, or Verona; however, I need to warn them about the wandering creatures, especially after what happened in Medina.

"What will you do once we reach Umbrich?" she asked to change the subject.

Marcy and Aimes stopped to stare at her.

"What do you mean?" the former replied. "Isn't that where you're headed?"

"I won't be staying there."

"Where will you go next?"

Coura pursed her lips since she still remained indecisive about going toward Dala. To her dismay, Aimes caught on to her lack of a destination.

216

"We'll decide when you do," he concluded, and the pair moved on.

Later in the afternoon, she tried again.

"You can't just follow me around Asteom."

"Why not?" Marcy chimed. "You're not doing anything important, are you?"

Why is it I'm the only one acting like an adult?

"You don't know my business. What makes you assume it's not important?"

"Why else would you slow your pace to escort an old man?" Aimes countered, winked at Coura, then laughed when she frowned.

"Come on you two."

"We go wherever serves us best," Marcy replied while twirling around and beaming. In the growing dusk, her skin and hair shone with a golden glow. "At the moment, that's in your company."

Coura pinched the bridge of her nose before shifting topics as the sunset disappeared over the horizon, darkening the world around them. "Are you sure we're almost there?"

"We decreased our speed when we abandoned the cart," Aimes answered and paused to stretch his back. "I'm certain we will reach it by noon tomorrow."

"It's about that time then," Marcy added.

She joined him, and the pair scanned the nearby fields for a suitable location to settle in. Meanwhile, Coura removed the map from her bag. Because of their timing, she could barely read the parchment.

If only I could create a flame right now to see this-

An invisible punch struck her chest mid-thought. She doubled over, dropping the map in the process, and gasped for breath from the sudden pressure. The strike felt immensely lighter than the first couple times yet still brought her close to fainting.

Not now!

Marcy hurried over to put a hand on Coura's shoulder. Aimes did the same a few seconds later.

"What's wrong, Paulina?"

"We need to get away." She pushed herself to her feet against a wave of dizziness and drew her sword. "One of the creatures is here."

But where? Coura searched around the road in an anxious manner. *Based on the previous encounter, which took an entire hunting party from the Sie-Kie to corner, it won't be easy to defeat. Would it really kill me? In any case, what matters now is getting these two to safety. I have to do what I can to keep the creature's attention on me. First, I need to calm down...*

Marcy interrupted her mental rundown with a serious tone that caught her off guard.

"Give me your bow."

When the pressure eased without the source appearing, Coura removed the weapon and quiver, set them on the ground, and positioned herself in a defensive stance with her back to the pair. Iris stamped uncomfortably while neighing and sidestepped to her left before tearing away from Aimes' hold to bolt into the field on their right. The older man called to the animal as Marcy gasped.

That's where you are! Coura gripped her sword tighter and faced the opposite direction the mare escaped in.

A nasty sound, like a deep horn, thundered nearby in response, silencing the peaceful atmosphere.

"What is that?" Marcy whispered without hiding her terror.

Neither companion answered. Instead, they all peered ahead as a shadow emerged from the horizon and approached, intent on reaching them. Once it came closer, Coura made out the beady, violet eyes and stag-like figure, which appeared identical to the first creature she had seen outside the training ground. It possessed excessive antlers and stood at least two heads taller than a normal version of the animal.

Despite twilight shrouding the land, there remained enough light for Coura to feel comfortable fighting. "I'll keep it busy while you get away."

"What?" Marcy squeaked.

"Stay on the road until you reach Umbrich, then tell their guards to produce enough lamps, torches, and fires to ward off this beast."

"We're not going to leave you," Aimes protested, though his bravery faltered given his shaky voice.

Coura smiled at their determination against her pounding heart and burning lungs. "You asked why my business is so important. *This* is what it is, to eliminate the demonic creatures before they can destroy and kill. I defeated others fiercer than this one before, but I'm not going to risk getting either of you caught up in it."

She thought they might linger until the stag-like being reared and landed with a powerful stamp. Then, Marcy and Aimes slowly retreated without a word.

Once they moved far enough for Coura to feel comfortable, she charged, releasing a cry that caused the creature's ears to perk up. She raised her sword and prepared to stab at the exposed chest, but it lowered its head to defend with its sharp antlers. In response, she adjusted her weapon in order to block them before leaping to the side. As she hoped, the beast turned its attention, and body, toward her and away from Marcy and Aimes' location.

She repeated the same strike-and-dodge maneuver to similar results after. The creature used its antlers to shield its torso; however, it connected with a weaker spot on her sword as she jumped away. The tips scratched against the blade, producing a sickening screech while etching marks into the metal and leaving globs of the slimy venom on its surface.

What a piece of junk, she brooded. *If this continues, I won't have much of a weapon left. I shouldn't have given Marcy the bow and quiver.*

This time, the demonic being went on the offensive. It galloped, raised its head, and swung the antlers at her before passing by, circling, and repeating the process. Fortunately for Coura, it wasn't as nimble as the lizard-like one from the Western Woods. She had ample time to slide or roll out of its path but couldn't strike when it came within range.

Is it planning on wearing me out? How can I attack if those antlers keep getting in the way? If they touch me, the venom will leave me useless.

The creature charged again, dipping its head in preparation for a swing, just as she expected based on its previous attempts. This time, she grounded herself, dug her toes into the dirt, and braced for the impact. When the antlers neared, she poised her sword to block them.

Its strength failed a split second after connecting with the blade. She grunted while pushing the head to the right, exposing its neck, then Coura brought her weapon up. The metal edge fell in a slash that split open flesh. Blood sprayed from the wound as the beast trumpeted in pain before dropping onto the ground. After a few seconds, the body went still and its eyes closed.

A sense of unexpected relief washed over her before she stepped near the enormous creature. The previous encounter in the Western Woods flashed in her mind, prompting her to place the tip of her sword above the creature's head in preparation for a killing plunge.

Suddenly, the violet eyes flew open. She stumbled when the head jolted upward to strike the antlers against her sword. With a stomach-turning snap, the top of the blade fractured, and the venomous tips scratched against the skin on her right arm as the antlers grazed her body.

Coura lost her balance and dropped onto her backside, then she stared at the remains of her sword in horror. Meanwhile, the creature rose, a frightening sight from where she sat underneath its gaze.

My weapon isn't completely broken; the end is sharp enough to use for stabbing. I just need to get close enough to-

A burning sensation flared along her right arm to interrupt the scheming and remind her of the substance on her limb.

Not this again!

Without an antidote, a proper weapon, or any chance for a retreat, she began to panic.

The being stalked toward her, and its eyes hovered on the blade. She prepared to scramble to her feet when its head snapped to look somewhere else. Night had crept upon the open area, so she wasn't certain what distracted it until a whirling noise sounded above.

An arrow? Did Marcy snatch the bow and quiver?

Twice more, a whiz cut through the air. The stag-like beast tilted its head at the sky, then it began moving back toward the road.

"Stop!" Coura shouted to the woman while climbing to her feet despite the dizziness accompanying her pain. "It's too dark to shoot!"

Either Marcy couldn't hear the warning or she ignored the protests. This elevated Coura's nerves until she observed the creature as it ambled on in the direction of the source.

The arrows are distracting it? I don't know if that's what Marcy intended to do, but it seems more intrigued than threatened by the missed shots.

She counted the whirls as she followed behind with her left hand gripping the sword's hilt. Soon, when they were close enough that she could distinguish the two figures ahead, the noises ceased.

Is the quiver empty? Perhaps they understand what threat we stand against.

In answer to Coura's thoughts, one of the silhouettes shifted before she heard another arrow fly. This time, it hit its mark.

The creature reared to kick at the air with a startled cry, providing an opening she felt more than willing to take advantage of. Just as its front hooves touched the ground, she sprinted to its left side and poised the remainder of her blade for its skull. The stag-like beast became too preoccupied by the sting of a new enemy to notice until the damaged metal grew too close to dodge. It attempted to sidestep, but Coura plunged the blade into its eye before the antlers could swipe at her. She leapt away to avoid them after, removing her sword in the process. Then, she rushed forward a second time. The bellows morphed into shrieks spurred by the wound.

Without vision on that side, she managed to stab the head twice more and avoid brushing against the venom. Her hands slipped off the sword's hilt during the final strike, embedding the weapon through the side of its head; however, that seemed to be enough. The creature's cries faded into moans as it dropped to the ground, pawing at the air for a few seconds before relaxing.

She took no chances. Despite the pain spreading to her chest, she hurried over, threw herself to her knees, and removed the sword to deal three additional blows.

"Paulina, are you all right?" Marcy's voice shook when she shouted from the road.

Coura ignored the question while the inevitable exhaustion set in to leave her panting. There, she waited, uncertain of the being's fate until her companions' footsteps neared. By then, she could no longer feel the right side of her body

"Is it dead?" Aimes asked. For the first time, his normally upbeat behavior seemed as dejected as his appearance suggested.

She didn't answer. A grip tightened around her throat when she recalled the past encounters with the demonic creatures, sparking an internal debate about whether or not she had gone too far.

I don't feel any different. Is the energy lingering, or did it fade away? What am I supposed to do if that happens?

"Let's move away from here," Marcy suggested and laid a hand on her shoulder.

Arguing would raise suspicion about her reasoning, so she allowed the woman to help her to her feet. Unfortunately, as soon as she stood, her body went limp and fell into Marcy, who hadn't been expecting the movement.

"Paulina! What's wrong?"

Coura tried to open her mouth and act on her own but couldn't. The pair lowered her onto the grass when it became obvious her muscles weren't responding.

"She must have gotten the beast's venom on her," Aimes added while the two knelt over her.

While they questioned their situation and commented to one another, their voices faded away as Coura embraced the darkness that swept over her.

Return to Dala

Outside the palace's entrance, Byron, Marcus, and Clearshot waited for their final companion to join them.

"Honestly, we were supposed to be departing before the sun rose," Byron muttered, more to himself than anybody else.

"Calm down," Clearshot replied from behind and held a hand above his eyes to shield them from the light. "We're in no hurry."

That morning, they met with Emilea to say their goodbyes. More importantly, Byron hoped to put precautions in place while he was gone. She promised to look after Aaron and Grace and use the Yeluthian as a means of communicating between Verona and Dala. The ambassador had been eager to assist in their plan yet grew discouraged when she couldn't locate Coura after days of searching.

It's unfortunate for our cause. We need some confirmation of where she's heading.

"I'm here!" Will jogged over from the gate bearing two, bulging packs presumably stuffed with his research equipment. The herbalist slowed to a stop as he approached before leaning on his knees to catch his breath. "Sorry I'm late."

"It's not like we're not used to it," Marcus commented with a grin from where he stood at the front of the group.

Byron readjusted his bag and gestured to the road. "If we're ready, let's be on our way."

When the king issued orders for the master mages to gather a team to find Coura and study the areas afflicted by the demonic creatures, Byron assembled another meeting between those previously present in his quarters. After discussing recent events, they reached the same conclusions.

Emilea's tutoring is benefiting Grace, and both are too valuable to put at risk when dealing with demonic energy. Will and Clearshot were more than happy to join me, but Marcus needed convincing. Because of Dillon's death, the assistant general is hesitant to leave Aaron's side.

"I hear the Sie-Kie are adjusting well to their new surroundings," Marcus began and glanced at Bryon.

"It's much better than we expected," he responded while shifting his thoughts to the present.

"A strange people they are," Clearshot commented from the rear. "Only a week has passed since they returned with the other dozen and already they're famous in Verona."

As their group strolled through the city, they noticed a handful of children running around nearby wearing headbands similar to the Sie-Kie leader's. Pieces of cloth or paper had been cut to mimic feathers, and painted or glued bits of glass added color.

Clearshot laughed at their behavior. "What did I tell you?"

They moved through the main road and went south to exit the capital. Marcus slowed to walk beside Will, and the young men began reminiscing about their memories of Dala. Meanwhile, Clearshot snuck up next to Byron.

"Do you think we'll encounter any demonic creatures?"

Byron nodded. He had yet to inform anybody aside from the council of General Tio's most recent letter.

It seems the same beast that showed up inside their training ground and others are slaughtering animals and humans left and right. An entire town to the south of the Western Woods has been devastated. If they're anything compared to what the Sie-Kie hunters described, I doubt we'll have an easy time finding a way to restrain them.

Clearshot handed over a piece of paper in a discrete manner, drawing his attention.

"What's this?"

"Emilea gave it to me before we parted. I believe it's intended for you."

Byron unfolded the parchment and skimmed the message. His eyebrows raised in the process. *This is a request from Aaron for us to travel to Fester instead of Dala. Why would he insist on changing our destination the day we are to leave?*

"She found it crumpled up on the floor of the high priest's room when she visited yesterday to discuss Grace's progress."

"He knows about the training sessions?" Byron frowned when Clearshot nodded.

"Hendal stopped by the ambassador's quarters and interrupted them one morning, so the secret got out. He's in favor of the instruction but requested they be cautious. Anyway, after finding this letter, Emilea's more suspicious than ever. I know you've been too. If you want to switch directions, we'd better do it soon."

Byron contemplated the contents of the letter before stuffing it into his pocket. "We'll continue to Dala. I trust General Tio's information, and they could use our assistance."

His friend didn't pursue the subject. Instead, they outlined their upcoming journey and expectations in the base, especially concerning the general.

On the third day, they passed through Sindaly, making excellent time by that point. The weather proved ideal for traveling on foot, and the roads were populated by travelers, merchants, and families. Still, Byron couldn't help but notice more people moving north rather than south.

That evening, the group camped under the stars alongside others resting for the night. As they sat in silence to enjoy the life around them while they ate supper, Will let out a displeased sigh. Byron decided to be nosy and see what bothered his companion.

"What is it?" he asked, causing the herbalist to glance up with a startled expression.

"I didn't mean to… Nothing's wrong. I just thought about Coura again."

"I see." Byron set down his empty bowl and gazed up at the stars. As he expected, all Will needed was a nudge before the young man shared his troubles.

"Ever since I began traveling with you, I can't imagine how somebody could wander around Asteom alone."

"Isn't that what you did before you met Byron and Coura?" Marcus interjected. His laidback tone reflected his amusement.

"I was a fool. Who knows what could have happened if they never found me."

Byron smiled, recounting the experience of discovering Will sleeping soundly in a meadow surrounded by flowers. "People should be able to travel without the fear of unnatural beings. I suppose that's what we're aiming to accomplish."

*

The majority of their trip remained uneventful, though everyone stayed on guard when the sun disappeared. Byron volunteered to keep watch most nights since he could become lost in his thoughts and concerns to repel sleep. With a fire to provide light and warmth, he didn't feel threatened.

We should reach Umbridge tomorrow, he realized during his shift and counted the days on his fingers. *I sure hope Coura's in Dala. Her involvement puts her in no position to interact with the creatures. Not to mention, we have our hands full from the murders in the palace. I don't want to be gone for more than a month at the longest.*

Somebody shuffled behind him, and he turned to where Clearshot crawled over while yawning.

"It's the middle of the night," Byron said in a hushed voice as his friend sat cross-legged next to him in the grass.

The soldier waved the words away. "There are a few hours left until the sun rises. You should get some rest. I'm awake anyway."

"I'd just toss around."

"Maybe if you stop worrying about her so much, you'd be able to sleep."

"I have more to worry about than Coura."

Clearshot sent him a disapproving stare. "I can rummage through Will's bags to see if he has a sleeping potion."

"I don't think medicine will help."

"Then what will?"

Byron opened his mouth before ultimately closing it, unable to answer.

"That's what I figured. You know, I face a similar issue with my wife and children. I ask them what would solve their dilemma when they're worked up, and they can't answer either. They just long to forget their problems and feel better."

Byron found himself giving Clearshot a crooked smile. "Are you suggesting I find a wife and have children to become as wise of a father as you?"

"You're joking! I have no idea how to fix their problems. Why do you think I volunteer to leave Verona so often?"

His friend slapped him on the back as the two chuckled. Already, his mood lightened because someone sat by his side and cared enough to listen. In response, he stood and stretched as his restlessness began receding.

"You can handle the rest of the watch. I might have some idea of what to do."

"Really?" Clearshot scratched his chin while Byron returned to his blankets and slept through the rest of the night.

***

For some reason, the high priest's quarters had been established on the southeastern corner of the palace's fourth floor, presumably because it provided more space than a regular room. That section also housed temporary guests, allowing Hendal to unwind in peace when no one occupied the spaces on either side of his. Despite this, he learned demons are not a species taught to respect privacy.

"You seem stressed," came the familiar, feminine voice from behind while he slouched at his desk, head in hands.

He released a displeased groan in response.

Soirée giggled and placed her hands on his shoulders. The unwelcome, unexpected gesture startled him enough to jump.

"*What* are you-"

"Isn't this what humans do? They find the touch of another comforting."

Her tone sounded innocent enough, but he knew better than to trust her kind. He pushed himself to his feet with the help of the desk's wooden surface before pacing the room. Soirée remained where she lingered behind his chair to observe him.

"Consolation develops between humans, most certainly not from a demon."

Hendal understood how much he needed to monitor his tongue around such a threat, yet his patience usually thinned when she showed up. Worse still was her sensibility. Her figure and beauty appeared more attractive than any woman he'd ever seen, and she learned how to use them to mimic human expressions and behavior in order to garner a desired reaction.

Illusions are alluring, but the truth is found within.

Just as she always did, the demon snickered, oblivious to his discomfort. "What is it this time? Could you be concerned about unleashing your precious angelic servants for this long? Perhaps it's the Yeluthian becoming an adept mage. You do remember she can speak to others at a distance."

"Of course I remember," Hendal retorted and spun to glare at Soirée.

Her amused expression didn't change. "Which is it then?"

A growl escaped him, then he realized he was fussing. He inhaled, released a calming breath, and focused on maintaining his dignity as he addressed the demon. "Jaspire and his group are smart enough to handle themselves. I doubt anyone will be able to contain your demonic creatures wreaking havoc in the south. The king is a pawn at this point, though he must continue to believe he's in control."

"Which is why you informed him the master mage received his message and is traveling to Fester instead," Soirée finished in a bored manner while examining her fingernails.

Hendal ignored her. "My only real issue at this point is the Yeluthian girl. Although she is nothing more than a figure for the alliance, I still think we should do something to prevent her from reaching out to Byron or the Dalan base. I would also like to rid myself of that meddlesome master light mage."

"Perhaps you could use her children as a bargaining tool."

Hendal stuck his nose up at the demon. "I'd rather not bring children into this."

In response, she smirked mischievously and crept toward him. "It could be fun to play with them a bit. It's been years since I experimented on a child. They're always so entertaining when presented with power."

A shiver slid down Hendal's spine. "You're revolting," he spat.

She shrugged, indifferent to his disgust. The action infuriated him, as did her lax behavior.

"I would be more decent if I were you. If you aren't, I could always send my angelic servants to find Coura and-"

At the mention of the young woman, the demon stirred, lashing out to seize Hendal by the throat. He choked incomprehensible words while attempting to pry away from the firm grip. The noises stopped when she brought her mouth close to his ear.

"If you or your pigeons break our agreement not to harm her, I'll vanish. How will you fare without my magic, High Priest?" she asked and threw the title in his face.

He intended to answer, but the sound came out as a whimper before the demon released him. While Hendal doubled over to catch his breath and process what happened, Soirée stood over him to utilize her menacing presence.

"You will invite the Yeluthian to meet you here after dinner with the excuse to discuss more about her home. Devise a lie about the alliance or the missing messengers, whatever convinces her to join you, and grab enough medicine to sedate her. Once you both arrive, I'll capture her. The potions will prevent her from using her ability."

"Won't I be suspected?" he asked and fidgeted under her resulting glare.

"Quit cowering. Nobody questions a priest. You will remain quiet about her disappearance. If anyone brings it up, inform them you met with her, but she left. Embellish her homesickness if you have to."

After a moment, Hendal cleared his throat and mustered the courage to comment. "I suppose this creates further strain on the alliance. All we seem to have done is intercept their messages."

"Now you're thinking," she replied before chuckling and reaching a hand toward him.

Although he braced for a strike, she merely patted him on the cheek. The gesture had him blushing with a mixture of flattery, shame, and rage.

*

For the rest of the afternoon, Hendal set the plan in motion. One of the healers was willing to listen to him explain his feigned headaches during the night and provided plenty of mind-numbing concoctions to help.

Dinner remained uneventful. The new king was quiet for most of it and spent time dancing with the ladies, who appeared too eager to hold his attention. Hendal pretended to appreciate the music and entertainment on the outside; on the inside, he prayed for Aaron to leave before the Yeluthian girl. Otherwise, he would need to create another excuse to meet with her alone. Luck seemed to be on his side, though, for the young man exited after wishing him a wonderful evening.

Hopefully, it will be, Hendal thought in a mischievous manner as he caught the ambassador's eye and gestured for them to exit the dining hall together.

"Good evening, High Priest," she greeted him and curtsied. Despite her political role, Hendal actually found himself liking her and the conversations they had.

She's always polite and considerate toward those in power. If only every person in Asteom behaved the same.

"Lady Grace, good evening to you," he responded as his jolly character. "If you have some free time, King Aaron and I were wondering if we could borrow you to discuss matters regarding the alliance."

Minor alarm flashed in her eyes as she tilted her head. "What kind of matters, if I may ask?"

"We hope to send another letter to Yeluthia via a ground messenger to inform them of the demonic creatures and the Sie-Kie men. Since there has been a lack of responses, we are hoping to converse about a more realistic method to connect with your people."

She pondered the offer before agreeing. Hendal assured her the king would be waiting, so he led her to the fourth floor.

"I cannot believe they have yet to contact Aaron," she commented when they stood in front of his door. "I am worried something might have happened."

Hendal rolled his eyes when she wasn't looking and opened the door. A single candle stayed lit on his desk. "All the more reason to figure this out. Come in. Allow me to light a lamp."

In the dimness, he couldn't see clearly and stumbled into his desk as Grace warily stepped through the doorway.

"I thought you said Aaron would be here."

"Yes, yes. I'm sure the king is on his way." He pretended to fumble with the candles for a while in order to buy time.

Do it, Soirée!

"High Priest, it is rather late," the ambassador started after a minute passed.

Hendal spun around to catch her retreating to the door. "His Highness is tardy, that's all! Really, it will be but a brief discussion..."

The door slammed shut behind the Yeluthian ambassador. He heard her gasp, begin to scream until the sound was abruptly silenced, then there came a thud. Hendal snatched the nearest candle, dripping hot wax onto his hand in the process, and crossed the room. His breath caught at the sight of the girl's body crumpled on the floor as Soirée leaned on the wall in her typical, casual fashion.

"W-What did you do?" he bumbled and knelt next to Grace. Her chest rose and fell, as if she were sleeping.

"I needed to detain her, correct?"

Hendal shoved aside his concerns to focus on the next phase of their plan. With some effort, he dragged the limp figure to the closet at the back of the room used to store several robes and ceremonial outfits. The clothing had been slid to the side or tossed onto the floor to make space. He also procured rope and tied one end around the girl's neck and the other to the horizontal, wooden bar where the robes hung. Finally, he went to the desk for a bottle of the sleeping potion, forced her mouth open, and poured it in. Her body reacted to the involuntary process by spitting up the liquid and jolting awake, but he possessed enough strength to secure her and managed to drain the vial before she realized what he had done. Once the Yeluthian settled down, Hendal waited until she fell asleep to close the door and lock it.

Soirée sat on his desk and watched him throw the key in its bottom drawer. "That went smoothly," she commented.

"It's not over." He paused to compose himself, then he removed a handkerchief to wipe away the beads of sweat dotting his head. "I trust you'll keep an eye on her."

The demon stretched her arms upward and closed her eyelids halfway, like a content feline. Being alone with her made him nervous, so he excused himself for some fresh air. Although she didn't respond, Hendal knew the demon heard him, as she always did.

***

"Are you still alive?"

The voice of a child broke the silence surrounding Coura, rousing her awake.

I think so, she thought after finding herself unable to speak.

"You shouldn't stay here for much longer," the child replied before giggling.

She lied on her chest with her right cheek pressed into the grass and dirt beneath, so she pushed herself up to her hands and knees. A glance around the area showed the open field where she last remembered fighting the demonic creature, though nothing else. A hazy twilight covered the land in a gray fog, which reflected her state of mind.

What happened? Where are Marcy and Aimes?

"It's just us."

Who are you?

The child didn't answer. In a brief amount of time, she forgot about her companions, the creature, and everything else as she stood and roamed around. No matter what direction she chose, Coura didn't get anywhere outside the grassy circle. Once she grew tired, she dropped to the ground without considering the environment until she fell into a deep sleep. Twice more she woke, wandered, then rested.

The fourth time she rose, a shadowy figure in the distance startled her. Her voice still wouldn't work, so she used her mind.

Who are you? Where am I?

232

"I warned you not to stay here too long," answered the silhouette in the distance, though Coura could hear the person clearly, as though they were in front of her.

How do I leave?

The question remained unanswered. The shadow disappeared, and she soon forgot the encounter.

*

Time halted in the fog-shrouded field, or it seemed to for Coura. She became uneasy and often ran until she wasn't able to move anymore. During other instances, she gave up and would instead lie on her back to stare at the void above until sleep took her. She woke and passed out often enough to lose count and remained unable to remember anything or escape the twilight.

When she moved to rise again, markings twisted along both arms, leading her to wonder about their appearance.

"Possessing pure demonic energy results in physical changes when the body can't contain it."

She looked behind her for the source of the voice and froze. A child lingered at her back, but it didn't look entirely human. Patches of purples, grays, and black spotted their naked body, like bruises highlighting their pale complexion. Dozens of scars were visible as well, some deeper than others, and messy, dark hair tangled in a mat on top of their head. The eyes, or lack thereof, haunted Coura. Instead of eyeballs, two voids matching the sky took their place.

"What's wrong?"

She flinched at the question and shook off the initial shock. *Who are you? I need to leave this place.*

The child produced a menacing enough laugh to bring Coura to her feet.

"I am what's left. A memory, you could say."

A gentle brush on her shoulder startled her into wheeling around. Human-like shadows ambled out from the thickening fog to surround them.

What do you want? she demanded.

The child tilted their head to each side. "It's too late."

233

The lack of emotion in their voice and expression became more than she could handle. She darted away from them in an opening between two shadows while their gazes followed. The farther she went from the group, the denser the fog grew until she wasn't able to see her hands when she held them in front of her face. This prompted a frightening thought.

What if I lost my eyes like the rest?

Shaking fingers flew up to her eyes as she closed them, and she felt her eyeballs moving underneath their lids, prompting warm tears to slide down her cheeks. The resulting amount of relief dropped her to her knees where she wept senselessly.

*

Coura woke with a start and sat straight up, covered in sweat and gasping for air. She threw off the heavy blanket that had been draped over her, stumbled to the nearby wall, then pressed her back against it to distance herself from the suffocating sensation. In such a confused state, her head swung from side to side until her breathing steadied.

"Where am I?" she whispered before moving to sit on the edge of the bed. One of her fingers traced the embroidery on the blanket as her memories from when she was last awake returned.

The demonic creature is dead, so I must have taken in its energy after Marcy and Aimes hurried over to me. If that nightmare isn't proof enough...

A tickling in her center, barely noticeable given the tightness in her stomach, made Coura consider if she could use the power; however, memories of the child and its warning became too distracting.

It felt real. They all have.

In order to avoid succumbing to the urge to remain alone, she decided to find out where she was. She still wore the same clothing and noticed her cloak hanging on a wooden chair, the lone piece of furniture next to the bed. Her pack had been hidden underneath, but the broken sword, bow, and quiver weren't around. As she donned the cloak, Coura noticed her damaged bandages had been replaced with clean ones. The reminder of the markings made her ready to leave before anyone could stop and question the injury, and evidently the demonic creature.

She shouldered her bag, slipped out the door, and walked noiselessly down the hallway outside the room. Voices reached her from beyond an opening at the end, motivating her to press her body against the wall and listen.

"How much longer then?" Coura recognized the frail words as Aimes'.

"I don't know," answered Marcy's, hushed and barely audible above the sound of boots stomping across the space.

Another man's baritone voice thundered when the footsteps ceased. "Well?"

"Is there any way we can work off the payment until she's awake?" Aimes asked.

Coura started at his question. *Are they talking about me? Why would they...*

A disgusting laugh rumbled from the stranger. "What? Sorry old man, but there's nothing for you to do. All the duties require labor, and I won't be held responsible for your untimely death."

His pause and next comment made Coura's skin crawl despite her not being able to peek into the room. "However, *you* are sure to find work here."

She had enough of the man and his behavior. A fiery anger rose as she threw up her hood and reached into her bag for the second money pouch before entering the space, which proved to be the lobby of a tavern. It smelled of unclean bodies and ale, and wooden tables and chairs filled most of the area.

"There's no need for that," she said to draw their attention.

The trio stood across the room near a counter. The back of a hefty man's hand caressed Marcy's cheek, but he removed it to stand straight and face Coura once she spoke. He growled in response, crossed his arms, and glanced between her and her companions, who appeared visibly relieved.

"Paulina!" Aimes exclaimed with genuine surprise and joy.

Coura gestured for them to move toward the front door. "Let's go," she ordered in a serious manner, even though she expected a confrontation.

The stranger dropped a heavy hand on her shoulder as she passed him, stopping her steps.

"You think you can just waltz out without paying for our services?"

"We gave you all we had!" Marcy snapped, desperation hindering the fierceness of her tone. "You agreed it would be enough until today."

"And when did today begin? It's already past noon. I could've found somebody to use that bed already!"

Aimes threw an arm in front of Marcy when the woman leaned forward in a challenge. Meanwhile, as she wondered how long she fell unconscious this time, Coura shoved the man's hand off her shoulder.

"How much is it for the room?" she asked calmly while dismissing her annoyance.

A grin stretched across his face, revealing yellow teeth, and he pretended to ponder her question. "Let's see, it's two silver pieces for the bed, and now I'll miss out on another for today, not to mention the food and drink included. I'd say it equals a gold piece, at minimum."

Coura was aware the man planned to rip them off yet opened the pouch in her hand and removed a gold coin, the last in her possession.

"Paulina, don't," Marcy whimpered as she and Aimes watched the transaction helplessly.

The tavern keeper bit on the metal to prove its authenticity while his eyes shone with greed.

Then, Coura glanced at her companions and nodded to the door. "Let's go."

"W-Wait now," the man stammered. "You just woke up. Why not stay for a meal?"

"I think not," Aimes replied with a scowl and was the first to head toward the exit. Marcy followed after him.

Unfortunately, the man grabbed Coura's arm before she could move. "I just remembered you owe me for the clean bandages! My wife mended your clothes and injuries as well. I'm a pretty generous person, so perhaps we could arrange for you and your friend to do some extra work."

She lost control of her temper and snatched the wrist of the arm holding her in place. "In exchange, I'll leave you and this disgusting building you call a business alone."

"What? You can't-"

"I can and will cause trouble if you continue inventing more idiotic excuses to keep us here."

His selfish behavior, the lust in his eyes when he addressed Marcy, and his lack of compassion fueled Coura's resentment. In response, she instinctively dipped inward to the tendrils of energy for emotional reinforcement. It hadn't been her intention to release the power into a spell, but a thin stream of smoke rose from underneath her hand on his wrist.

The man released a fearful cry before removing his hold and recoiling to cradle the scorched skin. "A mage," he muttered multiple times and stared at her with wide eyes.

She hid her own amazement by turning away. This time, he didn't interfere with the trio as they went outside.

Encroaching Darkness

From her memory of the map tucked in her pack, Coura figured they reached Umbrich. The town didn't boast noteworthy products or services in particular, but she instantly realized it was where the outcasts of Dala and the nearby towns lived. Since the prosperous areas were a day or two away, those who couldn't afford to stay chose Umbrich.

Now that I think about it, I don't remember seeing many beggars or sick citizens on the streets of Dala, she reflected while they crossed the main road.

People dressed in rags like Aimes', begging for money and food while hiding in the shadows. The sights and smells became repulsive, and she desired nothing else at the moment than to be out of the area; however, a more pressing issue than her discomfort awaited.

"You never told us you could use magic!" Marcy exclaimed and blocked Coura's path.

"Hush now," Aimes responded and chastised the woman as he shifted to walk on her left to urge the three onward.

"Now isn't the time to talk," Coura added to stall the questioning. The plan to escape on her own and keep her secrets to herself steadily crumbled.

"Why didn't you use it to kill the demonic creature?" Marcy continued. Although she lowered the volume of her voice, her excitement remained evident. "Did it prevent you from casting spells? Is that why you have markings on your arms?"

Coura said the woman's name in a forceful enough tone to silence her.

After a moment, Aimes shifted the topic. "Where are we going?"

"We?" Coura countered. "I believe I made it clear I would guide you here and no farther."

Marcy leaned over to bat her eyelashes in an innocent manner. "You wouldn't abandon us in such an awful place, would you?"

"Why not? Umbrich seems like your type of town. In fact, I'd venture to guess you're rather familiar with it."

The shame on their faces proved to be all the confirmation she needed. Still, they kept close to her until the trio journeyed an acceptable distance from the town. A few people passed them along the way, but everybody minded their own business.

"We should camp here," Coura suggested when they spotted a space in the tall grass flattened by numerous uses as a resting site.

Marcy and Aimes searched for food, leaving her to build the fire. *Has my dark magic actually returned?* she wondered with some hopefulness.

After focusing inward on her center, she recognized the shallow pool of energy, but it behaved wildly and slipped out of her invisible grasp. She put together a pile of leaves and twigs to use as tinder before finding herself unable to manipulate more than a thin line of the power. It provided enough to create a suitable fire, yet the limit upset her.

I doubt this is a result of not carrying demonic energy for months. That means it must be from Soirée's meddling.

"So you *can* use magic!"

She gazed over the flames to where Marcy joined her, trailed by Aimes, without responding. The two returned bearing handfuls of edible mushrooms and roots, which the duo roasted after they took seats around the fire.

While they ate, Coura sensed their eyes on her as they waited for the moment when she felt prepared to explain. She couldn't imagine another way to avoid the confrontation, so she lied down to relax her muscles and initiate the conversation.

"I'll answer your questions if you answer mine first."

Marcy and Aimes looked at one another without attempting to hide their eagerness, then they leaned forward in anticipation.

"Yes, that's fair," the latter agreed.

"What happened after I fainted?"

"We tried waking you and noticed the creature's venom on your arm, but we didn't know what to do. Thankfully, Iris returned as the sun started rising. We hauled you onto her and rode straight through the next day until we reached Umbrich."

Aimes paused, allowing Marcy to finish recapping.

"You were right about us living in Umbrich. When we left Dala, that had been where we stayed for a while. The tavern keeper controls the town, so we asked him to house you. We gave him everything in exchange, including Iris, but then you didn't wake up right away."

"And?"

"The keeper's wife tended to your arm, though she didn't find any injuries."

That piece of information startled Coura. "What?"

"The venom came off, revealing those markings. She rewrapped your arms since we figured you aimed to keep them bandaged."

Aimes shook his head as a melancholy expression crinkled his features. "After the fourth day, we weren't sure what to do, which was what we had been discussing before you arrived."

Coura jolted upright. "Four days!"

The two shared a look before nodding.

"I can't believe this," she muttered before placing a hand over her eyes.

A few seconds later, Marcy's sympathetic voice reflected her companion's behavior. "Do you need to talk about what happened?"

I can't avoid their involvement, and it seems they won't leave me willingly.

"No," she replied. "Let me explain why I'm traveling around this area. Then, I'll answer your questions."

Neither spoke when she returned to lying down after weaving together what exactly she wanted them to know. "I'm a mage from Verona assigned to locate and eliminate those creatures. They're connected with a demon and, as you saw, pose trouble for the entire country. Because I wield dark energy, I can take in a defeated beast's power so it isn't able to regenerate by possessing another animal, or a person. My magic hasn't been responding well to it, which is why I can't cast spells often. The one we encountered a few days ago is the last, so I'll be returning to the capital."

Now they should understand what's going on and why they can't remain with me, even if it wasn't entirely true.

When they stayed silent for a while, Coura ventured a glance across the fire. "Anything else?"

"What is Verona like?" Marcy asked next. An odd expression softened her features.

The unexpected, seemingly unrelated question took Coura back a bit. "It's nice. I suppose it's a lot like Dala."

"I heard there are festivals throughout the year."

"I've been to a few." For longer than she anticipated, she told Marcy about the city, even going into detail about the palace's structure and scheduling, while Aimes stared off into the distance. Memories of her old day-to-day life returned with a fondness she had not experienced in months. Although she kept her friends' names and titles private, she couldn't repress how much she desired to return to the place she recognized as home. What was worse, Marcy's interest in her life grew, focusing on the pleasant aspects of the capital city.

When her throat weakened enough to cause her to cough, the woman quieted. By that point, the hour became late enough for the three to begin yawning one after another.

"Verona sounds like an amazing city to live in," Aimes mused mid-yawn.

"Absolutely," Marcy added with a knowing smile. "That's why we're going to join you, Paulina."

"You'll what?"

"Verona seems to be the perfect place for people like us to start over."

Despite how comfortable she felt, Coura propped herself up on one elbow to glare at the pair when she realized what Marcy had been doing. "I can't believe you! What I shared is from my perspective as a soldier."

"You also mentioned how protected the capital stays, the opportunities available for citizens looking for work, and how friendly everybody is. I believe someone would hire us if we're willing to help. Because there's less farming to the north, it would already be easier."

Coura pressed her mouth closed. She grew irritated with the woman for manipulating her into saying what they hoped to hear. After a moment, she returned to her sleeping position and sighed in resignation.

"If you truly would rather live and work in Verona, I can't stop you from following me."

"Really?"

"It was that easy to convince you?" Aimes added, showing a touch of humor.

"You came this far. Besides, we're a day away from Dala. By using the northern road out of the city, it's eight or nine days to the capital, a simple trip compared to what we've been through."

"Paulina…"

A tearful Marcy wiped her eyes before lying down while Aimes put his hands together, as if in a silent prayer. Coura watched them with weary eyes and a sinking heart resulting from what she actually planned to do.

*

Sleep held her for a shorter time than she preferred, yet, as the days of traveling passed, Coura knew her body had been changing apart from her appearance. Either because of the energy she took into herself or the strengthening connection to Soirée, she slept and ate less without feeling any more tired or hungry.

It was a scary thought, being so attached to a demon.

She dismissed the notion, rose without disturbing Marcy or Aimes, who both breathed lightly as they slept, and went to her pack for the hunting knife. Before she went off on her own, she needed to test the recently acquired energy. In a sharp jerk, she sliced open her palm and waited.

As she expected, the cut mended itself.

I knew it! My healing ability returned. Then again, I wouldn't be here if that wasn't the case.

Coura returned the knife and shouldered her pack before tiptoeing onto the road, leaving behind only the pouch with her remaining funds.

***

The high priest avoided the urge to groan as he sat at his desk and listened to the angels recount their most recent experience in Dala. Jaspire prattled on at length, but Hendal understood well enough what had happened.

"The city has extra defenses in place because of the demonic creatures terrorizing the south," he interrupted the younger figure mid-sentence.

"That is correct," the group's leader replied with no small amount of displeasure. His eyes darted to where Soirée stood by the open window, her body a silhouette against the starry sky.

Hendal stood and clenched his hands into fists. "The point is you failed me again."

There came movement from behind Jaspire as one of the others stepped forward, a combatant named Drake. He proved the most skilled but also extremely outspoken.

"We would not have returned empty-handed if the demon could control herself," he growled and glared at Soirée.

A harsh laugh escaped her while she turned with arms crossed to address them. "You were unsuccessful because of your cowardice. Let's not forget who released my power with a misjudged attack. I don't have control over that energy, yet."

"Why not share your grand scheme then? It is quite obvious your intentions differ from assisting us and the high priest."

Hendal rubbed his temples. *They're turning against each other. This is dangerous.*

Soirée sauntered over to the desk. "I thought you had no interest in a demon's business. If that's the case, *I* would like to hear your plan too. What about your Yeluthian heritage?"

"That will be all for now," Hendal interrupted before their tempers heated further. "Jaspire, you and your companions are to remain in the area for now. Stay close but out of sight. I will send for you when I have need of your assistance."

"But-"

243

He pointedly glanced away from them as a clear dismissal. From of the corner of his eye, he caught Soirée waving at them with her fingers, like a child. Soon, the room fell silent, and he breathed easier.

"Why do you insist on goading them?" he asked the demon.

"Because I despise their kind," she replied and shrugged. "Why do you insist on keeping such company?"

"You know as well as I do we need them to intercept the messengers between the palace and Yeluthia. We wish to see the rise of a new Asteom."

Soirée said nothing after.

Hendal walked to the closet, removed its key from his pocket to unlock the door, and opened it. Inside, the ambassador sat hugging her legs to her torso. The week without a bath or proper lavatory left her skin unclean and hair lackluster.

He knelt and grabbed her chin. "Let's see that pretty face."

"No," she protested as tears slid down her cheeks.

The lack of movement or proper nutrition, in addition to the potions, left the Yeluthian weak enough to manipulate. He tilted her face upward and squeezed her cheeks so her mouth parted before grabbing the potion from his other pocket.

"Good girl."

With his teeth, he twisted off the cork sealing the bottle and prepared to pour the liquid down her throat until a knocking from the other side of the room caused Hendal to jump. The potion slipped from his hand and dropped to the ground where the fragile glass cracked into three pieces. He mumbled a curse for his clumsiness and pushed the ambassador back inside. She let out a squeak but nothing more as he shut the door.

The knocking continued.

"Who could possibly need to visit the high priest?" Soirée asked while pretending to act naïve from where she stood across the room.

Hendal ignored her to hurry and take a candle in hand. "Forgive me, I'm just preparing for bed," he lied and fumbled to open the door.

Outside stood the new king, still in his formal dinner clothes. "I must have come later than I thought since you're about to settle down for the evening," Aaron began with an awkward smile.

"I… Y-Yes, Your Highness. I don't see your guards. You didn't venture all this way by yourself?" Hendal prayed his feigned concern explained his nervousness.

The young man expressed some hesitation before a seriousness passed over his face. "I requested they wait near the staircase down the hall to give us privacy, though they are well-aware of what this is about. High Priest, I'm hoping we could discuss the disappearance of our Yeluthian ambassador and the past murders. I proposed a thorough search of the palace led by General Casner and General Tont and spoke with them already. They agree we shouldn't exempt anyone from being a suspect."

Where is this coming from? And at a time like this!

"Y-Your Highness, I don't understand. What if our guest left of her own accord? As for the murders…"

Hendal struggled for the words to usher his uninvited guest away when there came a gentle pounding. The Yeluthian's frail voice strained beneath the nearby noise.

"Help! Please, somebody!"

Hendal's mind went blank.

"What is that?" Aaron asked while peering into the room.

"Nothing, Your Highness. I often hear the residents on the floor below. You know how rowdy the soldiers can be!"

Again, the girl cried a bit louder.

What are you doing, Soirée? Stop her!

Hendal attempted to close the door and babble an apology, promising to discuss matters tomorrow; however, the new king wasn't deceived. He slid a foot between the opening, preventing the door from closing.

"High Priest, what are you-"

"Aaron?"

Despite his poorly composed façade, Hendal couldn't help but gasp at the Yeluthian's unmuffled voice. He spun around to spot her pale figure on the floor as she crawled toward them.

How did she free herself from the rope?

"Grace!"

Before he knew what had happening, the unwelcome visitor pushed past him to kneel at the girl's side.

"W-Wait, I can explain…"

"Are you all right?" Aaron asked while placing his hands on her shoulders.

What should I do? Where's that cursed demon! As Hendal began to panic, the young man rose and faced him.

"High Priest, why is the Yeluthian ambassador in your quarters?" A hand rested on the hilt of the sword at his waist.

Hendal pursed his lips. *This child has the audacity to turn on me? How dare he barge in here!*

Just when he prepared to throw those words into Aaron's face, if only to release his frustration, the door gravitated from his grasp to close.

"This is becoming painful to watch."

"S-Soirée?" he whispered and glanced over his shoulder to where the demon stood in the shadows.

"Who's there?" the young man demanded and drew his weapon.

"I mean honestly," she continued and strolled past Hendal. "I must do everything myself."

When she halted in front of Aaron, whose eyes went wide at the sight, an ugly grin stretched across Hendal's face. *He's struck dumb by the presence of a demon.*

"What do you think, Your Highness," he began in a venomous tone. "Does such a powerful creature paralyze you with fear?"

As if the words broke a trance, the new king stood straighter. "I'll admit, it scared me the first time."

"The…first time? What's he talking about?" Hendal bumbled to the demon.

Soirée eyed him up without hiding her exasperation. "As a priest, you really need to learn how to listen. When you sent me to Dala with the pigeons, I saw him, Coura, and the others from the palace."

"You never told me that," he snapped.

Soirée raised a hand, causing him to flinch since he believed she would strike him. Instead, she pointed at Aaron.

"Oh, Hendal," she continued in a playful tone. "Are you so focused on the past that you can't see what I've done for you? By releasing the girl, I lured him right in front of you, fresh for the taking."

He paused to consider the realization.

Meanwhile, the young man's eyes never left Soirée, even when he addressed Hendal.

"You've been conspiring with a demon this whole time? I warned you already, my guards know my location. If anything should happen to me, they *will* be here to capture you."

He's right. Why would she bring him to me if it will only result in my death? Cunning creature, what am I supposed to do now?

As if Soirée read his thoughts, she released an annoyed sigh and shook her head. "I don't mind doing most of the dirty work, but apparently I must do all the thinking as well!"

Immediately after, she launched herself forward. Aaron saw her coming and shifted his sword into a position to prevent her from attacking. Hendal held his breath since he knew the potential noise would alert the guards down the hall.

Soirée allowed the new king to swing at her before reaching out and grabbing the blade. Blood dripped onto the floor from where it scratched her palm in the process. The Yeluthian scrambled out of the way while Aaron tried to pull his weapon free. When he opened his mouth, Hendal prepared to shout an order for the demon to silence him until her other hand clutched the lower half of his face. His resulting scream muffled, and the force from her arm accompanied by a kick to the side of his knee dropped him onto his back. After, Soirée balanced herself above him without removing either grip.

"Allow me to show you a trick," she said to no one in particular.

Hendal longed to scold her for being reckless and order her not to harm the young man, but she continued before he could vocalize the words.

"When a demon possesses a living being, we merely extend a tendril of our power into their body. Human mages reserve energy in their center, yet movements, such as waving or walking, are controlled by the brain."

He felt nauseous when he sensed her power rousing, and the new king began fighting harder against her physical hold.

"Like dripping blood into a basin of water, the energy spreads to dominate the human mind, putting it in the possession of the more powerful source."

Within a few seconds, her victim quit moving, and Soirée stood with an almost excited smile. The Yeluthian ambassador said his name in a shaking voice.

"Why don't you rise and put your sword away," the demon ordered.

In response, Aaron pushed himself to his feet and returned the weapon to its sheath while wearing a blank expression.

A shiver trailed down Hendal's spine, though he didn't know if elation or fear prompted it. When Soirée stepped toward him, he understood which it was.

"Don't you dare think of doing *that* to me," he growled between his teeth.

Still, he didn't resist when she rested a hand on his head. A chill grew in his midsection, as though he had swallowed ice, before she backed away.

"I wouldn't dream of manipulating a mind like yours," she replied with an eyeroll. "I forged a portion of my energy into you. Why don't you try it out?"

Soirée glanced at the young man, who stared ahead with lifeless eyes. At his feet, the Yeluthian girl sobbed and muttered his name.

Hendal cleared his throat. "Your Highness, return her to the closet."

Aaron seized the ambassador's wrist, then he dragged her across the room against her weak protesting. Meanwhile, Hendal returned to his desk for another sleeping potion. Together, they forced her to drink it amid her crying. He re-tied the rope tighter around her neck before locking the door and hiding the key once more.

"I must say, this is quite handy," he mumbled while observing the royal figure, who awaited his next command.

Soirée waved the comment away. "You possess the ability to use the energy linked to me, but don't overdo it. Reach into the pool of power when your hands are on the victim's head and order it to control their mind."

"That's it?"

"Magical energy is alive. Mine happens to feed off its hosts to survive and grow."

The idea of devouring someone's life didn't sit well with Hendal, yet he knew it would allow him to achieve any goal he set out to accomplish.

"Your Highness, return to your quarters and rest. Carry on with your daily routine without mentioning what took place tonight."

"Yes, High Priest."

"You're not so much a victim as a servant, aren't you?" he teased.

The young man nodded in response before the pair exited, strolled across the hallway, and met the four soldiers waiting for their leader. The guards greeted them before descending with the new king in the middle.

Despite his narrow escape from capture, Hendal entered his room, closed the door, and leaned against it while panting. His face grew sweaty, and his body trembled, so he hurried to fall into his desk chair and retrieve a handkerchief.

"With this magic, I can possess anybody in the entire country," he mumbled. "The king is under my control. Who do I need next? Or should I wait to act until the creatures to the south weaken Dala? I already have Jaspire and his group. Yes, perhaps it is time for a break."

Somewhere in the room, Soirée chuckled. "Whatever helps you sleep at night."

When Hendal glanced around, the demon was nowhere in sight.

Trouble in the South

ala seemed exactly as Byron and his companions remembered, except for an increase in their defenses. When the group approached the base's northern entrance, they noticed eight guards posted instead of the usual three or four. More surveyed the area around the moat in a casual manner to show they were accustomed to the routine, and no hallway ever emptied inside. Many of the troops recognized and saluted the four with personal greetings, including the ever-attentive assistant general.

"I figured the outer wall's guards had been standing in the sun for too long when they reported your arrival," Calin said before leading the four into the center.

Byron rubbed the back of his neck while allowing his eyes to wander. "We would have sent word ahead, but traveling isn't safe enough to justify a messenger unless necessary."

"You're right. The general understands," the soldier replied without a hint of apprehension.

He raised an eyebrow yet didn't comment. The basic layout remained easy to remember, giving him a sense of comfort after the week and a half on the road.

They found General Tio in his meeting room huddled over several documents scattered around the table. At his assistant's announcement, the man dismissed whatever he'd been preoccupied with to give them a proper welcome.

"What a surprise this is. Let's have some food and drinks!"

While Byron, Clearshot, Will, and Marcus took seats around the table, Calin slipped out and returned when they moved on from the pleasantries, reminding the group of the general's preference for diving straight into business.

"It's been weeks since your last letter. What's been going on in the capital? Are they any closer to finding the people responsible for the murders?"

"Not yet," Byron answered. "I don't have much confidence in our situation either."

"Why is that?"

He chanced a glance at Clearshot, who sat across the table next to Calin. His friend nodded, urging him to continue. Without hiding the details, he informed Tio and his assistant about the quarrels during the council's meetings, the other generals' views, and about his suspicion regarding the high priest.

"King Aaron wrote to us requesting we change our route to head toward Fester, according to Clearshot and Master Emilea. I'm not sure why, but I think-"

"Someone's feeding him information," the general interrupted to finish. "I'm guessing not all of it's true."

The room fell silent while they each contemplated this until Marcus shifted topics. "Excuse me, but there's more to our mission. Byron was ordered to stay here because of the threats posed by the demonic creatures, and the rest of us agreed to join. Is it true they're increasing in numbers?"

"Aha!" Tio shouted before gathering the papers in front of him and tossing them to where Marcus and Will sat at the opposite end. Some of the pages flew apart, so Byron slid the closest one over to read it.

REPORT FROM MARINICH BY SECOND COMMANDER LYSON: SURVIVORS OF THE ATTACK ON MEDINA ARE SETTLED AND EMPLOYED. ONE IS MISSING BUT EXPECTED TO HAVE LEFT TOWN TO MOVE WEST. WE ARE STILL KEEPING DEFENSES HIGH EVEN THOUGH WE ONLY FIND AVERAGE-SIZED BEASTS. THINGS ARE RETURNING TO NORMAL, BUT WE WILL KEEP THE NIGHTS LIT UNTIL

NOTHING CAUSES TROUBLE FOR TWO MORE WEEKS. PLEASE, WE ASK THAT YOU RESPOND TO OUR REPORTS WITH BETTER NEWS.

This is dated six days ago, Byron realized before looking up at the general. The man leaned on the back of his chair in a bored manner.

"These are all reports?" Marcus asked while glancing between two documents.

Meanwhile, Byron noticed Will paling as the herbalist stared at a page. Tio did too and pointed to the paper the herbalist gripped.

"*That* is what we're dealing with."

Soon, Will handed the document to Marcus, then it went to Clearshot, and finally Byron. The report came from the same commander in Marinich and described an attack on Medina, as well as the results. The thought of an entire town being slaughtered by just one being baffled and concerned him.

"We can't seem to locate the creatures now," Calin continued in a gentler tone. "One day, they're said to be near Clearwater; the next, we'll have sightings outside our city's borders."

Clearshot scratched his chin. "If they're similar to what showed up in the center of this base, I get the feeling they're able to appear without warning."

"What's worse, the generals in the capital threatened to send their troops here to command the base," Tio added while holding a page that seemed to have been crumpled multiple times. "They threatened my authority as a leader! If they even dare to consider assigning soldiers without my permission, I'll make them regret it."

He balled the paper up in his fist and threw it over his shoulder after, though Byron ignored the personal grudge to focus on the current issue.

"Perhaps there's more to it than merely assisting you. I admit, there's been talk at the council meetings regarding the distance between Dala and Verona. They might be hoping to reestablish communications."

"Either that, or they're aiming to stretch their control south," Calin countered.

Byron couldn't argue against the notion. An uncomfortable break in the conversation followed while they collected the documents, then Tio rose to stretch.

"I'm sure you're used to it by now, but it's rude to bring you right into the middle of this without letting you settle in. Calin, let's find some rooms for them. We'll concentrate on the creatures once we're rested."

*

Despite the severity of the threats and an urgency to find solutions, Byron sensed their group unwinding during the evening. The soldiers and mages who recognized them wished to partake in casual activities, so they separated and enjoyed the new company. One day became three in the blink of an eye, yet they hadn't been summoned by the general.

He conversed with Clearshot about it as they lounged under the shade of a fruit tree in the garden space.

"Should we approach him?" Byron wondered aloud, allowing his concern to leak into the question.

"Has it really only been a few months since we were last here?" his friend asked instead of answering while gazing at the colored canopy. The fall season already arrived in the south, though Byron had not given it attention until that moment.

"Will you focus?"

Clearshot lowered his chin to stared across the field. "What else is there to talk about? The general will fetch us when he needs us or learns new information. There's no reason to bother Tio or Calin, especially since it's been less than a week. Do you want to know what I think?"

Byron waited as the other man looked him over.

"Politics aside, the people here live in fear of the demonic creatures. There's never been this impactful of a natural threat, so something has to be instigating it."

"We already know it's a person in the palace," Byron added and rubbed the bridge of his nose.

"Exactly, and the same person is working with the rogue angels and a demon. Our main priority should be discovering who they are and what it is they're plotting."

"You can't expect us to return to Verona so soon. What about the attacks in this area?"

"True. If a beast like what we faced last time shows up again…"

Clearshot didn't finish the sentence, prompting Byron to groan in dismay.

I possess the experience and skills necessary for protecting the base and towns beyond from demonic creatures, as well as for instructing and leading the soldiers and mages with Clearshot and Marcus' assistance. Aaron not only knew that but understood we wouldn't allow innocent people to become victims. If that's the case, why did he wish to send us to Fester instead? Is the priority to search for Coura and return with her to train the teams and send them out, or are we supposed to support the southern base's efforts first?

His friend echoed his thoughts. "There's more to our assignment than fighting alongside the troops here. Remember, we're supposed to find Coura. Something tells me once we do we'll learn more about what's going on."

"Sure." Byron's eyes lowered to the ground as a wave of nostalgia washed over him, and he longed for the life they led before the murders.

Clearshot put a reassuring hand on his back. "Lighten up. You always overthink our problems. Don't you trust the general to know what he's doing in his own base? If you don't, I'd like to be there when you tell him that."

The idea of approaching Tio with such a message made Byron smile. "You're right."

"I know." The archer patted his back with a chuckle.

As they studied the soldiers and mages farther ahead, Byron decided to map out their next steps. "I'll ask Marcus and Will what they prefer to do instead of expecting them to listen to us."

"Why?"

"I trust the general and his troops to take care of them if they stay to aid the efforts in Dala and the surrounding towns."

"You know what their answer will be."

"Yes, but I'd like to give them the choice. At least then we would-"

Mid-sentence, he sensed a surge of vile energy in the distance. Clearshot said his name and shook his arm as he recognized the power.

"It's one of the creatures," he explained while rising.

His friend did the same except with widening eyes. "Is it here?"

"No, it's…" Byron hoped his sense of direction was misguided, yet his heart sank. "It's between the city and base, just past the southernmost section of the moat."

Clearshot swore and sprinted to the nearest door, presumably to grab his weapon. The mages nearby huddled together, causing a scene among the soldiers until a horn sounded to alert them of the enemy.

***

The city Coura became so accustomed to earlier in the year hid her for a couple days while she tried to wait out her stragglers. From the moment she arrived in Dala, she kept her face and body hidden beneath the cloak and found an alley to settle in with several beggars. They paid her no attention since she didn't attempt to bother them.

The next morning, as she wandered in search of a breakfast to snag, she spotted Marcy and Aimes wandering along the main road. The two peered down each street, appearing just as worn and hopeless as the people who called those places home. She muttered a curse and kept a close eye on the pair.

I thought it would take longer for them to get here. They have directions to Verona, so why are they lingering in Dala? Perhaps they're worried about being attacked on the way. They should be safe as long as they continue north with the other travelers.

She attempted to persuade herself they would go to the capital on their own and that there was no reason for her to follow. Still, she'd grown attached to her former companions, especially after they sacrificed so much. With a vow to watch over the pair until they left the city, Coura trailed them from the shadows.

Her impatience rose over the next two days when it became obvious Marcy and Aimes were adamant about finding her. She felt torn between approaching them and leaving on her own before forcing herself to do the latter.

I need to trust they'll make safe decisions, she reflected and hurried away to the northern road. Despite her body's extra reserves, she grew tired of pretending to be a street dweller, and she desired nothing more than to move under the cover of the forest and locate a pond or stream.

People crowded the main street, though none seemed to be heading in or out of the city. Just as Coura wondered about that and how it would affect the journey, a tightness swelled in her chest to signal danger.

A creature is here? she thought while frantically scanning the surrounding space.

For a while, nothing happened out of the ordinary; however, the pressure on her body steadily increased until she started leaning against a building in order to breathe with effort. The source had to be bearing Soirée's energy, yet she couldn't imagine how a creature similar to the other three could sneak into the populated city.

In the distance, a horn blared followed by a second as the base raised the alarm.

A heavy, unified pause resulted for a moment when the people heard the warning. Then, everyone took off in various directions, showing equal panic. The noise from the citizens' shouting, cries, and shuffling feet hindered Coura's ability to concentrate beneath it all. A bulky object soared through the air farther down the road to crash against the houses, shattering into pieces while smashing the fronts of the structures. A group of soldiers hurried by in front of her with swords drawn, preventing her from observing what caused the chaos. When they passed, she trailed behind against the current of people fleeing in the opposite direction. Soon, they stood at the edge of the city and could see what awaited them.

The oversized, wolf-like beast was the same one that entered the center of the base three times when she had been recovering. It appeared shorter than the previous encounters due to the buildings lining the main road, yet it still loomed twice her height and bore teeth identical to knives. The violet eyes flickered to study the humans below before a paw raised to strike the nearest building, causing the corner of its roof to collapse.

The troops slowly surrounded the giant creature with weapons at the ready. Abandoned carts, booths, baskets, and more items discarded minutes ago provided cover for them to use. The creature took the nearest table in its mouth and flung it toward the soldiers, then it repeated the attack. Most people jumped out of the way, but those without sharper reflexes were knocked off their feet amid a clanging of armor or weapons.

Somewhere, a woman screamed. There came shouts from men who refused to part with their belongings, or who took advantage of the opportunity to loot their neighbors. Tied-up animals struggled to break their bonds while the ones able to free themselves from their pens squealed in fright and turned tail, just as Iris had done.

Coura froze, unsure of what to do before retreating into the nearest alley in order to peek out at the fight. To her amazement, others lingered on the road, in the shadows, and from inside buildings, displaying a dazed interest in the scene.

Why are they staying here? In fact, why am I still here? Should I try to help? I don't have a weapon. Would the creature follow me if I leave Dala?

While she struggled to decide, a faint yet unmistakable burst of dark energy erupted nearby. A blast of fire hit the beast from behind, knocking its body forward onto its face in an awkward position. The soldiers on the road regrouped to guard the front and began ordering the spectators to evacuate. Most of the noncombatants ran once they saw the spell, but the rest, including Coura, became more invested in what was about to take place.

The creature pushed itself to its full height while growling, a sound like thunder rumbling in the air. Because the narrow area prevented it from turning around or entering farther into the city, it grew visibly angered and lashed out at whatever remained in range. Carts and booths were launched by strikes or thrown from its mouth, and with so much movement, it became impossible to catch what was happening on the opposite side. Arrows began flying while more troops joined those at the creature's front end. Even a duo of mages around Coura's age launched magical projectiles, which did nothing except distract their opponent.

"Drive it back!"

A commanding voice rose above the others as Calin sprinted straight past her hiding spot to stand behind the row of troops. Behind him, additional soldiers reinforced the line; among them, to Coura's surprise, was Marcus.

"We've got the advantage," Tio's assistant shouted and pointed his sword at their enemy. "While those in the field are distracting it, we must push it out of the city!"

Each man and woman confidently raised a weapon or fist in response before marching forward. Meanwhile, Calin took Marcus by the arm and called over several men closest to the pair, then they conversed for a brief moment. The assistant generals split apart after with Calin joining the mass and Marcus leading the chosen soldiers away where they ushered the remaining citizens to safety and tended to those who were injured by the previous attacks.

What's Marcus doing in Dala? Coura wondered. Her heartbeat settled as she studied the coordination of the troops, yet she remembered how much she remained directly involved. *I'll take my chances by fleeing and hope it abandons its efforts here. Otherwise, I need to put faith in the soldiers and mages holding it off. Perhaps they can weaken it enough to kill. If that happens, I should keep close enough to absorb the demonic energy.*

Although she didn't feel confident in the plan, she removed herself from the alley, held her cloak's hood tight over her face, and hurried to cross the road. The people scattering in her path ignored the movement as her destination became another street shielded by a set of multi-leveled structures. Seconds ticked by until she prepared to slip under cover once more.

Out of the corner of her eye, she caught something airborne to the right. Whatever the creature had thrown crashed into the nearest building, raining fragments of wood and rubble over her goal. She clenched her fists tighter in preparation to continue through the debris, even if it meant risking her physical safety.

"Don't move!"

Someone grabbed her left arm and yanked her backward. As she stumbled, the person sidestepped to place their body between her and the wreckage while wrapping their arms around her to act as a shield. The resulting planks, metal attachments, and brick shards smashed a few steps in front of where they stood to kick up a cloud of dust.

When nothing else dropped to the ground, her rescuer loosened his hold. "Are you hurt?"

Coura recognized the voice as Marcus' before pushing herself out of his embrace. In order to avoid showing her face, she kept her head down while brushing aside her relief at reuniting with her friend before jogging along the edge of the road. When another opportunity presented itself, she dipped into a side street and went along its winding turns until the outer farming homes became visible. Only when fencing prevented her from continuing ahead did she stop to catch her breath before climbing over the wooden barrier.

Although she was no longer near it, the fighting stretched into the clearing between the base and city as the troops successfully drove the creature away from the buildings. Mages lined up in rows to backtrack while attacking the head with a single man controlling their group.

I knew I sensed Byron's energy earlier, Coura recalled.

Watching her former mentor participate in an event where he seriously used his intellect and abilities always gave her a thrill because he never bragged about the power he could control. At that moment, he manifested lightning bolts in his hands, bending their form until the time came to release them one after the other. Behind him, the other mages did what they could to seclude the creature with shielding spells or copy the master mage to lure it farther into the open area.

Once the beast moved within range, a volley of arrows flew from near the base. Coura crept closer to the combat and noticed Tio barking orders. The general organized his soldiers to circle the outside of the mages' shield, halting the creature without allowing an opening for escape.

I understand their strategy now. Because of its size, they need to trap it in one location in order to weaken it. The shield and soldiers are preventing movement while Byron, the dark mages, and archers are attacking consistently. Its attention isn't on the innocent anymore but those causing it pain.

As she predicted, the demonic creature dug its claws into the ground and battered the shields, which were replaced before they completely shattered. Archers and mages chanced shots between openings when the soldiers' weapons kept it at bay.

Coura cautiously inched nearer as the fighting continued. She wasn't the only noncombatant who felt compelled to approach the troops either. Men and women brave enough to venture from the city did so while carrying makeshift weapons, such as pitchforks, metal bars, and kitchen knives. They all seemed to freeze like rabbits when Tio noticed and spun around to face them; however, instead of sending them away or insulting their decision, he let out a cheer echoed by his soldiers. The citizens hurried forward at the support, so she joined them to stand behind the general's line. People spewed insults and curses at the demonic creature while it couldn't break free from the routine, and she questioned if they were aware of the risk to their lives.

For a few minutes, the repetitive action went on, sparking enthusiasm from each group when they didn't participate. Meanwhile, Coura's hands twitched nervously under her cloak.

This is taking too long, she realized with a glance over the troops.

The general must have reached the same conclusion because his orders changed. "Outer squad, accompany these men and women to Dala and move the citizens to the western side. Guard them until you hear from me."

Protests and confusion sounded from multiple people, mainly his soldiers, but it became apparent how frequently the shields were coming down. As if to emphasize that point, the demonic creature rammed into the tallest section until the wall cracked, then it growled in Tio's direction.

This scared most of the people who emerged from the city, and they fled with the outer squad at their heels. Still, Coura and half a dozen onlookers remained despite the general's glare.

"If you ignore my order, you better be smart enough not to get in my way unless you prefer to be killed by my hand!" With those words, Tio called for a retreat.

She followed behind the troops as they returned to the base. *The soldiers can't hold it off without the mages' shielding, which is barely able to withstand a blow or two. There's no doubt they wore it down, yet I can't imagine how we're supposed to defeat it if it's mobile again.*

While the others crossed the moat, the general issued another order for the archers.

"We're going to draw it here for a final stand, even if it means sacrificing the base. Decide whether you want to remain by the bridge or head inside."

There rang a resounding confirmation, then another volley of arrows launched ahead. Coura kept out of their way by not crossing over, instead remaining closer to the clearing and watching those still engaged.

Byron must have given his own commands as the mages dropped back one by one to jog into the groupings of trees farther east or toward the base. Tio said nothing to those who passed by where he stood on the bridge. Only four dark mages lingered to construct a final shield while the rest fled.

A man shouted from the among archers before a sound like shattering glass echoed, and the demonic creature bristled amid a shower of shimmering energy from the magical wall. The mages, soldiers, and Tio wore expressions of uncertainty and horror when the beast circled around to head toward the city.

Desperate to prevent disaster, Coura considered what she could do and remembered what hindered the same creature when it attacked inside the base. She looked inward to focus on the connection to Soirée's power in her center before mentally screaming for it to stop.

Somehow, she knew the demonic creature heard her. It abruptly halted, turned, and scanned the humans between it and the base in a confused manner.

It can't tell where I am, she realized and started when it stepped backward to reach the city's perimeter. *Perhaps I can lead it away.*

She swallowed her doubts and prepared to sprint across the clearing. The creature moved before she did, though, sending her hopes plummeting. With its massive jaw, the beast ripped off a wooden beam from the roof of the nearest building, steadied its stance, then threw it in the direction of the base.

It landed far from the moat, yet Tio swore before abandoning his position to regroup with the troops across the bridge. Instead of joining them, Coura hurried toward where the beam skidded to a stop.

The trees to the east near the mages might prevent it from catching me or damaging more of the city. In any case, we're vulnerable out in the open.

The demonic creature hurled another chunk of the building at the dark mages, and it landed behind where they decided to huddle together, causing them to scatter. Two went for the trees and two for the base, though a boy heading in Coura's direction stumbled multiple times as a result of his weariness. She considered assisting him but thought otherwise and eyed the nearby brush until a glance over her shoulder at the beast had her sliding to a stop. It held what appeared to be a metal sheet, either somebody's roof or a door, and its eyes darted her way. With a jerk of its neck, the creature released the object to let it soar through air toward the fatigued mage, who kept his attention on the base.

Her voice broke as she screamed for them to run even when her feet moved in their direction. She willed her body to go faster when the mage stopped to stare at her before noticing the projectile. When he didn't respond, she did the only thing she could think of and charged into him at full speed. The tackle knocked them both to the ground just as the metal sheet crashed and bounced across where he had been standing. Together, they tumbled to the side and rolled to a stop in the grass. The effort of exerting her body, as well as the pressure weighing on her chest, made Coura dizzy.

She managed to push herself to her feet and mentally shouted at the beast when her patience dwindled. *Here I am, you monster. Quit playing games!*

The demonic creature narrowed its eyes and curled its upper lip into a snarl. She didn't plan on waiting for it to strike first, yet her idea to lead it into the woods vanished when the distressed mage stumbled in that direction. Her next best option was to obey Tio by bringing it to the base, so she retraced her steps and hurried toward the bridge. The ground rumbled beneath her feet as the beast charged across the field. Up ahead, the archers readied their bows.

Coura spun around once she reached the moat to find their enemy slowing. It was then she remembered her lack of a weapon, and irritation replaced fear.

I can't do this alone.

The sole intent to possess something for defense forced her to interact with Soirée's energy. It hummed in her center, as if eager to be released, though it proved impossible to grasp a substantial amount. At last, she abandoned the attempt at a spell and focused on manifesting what had benefited her in the past. She commanded the power to take shape into her open palm, and a mixture of shock and elation struck when a weight she had grown accustomed to fell into her hand, that of the black sword crafted from demonic energy.

The creature already paced in front of the bridge before swiping with its deadly claws. She managed to dodge while bringing up the sword she summoned, and its charcoal color glistened in the last light from the sunset. When the beast swung again, she slashed at its exposed front leg. Her blade swept through the slick skin in a deep cut, causing blood to drip onto the grass, and the wolf-like being released a shrill cry while backing away. Coura held her ground for a moment as it cradled the injury; however, once the wound healed, it tried again.

Twice more she injured the creature while targeting the legs. The original idea had been to avoid confrontation and hurry inside to the base's training ground where she would see if it would follow, lose interest, or flee. She reconsidered the idea after noting its exhaustion and her confidence with the sword.

"Hey!"

She chanced a look at the source of the shout. From the opposite side of the bridge, Tio, Clearshot, and five other archers stood in a line. The general made a shooing motion with his hand.

"Get out of the way!"

Coura rolled her eyes at the man but obliged. She wasn't able to move around the beast since it kept its front side to her, so she charged under the front legs and hoped to lose its attention. After scrambling away to avoid being sliced by the claws on its hind legs, which kicked in an attempt to find her, she dropped to crouch in the grass.

Tio yelled once it moved into a position near the moat, prompting the archers to send arrows at its face one after the other. Even though their numbers were minor compared to the dozens of volleys from earlier, each buried into the nose or eyes. Coura marveled at the skill necessary to hit such a specific, narrow spot as she rose to her feet. Then, she debated whether or not to attack the legs again until the sound of footsteps came from behind. In an instant, Byron jogged up to her side. Sweat drenched his face and clothes, which had also been splattered with dark blood and smeared with dirt, and he breathed heavily. Otherwise, he appeared focused.

"Push it toward the moat," he ordered in a hoarse voice. "I doubt it can climb out of there, at least not easily."

She considered the idea yet wasn't certain how deep the water went. Before she could question the suggestion, the master mage mustered more of his energy into a flame spell, leaving her to join him.

Their target still kept its attention on the archers and general, who skirted away from the bridge while sidling the moat's drop off. In response, the creature planted its front paws on the edge, as if it intended to leap across.

"Go now!"

Byron's words acted like a physical shove to send Coura ahead, and his power pressured her from behind. The oversized body lowered closer to the ground, giving her the opportunity to slip along its stomach and slice at its underbelly in a single, wide motion. At the same time, her former mentor's fireballs slammed into its backside and created a cloud of smoke to fill the air with the smell of burning hair.

A wave of heat blew against her face, causing her to cough while squinting in order to avoid the creature as it tumbled forward. Because of the approaching night and gray smoke, she couldn't see much, though, and one of the hind legs rammed into her shoulder before she could get clear of the mess. As she stumbled to catch her balance, the ground underneath her right foot disappeared, sending her falling over the edge of the moat.

By some clever design, the surrounding structure had been built with a steep slope narrowing at the bottom into a dip. Coura's body slid along the wall instead of falling straight in the water, slowing her descent. She also dug her fingers into the earth with one hand while thrusting her sword into the dirt wall with the other. The blade sunk in enough to stop her from moving farther down. Meanwhile, a loud splash signaled that the creature already plummeted. When she could look, only its front paws stuck up before sinking. She thanked whoever possessed the creativity to build such an impressively wide defense before returning to her current dilemma.

She shifted her weight to glance upward, placing both mud-covered hands on the hilt in an attempt to steady herself. A second later, the blade dipped sharply from the movement, and the jerk caused her grip to slip. With a gasp, she resumed sliding against the wall before dropping into the water.

Terror took hold of Coura's mind when her body went under the surface and her legs stretched without being able to touch the bottom of the moat. There had never been a reason for her to learn how to swim in any pool greater than a pond given the location of Neston and the Magical Arts Academy. Her arms waved from side to side as the cloak's hood stuck over her head to shroud her vision. When she went above to inhale, she would find herself unable to remain there for long.

Someone will...help... I can't...

A pain sprang in the back of her head so sudden and unmistakable she was amazed it didn't render her unconscious. It flared once she reached the surface again, hurting enough to have her opening her mouth to scream. Instead, water flooded into her lungs, choking out the last of the air she inhaled. Her body began to stop moving and relax in response.

For a moment, she figured she had died until something wrapped around her torso and pulled her upward to the surface.

"Wake up," a man urged but didn't attempt to remove the hood or touch her head.

Clearshot's familiar voice revealed her rescuer, yet Coura felt too exhausted to reply. He spoke to her more in a firmer tone before she bothered to open her eyes. They waded over to the wall where he stabbed a knife into the dirt and held on to prevent them from sinking while keeping his other arm around her waist.

Her head throbbed, and she wished to breath fresh air. Clearshot tried to sooth her with reassuring words as they waited for help. Night fell over Dala to cool the area as well, making her tremble; she even felt her rescuer shaking. Underneath the problems, she wondered if he, or anybody else, recognized her.

Someone shouted to them from above before tossing a rope down.

"I'm going to tie you up tight," Clearshot explained while securing the end around her waist. "It'll be rough when they pull you from here."

He sounded satisfied when she clutched the line, then he tugged it twice with his free arm.

If Coura felt horrible before being dragged up the side of the moat, she underestimated the ease of her rescue. It didn't take long to be raised to safety, but the dirt coated her wet back and limbs in mud to weigh her down. She squeezed her eyes shut against the pain in her head threatening to throw her into unconsciousness.

As soon as she had been hauled onto the ground, a man removed the rope. Dozens of voices and noise filled the area, but she remained frozen on her hands and knees, both from physical and mental strain, until she started coughing up the water that found its way into her lungs. That alleviated most of the trouble in her chest, allowing her to chance a look around the busy space.

Six soldiers lined up behind Tio by the moat to tug on the rope used to haul her to safety until Clearshot's body flopped onto the grass. He remained sprawled out on his back to catch his breath after.

"Can we get some light over here?" a woman called from the group.

By that point, the scattered mages, soldiers who retreated into the base, and citizens figuring the danger had ended made their way across the damaged field with torches or lamps in hand all while murmuring. Coura stared at the ground when more people moved closer, ignoring them until someone gently touched her back.

"Where are you hurt?"

She glanced up to where a woman in a white tunic knelt at her side. *I can sense how spent her energy is. I shouldn't startle her, especially since she might sense the demonic power.*

"I'm fine," Coura began, projecting as much reassurance as she could muster. "You should go inside and rest."

"Don't hide your injuries. I can heal whatever that creature did to you."

After more encouragement, the mage seemed satisfied enough to leave her alone, though the woman promised to return with blankets and medicine to prevent her from catching a cold. The concern about remaining hidden returned then.

I should leave before anybody else decides to question me, she decided and pushed herself to her knees. The movement triggered another flare up in her head, blinding her momentarily. Coura squeezed her eyes shut, placed both hands over her ears, and hunched forward while repressing a groan.

Time passed, and she settled enough to open her eyes again. When she did, she found the clearing even more populated than before, showing the excitement from the evening wasn't going to die down soon.

"Listen up," Tio's gruff voice said above the others as he waved a torch in his hand to silence the crowd. "The creature plaguing our city is dead!"

His words were met with weary cheers and clapping.

"We can celebrate tomorrow when we're well rested," the general continued. "For the remainder of the night, all troops should check in with me at the base, then you're dismissed. Outer squad members, you're on guard duty in the city. Everyone else can report injuries, missing persons, and property damage to Assistant General Calin. It may be safe for now, but we can't count on that. I'm too worn to babysit, so stay out of the clearing and off the roads!"

Coura smiled at how the man handled his people in such a personal manner. *He's a character, there's no question about it. Even so, anybody who knows him can tell he truly cares about the citizens and soldiers in Dala.*

After Tio's announcement, the area started to empty, and the noise with it. She shifted into a sitting position and deflated when the effort made her dizzy enough to forget running away. The aching in her head left her unable to think about what to do next.

Calin and Tio met with person after person despite their obvious exhaustion as the crowd broke apart. She caught Marcus speaking to a pair of soldiers and Will, who she didn't entirely seem surprised to see accompanying those from Verona. Byron and Clearshot also chatted near the general. Her rescuer stood wrapped in a blanket and wore his characteristic grin. Their eyes moved in her direction before returning to each other again, causing Coura to shutter.

I don't care to find out what they're saying about me.

She winced at the idea of facing her former mentor and friends in her current condition and pulled her hood down a bit farther. The sopping cloak and clothes beneath remained heavier than normal and chilled her body, causing it to shake uncontrollably.

When she glanced up again a minute later, Byron and Clearshot began walking toward her. She considered rising when a woman's voice rang through the space like a bright bell.

"Paulina?"

Two figures emerged from one of the groups gathered nearby. Coura instantly recognized them as Marcy and Aimes and kicked herself for giving her identity away by reacting to the call. The pair appeared relived, though, and hurried to kneel in front of her.

"It *is* you!" Marcy exclaimed as she placed her hands on Coura's shoulders. "We searched everywhere in Dala. Once the demonic creature attacked, we assumed... You're soaking wet! Take off that cloak before you get sick."

Aimes put a hand on the woman's arm. "I don't think now's the time. Am I right, Paulina?"

At first, Marcy looked between them without comprehension before her eyebrows rose and she nodded. "I remember now."

Coura glanced past them to where Byron and Clearshot had paused their steps. Both of their expressions appeared perplexed, and they spoke to each other again without attempting to approach the trio. Aimes tugged on her arm to bring her attention back to the discussion.

"In that case, we should find a place to rest," the older man began. "Perhaps we can convince somebody to keep us in their home for the night. We can pretend one of the destroyed buildings had been ours, so we have nowhere to stay."

Coura's knees wobbled as the two lifted her to her feet. Their grip on her arms reminded her of the loose bandages underneath the cloak, which unraveled with each movement. While Marcy and Aimes looked around and whispered suggestions, she forced herself to face what she had been dreading for days.

I can't do this on my own. The effort necessary to simply exhaust this demonic creature before finishing it off required dozens of soldiers and mages. This has been the strongest of the four I've encountered. When I leave here, Marcy and Aimes will follow too. She eyed up the man and woman clinging to each of her arms. *They know nothing of who I was...or rather, who I am...yet they trust me to lead them to a better life in Verona. I don't understand why, but I want to do that. The only way I can protect them and absorb Soirée's power is to ask for help.*

Coura instructed her companions to wait while tugging her arms free. Marcy and Aimes watched as she moved across the clearing toward Byron and Clearshot while praying for the strength to reach them without losing her nerve.

An Overdue Reunion

The night was still young, yet Byron felt exhausted. He could only sense a dim pulse from deep within his center; that, plus a weariness thickening the air in the field. Fortunately, Tio and Calin chose to burden themselves with the responsibility of organizing the people and didn't request his assistance.

I haven't expended this much energy in months. I'm not completely depleted, but there's no reason for us to stay here much longer. He shared as much with Marcus and Clearshot when they came to him after the chaotic finish.

Many questions continued to keep his mind active; the most prominent related to the stranger who appeared to rescue one of the mages then help him drive the demonic creature into the moat. He refused to jump to conclusions or entertain suspicions until he spoke to them, and he had the feeling Clearshot thought the same. They discussed as much beforehand and moved to investigate.

"Paulina!"

A woman shouted the name before breaking away from the crowd with an older man to meet the stranger. The lack of proper lighting prevented Byron from seeing if he recognized them, but he hesitated to go over once the pair lifted the cloaked figure to their feet.

"I don't know anybody named Paulina. Do you?" Clearshot asked through chattering teeth.

Whatever prompted him to dive into the moat and save the stranger Byron didn't know. His friend had shrugged off the question, begged for a blanket, and remained by his side, not leaving even for a change of clothes.

"No."

"Do you think they're a soldier, maybe someone off duty?"

Byron shook his head as his original suspicion rose again. "They're trained and experienced, especially in front of a demonic creature. Although, I have a hunch…"

The stranger started walking toward the pair.

"I think we're about to get an answer," Clearshot mumbled.

I refuse to believe it's Coura unless I see her, he told himself against a sense of anxiousness. *There's a slim chance she would be in Dala to begin with since she would've had to travel straight from the western coast.*

Byron shoved aside the notion when the still-cloaked figure stopped in front of them and stared at the ground. The three of them remained silent, waiting for another to start the conversation. Then, he heard a weak yet familiar voice.

"I'm glad you're here."

He glanced at Clearshot and found his friend grinning with jittering teeth. The soldier raised an eyebrow and dipped his head to confirm the stranger's identity. That shut out any doubt, allowing Byron to pull his former student in for an overdue embrace, wet clothes and all. A second later, she put her hands on his back to return it.

She could have been killed, he recalled when he noticed her body trembling against his. *She almost drowned!*

He released her and opened his mouth to begin asking the questions floating in his mind before remembering the condition they were in. Instead, he peeked under her hood and met the glittering, blue eyes underneath.

It really is her. What a relief!

"I'm glad to see you too," he responded.

"We can catch up tomorrow. Right now, can you help us find rooms for the night?" Coura looked over her shoulder to the woman and older man waiting nearby.

Clearshot answered for him. "You and your friends can stay in one of the spare medical station rooms. Nobody will be needing them tonight thanks to you and Byron. Besides, I'm about to shake the skin off my bones if we stay out much longer."

Coura thanked him and gestured for the two others to join her. They trailed behind without a word as Clearshot led the trio inside.

Meanwhile, Byron went to Marcus and Will. He didn't mention Coura since he hoped to give her whatever privacy he could for the evening but encouraged the boys to rest. With his final concern taken care of, he entered the base and went to his quarters, trusting Clearshot to take care of himself. He collapsed onto his bed after peeling off the dirty clothes but woke during the early morning to a faint idea.

It took some effort to drag himself from the comfort of his blankets and get dressed, yet he did so in order to search for the nearest guard posted by the medical station located on the south side of the base. The man appeared ready for a break as he greeted Byron with the common salute.

"What can I do for you, sir?"

"Has anyone left these rooms since last night?"

"Not that I've seen. Should I keep watch for somebody in particular?"

After pondering the notion, he nodded. "Three guests are in here: two women and an older man. I'm afraid they'll try to depart from the base if they don't meet with me today. Alert me if they do, even if it means waking me."

"Yes, sir!"

The guard saluted him once more before he returned to his bed.

*

Byron's dreams were interrupted by a pounding on the door. Instinctively, he jumped to his feet, rushed to open it, and prepared for an issue when he found a guard on the opposite side. A moment later, he remembered his earlier request.

"Master Byron, you ordered me to wake you when the guests in the medical station moved out of their rooms."

"That's right. I'm assuming they're up now?"

The guard nodded. "I caught two of them exiting and mentioned how you wanted to speak with them. The woman asked for directions to the mess hall, then she requested new clothes for herself and the older man at her side. They didn't mention anything about a third companion. I led them to the dining area myself before coming to find you, though they promised to wait in the medical station until you arrive."

Byron thanked the soldier before closing the door. While he dressed, put on his boots, and combed his hair, he contemplated what to do next.

Our assignment consists of finding Coura and bringing her back to Verona with us while assisting the efforts in Dala, yet I can't help myself from doubting the intentions behind the council's decision. With Hendal's behavior and Aaron's note about Fester, it might be best to avoid returning for the time being. Perhaps Tio will have a better idea. Would he need us to stay and repair the city alongside his troops? I'd better talk to Coura first, especially since Marcus claims she left to do something about the demonic creatures. Could she have discovered a way to eliminate their source of power? If not, what are we supposed to do?

The base steadily came to life as the troops moved about after the eventful evening. Most rubbed their eyes and trudged away while others, like Byron, seemed wide awake with a purpose for the morning.

He made his way to the opposite side of the base and the rooms used for treatments, healing, and recovery. The doors of the unused spaces remained open, yet he peered inside just to be sure the area was empty. When he came upon the lone, closed one, he knocked, twisted the knob to crack it open, then gave his name to avoid startling those presumably awaiting him; however, he didn't receive a response and entered to find nobody inside. The trio had definitely used the room because of the unmade beds, discarded clothing on the floor, trays of half-eaten food on one bed, and wrinkled bandages on the side table.

"She wouldn't..."

The idea of Coura lying to him sparked his anger, leading him to march toward the mess hall to search for her at the busiest location. He heard his name from farther down the hall along the way and recognized the base's assistant general jogging over to meet him.

"What is it?" he asked as Calin slowed to walk at his side.

"The general wishes to speak with you in the garden."

"About what?"

The assistant general appeared weary, judging by the bags under his eyes, yet he chuckled. "It's about the visitors from last night, the people Clearshot brought into the base and you had a guard supervise."

Byron didn't question the request further. They passed through the double doors into the centermost space where the sun beat down on those outside and blinded him for a second. They spotted the burly man standing under the shade of a nearby tree and approached.

"I haven't got all day to spend sweating in the sun!" General Tio's worn voice barked.

Calin left them then. Once the two were alone, the man cleared his throat while looking Byron up and down. "I'm surprised you're in such reasonable shape after the work you performed last night. That magic of yours is amazing stuff."

Byron thanked him for the compliment while noting the general's exhaustion.

"I've been told your former student returned to Dala."

Before Byron could answer, Tio waved his stubby arm to dismiss an explanation.

"Clearshot found me this morning and shared everything. I ordered Calin to make sure a guard checked in on them, but it seems you had it taken care of. Well, as I'm sure you've already noticed, they left to head north about an hour ago."

"An hour ago!"

"Don't get yourself too worked up. From what Calin saw, the three snatched some food from the kitchen and weapons from the training ground before departing. It didn't appear as though they were trying to hide their intentions."

When the general finished, Byron knew the man waited for his reaction. *Why couldn't she be more patient? In order to chase after her, I would need to abandon Dala. Why is she avoiding me instead of talking here in the base?*

He gazed at the sky as a group of seabirds flew overhead. "What do you recommend I do?"

Tio chuckled at the question. "No one ever asks for *my* opinion!"

For some reason, the notion was hilarious. When the harsh laughter continued, Byron found himself joining in. Their noise faded soon after, then they savored the peacefulness of the empty courtyard for a minute.

"No matter how hard I try to solve the problems in front of me, there seem to be more lurking around the corner," Byron admitted. He stretched his arms upward and winced at the sore muscles.

"Perhaps you should focus on your own problems instead of everybody else's for a change."

The general gave him a sidelong glance, and he could only groan at the truthful statement.

"You asked me what I think you should do. My answer is to gather your group from Verona and head north to find Coura."

"But-"

"The creature from yesterday has been the worst of what we've encountered around here. The others we can handle. I'm also certain it meant to be in Dala at that exact moment, if you understand me."

"We can't be certain another like it won't show up," Byron protested.

Tio shook his head. His next words involved an unusual amount of emotion. "*I'm* sure of it. Besides, your mission from the king is to find her and return to organize and train the troops there. You're still involved in stopping the attacks, more directly than anyone else. Ever since those angels showed up in the Valley Beyond, I expected some details tracing deeper in Asteom. If I could, I would lead my soldiers on a hunt across the country, then I'd bombard the capital until these killings are solved. Regardless of my enthusiasm, my home is here. Who would keep this base in order? What other general is familiar enough with the citizens to lead them properly? We all desire to rush out and be heroes, but we have our own positions to manage and places to be. Mine is here with my troops. At the moment, yours is with Coura."

Byron contemplated the man's passionate encouragement. "What makes you so confident?"

"It's mainly because you're a part of more diverse assignments. For you to use your time to help solve minor problems sprouting all over is foolish thinking. You're only a single person, and not just any ordinary person either. Don't waste your unique abilities on issues others with less skill can fix. This base can withstand the demonic creatures and protect Dala and the southern towns, but none of us can face what you must in the capital. We don't possess your magic or brains. Frankly, it's insulting to you and demeaning for us if you stay."

Byron found himself speechless after Tio's praise, as well as the general's blunt honesty. When he felt composed, he expressed his gratitude with a sincere smile. To his amazement, the man's cheeks flushed.

"Don't thank me for rambling, just get out of my base," Tio raised his voice to yell. After, he crossed his arms and left for the doors while muttering about the heat.

Although amused by the general's behavior, Byron knew he needed to get going if they planned to catch up to the trio possessing a head start. *So, we're back to the original plan then. Coura's on foot with two others who probably won't maintain a steady pace. If they weren't hiding when they left and knew I needed to speak with them, I believe they expect us to follow. I suppose it's time to gather the other three.*

He visited Will and Marcus first and instructed them to be ready to leave the base as soon as possible. Both expressed their confusion until he mentioned they would be meeting Coura as she had been present during the previous evening's attack. After he moved on so they could prepare, he found Clearshot exiting a room, packed and dressed for the journey.

"You knew we'd be going after her?" Byron asked.

His friend winked. "Let's just say I had a better hunch after speaking with Calin earlier this morning."

They caught up as Byron readied himself, then they stopped in the mess hall for breakfast. When they stepped outside the base, Marcus and Will were waiting.

"Where have you been?" the assistant general demanded.

Byron watched the young men fidget with their bags and travel cloaks before ushering their group forward. *I can't believe I'm more relaxed about this than anyone else.*

To apologize for keeping the pair waiting, he handed them each a wrapped meat pie from breakfast. "We didn't see you in the mess hall, so I grabbed these just in case. Clearshot stuffed our bags with plenty of food to last for a couple days."

Marcus and Will vigorously dug into their meals as he halted to adjust his pack and glance behind once more at the enormous structure he had come to enjoy visiting.

***

The road turned out to be busy on and off throughout the morning while Coura, Marcy, and Aimes traveled farther from Dala. It took until noon for the trio to find a proper spot to settle in where they wouldn't be accidentally disturbed. A trail branched off the main path into a clearing wide enough for a dozen people to sit comfortably under the cover of the surrounding forest.

Coura thanked their luck and dropped down next to the firepit at its center with a sigh before removing her hood to cool her neck and head. She reached into her center of power, admired the energy restlessly stirring inside, and gestured to the remaining logs. Her magic successfully caught on to produce an adequate fire, and she felt grateful she could at least manage casting such a basic spell. Meanwhile, Aimes and Marcy remained on their feet to scout the area.

"How long are we planning on staying here?" the former inquired before lowering himself to sit cross-legged on the opposite side.

"I'd guess a few hours; at least until the people I told you about catch up."

When they had been placed in the medical station after the creature's defeat, she informed the pair of who Byron, Clearshot, Marcus, and Will were. They asked plenty of questions to keep her awake for a while, but eventually she opted for sleep by promising to speak more about it after they left Dala. At the moment, she regretted the agreement.

Marcy spun around from where she stood at the entrance. "Until they what? You *want* them to track us down?"

The woman's voice tightened with disapproval, and even Aimes cast Coura a doubtful look. Still, she held her ground.

"I tried leaving others out of my problems. Why do you think I didn't meet up with you in Dala? I realized how difficult it will be to

277

defeat the remaining demonic creatures when that one attacked the city. I can't do it by myself."

"But you have us!" Marcy blurted and extended her arms.

Fortunately, Aimes seemed to understand Coura's point and shook his head while knitting his brow. "She's right, Marcy. We were helpless when the city was in danger. The mages and soldiers keep the beast at bay."

"We were unprepared," the woman responded, yet her expression softened.

With a yawn, Coura lied on her back and closed her burning eyes. "I'm not saying I don't want you accompanying me. We're still going to Verona, but we can't challenge creatures like the one from last night without their help. You'll see why once you meet them."

That satisfied their concerns for the time being, allowing her to relax. The power she took in helped her sleep, though it brought upon the expected, nightmarish visions. Her body needed time to properly rest, even if there wouldn't be enough for a full recovery.

I'll accept what I can get, she thought while turning on her side, ignoring her companions' next conversation, and drifting off.

*

No dreams muddled Coura's mind while she slept; however, tense voices had her awake in an instant. With a start, she opened her eyes and winced at how drained her limbs continued to feel.

"That's enough. Lower your weapon."

"Not until he does!"

"Marcy, stop this."

She recognized each person, which calmed her nerves, and she sat up while covering a yawn. A glance at the trail showed Marcy blocking the way into the clearing with the bow and arrows they stole from the base. Aimes had stepped in front of her and put his hands up, as if to assure her they weren't in danger. Behind him, she saw Byron first, then Clearshot with his own bow drawn. Although she couldn't see Marcus or Will, she figured they kept to the rear.

"Marcy," she started in an annoyed tone. "I thought I told you they would be arriving soon."

The woman didn't answer.

Coura rubbed her eyes until she saw colorful spots before rising. At that, Marcy caved in and returned the arrow to its quiver along her back, prompting Clearshot to do the same.

"I wanted to make sure," the woman added as she strolled to the opposite side of the firepit with her chin held high.

Aimes behaved in quite the opposite way, leading Byron, Clearshot, Marcus, and Will over. He shook their hands and began praising them for their participation in Dala's fight against the demonic creature in an overly polite manner, which reminded Coura of the encounter that ruined his life in Clearwater. "

To think, our soldiers possess such extraordinary skills. Thank you for protecting the city and, more importantly, us!" A chuckle afterward eased the tension.

Byron offered a smile. "I appreciate your hospitality…"

"Aimes," Coura supplied. "The woman you first met is Marcy."

The master mage glanced between them in a calculating manner. "I must apologize for startling you. We've been inspecting any sites along the way and noticed fresh footprints leading here. Perhaps we should have called out before stumbling into yours."

Coura caught Aimes blush at the apology, and Marcy even smiled as a result of his sympathetic tone. *Byron's always been a people pleaser.*

"How about some lunch?" she offered while grabbing her bag, which had been filled in Dala's kitchen.

Byron turned his attention to her without any of the warmth from his apology. "We need to talk."

Coura selected a piece of fruit before handing the sack to Marcy, who removed her share and passed the beg around.

"It can wait, right?" Clearshot asked and patted Byron's shoulder.

To her relief, he and Will joined Marcy and Aimes by the fire and accepted the offered food. Byron and Marcus remained standing to observe her with unreadable expressions.

This is the first time we've seen each other in weeks. Byron should have noticed the blade I summoned against the creature last night as well. I suppose I should clear this up in front of everybody at one time.

"We can talk while we eat," she suggested and dropped to the ground again.

Marcus accepted it and sat, leaving Byron to do the same. They ate in silence, seemingly waiting for somebody to begin the questioning. When no one did, Coura decided it would benefit her not to prolong the torture.

"Well? What do you want to know first?"

The assistant general spoke right away. "Why did you leave Verona by yourself?"

She sensed distress in his voice, which she found understandable given how they ended their discussion on the bridge outside the palace.

"I guess the best place to start is before Aaron's coronation."

"That far back?"

She nodded, took a deep breath, and dove into the past.

***

Marcus knew it would be interesting to speak with Coura again, but talking with her raised an uncomfortable sensation in his gut. Her behavior seemed more reserved than usual, preventing him from connecting with her as they had ever since they became friends. Then, while she recalled her experience away from the capital, he found himself growing concerned.

I can't believe I didn't notice something was wrong after she disappeared that morning in the training ground. The ceremony and celebration were fine, which was why I couldn't understand her departure. I should have gone along, or at least mentioned it to Byron or Aaron sooner. What's worse, she traveled west and south to fight demonic creatures and collect their power for a demon. Even after Byron told us about her bond with it, I promised myself I wouldn't blame her for its manipulation. Now, it's not controlling her, but she's helping it?

His friend concluded her explanation, returning his mind to the present.

She looks exhausted. How much of a burden is this taking on her?

He prepared to ask until Clearshot cut him off.

280

"Let me get this straight. You ran off to kill creatures carrying energy from the demon you let inhabit your body just to take it for yourself. Does this mean it's getting the power returned too?"

"I don't know," Coura replied. "Right now, I can't sense a connection to her. That makes me believe she actually needs me in order to recover what we lost. What's more worrisome is the increase in the original amount. Soirée once told me demons possess living beings in order to steal their energy and add it to their own. Hers has been roaming the country doing just that, finding host after host to mutate and steal from."

"Why couldn't it collect the energy by itself then? Why send you?"

"Because it's busy meddling in the palace," Byron finished for her in a frighteningly calm manner.

Coura glanced at him before nodding in agreement. Marcus' eyes lowered to stare at the ground as he contemplated their situation, and a fog of despair fell over the group.

"I hate this," Clearshot muttered, then he raised his voice. "We're supposed to stop the demonic creatures from destroying Asteom by killing them, then you absorb their energy and return it to the demon?"

"No."

The single word cut through their gloomy mood, and the determination across her face supported her serious tone.

"At first, I left to protect people from the creatures because I'm the only one besides Soirée who can stop the energy from spreading. My magic is returning, and I'm grateful for that, but there isn't another way to prevent her power from ever finding new hosts and continuing to terrorize the country, except to end it at the source. I'm still bonded to Soirée; I think we should use that to our advantage."

"What do you mean?" Marcus found himself asking.

Coura stared up into the canopy before explaining. "I saw what those monsters can do, and what Soirée's done. Once I possess enough of her energy, then I'll kill her."

"You can't be serious," Clearshot snapped, causing her to glare at him.

"What better option do we have? Besides, you don't understand what she can do."

"Can a demon even die?" Will wondered out loud.

They ignored his comment.

"How can we trust it won't steal back all the power once you encounter it again?" Clearshot countered a moment later. "We have our own problems to worry about too. That demon, and possibly the rogue angels from outside Dala, are still involved with the murders in the palace, or at least know who's responsible."

"You haven't figured anything else out?" Coura asked, though she appeared more startled than upset. When no one responded, she rubbed at her eyes. "What were you doing this whole time?"

The firewood crackled in the resulting silence, sending glowing sparks into the air. Marcus wasn't sure what to say, so he watched Clearshot and Byron instead. The former frowned, yet seemed to have calmed down. On the other hand, the master mage appeared unaffected by their conversation and removed his waterskin for a drink.

"You're awfully quiet," Coura addressed Byron with an edge to her voice.

He sighed, replaced the waterskin, then stared at the flames once again before commenting. "I'm just wondering why you three would light a fire in the middle of a summer day. Let me guess, Coura struck it up as soon as you arrived. It's too hot out here as it is, and the smoke is easy to spot and smell. Seems like a foolish idea."

Marcus' mouth fell open a bit, then the corners twitched as he tried to hide a smile. *Has he been paying attention to our conversation at all?*

The older man named Aimes started to laugh. "That's an accurate assumption."

Marcus glanced at Coura, who narrowed her eyes at Byron.

"That doesn't matter. I can light a fire whenever I want to. Were you even listen-"

"It's unnecessary and was done thoughtlessly," the master mage interrupted without missing a step. "Your years at the academy should have taught you better than to throw spells around. My concerns stemming from you wandering the country alone have been justified in numerous ways, yet your inability to consider such simple concepts while traveling shows your lack of experience out in the field."

Marcus winced at the insults and instinctively prepared for his friend's predictable outburst.

"Maybe I have more important issues on my mind than setting up a temporary camp," she spat back while rising to her feet and turning away to hide her scarlet cheeks. "I didn't ask for you to follow me, and I didn't need to wait for you to catch up either. Instead of worrying about me, you should be concerned about how soon you're going senile!"

With that, she stormed into the woods behind them as everybody else watched. The woman, Marcy, stood and hesitated to go after Coura while muttering the name Paulina.

"Don't worry. She'll return when she cools off," Byron reassured her. His expression shifted into one of relief, and he wore a slight smile.

"Why did you do that?" Marcus decided to ask.

"Given what she's been through, and her normal temper, I was curious to see how she would react to my prodding."

Although he didn't completely understand, Marcus placed his faith in the master mage's intuition.

*

When Coura returned, she seemed to be in a better mood, so the group planned their next moves. They would travel from their location north of Dala straight to Verona during the afternoons and evenings in order to hunt the demonic creatures along the way. They were in no hurry yet understood they should avoid major cities or towns. Then, they all agreed to let Byron take the lead as he had grown adept at charting their location in the area.

While Marcy kept to Coura's side, Aimes felt open to talking, and Marcus instantly took a liking to him. The man got along well with Will right after mentioning their hometown of Clearwater, sounded polite any time he spoke, and cared for both his female companions. Clearshot stayed in the front by Byron for the start of their journey but slowed his steps to drop back to Coura's other side after the conversations died down.

"I couldn't help but note your interest in archery," he said to Marcy in his cheerful manner. "How much experience do you have?"

The woman appeared surprised at being addressed. "Not much. When we first met Paulina…I mean, Coura…I picked it up again."

"You haven't been trained?"

"I learned as a child and practiced on and off."

Even though Clearshot behaved sincerely, Marcus sensed Marcy's distrust. Still, the soldier wasn't one to give up on developing a friendly relationship. He removed his weapon and drew the bowstring half-heartedly.

"Do you mind if I show you a few pointers? You have a lot of potential."

Her eyes widened before she cast Coura an unsure gaze.

"He won't bite," his friend responded before slowing to walk on Will's right.

Marcus remained on the herbalist's other side, and they watched as Clearshot began his lesson. Over time, Marcy eased up and even giggled at his carefree attitude.

Byron led the group left at a fork in the road as the sun set behind a wall of gray clouds. Marcus became so preoccupied with the sky that he missed part of the discussion happening next to him. Will updated Coura on the palace, Aaron and Grace, and various events taking place in Verona before they had been assigned to Dala. The pair noticed his attention, and Coura leaned forward to look past Will.

"You barely said anything today, Marcus," she commented, as though they hadn't been apart.

"It looks like it's going to rain."

Although he didn't intend for it to be a joke, his friends laughed. It was a sound he appreciated, one that brought a smile to his face.

"*That's* all you can think to share?" Will chided with a tilt of his head.

"What do you want to know?"

"I thought you would come up with more to ask," Coura replied. "I visited several guard stations, met the Sie-Kie, and fought the demonic creatures. You've always been interested in stuff like that."

"I have a question," Will interrupted.

"What is it?"

"Why do Marcy and Aimes call you Paulina? I noticed it multiple times earlier this afternoon."

Coura rubbed the back of her neck in a bashful gesture while Marcy glanced around to answer.

"It's how she introduced herself to Aimes and me when we met."

"That makes sense. It's a pretty name."

"It was my mother's," Coura responded and averted her eyes.

The first raindrops began to fall then, halting their progress for the day, so Byron called everyone over to a nearby path stretching into another campsite. In order to stay dry, for the most part, their group slept huddled against the trees' trunks.

Too Far Gone

The showers continued for three days. Initially, they hoped to wait out the storm, but each time it cleared up for a few minutes, more would follow. In the end, their limited supplies forced them to push forward, though the weather brought a relief from the heat and filled their waterskins.

Marcus pulled back the hood of his cloak to let some of the rain wash away the sweat and grime on his face. He was the only person taking advantage of the opportunity.

"We should reach another campsite by nightfall," Byron shouted from the front.

"Nightfall?" Marcus muttered to himself with disappointment.

"Isn't there anywhere closer, or a town we can stay in to dry off for a while?" Aimes asked from the rear where he strolled next to Marcy.

"I'm afraid not," their leader answered before putting his head down and trudging ahead.

Nobody spoke until they reached their goal where they rested under the shelter of a suitable canopy. Marcus slumped against a tree trunk to catch his breath and noticed Coura kneel and attempt to cast a fire spell on a pile of wet logs in the designated firepit. Will joined her, used a knife to whittle down the less suitable parts, and hurried to scrounge for drier materials.

Eventually, long after it grew too dark for Marcus to see anything except Coura's magic, the pair managed to build their weak fire into one stable enough to last for a few hours. Will huddled close for warmth before Aimes and Marcy accompanied him. Byron snored where he had propped himself up when they arrived, and Marcus remained where he sat. Those by the fire conversed until they fell asleep, and soon he found himself nodding off.

"Get some rest," came a voice from above.

He glanced up to see Coura standing and leaning on the same tree trunk with her eyes on the flames.

"I don't think I can stay awake even if I tried," he admitted. With her permission, he released the tension in his muscles, relaxed his body, and drifted to sleep.

*

Marcus didn't expect to be roused so soon, or by a vicious snarling sound. His eyes flew open and scanned around before he pushed himself to his feet. Against the dying embers of the fire, a shadowy creature paced across the clearing. The rain had stopped, leaving the night unnaturally silent.

He grabbed his sword from next to where he slept and unsheathed it as he located the others, who already prepared for a fight. Clearshot waited on one side of the firepit with his bow drawn while Byron lingered on the opposite end, seemingly unarmed. Coura still stood next to the tree trunk on Marcus' left with her blade in hand, and Marcy raised her bow from where she positioned herself in front of Aimes and Will. The latter pair had backed farther into the partial cover of the brush, though Marcus noticed his friend gripping his sword using both hands while remaining between the older man and the creature. After approving of the herbalist's bravery, he returned his attention to the beast.

There was no mistaking it as a normal animal. In the remaining, reddish glow, he could study how it crept on all-fours at eye level with him. "What should we do?" he chose to ask just loudly enough for everybody to hear.

"Coura?" Byron offered next.

It took her a moment to answer. "If it's like the others, its sight, smell, and hearing will be sensitive. The claws and teeth probably contain venom, so avoid them. Also, it shouldn't be able to follow each of our individual movements if we split up to surround it. I can act as a distraction."

"How do you plan to do that?"

Even as Byron spoke, the creature's head swung toward her and tilted from side to side, as if it became intrigued with her specifically. Marcus stepped forward and prepared to slip behind Clearshot when the master mage held out a hand for everyone to pause.

"I have an idea. We'll take advantage of its strong senses to provide an opening. Move to surround it and strike when I give the signal."

Step by agonizing step, Marcus remained a generous arm's length away from Clearshot, who reached the far end of the site closest to the creature. All the while, its attention stayed on Coura as she raised her sword and proceeded to meet it head on.

When Marcus nearly moved into place, Byron released a fire spell that flashed in the darkness and made him jump. Both the master mage's hands extended to either side of the beast, aiming to scorch the wet grass around it. A black cloud rose, and when the creature backed away with a growl and rubbed its nose, they understood what he did.

He's abusing its heightened sense of smell by creating smoke. What can we do about its sight? Even as he thought of it, Marcus heard the familiar whirl of an arrow to his right.

While the beast retreated from Byron's spell, Clearshot launched arrow after arrow into and around its left eye. The beast howled in pain and reeled to face the source.

My turn!

Marcus stood far enough away from his comrade not to be in their target's line of sight, so he charged. Coura shared his mindset and adjusted to attack its backside, slashing off the bushy tail in a single swing. At the same time, he stabbed its side.

The creature was swifter than he expected, though. It spun to snap at his friend then at him with its canine-like snout. Between Marcus, Coura, and Clearshot, and without one eye or its clear sense of smell, the beast could only focus on so much. Their coordinated strikes injured it repeatedly until it attempted to escape twice.

Byron's precise magic prevented it from going too far; however, Marcus began to tire of the routine and figured the creature would too.

"What should we do now?" he called to the others when the violet eye rested on him.

"We need to end this," Clearshot responded before launching another projectile into its damaged eye. "That was my last arrow."

Marcy's wavering yet hopeful voice close behind startled him. "I have a full quiver!"

"Stay where you are," Byron ordered. "It's too risky to be near it when it's wounded."

"We should attack at once," Marcus suggested while tightening the hold on his weapon's hilt.

Coura shared her agreement and again offered to be the distraction. Before anybody could accept or deny the plan, she lunged to drive her blade into the creature's shoulder as it snarled at Marcus. There came a yelp, and it whirled around to snap at her, but she fended off the strikes with wide swipes of her sword. As he thought, their target grew weary of their strategy.

Without Clearshot to act as the third means of distracting the beast, it towered to its full height and used the advantage to lunge at Coura, pressuring her into backtracking despite Marcus' deep slices to its back half. He figured it planned to focus on a single person instead of switching when it refused to turn away from its current prey.

Size won out as the creature pounced to knock his friend to the ground and stand over her until Byron intervened. A blast of lightning connected with its shoulder, sending it stumbling sideways, yet it hadn't become weak enough to fall over. The snapping jaws went for Coura when no one made a follow-up attack.

Marcus hurried ahead and saw how she kept one hand on the hilt of her sword and the other on the blade in order to position it horizontally and shove the metal against the beast's mouth, preventing it from biting her exposed torso. Blood and saliva dripped onto her body as she fought for her life.

Despite the danger she faced, he knew this was the opportunity they needed. The creature's left eye had been mangled by arrows, allowing him to sneak up and bring his sword down on its neck with all his strength. To his surprise, the sensation didn't feel any different from slicing through a normal animal's flesh. The edge cut into fur then skin and tissue with a nauseating squish until his swing stopped to settle about halfway through the creature's throat. Without considering its current fate, he yanked his weapon free, raised it once more, and cut down to finish decapitating the beast.

Marcus hunched over his kill to observe the remains, panting and sweating as the exhilaration wore off. Then, he remembered Coura lied beneath the body. She let out a disgusted groan and stared at the head twitching on her lap before shoving it away. Although it grew darker than before, blood pooled into the grass, reflecting what light remained from the embers. He offered a hand to Coura after, which she accepted.

"Not bad for your first demonic creature," she said and elbowed him in the side once he pulled her to her feet. The cloak she wore became soaked with blood and organs from the head, but she ignored her appearance entirely.

They waited while the rest of their group joined them.

"Is it…" Will started but didn't finish the question.

Byron eased their concerns after a brief inspection. "Unless it can return from that, I doubt we need to worry about it anymore."

"Are we going to remain here tonight?" Marcy asked next with eyes glued to the creature.

"It might be best to gather our belongings and distance ourselves from this mess. We should be safe once we reach the road, especially because the rain has ended." Byron created a flame in his hand to help them to see better and returned to the firepit.

As everyone shuffled along behind him, Marcus noticed Coura linger to stare at the lifeless body and wondered if she had been harmed by the encounter. "You're not hurt, are you?"

"No, I'm fine," she answered in an odd, hollow voice.

He wasn't entirely convinced but hurried to clean his sword on the grass, return it to its sheath, and walk over to where his pack rested by the trunk he'd slept against.

"Coura, come on," Clearshot called after, prompting Marcus to look over at where she still stood beside the creature.

She turned, took a couple steps, then stopped. He knew something was wrong, yet he remained too far away to do much. Her stance wavered before her body dropped to the ground with a light thud.

Byron sprinted over and knelt beside Coura before anybody else could comprehend what happened. Marcus shouldered his bag and joined the others steadily surrounding their companion.

"There's too much blood to tell where she's injured," the master mage explained while wiping his forehead.

"We need to find water," Will interjected. Already he had removed bandages and various vials from his belongings. "If she is hurt, even a scratch, there's a chance the venom she mentioned is in her body."

"I'll see what I can find. Marcus, come with me," Clearshot ordered before requesting Byron's magic to create a makeshift torch and charging into the woods to their left.

Marcus hesitated when he noticed Marcy and Aimes hanging farther back. Their expressions and posture didn't mirror everyone else's concern, which he found odd given their dependent behavior. When he considered their past experiences, a possible reason came to mind.

"Has this happened before?" he asked the pair.

Marcy chewed on her bottom lip as Aimes nodded. "Only once before," he shared. "After we met her, she killed a different creature and fainted for four days, though she had an injury with its venom on her arm too."

"Four days?"

"That's right. Marcy and I brought her to the nearest town for treatment; however, she didn't wake after the wound had been cleaned and mended."

Marcus contemplated what they revealed against his rising nerves. He glanced to where Byron and Will still knelt and met the latter's eyes, which appeared as unsure and confused as he felt.

After a minute, the master mage spoke in a controlled tone. "If this happened before, I believe it's connected to the demon's energy. Perhaps her center of power must adjust to the additions she takes in. Even now I can sense it, albeit faintly. With that being said, we shouldn't stay around here as long as the creature's remains are too. Once Clearshot returns, I'll clean up the blood and search for venom just in case."

"I should come too," Will offered.

Marcy stepped forward and demanded to go along as well.

"Fine," Byron snapped. "Marcus, Aimes, be ready to leave once we return."

Clearshot burst through the bushes nearby a minute later and described the location of a nearby pond. Marcus helped place Coura on Byron's back before the designated trio moved out behind their guide. When they were gone, he started pacing.

"I'd like to follow them," Aimes startled him by mentioning.

"We should wait for everyone else to return," Marcus commented half-heartedly. A glance around the camp showed only Coura and Byron's packs as the rest of their group grabbed theirs earlier.

Aimes shook his head, gripped the straps of his bag tighter, and apologized before turning around. Then, he hurried toward the bushes the others disappeared through and shuffled beyond the brush despite Marcus' warning.

He just left…

Marcus gaped at the older man's decision until his mind recovered. The pacing continued until he had enough.

"We're heading to the road anyway," he muttered to verbalize his annoyance. "Why should they need to return for me? Besides, what if Aimes gets lost? I guess I'm responsible for him too."

He rushed over to collect any remaining items, which proved to be just the two packs, and carefully maneuvered into and through the forest area. Fortunately, his companions created more noise, leading him in the right direction. He spotted Aimes ahead and caught up without frightening the older man. Together, they emerged into a less than ideal situation.

Byron must have had the idea to light a fire, so the flames brightened the area against the night's darkness. Marcus held back a branch for Aimes to scramble past and heard the master mage's raised voice yelling curses. His eyes went straight to Coura, who had been laid next to the aforementioned pond. Someone removed the filthy cloak, revealing bruises along her arms, and her face winced slightly to reflect her internal distress. He noted a pile of unwrapped bandages at her side and figured the situation must be a result of the venom.

"What's going on?" he demanded when nobody bothered to explain.

Will and Marcy ignored the question to watch Byron instead while the master mage stopped swearing and leaned against a tree trunk away from them. Clearshot covered his mouth with a hand, as if in thought, while scanning the woods in the opposite direction.

Aimes approached Marcy and took her hands in his, drawing her attention. "What has everyone so worked up?"

The woman glanced down at Coura, then she returned her gaze to him and answered at a quieter volume. "Do you remember those markings she always wrapped up? The mage claims they're appearing because she's been killing the demonic creatures. It's hurting her and damaging her source of magical energy. I don't quite understand it myself."

Despite his suspicion regarding the pair, in that moment, Marcus could sense how much they cared for his friend. Aimes left Marcy to kneel beside Coura and dip his head in a prayerful posture. Will watched them too from where he sat hugging his legs.

"Is what she said true?" Marcus asked while addressing the three others from his original party. When no one replied, he ground his teeth and repeated the question. "Is Coura going to be okay?"

"We don't know," Clearshot snapped.

He looked at Will. "Isn't there anything you can do? Can't you at least wake her up?"

"My medicinal treatments don't work like that," Will answered with a defeated shake of his head. "Physically, there are no injuries. It's rooted in magical energy. Someone who is familiar with the concept might know what to do."

The response didn't satisfy him, and a hot anger burned in his chest at the notion that none of them could help. He prepared to interrogate Byron for more information next; however, as he faced the master mage fuming off in the distance, the swelling emotions ceased altogether.

I don't think I've ever seen him like this, Marcus realized. After a moment of consideration, he confirmed the thought. *No, Byron doesn't get mad about much. This just makes me worried about how severe the problem really is.*

***

The bells in Verona chimed five times behind Emilea to signal the beginning of the evening while she passed through the palace's front gates. The guard nodded to her, which he'd done all week, and she offered a polite smile before holding herself to a steady walk through the hall and up the grand staircase. It was time for another meal in the private dining hall, and she'd be late.

Why do I put myself through this? she wondered with a shred of guilt. Her footsteps echoed down the corridor to emphasize its emptiness.

Nothing changed much with her husband and Byron away, at least not until eleven days ago.

Nearly two weeks earlier, she felt a surge of dark energy unlike anything she picked up before except when she brought herself face to face with the demon in Dala. Remembering the horrific experience still sent a shiver down her spine, but she brushed it off, raised her head higher, and entered the dining area.

As usual, no one paid her any attention while she accepted her seat beside the high priest. The chair on her other side remained empty, as it had been ever since Grace returned to Yeluthia.

Too many concerns, she thought, prompting a deep sorrow at the reminder of the severed alliance. *There's so much on my mind, I can barely stand to keep up appearances.*

Fortunately, Hendal started a conversation to distract from the depression. "Lady Emilea, how fare your students?"

She returned his smile with a pleasant one of her own. "They are well, I suppose. Although…"

Hendal studied her while she contemplated her suspicions regarding the haunting presence lingering in the palace. Of course, they discussed the subject a handful of instances already. After the initial experience, which anybody possessing magical capabilities could sense, an unspoken fear rose within the palace, especially at night. He heard about it as well, yet neither could think of a way to identify the source.

That conversation took place a week ago. When it became apparent the power wasn't going away on its own, Emilea moved herself and her children into Lady Katrina's home in the city. The woman waved her worries aside, claiming to not understand topics relating to magic, and acted eager to host guests nonetheless.

I don't believe she will ever comprehend what her generosity means to me and the children.

As if he read her mind, the high priest laid a hand on top of hers in a supportive gesture. "How are Mace and Lexie doing?"

"They're much better being around other people," she answered before sighing at the memory of her magic-sensitive children's initial fright. At least *she* recognized demonic energy; Mace, who began to practice dark magic spellcasting, went cold and paled, and Lexie had burst into tears in her arms. Emilea's son didn't speak a word after that until they were in Verona.

"I'm afraid I'm no closer to finding a reason for this," Hendal admitted as he removed his hand. "I just don't know what to do."

"Has King Aaron noticed the issue as well?" Emilea dared to ask and allowed her eyes to slide over toward the motionless figure on the opposite side of the high priest.

"Yes, of course. Our vigilant king is always watching for clues."

Something seemed off about Aaron, that she became certain of. She noticed it during her first dinner in the private hall after moving into the city. He didn't greet her when she approached and gave brief responses when she struck up a conversation. Hendal dismissed his behavior, though, claiming the king had been weary and restless due to their accruing issues.

For three days, she tried breaking through to Aaron, even going so far as to mention Coura with the hope of sparking some emotion from him; however, no personality radiated from the young man sitting nearby. His vacant eyes stared off into the distance, and his lips pressed into a thin line.

Emilea decided it wasn't worth the effort to push for more on the topic. She ate as much as she could against the knot in her stomach and shifted the rest of her food around with her fork. All the while, the high priest continued chatting about this and that. She cared little for the gossip of the palace or Verona, yet one item he listed perked her attention.

"I can't believe the fall season is almost upon us," he commented at first. "It will be an interesting time of the year indeed, especially with General Tont's information, but Asteom has more of a reason to celebrate now than ever. Why, if we start to-"

"What did you say?" Emilea interrupted despite her normally well-mannered behavior.

Hendal paused mid-sentence before working his mouth to backtrack his words. "I-I'm hopeful for the upcoming season is all," he managed.

"You mentioned General Tont has information. What is it about?"

The high priest rubbed his arm in a nervous manner, an action Emilea found odd.

"Haven't you heard? The general sent one of his assistants north to speak with the Nim-Valan army."

"Nim-Vala! What did they report?"

Although she didn't often dabble in the generals' business, many people were aware that the northern country had lined the border they shared with Asteom several months ago. The unexpected movement from hundreds of troops troubled some citizens while others wondered if the reason related to preparation for an attack or extra defense.

"They wish to negotiate with His Highness about an alliance."

When he stopped, Emilea raised an eyebrow. *Why is he being coy?*

"Isn't this positive news?" she pushed.

Hendal frowned but gave no other indication of his discomfort. "At the start of the upcoming winter season before the weather changes, they requested to send one of their generals and two hundred soldiers."

Again, Emilea's eyes scanned over Aaron. "Why hasn't he called a council meeting? This involves more than General Tont and the man's assistant."

"There are worse concerns plaguing us all."

She found his bitter tone displeasing and dropped the subject. The servants brought dessert after, and a trio of singers performed their series of pieces. On an ordinary day, she enjoyed the entertainment and dancing, but that night, the mood grew heavy around her.

Hendal rose once the music began and left with Aaron trailing close behind.

*

The following morning, Emilea took it upon herself to speak with General Tont. She roamed the palace in search of the man while making a point to monitor her fellow mages. Before Byron departed for Dala, each of the master mages designated several of their subordinates to act as leaders and instructors. By dividing the workload, they could free up time without diminishing the quality of their pupils.

Many of her former students were practicing in the training ground and greeted her, along with some dark mages and soldiers; one of the latter she knew reported directly to the general.

"Excuse me," she began while reaching out before he could return to his sparring session. "I'm looking for General Tont. Can you tell me where to find him?"

At first, the soldier appeared startled by her familiarity with him, then his face scrunched as he considered the request. "He mentioned something about a meeting involving King Aaron. He seemed to be in a real hurry, so he didn't mention any details."

"That's all I need," she reassured him. After expressing her thanks, she entered the palace and realized how pleasant it felt being outside compared to staying within the stone walls.

How strange, she thought as she strolled alone and once again sensed the lingering, unnatural energy. *Could there be some sort of object or spell causing such a presence to remain here?*

General Tont had always been a busy person constantly on the move, a characteristic she understood from a dedicated leader. Because of this, she rushed to catch him before he left the meeting chamber, but ironically, she ran right into him while rounding a corner on the second floor.

"General! Forgive me for being so careless."

Emilea flushed a bit with embarrassment until she glanced into his face, then the blood drain from hers when she recognized the expression he wore appeared identical to Aaron's. His cheeks hollowed and bags drooped under his eyes, as if a shadow crept over his body. Although his hair and beard remained trimmed and combed, the lack of emotion gave her the impression he wasn't concerned about much. She didn't recall the regular color of his eyes, but his pupils dilated enough to make them look devoid of life.

As she stood analyzing him and wondering what to do, the general continued walking, as though nothing had happened.

What's going on? He's not himself... The meeting chamber. I must find His Highness!

Emilea jogged the remainder of the way to the center of the floor, and a gripping panic closed in when the unnerving power grew stronger. After approaching the unguarded door to their council room, she sent up a prayer and entered.

As soon as the door opened, she saw how lamps along the wall and candles on the table lit the space. She expected to see Aaron inside with a couple guards at least. Two, familiar voices conversed, but they fell silent once she appeared. The air became practically unbreathable because of the energy weighing down her body. Still, she walked into the chamber.

Her eyes went to the king on his throne and the high priest standing at his side. Six noblemen she recognized from previous meetings and social events sat around the table.

Hendal stepped off the raised section and took a couple steps toward her. "Emilea? Is something the matter?"

It's either now or never.

"Tell me what's going on here," she demanded while swallowing her rising fear.

At first, he recoiled at her harsh tone, and the pause provided an opportunity to analyze the others in the room. Somehow, she wasn't surprised by their shared, blank expressions.

They're behaving like Tont and Aaron. Only Hendal isn't affected...

A change came over the high priest then, as if he understood she made that connection. "Please join us, Master Emilea," he offered with a gesture for her to move toward the throne.

Her instincts screamed at her to turn and flee, to sprint outside, inhale the cleaner air, and find help. For whatever reason, she decided against it. No one else attempted to act while she proceeded to stand in front of the man.

"What drove you to interrupt our merchant meeting?" Hendal asked nonchalantly.

"I found General Tont and tried asking him about the news from Nim-Vala. He didn't even acknowledge me."

"As I mentioned last night, such business is not your concern," he responded with a hint of irritation.

Emilea ignored it. "Something happened to him, and to King Aaron. They share an unresponsive expression and refuse to speak or react, even when I reach out to them. Worst of all, I seem to find *you* right in the middle."

This time, he appeared taken back. "How could you say that?"

While he fumbled for his next words, she noticed how he seemed offended by the accusation rather than shocked. The high priest composed himself by clasping his hands behind his back, releasing a sigh, and shaking his head.

"Oh, Emilea," he began and flashed a sympathetic smile. "I shouldn't be upset. After so much trouble, I know your mind is full of worry. Your husband left to accompany Master Byron on an assignment, forcing you to manage both your children and the rest of the mages. We have monstrous beasts roaming the country, threatening the people's livelihoods alongside a demon and rogue angels. You've been alone since the Yeluthian ambassador went missing, and now I added an extra burden by revealing the news about Nim-Vala. It's been a lot for us both to handle, don't you think?"

He paused to wait for her response; however, Emilea barely heard his question. She became too appalled by his previous comment to answer and instead narrowed her eyes into a glare.

"What do you mean Grace went missing? We were told she returned to Yeluthia."

Hendal's expression faltered. His eyes widened as she continued.

"If I remember correctly, *you* insisted she must have been too homesick to remain in Asteom and respecting her decision was the best option. If that's the case, why did you say she went missing?"

The high priest's mouth opened and closed several times before he cleared his throat and began babbling a response. Although Emilea felt disgusted with herself, a sick satisfaction came over her as he tried to rescue his reputation.

"Well, I didn't mean missing in the way you interpret the word. It's been so long since our discussion that my tongue slipped. I'm sure the ambassador will return soon from Yeluthia or send a letter explaining the situation."

"You're lying." Her response projected at a volume just above a whisper due to her rising anger and repressed fear.

In the resulting, uncomfortable silence, Emilea became aware she stood alone in an enclosed room with seven men under Hendal's influence. She took an involuntary step backward toward the door, but something cold pressed against the side of her throat, stopping her dead in her tracks. When she strained her eyes to study the object, a glint from the lamplight revealed it as a metal blade.

The bearer noticed her attention and pushed the sharp weapon harder into her skin, sending a trickle of blood down her neck. It tickled, yet she could barely feel the sensation. Her whole body grew numb from the source of the unnatural energy standing behind her.

I'm trapped! A gasp escaped her upon realizing this.

Hendal's movement drew her focus forward once again. He stalked toward her like an arrogant wolf who cornered a rabbit with a greedy hunger in his eyes. That man was no longer the high priest she had known for years.

"You're clever," he started once he moved in front of her. He then raised a hand and placed it gently against her cheek in a patronizing gesture. "It's such a shame you found out like this."

Emilea strained her patience to remain as calm as possible. Her voice didn't waver, yet she couldn't help her knees from wobbling. "What have you been doing?"

The hidden figure behind her caught his attention for a moment before he knit his brow and spun to sweep an arm at the throne.

"Look at the young man there," Hendal yelled with a ferocity that startled her. "Asteom's lineage stems from a rein of kings who add their own, personal touch to our history. I've done my research. Kings and queens rely on alliances to stop countries from interfering with their visions. Some aimed to expand by claiming the wild lands, others to create art and traditions worth celebrating later, and still more build defenses to protect the borders In all that time, nobody ventured to learn more about the processes their own people are involved in. Not one ruler of Asteom truly wished to change the country! I say, why follow a leader who ignores the wants…no, the *needs* of its citizens?"

He turned around again, yet his gaze stayed over Emilea's shoulder. "I shall act as the representative of the people, an ambassador for the rest of the magic-less world. The angels and demons will have reason to join with us humans once we prove ourselves equal without abusing their power. Before the founding of this kingdom, dark and light mages had been born above us normal individuals. Imagine how terrifying Asteom will be in the future."

Emilea could only stare and gape without comprehension at Hendal's ravings before blurting the first protest that came to mind. "Humans, angels, and demons are separate beings from one another. You claim to know Asteom's history, yet you are blind to why we can't be joined together. Living beings think and behave in the manner best benefiting their evolution. Not every human wants what you desire. Don't claim to be the voice of a people when you rely on assuming what lives they should or shouldn't lead."

Her rebuttal struck him like a physical blow. He winced, glanced away, and flinched at the final words. After, he glared at her, first with frustration then disgust until some idea twisted in his mind to draw him closer once more. Emilea remained too afraid of the blade pressed against her throat to move.

"Your abilities separate you from those of us without magical gifts," he continued in a soft voice yet with the same, venomous tone. "You could never understand our weakness in the face of true power. Once we unite to overcome such adversity, the future will be brighter."

Before she could even consider a response to the madness, a female voice cut in.

"How shall I dispose of her?"

Emilea knew the demon stood behind her because of the hostile energy, but hearing its voice still startled her enough to flinch. She couldn't raise a finger without being killed, which Hendal was aware of as he contemplated her fate for an agonizing amount of time.

"I'll give you a choice," he offered. "Those in this room are kept under my spell of obedience. Although you would be a valuable asset, if you're catching on to their inability to act as they once did, soon others will too. I'd hate to explain myself to people of lesser importance if you behave differently too, so you can choose to serve me or leave Asteom. Which will it be?"

Emilea couldn't stop a tear from sliding down her face as she considered the offer. No matter what she decided, she would lose her freedom, and the high priest, demon, and those under his control would watch. Another tear escaped when she thought of Clearshot, Mace, and Lexie. Against her nightmare, though, the value of their lives brought her strength.

I can't do this. I can't stop them by myself. The palace is being compromised one figure at a time, and I suppose it's my turn. The situation is out of my hands for now.

"I can't agree to serve you, but I know when I'm beat," she responded without any shortage of dignity. "Please, have mercy and allow me to take my children home. I promise to stay there and not interfere with your plans. Put me under the eyes of your guards or strip away anything I possess, and I promise not to take action. I won't leave my children motherless; your options would do just that."

A chilling silence filled the chamber while Emilea closed her eyes and prayed for her request to be honored. She couldn't bear to look at the man who held her life in his hands.

"Fine," she heard him answer at last. "I won't force you to choose between the fates I designed. Besides, I might find use of you here soon; however, they are more merciful than what will happen if you disobey. You will return to your home in the woods with your children. My companion will make sure you don't go against what I so generously permit. I believe a fitting punishment for any disobedience will be the lives of your children, which I can tell you view as worth more than your own."

The thought of losing Mace or Lexie became too much to handle. With a bow of her head, Emilea accepted Hendal's terms and admitted defeat.

Making Amends

A severe pounding in Coura's head woke her from the unexpected sleep. She wondered what happened before squeezing her eyes shut as sunlight poured onto her. Next, she moved her fingers and toes, then her arms and legs. Everything hurt but nothing more so than the tender skin on her stomach and chest. At first, she attempted to remember if a spell had burned her since the sensation felt familiar, yet she couldn't recall any recent event where she had been near magic.

What was I doing? Where am I? Where's... That's right. Marcy and Aimes traveled with me, then Byron, Clearshot, Marcus, and Will. A demonic creature showed up, and we fought-

Another sharp jab interrupted her thoughts. It continued as she steadily outlined the encounter with the wolf-like beast in her head.

I must have lost consciousness after Marcus killed it, she concluded and opened her eyes to watch the darkening sky. *That would explain why my body feels so terrible. Where are we now?*

It took time, but eventually she longed to stand and stretch her stiff muscles. After pushing herself into a sitting position, and nearly blacking out again from the throbbing headache, she noticed a stream across the grassy opening.

"Hello?" she called despite the soreness of her throat. "Is anybody here?"

The sounds of the wildlife around her remained the only noise. Above, the sky shaded with the vibrant colors of the sunset visible behind the tree tops.

Until the group returned, Coura figured she could utilize the fresh water. She stripped off most of her clothing then slid into the water while attempting not to hesitate and prolong the initial chill. It wasn't deep at the edge, and the brisk temperature shocked her weary body. By the time she dressed and dried, she felt wide awake with only minor pain in her head and limbs. The burning on her stomach and chest left as well, though she noted new markings there as a result of taking in the demonic creature's energy. The ominous realization had her shivering in the approaching night.

She waited until it grew dark to begin exploring for signs of her missing companions. When she couldn't find any, her irritation rose. *We defeated the creature and were preparing to move on. Did they actually abandon me when I fell unconscious?*

With nothing else to do, she focused on creating her own light and heat source. A reach into her center would trigger a fire spell, which she prepared for by extending her arm with the palm facing upward; however, what she found shocked her enough to jump.

The same level of power she and Soirée shared in the past had returned. Another venture into the pool of energy proved it wasn't a trick or illusion. The amount equaled what she possessed when she encountered the rogue angels in the Valley Beyond, except it remained wildly active, like a buzzing beehive.

She couldn't deny her growing excitement, as this meant the end of her journey to hunt the demonic creatures as well, so she closed her eyes and extended her hand again. From the tendrils of energy whipping around inside, she seized enough to sustain a controlled flame and drew upon it. A heat radiated against her fingers, so she opened her eyes to see a ball of fire balanced in her palm.

My magic is back to normal, she thought with a smile while releasing a content sigh.

A second later, her control slipped. The steady flow of energy fluctuated into an unexpected burst and shot through the established exit in her palm. The blow to her center was minimal, yet it resulted in the flames increasing in size and losing their shape. Coura yelped as they engulfed her hand for a moment until she cut off the spell. Her arm burned from the elbow down where the fire singed her skin. In an attempt to ease the pain, she hurried to the pond and plunged it in with a hiss. The healing already progressed to send soothing relief to the inflicted area, and she removed her arm once she no longer felt that power.

As she stared at her trembling hand and tried to dismiss the welling fear, she questioned what just happened. Never before had she struggled to balance the flow from her center, and the notion reminded her of how she always had Soirée to monitor her progress, whether she was aware of the demon's presence or not.

Could this be what she meant when she said her energy would increase with the creatures it possesses? Will I be able to control my dark magic without her?

A shuffle in the bushes off to her left snuffed out the concern for the time being, and Byron's deeper voice filled the entire space above the nightlife.

"Glad you're awake."

Coura caught his silhouette walking farther from the trees and stood to meet him. "Where's everyone else?"

Although she couldn't see the gesture, she figured his next movement was to point a thumb behind at the brush. His tone sounded unpleasant when he answered.

"We set up camp in another location. While you were resting, we managed to cover some ground. The main road brought us just outside Sindaly, but we didn't want to carry you into town because of the malicious energy surrounding you."

"So, you decided to leave me here alone?" she asked next without hiding her disbelief.

"Like I said, the demonic presence scared off most living creatures," he retorted. "In order for us to hunt and travel in the populated places, we needed to keep you somewhere secluded and safe. Don't worry; we took turns monitoring you."

Coura couldn't think of anything else to comment on. She sensed Byron growing upset with her and arguing would escalate their negative emotions. Instead of continuing the questioning or defending herself, she chose to accept the blame for their problems.

"I suppose we should join the rest," she concluded before moving to pass into the bushes he emerged from.

He reached out to seize her wrist and held her at his side. "We are not done yet," he added forcefully enough to startle her before raising her arm upward.

The action confused her for a second, then she noticed the exposed patterns against her skin. Until that moment, she forgot about the missing bandages that hid the abnormal markings.

"How do you explain what you've been doing?" he shouted at her. "How can you *possibly* justify your actions?"

She yanked her arm free and rubbed the spot he grabbed. "I already told you what I planned to do. I needed to find the creatures-"

"You're only human, Coura! Don't you realize how meddling with demonic energy is harming you?"

Her patience thinned as Byron's booming voice caused her head to throb again, and she matched his volume to reflect her own exasperation. "What do you know about it? Soirée spoke to me. I've seen what those creatures can do. Without me, the power would have continued to grow and spread!"

"You never had to do this by yourself. You never had to throw your life away."

His statement rang in her mind, emphasized by the amount of distress he projected. By that point, they were fully yelling at each other.

"I'm sure with time and extra assistance we could have done enough to stop the demonic creatures and seal or eradicate their energy," he continued. "We had respectable lives in Verona. Your friends were there. Marcus helped train you to become a permanent soldier. You had such a bright future ahead of you! If you would just stop acting without thinking about the repercussions and taking these problems on alone..."

"That's not the kind of life I want."

Byron's face dropped at what she admitted.

I've been trying to fill a role that isn't meant for me and pretending I'm not involved in Soirée's mischief.

Coura composed herself and brushed a hand along her left side. "I never completely healed after the injury in the Valley Beyond. Throughout my entire life I never desired a simpler life where I'm meant to follow routine directions. It's why I could never be an ordinary soldier, especially not without magic. Every day we stayed in Verona, I needed to force myself not to think too much about the past or the future. Otherwise, I'd panic."

"Why didn't you say anything to me?" he asked while showing as much emotion, which made her chest ache.

She paused to consider his question but ultimately couldn't come up with an answer and admitted it. "I don't know. I didn't understand what was happening until after I left the palace. When I explored the country, especially what people had to go through because they didn't have protection from the creatures, it became my responsibility to put an end to the demon instigating the trouble."

"Plenty of others are involved in this."

"Not the way I am. I let myself play along and ignore the risks. Whether it had been intended or not, Soirée's power got released and grew because of me after she escaped the prison I kept her in. The person I was meant to be before I met her is gone."

Byron fell silent for a long time.

This isn't about Soirée... It's about me and my mistakes.

At last, he responded. "Your life may never be normal, and you're still connected to a demon, but that doesn't mean you should throw everything else away. The people who are waiting for us at the camp and many more don't want you to sacrifice yourself. If we work together, there might be another option besides using the creature's energy, or at least one to prevent it from harming you."

Coura glared into the trees. *Why doesn't he understand? They should trust me to defeat Soirée and restore peace. There's no use endangering their lives when I can handle whatever she does to me. There are people who need him and issues that become easier to solve when I'm involved.*

She opened her mouth to say as much when her eyes found his, and he stared at her with the most heartbroken expression she had ever seen.

Somehow, in their shared gaze, she understood why he spoke to her the way he did.

"Byron…"

"That unnatural energy is causing you an amount of physical pain I can't even imagine," he began again. "Do you know what it's like to watch somebody you care about suffering and have to accept there's nothing you can do about it?"

This was never just about eliminating the creatures. He cares about me, and I would bet the others at the camp feel the same. If I go after Soirée, I'll probably die. If I'm alive after killing her, our bonded soul might cause my life to change for the worse as well.

A wave of guilt threatened to choke her until she pulled her eyes away from his. She expected the idea of dying to scare her; however, her resolve strengthened when it didn't.

"You always believed in me, even when you learned I was connected to a demon. I don't think I could ever have more faith in anyone than I do in you. That's why I'm trusting you to let me see this through to the end."

Byron made a sound to protest, but she went on before he could interrupt.

"Sometimes soldiers put their lives in danger for the kingdom's sake, right? I'm willing to suffer in order to pay the price for my past mistakes and the safety of Asteom. My relationship with Soirée puts me in the best position to stop her for good. I can't go back and erase what she's done, but I can at least make sure she doesn't meddle with anybody else ever again."

Coura understood Byron's desire to speak against her decision; it was written across his face. She paused to give him a chance to do so, yet he caved in to her request instead.

"If that's what you're set on doing, I suppose I can't dissuade you. Don't you dare expect to return to Verona alone, though. Even if I choose to move on, no one else will abandon you."

A weight lifted from her shoulders as she thanked her former mentor, then she followed him into the brush.

***

Marcus fidgeted from where he lied on the grass staring up at the stars. The restless shuffling of the others attempting to sleep didn't calm his nerves.

I haven't heard any noise in a while. Perhaps I should go check on them.

Byron left to return Coura to the campsite while the group finished their evening meal at sundown. Marcus had his own opinion on leaving his friend in the middle of nowhere but allowed it when they arranged a schedule for somebody to be with her throughout the afternoon while Clearshot hunted. With Will and Marcy's assistance, he caught and cleaned their dinner, which provided the first healthy portion of food they had eaten since leaving Dala. Despite that, a full stomach couldn't counter the concern for their absent companions.

Shouting reached them from within the woods as they prepared to sleep. The words weren't discernable, yet they recognized Byron and Coura's voices.

I hope he was able to talk some sense into her, Marcus thought after remembering her intentions.

Nobody fully understood or felt comfortable with the toll the demon's power took on her, and the possibility of losing her continued to rise while she remained unconscious. He rolled onto his side, then he sat up against his body's desire to relax.

"Can't sleep?"

Marcus caught Will sitting as well and started to respond when another voice cut in.

"Not a wink." Aimes popped up and stretched from where he positioned himself next to Marcy. "It's been a while since the master mage went to fetch Coura. Perhaps one of us should make sure they're safe."

"I'll go," Marcus and Will offered at the same time before pushing themselves to their feet.

In the resulting hush that fell over their camp, those who were still awake heard approaching footsteps. Byron appeared first in the glow of the dimmed fire, then their friend. Marcus pressed his lips together to avoid commenting on the prominent designs along her exposed limbs.

I didn't like the look of them when I initially noticed. Now that I know what they are, I definitely don't approve of what she's doing.

Along their journey during the days prior, Byron explained his analysis of the markings, as well as why he became furious with Coura's decision to pursue the creatures.

"A mage's energy is kept in their center," he began while pointing to the middle area above his belly button and below his ribs. "When we cast spells, the energy is led to an exit point, which is generally in the palm of your hand. Once the spell is complete, we cut off the trail of energy, and it adjusts to what's left along the line. That's why when a mage uses most of their power, it requires time to recover. We must replenish what was lost, just as anybody without magic needs to do when they're physically weakened or exhausted.

In Coura's case, her center is overflowing with the demonic energy to the point where it needs to find an exit point in order to avoid overwhelming and probably killing her. From what I can tell, it's doing this regardless of what she wants, creating those bruise-like patterns. I would imagine the process is especially painful because the power is forcing its way out."

"How can she recover from something like that?" Marcus had asked as his stomach twisted upon hearing Byron's theory.

The master mage frowned while he contemplated the question. "She would need to use all the energy up since her center doesn't naturally produce it. The problem is, her center has adapted to possessing and absorbing it, most likely due to her deeper bond with the demon. I don't expect she'll ever be able to stop. By taking in a power that doesn't belong to her, willingly or not, she's permanently damaging her body."

And she still plans to continue playing host for the demon's power? Marcus longed to counter, but he figured he already knew the answer.

While the two entered the camp and took seats around the firepit, he and Will returned to their sleeping positions.

"How are you feeling?" Will asked Coura.

She shrugged and stared into the embers.

"Would you mind keeping watch since I'm assuming you won't be able to sleep tonight?" Byron asked her before yawning and lying down.

They accepted her silence as a confirmation, and soon Marcus could rest with less worry. In the morning, he found he slept in the latest. Everyone else enjoyed a simple breakfast of dried meat, berries, and bread purchased in Sindaly the day before. Nobody commented on his lengthier snooze while he packed his belongings and scuttled over to sneak some food. Once he felt content and the remainder of the meal had been picked through, Byron cleared his throat to get their attention.

"Since we're ready to move on, I'd like to discuss what to do next."

"Are we not heading back to the palace?" Clearshot added with a raised eyebrow.

Marcus could tell his fellow soldier intended to see if Byron planned on resuming their original orders. When the master mage shook his head, a sense of relief spread around the circle.

"Although I wish I could trust the council members, there's still the threat of the man working against Dala, and ultimately Asteom. I'd like to consider the possibilities before storming in, especially since we're together now."

Clearshot directed his next question at Coura. "What do you plan on doing?"

"I'm going after Soirée."

After her answer, everyone besides their leader voiced their objections.

"You can't be serious!" Clearshot shouted while shooting her a disapproving glare once the others quieted.

Marcus was astonished by his friend's patience throughout their arguing given her regular temper. She didn't avoid their concerned or disagreeable expressions, and her own softened when she responded.

"I know you don't agree with me, but if I stop Soirée, there's a chance she'll share more about what's happening in the palace. When she's gone, it'll also deal a significant blow to whoever is pulling the strings. Whether any of you like it or not, she's my responsibility."

Aimes and Clearshot growled their frustrations regarding the entire situation while Will and Marcy begged her to reconsider. Meanwhile, Marcus caught the master mage's eye as Coura defended herself and found acceptance reflected in them.

Byron already tried to change her mind, he realized. *If that didn't help, I don't think any of us will be able to convince her.*

"Are you sure you can fight a demon alone?" he asked when the others didn't speak. "Why not wait until we approach the traitor and put him to justice? Then, we could take it on together."

Although he attempted to not sound disappointed, he couldn't prevent his words from leaning that way. *None of us agree with what she's choosing to do, but it's going to happen. So, let's start figuring out a strategy.*

To his satisfaction, Coura seemed to understand what he was getting at and nodded. "It would be better to target them individually. Because of our connection, I'm certain Soirée can still wield the energy I collected. If worse comes to worse, I can lure her away from the palace."

"I agree," Byron surprised them by interjecting. "It's smarter to stop one part of this mess than to let the demon, rogue angels, and our interfering traitor call upon each other."

"With that being said, there's another creature wandering around," Coura added. "I say we decide what to do next when it's out of the way."

"Another one?" Will exclaimed, mirroring everybody's surprise. "How do you know?"

"I can sense it nearby. Can't you, Byron?"

The master mage closed his eyes to focus before opening them with a slight, bothered groan. "I can, but I wouldn't say it's near us. It's farther north."

"Outside Verona?" Aimes inquired with wide eyes. Marcus noticed both the older man and Marcy behaved in a reserved manner while the others discussed magic, so he assumed they were unfamiliar with the concept. For the most part, the pair listened instead of questioning the subject.

Byron nodded to acknowledge the location.

Clearshot rose first to move in the direction of the trail. "I don't like the idea of those monsters roaming around my home," he grumbled in an uncharacteristically serious manner.

That ended the conversation as the rest of them joined him after.

***

Sindaly proved to be uneventful, mainly because no one would go near them. Like a group of treacherous-looking bandits, the citizens gave sidelong glances and curious stares yet never approached or spoke to any of them. The reason for this, as Byron mentioned to Coura before their argument, was the demonic energy, which became great enough to unsettle even those without the capability to wield or sense magic. She was grateful her companions didn't mention this as they passed through without needing to linger any longer than necessary.

Byron continued leading them on the main road for another day, yet the next morning Clearshot demanded they take a shortcut.

"What do you mean there's a back path to the capital?" the master mage asked from where he sat across their breakfast circle.

"It's to the east of the main road entering from the south," Clearshot explained around a handful of freshly picked berries.

"I never heard of it."

"Where's your map? I'll show you."

To Coura's surprise, Byron stood, rummaged through his bag, and dug out the rolled-up parchment. Everyone leaned closer to catch a glimpse of the supposedly hidden trail.

"Look here," Clearshot ordered and placed a finger on Verona. He moved it down and along a trail marked in a faded, yellow color. It curved east to skim a darker green space, which portrayed the line of trees, before dipping straight south into Sindaly. "The main road we've been on goes around the forest to the south of the palace. This is because there isn't enough space through the trees for travelers with animals and wagons. My home is at the uppermost section of the woods."

Again, he pointed to an unmarked spot at the top of the dark green space, then he slid his finger straight down until it connected to part of the yellow road. "We're coming up to the intersection leading north. It's more difficult to move through since it isn't in use, and it doesn't lead straight to the city, but it would take a day or so to reach my property."

"We would get there sooner without needing to avoid being spotted near the capital," Byron muttered.

Clearshot dipped his chin and leaned back with his arms crossed. "It's your decision. *I* would prefer a comfortable bed and hot food to another night outdoors. Not to mention, we wouldn't tempt danger on the main road either."

"He has a point," Marcy added as she glanced over at Coura. For some reason, their newer companion still didn't trust anybody besides her and Aimes yet.

"I don't care what we do," she replied to the woman's comment.

Actually, I'd hate to lure a demonic creature near Clearshot's home. It's strange since I have a feeling he would prefer that to our other options. At least this way we're sheltered far from the city. I wonder what Emilea will think... She shuttered at the idea of facing the light mage while possessing such incredible, unnatural energy after they seemed to reconcile.

She's going to kill me, a tiny voice chirped in the back of her mind before Byron's response brought her attention to the discussion again.

"I would like to keep innocent civilians at a safe distance as well, but I'm not entirely comfortable with the idea of traveling in a place that limits our movements; however, I'm not the only one invested in this. Who's in favor of taking the shortcut?"

Clearshot and Aimes raised their hands. A moment later, Coura and Will lifted theirs.

"Four of seven," Byron tallied with a smile. "It's settled then. We'll head out and make for the woods."

Serpent's Venom

The entrance to Clearshot's secret path hid behind the remains of an old guard station just off the main road. Vines covered the sides in a layer of green while tree limbs sprouted from its open windows. Not only was the entrance overgrown with foliage, but the trail itself appeared to be nothing more than a dirt line, which became difficult to discern from the grass patches and fallen leaves. If they hadn't been traveling with someone who knew what to look for, Coura didn't believe anybody would have noticed it.

"Are you sure this is the right direction?" Marcy asked while holding a flexible branch out of their way.

"Without a doubt," Clearshot answered while returning to his optimistic attitude.

Coura rolled her eyes before glancing around for any sign of movement. To her relief, the forest seemed normal. Birds darted by overhead in the sky and canopy with chirps, and though she couldn't spot the animals on the ground, there were plenty of sounds to assure her they took notice of the strangers. She didn't realize how wary she acted until Will pointed it out.

"I guess you still don't care for the woods," he commented in a sly tone while sneaking to her side. Most of the trail became too narrow for them to stand beside each other, but her friend took advantage of the opportunity to make a jab at her.

Coura shot him an unamused look. "I wish you would stop bringing it up," she grumbled.

Marcus glanced behind from where he walked in front of her. "I forgot about that!"

He laughed at the reminder, and Will joined him before they recapped their first journeys with Coura and Byron after Marcy inquired.

"We traveled across the country in such a short amount of time," the herbalist concluded, disbelief emphasizing the words.

"You shouldn't act so shocked," Aimes added. "After all, being young and leaving Clearwater to head north must have been a harrowing experience."

"Not so much. I enjoy exploring yet having company makes it more worthwhile."

"Was it really that long ago since we met?" they heard Byron ask from the front.

Coura tried counting the months in her head while Will used his fingers.

"About a year and a half ago," he concluded.

I'll be eighteen in two months. How incredibly fast the weeks seem to fly by. I could never imagine myself where I'm at now.

They continued hiking and chatted about random topics until the sky darkened to signal late afternoon. By then, they were ready for a break.

"I spotted an opening up ahead," Clearshot called from where he led. "We can stop there to rest."

Once their group reached the spacious area, Coura stretched her arms and drank from the waterskin being passed around as Marcy offered the remaining jerky and fruit. Byron and Clearshot huddled over the map near the trail, and everybody else sat in the cool grass.

"I can't believe how wonderful the weather is," Will commented, initiating a conversation with Aimes, Marcus, and Marcy about the changing climates compared to Dala and Clearwater.

Meanwhile, Coura extended her senses for any sign of the demonic presence. Unlike earlier, nothing became conspicuous, which had her wondering if she would need to lure it toward them, as she had done to the previous creature and the one in Dala. A yawn escaped her then, interrupting the idea. She rubbed her eyes and stood when Clearshot called for them to go.

I don't know how much longer I can rely on Soirée's power to avoid a real night's sleep. Perhaps it will come easier once we can lie in actual beds.

Clearshot prepared to take the lead again until Byron extended an arm to halt their steps.

"Don't move."

His vigilant expression and signal caught the group off guard, and they froze. Several seconds passed by in complete silence.

It's too quiet. Something spooked the wildlife. Coura swung her head from side to side as she peered into the trees.

"What happened to the birds?" Marcy whispered, but Marcus shushed her.

Coura met Byron's eyes and sent him an uncertain look to try and convey that she didn't sense hostile energy. He shook his head in response, as though he understood what she meant.

A gentle rustle in the bushes alerted them of an intruder. She manifested her blade as she spun around to catch something emerge. Her breath caught at the sight of what appeared to be a tentacle-like limb stretching from deeper in the woods.

"Look out!" Marcus shouted. He seemed to be the only person who noticed it move to strike the nearest person, who happened to be Marcy, and had enough time to act.

The limb poised to swipe horizontally, so he lunged forward, grabbed her by the shoulders, and dragged her to the ground with him. The tentacle swung over their heads in a blow forceful enough to break bones.

Coura grasped her sword in both hands and charged to stab the exposed limb before it could retreat. A hissing sounded from farther in the trees, then it receded. She prepared to give chase, but Byron instructed her to wait.

"We're almost to my home," Clearshot said with a motion for them to follow. "It's a straight shot into the backyard. Let's lead it into a wider space."

"It's right here!" she protested while using her blade to point in that direction.

Even so, Byron was already waving everybody else onto the trail. "This isn't the place for multiple archers, swordsmen, and mages to engage in a fight. Now, hurry up!"

Against his wishes, she kept to the rear while their group jogged as swiftly as they could manage behind Clearshot. The forest around them remained still, so the sounds of their scrambling through foliage, footsteps on crumpling leaves, and panting from the unexpected pursuit seemed amplified.

Eyes forward, she told herself. *I won't be useful if I trip over my own feet.*

A shadow against the graying sky in the canopy caught her attention. Coura slowed to track its movement in the trees until it waited directly above the trail. Before she could put together a warning, the creature dropped to plop itself on the path in front of Clearshot. He extended both arms to his sides and stepped backward at a steady pace, pushing the group into retreating.

With how narrow the trail was, she couldn't identify what the creature looked like until the black figure rose to its full height, roughly the size of a house and a head taller than the beast from outside Dala. Like the previous creatures, it took the form of the animal it possessed, which in this case happened to be a giant serpent. The body appeared as thick as a tree trunk, one she doubted she could wrap her arms around, and the limb she mistook as a tentacle had actually been its tail coiled beneath the body. With a hiss, its mouth parted to reveal a pair of dagger-length fangs.

"Is there a way around?" she heard Byron lean over to ask Clearshot when the creature took notice of them. Her stomach dropped when she noticed the archer didn't have his bow drawn.

They need to let me up there, she thought amid a rush of fear. Marcy stood in front of her, and although she attempted to shove past the woman, there simply wasn't enough room without climbing around the bushes and saplings off the trail.

Everybody began shuffling when the snake-like beast raised its tail and whipped it forward with less force than earlier. Clearshot raised his arms for protection, and the limb pushed him back into Byron, who lost his balance and fell into Will. Since their group merged so closely together, they all tumbled onto one another, though Coura purposefully made sure Marcy landed on her instead of the ground. It proved a successful method to both incapacitate and embarrass them for the moment. It also amused the creature, which became evident when it swayed its head from side to side and flicked a bright red tongue.

Irritation swelled inside Coura as she pushed herself to her feet and instinctively raised her weaponless hand to manifest a spell. She dove into the power, but her previous attempt to use magic flashed in her mind, prompting her to clench the hand into a fist and lower her arm.

When I used the energy before, I lost control. I won't risk the same result with everybody close to me.

"I'll keep it distracted," Clearshot shouted from the front, using the opportunity to draw his bow and nock an arrow.

"Return to the clearing and spread out as much as you can," Byron picked up without turning to face them.

Because she stayed at the rear, Coura's position forced her to lead the others to their previous resting spot. They reached the area without issue, drew their weapons, and adjusted themselves. Byron and Clearshot hadn't retreated, so they waited.

"Should we help?" Marcy was the first to ask.

Marcus kept on the trail and glanced in their missing companions' direction. His face remained set in a steadfast expression. "They ordered us to go here. I'm sure they're hurrying."

Coura held her breath to the point of dizziness until they heard footsteps.

"I see them," Marcus shared before stepping inside the area.

The two jogged into the space to rejoin the group a moment later.

"What happened?" she pressed right away.

Clearshot wheezed and told her to give them a minute to catch their breath. Both bent over with hands on their knees gasping for air while she tapped a foot. Byron glanced to the trail where Marcus continued to keep watch before standing up straight.

Meanwhile, Clearshot lowed his head and groaned. "I hate running for my life!"

"Is it still there?" Will asked.

"Yes, but we were able to put some distance between us thanks to Byron's magic."

"Arrows aren't effective on its tough skin," her former mentor explained without removing his eyes from the trees. "Grazing it with a sword won't work either. It'll take either a committed stab or magic to do any damage."

"How inconvenient," Coura heard Aimes mutter.

His words drove her to approach the path. "I can lead it away from here," she started while mirroring Marcus' glance.

He stepped back and waved his sword at her. "Have you lost your mind? You can't do this alone; you said so yourself."

To her dismay, he was the only person to protest her idea.

"I'm not going to let it get a chance to hurt the people who can't fight. If arrows and weak swings don't help, where does that leave most of our group? Besides, if I can draw it ahead to the wider yard like Clearshot suggested, the rest of you will be able to follow."

No one could reasonably dismiss the idea, so Byron and Marcus moved away from the trail.

"I'll locate you in a few minutes," the former added. "Those of us who can fight will support you too."

She gave a curt nod to acknowledge his comments before sprinting down the path.

*

For a while, Coura's panting and footsteps seemed to echo in the woods as she focused on avoiding potential hazards. Her inner voice taunted the creature and beckoned it to come after her multiple times. Without much else to do, she continued running.

The trail stayed even and straight, which allowed her to cover plenty of ground in the minutes since she left, though she slowed her pace in order to observe her surroundings.

Why hasn't it revealed itself yet?

Twice more, she paused to search for the shadow to no avail. A sudden pang of terror sprang up when she considered it attacking the rest of her group instead; however, she reminded herself of Byron's magical abilities and the need to fulfill her part of their plan.

As the forest grew dim with the setting sun, she blinked more frequently to adjust her eyes. The trees' spacing didn't thin, but she could see the opening ahead and burst into the promised clearing. Above, stars shined even brighter against a clear backdrop, and twinkling, yellow-and-green light bugs kept her company as she came to a stop farther in the area. Clearshot described the land as his backyard, yet it stretched away from the lone building into its own field. She spotted two windows glowing from inside their home and felt relieved to know someone, probably Emilea with her children, was at home.

In order to monitor the area and keep her muscles from growing too tense, Coura paced while listening for any sign of danger. This became easier than she expected due to the quieted environment, and she returned to the trail's entrance when enough time passed to leave her anxious. The crunching of footsteps caught her attention soon after, then she sensed Byron's energy, though faintly at such a distance.

Marcy had been the first sent along and passed through the opening while shouting in a concerned manner.

"I'm here," Coura replied and approached. When she did so, she realized the woman came alone. "Where's everyone else?"

Marcy answered in gasps since she had been sprinting. "That creature…found us on our way…to meet you. They're coming, but…I hurried ahead to warn you."

While the woman continued catching her breath, the sickening twist in Coura's stomach returned. In response to her worry, the energy in her center hummed, as if it prepared to be released. The primal sensation helped her to focus rather than urge her into action, so she allowed herself to sink into its embrace.

"Marcy," she began while placing her hands on her companion's shoulders. "I need to request a favor."

With wide eyes and apparent fright, the woman faced Coura and bobbed her head.

"Clearshot's home is just across this field. His wife is a master light mage and can assist us. Go find her, say Byron sent you, then explain what we know about the creature. There will be children with her; make sure they stay inside where it's safe. Watch over them until we meet up."

Marcy dipped her head again, showed more confidence, then took off toward the house. When the woman made it about halfway, somebody else emerged from the trail to jog by Coura without even noticing her. When they halted to glance around and speak, she recognized it was Will.

"Where are you?" he whispered while she walked over.

"Here, right in front of you," she replied and reached over to gently grab his arm.

At first, he jumped at the touch but did the same to her with his other hand. Grumbles and footsteps on the trail distracted them from conversing.

"Can't you move any faster?" That voice belonged to Aimes. The older man hobbled into the clearing while another figure scrambled behind him.

"I already told you, we're almost there." The second voice came from Clearshot, who emerged after.

Coura kept a hold on Will while they approached and inquired about the creature's location. Even as she asked the question, she felt another surge of her former mentor's energy to alert her they were nearing.

"Marcus and Byron are keeping it back for as long as possible. I think we should spread out and let them lead it to us."

She bit her bottom lip as she considered his strategy. "We can't kill it without using a powerful spell, and the attack would need to land accurately."

"What do you suppose we do then?" Clearshot retorted.

Another sense of panic threatened to overwhelm her until she dove into her center for the demonic energy, which soothed her nerves enough to not to be a distraction. "Marcy went to fetch Emilea and watch Mace and Lexie. Will, Aimes, you should head there for safety too."

"No," Will protested. "I'm not going to-"

"You're useless here," she cut him off as she sensed Byron's power again. "We don't have time to mess around."

"Come on," Aimes ushered her friend and stepped toward the house. "She's right. If we're going to get out of the way, we need to go now."

Will didn't argue a second time and left while continually glancing behind.

"What should we do?" Clearshot continued once a thumping sound grew louder.

She walked away from the noise and toward the middle of the clearing. "You know, there's not much you can do either. I wouldn't judge you for going with them to your home."

Even before she spoke, Coura knew what his reaction would be. He moved to stand by her side with his bow drawn and an arrow pointed at the trail.

Marcus appeared seconds later with his sword in hand. He didn't slow his pace until he reached them, then he slid to a stop. "Who's there?"

"Clearshot and Coura," the former answered.

Before the assistant general could say more, Byron crept toward the trio from the path with his back to them. In the darkness of the woods, Coura assumed it became impossible to see the creature clearly. He shot a blast of fire once before turning to jog over and join them.

"Where is it?" Clearshot asked at a lower volume.

"I don't know."

"What do you mean you don't know?" Coura couldn't help herself from snapping.

Byron's response sounded patient, yet he kept an edge to his words. "I managed to scorch its belly before it hid in the trees again. My last spell lit up the area, but I wasn't able to track where it disappeared to."

"Should we retreat?" Marcus suggested next.

Before anyone could respond, there came a rustling in the bushes next to the trail's opening. They heard a deep hiss comparable to a growl, and the four spaced themselves apart in preparation for the demonic creature to reveal itself.

Coura squinted to peer ahead in an attempt to better observe the shadow as it slid its oversized head out. A glint from each eye shined when the head glanced both ways before settling on their group. Its mouth parted again to display the sharp fangs as the rest of its body slithered into the open, and it gave up on sneaking through the foliage.

Byron's voice broke the silence. "Marcus and I will keep its attention since that's what we've been doing so far. Coura, prepare to strike when the moment is right."

She hoped to agree, but the words were stuck in her throat as she remembered the lack of control from her last spell. *What if it isn't an accurate blow? I also need to stay away from them in order to use it, otherwise...*

Without waiting for a reply, the master mage sent shards of ice directly into the creature's face before following with a blast of fire. He sidestepped to the right after releasing the spells, and Marcus trailed behind him.

"Wait!" Coura cried, but the magic connected with its target to drown her voice out.

The creature bit at the air before shifting its focus on Byron and Marcus, who waved his sword in a showy fashion. For a heartbeat, she recalled facing the lizard-like beast alongside the Sie-Kie hunters and how they manipulated its position in order to strike from behind.

"Let's go," Clearshot called as he hurried toward the tail.

She followed while studying their opponent's body. Attacking the head had been the most successful method during her previous fights with their kind, so she mustered her power and decided to aim a spell at the back of its skull.

While they moved, the creature caught on to Byron's pattern of attacks, and its head swerved to dodge the fire and ice he released. Once, it paused to slam its tail against the ground in front of him with such speed that an accurate strike would be detrimental, if not fatal, to the victim.

Coura slowed to a halt away from Clearshot, raised her arms and placed the palms outward to aim at her target's head. Then, she secured a tendril of energy in preparation for a single bolt. The power cooperated at first, allowing her to lead it to the exit points in her hands, but it swarmed out of control before she could release the spell. The thin river stretching from the pool overflowed with a mind of its own. By then, it was too late to abandon the attempt.

A bright scattershot of lightning blasted to hit the creature in several spots, including in the back of the head. How much damage the attack actually did, she couldn't guess. Her arms shook from the uncontrolled sparks escaping at the top of her hands and forearms to burn the skin and stun her muscles. It hurt terribly, and she let out a yelp before being pushed backward by the spell's force. Once it ended, her arms dropped to her sides and remained numb until the healing began.

The smoke created from the lightning cleared as the creature writhed in pain while shrieking into the air. Already, she could tell none of the bolts had been precise enough for a single hit to be lethal. If anything, it served to irritate the snake-like beast, which proved true when it spun to hiss at her.

"What was that?" Clearshot yelled from where he scrambled to stand away from her magic.

Coura ground her teeth in distress influenced by her continued inability to control the growing power. Despite how upset he felt, her problem became too complicated to explain, if she could even do so at all.

The creature slithered in a circle to fully face them with its tail pulled back in a position to attack. In response, Coura and Clearshot retreated at a sprint to put some space between them and the beast.

Our roles are reversed, she realized as she remembered Byron and Marcus. *We need to be the distraction for those two.*

Once they reached the edge of the clearing and the forest looming beyond, they stopped and spun around. The creature kept itself at a distance, dancing from side to side once again. Coura's arms started aching instead of stinging, which she knew from experience meant the healing was nearly complete, and she opened and closed her hands to test the muscles. Clearshot echoed her previous thought while she did so.

"It looks like it's focused on us now, so we need to keep it busy for Byron to use his magic."

"Right," Coura muttered and mustered more energy.

I may not be able to cast a single spell correctly, but what I did before seemed to become a meaningful enough diversion.

She raised a hand against a warning from Clearshot and launched a fireball into the creature's face. The flames singed her palm yet not as badly as the lightning spell due to the lesser power she utilized. Still, it didn't matter.

The snake-like beast attempted to dodge the blast but proved to be too bulky, causing it to recoil in a jerk. Just as Byron had done earlier, she sent another, much weaker bolt meant only to hold its attention. This time, instead of moving backward, it slid its head forward into the spell. The lightning connected with its skin and had no effect.

Can it sense how much energy I expend in each spell and then judge whether or not to accept the blow or dodge? This creature is intelligent.

"I think we overworked that strategy," Clearshot added from where he sidestepped to meet her. While she had been wielding her magic, he sent arrows across the clearing with the hope of hitting the oversized target.

Before either of them could decide what to do next, the creature curled forward in a sudden lunge, and Coura felt Byron's magic at work. An icicle identical to a sword flew over where its head had been seconds ago.

"It ducked under his spell?" she heard her companion mumble in disbelief while she gaped and sensed amusement from their target.

In a similar motion, the snake-like beast shot its head forward, snapping the air with a heaving noise, then fixed its eyes on them. She prepared to ask what they should do next when something struck her right thigh. The unexpected force sent her to one knee, and she noticed Clearshot's body fall to the ground. She managed to say his name before gasping when whatever stuck to her thigh began stinging worse than any of the burns, leaving that leg useless. The demonic energy swarmed the spot, but no relief came.

What's happening?

Coura chanced a glance at the creature and found it had circled around again to continue toying with Byron and Marcus. She couldn't see much, so she occupied herself with figuring out a solution for her current dilemma.

No object impacted her leg to create an injury, yet the pain was triggered by some substance on the skin. Tentatively, she brushed a finger over the inflicted area. A hot liquid coated it, then the stinging began on her hand. She cursed aloud once she understood and wiped the skin clean on the grass.

It hit us both with venom. My magic is strong enough to prevent the affliction from spreading throughout my body, yet the area isn't healing.

She looked over to where Clearshot remained sprawled on his back unmoving. When she called his name, he groaned in response. Next, she analyzed her remaining power. The energy became preoccupied with restraining the venom, an automatic action steadily draining her reserves.

This is bad...

Without considering their plan aside from enabling herself to be mobile again, she stripped off her pack, dug out the cloak, and scrubbed the liquid away. Hot tears flooded her eyes and she let out several whimpers behind her teeth from the pain, but once it had been removed, the healing strengthened. She dragged herself over to Clearshot after to assess the substance on his left shoulder.

"This is going to hurt," she warned, though he didn't even make a sound at her comment. The lack of a reaction reminded her the man didn't possess the same ability to recover, meaning he was most likely paralyzed at the moment.

Coura proceeded to wipe at the liquid without pressing on his body as much as possible, then she listened for a heartbeat. A sense of relief washed over her when she heard one, though the rest of her inspection proved he fell unconscious and his breathing became shallow.

Byron's continued spellcasting lit up the night with flashes of lightning and glowing fire. A silhouette slipped around the oversized creature's body, and she recognized Marcus as he hurried over to kneel on the opposite side of Clearshot.

"What's wrong?" he started.

"It spit venom at us."

His eyes lifted from their companion to examine her body.

"I'm fine," she added to answer his unspoken question. "My healing prevents it from spreading, but we'll need Emilea to help him."

Marcus seemed to hesitate when a familiar presence answered their prayers, and Coura glanced at the creature in search of the source. She noticed Byron's figure limping toward them and assumed he grew fatigued from the constant use of his magic. Behind him, an enormous, silver wall of shimmering energy prevented the beast from following. It hissed in frustration and began to slam its tail and head against the shield, which fortunately didn't budge.

"What happened?" Byron demanded between breaths as he approached.

"The creature spits venom," Marcus answered before Coura could. "It's off his body, but Clearshot's unconscious."

A flash of concern passed over Byron's face until his eyes went to her. Then, anger replaced his worried expression. "Why didn't you use a single-striking spell and aim for its head? You have enough power. Releasing it in a scatter just did minor damage. You should know better!"

Coura stared down at her hands in response to his scolding. "I tried, but the energy overwhelms my direction. When I use a certain amount to cast a spell, more is released and goes back on me. I can't wield it for a precise attack."

For a moment, the only sound became the creature's persistent attempts to reach its prey.

"I don't believe that."

She fully expected her former mentor's wrath for her diminished skill resulting in their failure to kill their opponent and Clearshot's status. The unfaltering words had her raising her eyes in bewilderment.

He knelt beside her after, placed a hand on her shoulder, and met her eyes with a mask of fortitude. "I don't believe you can't control your magic. We've never had this issue before, and it shouldn't change now."

"You saw what happens," she argued and shook her head against a wave of nausea.

Despite her protest, Byron remained unphased. "If you aren't able to release the energy through a narrow point, create a wider exit."

"The spell won't stay together."

"Not without a greater amount of power being pushed through the same space. Send everything you have for one blast."

"How can you be so sure it'll work?"

"We'll know when we try."

Without asking for her permission, Byron grabbed her arm and lifted her to her feet. They limped away from Clearshot and Marcus, who remained motionless, until they were in front of Emilea's wall. In the back of her mind, Coura wondered where the light mage hid herself. They could see the shield cracking under the repeated blows and understood it would shatter after a few more strikes. Byron released his hold then, forcing her to stand on her own, and the pain in her thigh returned twofold.

"Remember what I said," he shouted while backing up. "Envision the spell, create a satisfactory exit for the energy, then send through as much as you can."

How much is this going to hurt me? she longed to ask.

Her heart beat deafeningly loud while she narrowed her focus to the target. She trusted Byron, yet her instincts screamed at her to abandon the attempt. In order to ignore the doubt, she repeated the instructions again and again, preventing the fear from rising.

A faint, almost haunting sound of breaking glass filled the air when the wall shattered seconds later. Glimmering pieces of silver light faded as they floated from the sky and onto the grass.

"Now!" Byron ordered above the noise.

Coura raised her right hand toward the creature's head on his command. Instead of her usual process of guiding a tendril of energy along a directed path, she released as much as she could force through her body in a surge of lightning.

The burning sensation was to be expected. Parts of the spell lashed against her face and chest like whips, but Byron's guess was correct. The resulting push of raw energy propelled the bolts forward instead of allowing them to scatter like they did earlier. Luckily, the creature had been too preoccupied with Emilea's shield to notice the lightning until it manifested. By that point, it became too late to avoid her spell. The bolts struck home, tearing through its head to scorch and shred its flesh into pieces.

Coura didn't see the aftermath. When she felt her center drained, the energy cut off on its own, and she dropped onto her knees and leaned forward on her left hand. Her damaged right arm could do no more than hang limply at her side. Every bit of physical stability vanished, leaving her gasping for air in order to remain conscious.

There was no question in her mind that the snake-like beast had been killed, though. If it didn't die, her former mentor wouldn't have knelt beside her to rest a comforting hand on her back. That, and the disgusting stench of a burned carcass filling the clearing.

"Byron!" Emilea's voice rang as the light mage's footsteps shuffled closer.

A second hand rested on Coura's shoulder before the woman's healing energy began flowing. She couldn't help from pushing herself up to her knees and swatting the hands away.

"Go!" she managed to say despite their alarmed expressions.

"Hold still," Emilea replied and attempted to reach out once more.

Coura shoved the light mage away a second time, then she huffed Clearshot's name.

Byron swore once he remembered their companion's condition and mentioned the need for Emilea's magic; however, the pair lingered next to Coura.

She swallowed to rouse what remained of her voice. "I can wait."

The sentence came out as strongly as she hoped and proved enough to convince the master mages. Byron rose and hurried ahead while Emilea followed close behind. Once they were on the move, Coura fell forward to collect herself, and for a while, she remained in that position.

Then, the energy from the dead creature found her.

Each part of her body sang with a new pain more extreme than what she experienced before. It seemed as if her limbs, chest, and back caught on fire and steadily flared with every passing moment. She wished to scream, yet her throat wouldn't respond, leaving her to open and close her mouth while sharply intaking air. Her muscles strung tight and trembled despite her inability to move, and tears blurred her already-hazy vision until she squeezed both eyes shut and waited for it to end, to black out and recuperate in sleep.

Unlike the other instances involving the demonic energy, though, her mind and body stayed awake to endure each agonizing second. In a lone corner of her mind where she could still think aside from the torture, she prayed for help.

Summoning Wings

For one of the few times in his life, Byron felt powerless as he watched Emilea kneel in the grass and place her hands on Clearshot's chest. Not only did his friend lie paralyzed and hurting, but his fellow master mage needed to do her best work in order to save her husband's life. Sympathy for the couple passed over him while he observed her heal with closed eyes and tears silently sliding down her cheeks. He stayed beside her just in case she requested support, not that he could do much in his exhausted state. Marcus stayed present and vigilant as well but in the same position.

Using the full moon above, he began to count the time in his head. After nearly ten minutes, he began drifting off and shook himself awake.

Emilea lifted her hands from her husband with a weary sigh moments later. "That should do for now."

"Will he recover?" Byron asked at a quieter volume.

Her eyes didn't lift from Clearshot. During her spell, his short breaths became drawn out until they seemed normal while he rested. "He'll be fine as long as I can keep an eye on the infected area. The creature's venom acts like a type of toxin that paralyzes once it comes in contact with the skin. A large quantity like this spreads rapidly. I managed to block the pain, but it'll take a few days for the muscles and nerves to function regularly."

Byron mirrored her sigh. "That's a relief," he commented before glancing upward.

It's well into the evening. I suppose we can regroup since the creature has been dealt with.

Marcus scrambled to his feet and helped Emilea to hers, to the light mage's appreciation.

"Let's head to your home for the night," he suggested. "Clearshot was guiding us there since this morning."

She nodded and wiped away the lingering tears from her cheeks. "How will we get him across the yard?"

They considered the issue until Marcus shrugged off his pack and stated he had an idea. From the bag, he removed the cloak he stuffed inside and laid it next to Clearshot.

"If we can lift him onto this, we won't need to carry him," the assistant general explained.

"That's a wonderful idea," Emilea said with more enthusiasm.

The two must have known how weak Byron was, for they took it upon themselves to move their companion without allowing him an opportunity to assist. After, they each seized a sleeve of the cloak and pulled together. At first, he moved to join when their burden didn't budge, but once the two were able to start dragging the cloth across the ground, he struggled to limp behind.

I can't believe how much I overworked myself, he thought and held his side against a looming cramp. His eyes wandered around, and he slowed his pace when he spotted Coura, who still looked to be recovering. *Speaking of overworked...*

Byron pointed to his former student and called ahead to tell Emilea and Marcus they would catch up. If the pair heard him, they didn't acknowledge the words. He decided it didn't matter as long as he could walk. So, with a shift in direction, he steadily made his way to Coura.

Watching her gasping on her hands and knees brought on another wave of sympathy, as well as a hint of guilt after he recalled his lessons about exhausting one's power. *'A mage should never release all their energy into a single, massive attack' I would say. Not only does doing so backfire on their body because of the lack of control, but it depletes their reserves, rendering them useless if they don't pass out right away. It requires days to recover from the shock, both physically and mentally. In this case, I'm glad Coura didn't remember that. She carries too much demonic energy for her center to handle. I doubt it's completely drained, and the blast had been enough to kill the creature. I just hope she can forgive me for thinking so recklessly.*

Byron approached and stood beside her, wincing at the effort it would take to kneel. "How are you holding up?" he asked in a gentler tone.

When she didn't respond, he decided to remain out in the clearing until they were able to somewhat move on their own and groaned as he sat next to her. He could sense the demon's power surrounding her as her center replenished, so he chose to leave her alone for a moment. Without anything else to add, he leaned back on his hands to relax, content to savor the odd peacefulness resulting from the fight.

Soon, he felt himself drifting to sleep again and remembered Emilea's home; the reminder of a featherbed brought his mind back to their situation. He glanced over at Coura. "Are you strong enough to stand?"

She hadn't shifted positions and continued gasping for air, as though unable to calm her breathing. That was when he became concerned.

After saying her name, he placed a hand on her shoulder. Underneath, she trembled, and her skin radiated an unnatural amount of heat beneath her shirt. Byron reached out to her twice more until the results of the creature's death dawned on him.

She's taking in its energy, he realized and looked between Coura and the charred remains. *Last time, she fainted right away and stayed unconscious for days. How much more powerful was this one to cause her to freeze like this? There's also the venom that struck her leg. I wonder if it's affecting her as much as it did Clearshot.*

"Can you move?" he started with a growing tenacity.

She didn't answer.

"Can you talk to me?"

Again, only her labored breathing came after his question.

"I can't carry you there on my own," he said, more to himself than to her. He tried tugging on her arm next in order to shift her position. When he did, she let out a pained yelp, causing his hand to recoil.

Forcing her to do anything while she's in this state is going to hurt her more. Should I wait for Emilea? Can she even help when there's demonic energy involved? Byron didn't think so. His heart sank as he felt useless for the second time that evening.

Despite the ineffective attempts, he racked his brain for a solution. A faint memory seemingly popped in his head when he considered his experience with unstable magic traced to an individual. Years before he had ever known Coura, he needed to subdue a young man who discovered his potential later on in his life. The revelation frightened the wielder into casting spells without controlling where they were directed. The outcome involved incapacitating him by using a physical blow to knock him out and abruptly end the conscious release of energy.

Byron hated the idea of doing the same to Coura since he worried it would harm her instead of help; however, waiting it out became his only other option. Because of how unique the situation was, leaving her struggling and vulnerable in the open didn't feel like the best alternative.

"I'm sorry," he whispered once he made up his mind, then he drew the blade at his waist.

After locating the area below the base of her neck, he twisted the sword sideways in his hand and struck a deliberate, precise blow to the back of her head with the flat bottom of the hilt. The strike hit true and rendered her unconscious despite any additional pain it may have caused. Her body relaxed, and she crumpled onto her side with no indication of trouble except her twitching fingers and shallow breaths.

He ran a hand through his hair several times when he couldn't find something else to do with himself. Nobody left the house to check on them, which surprisingly upset him, but it became motivation for him to struggle to his feet. To his dismay, the body of the creature rested between their location and his goal.

"Hey!" he called toward the lone building while walking over. As he found his way around the remains, he continued shouting with the hope that at least one person would hear his voice and investigate.

At last, when he nearly reached the front door, it opened. The lights from inside were jarring, but Marcus jogged over to join him with Aimes behind.

"Where's Coura?" the assistant general asked when they realized Byron stood alone.

"She's unconscious back where we left her."

As he expected, the young soldier glanced over and hurried past after noting he appeared capable of acting on his own. Aimes seemed to be unsure about following and stared out into the darkness.

"It's safe," Byron reassured the older man. "The creature's dead. Take a light and go after Marcus. He'll need your help in order to carry her inside."

Aimes grunted in confirmation, returned to the house, and emerged bearing a lamp as he chased after the assistant general.

Meanwhile, Byron stepped through the doorway and spotted an open armchair on the left side of the sitting room. He dropped into its comfortable embrace, and his eyes drooped to close against his will. As he settled down, the energy in his center started to replenish, and he knew it would be foolish to sleep without eating and drinking enough first.

He hadn't noticed anybody else in the room until he prepared to rise and saw four sets of eyes watching him. On the chair across from him sat Marcy, like a mother bird with a child under each arm. Behind them, Will had positioned himself at the dining table. Each of them projected a sense of concern.

I'm too worn out to deal with this, Byron thought and licked his lips.

"Will, can you bring me something to eat and drink?"

The young man appeared startled by the request but rose and moved into the kitchen. He returned a minute later holding a mug and a piece of bread with an herbal paste stuffed inside. Although his mouth watered at the sight of decent food and drink after spending days on the road, Byron's stomach tightened as it always did when he exhausted himself. He scarfed down the bread without tasting its contents and sipped at the cooled cider.

Before he finished and felt ready to explain their situation, the front door burst open with a ruckus. Marcy, Will, and the children leapt out of their seats upon hearing the sound, but Byron remained unphased as Marcus entered. Coura had been draped on his back, and he went to the stairs. Meanwhile, Aimes replaced the lamp he borrowed, slid the locks on the door in place, and trailed the assistant general to the second floor. Neither of them said a word or gave any attention to Byron or the others.

He cleared his throat to get the group's attention once they were alone again.

"Where's Mother?" Lexie whimpered.

"She's upstairs," Marcy answered before the child could make more noise.

I shouldn't say too much about tonight's events in front of the children. Besides, I'm sure everyone else would like to be present for a discussion in the morning.

In order to emphasize his weariness and suspend their questions, Byron decided to utilize his authority. "It's far too late to talk tonight," he began while glancing between Will and Marcy. "Emilea is tending to Clearshot, so there's no need to be concerned about them. Coura exhausted herself, and I'm about there as well. The creature chasing us is dead. Let's sleep in peace, recover, and reorganize ourselves tomorrow."

"I want to see Father!" the girl whined without processing his words.

He shot Marcy an exasperated look, rather like a plea for her cooperation. To his relief, she caught the message about Emilea and Clearshot and pulled the children closer.

"He's right," she offered in a soothing manner while addressing them. "Your mother is the strongest healer in the kingdom. Don't you think so?"

They didn't reply yet both continued listening.

"Mages need time to work and for it to be quiet. Your mother would want you to head off to bed and let her take care of your father tonight. There are plenty of powerful people here to protect you."

She stood after those words, and the children stepped away. Byron was pleased when each accepted one of Marcy's outstretched hands, then the woman led them up the stairs while murmuring words of comfort.

"I guess I'd better go too," Will added after.

Byron expected him to be the one to stay in the room, or go to Coura, but he climbed the stairs in silence.

"That was easier than I expected," he muttered when he was alone and closed his eyes once more. At some point before he fell asleep, he heard footsteps near the kitchen yet didn't care enough to investigate.

*

Although nothing woke him until later in the morning, Byron felt horrid when he stirred. His body had grown stiff from remaining in the armchair, his stomach knotted with hunger, and an all-too familiar hole rested in his center.

There's no doubt about it, he thought as he rubbed his eyes and stretched. *I drained most of my reserves. I hate being in this state.*

Seeing Marcus sprawled out and slumbering in the seat across from his spot did surprise Byron. The reminder of the young soldier's persistent sense of responsibility made him smile as he repressed a groan and rose.

Subtle noises came from the kitchen to capture his attention next, so he snuck around the room and entered to find Emilea digging through a worn satchel. She removed several pieces of fruit, set them on the counter, then replaced the bag where it had been hanging on a hook.

"Good morning," he greeted her softly in order to avoid startling her.

A hand flew up to cover her mouth as she yawned before answering. "I didn't expect you to be up for a while yet."

"Neither did I," Byron admitted with a chuckle. "How are you doing?"

Emilea released a shaky breath and turned her head toward him, revealing reddish eyes and a paler complexion. "I'm managing. The worst is over."

Although her words comforted him, he couldn't help asking about Clearshot.

"He should be awake soon," she replied in a controlled tone. "I'll be able to assess what I need to work on then."

That was that for the time being. He didn't intend to push either of them into processing more than necessary when they were still weak, both physically and emotionally. After an expression of gratitude, he prepared to return to the living room when Emilea stopped him.

"Wait, Byron. There's a lot we need to discuss."

The unexpected comment concerned him, and he sensed a headache creeping behind his eyes. "We can talk when everybody is present and recovered."

"I would, but I don't know if you're safe here," she went on, allowing her emotions to bleed through the words.

He stared at her without understanding. Although he wondered what could possibly cause her to become so flustered, he decided neither of them were able to think clearly in their current conditions. "Whatever comes our way, we can handle it together," he assured her before returning to his seat.

The light mage didn't pursue, and eventually he drifted into an uncomfortable sleep as he tossed around in the limited space.

***

An echo of laughter faded in and out of Coura's dreams. In them, she fled from unseen forces and creatures similar to the ones she faced when she had been awake.

It's a vision. It's not real, she repeated to herself in an effort to calm her frantic heart and mind.

Against her attempts to be courageous, the dark place she dwelt in felt too lifelike to brave without consideration for possible consequences. Her feet slipped on or got stuck in puddles of an unknown liquid, and vines appeared out of nowhere in the sky to wrap around her arms and neck while she moved. It seemed like an eternity until she could free herself from either before choosing a direction to flee in. When she did so, her breathing came in gasps that had her wondering if there was a limited amount of air.

It's not real. They're just illusions.

Due to the shadow-filled environment, she didn't notice the gaping fissure across the ground until she found nothing beneath her feet. She tumbled forward into the crack splitting the earth, screaming at the top of her lungs and expecting any second to be her last.

For what seemed like hours, she continued falling. Her throat burned as she tried to make a sound, yet it grew too raw and damaged to use. Against the terror, she squeezed her eyes closed and tried to count the passing time until she blacked out.

*

When Coura came to, she lied on the dirt floor of a cavern with one cheek pressed against the ground. Its walls glowed crimson from a source below the circular platform, and she stared up into an abyss where no ceiling limited its depth as it swallowed the light. The space proved to be unbearably hot, and after a brief inspection at the edge of the rock structure, she became awestruck by the sight of molten earth far below. It crackled, bubbled, and released smoke and steam, which rose to burn her exposed arms and face.

She backed away from the ledge but froze and spun around when several, giddy laughs in various pitches started behind her. Shadowy creatures pulled themselves onto the platform or leapt over from others all around the space. No two beings were alike, as some remained crawling on four legs and most stood on two. Some displayed sharp, jagged features jutting out from their bodies, like horns or spikes, and still more bore extra limbs, growths on their heads, arms, or torsos, and fangs that dangled from their grinning mouths.

Despite their individual differences, she noticed how each gazed at one another with violet eyes, and their skin appeared like black, shiny silk. She instantly realized where she had fallen and what creatures roamed in front of her.

They're demons. I must have landed into the deep reaches where their race dwells. Even though Coura knew in her heart it was merely a vision conjured from her poor physical and mental state, she couldn't help but stare in amazement and fright at the discovery.

None of the creatures paid her any attention. Instead, they made strange sounds to communicate with each other. For the most part, they seemed amused. A handful of those on two legs moved by swaying along the ground to thread around their companions, like a dance.

As she watched their behavior, a menacing sensation overwhelmed her, and she found herself searching for the source. The demons changed too. A pair screeched at the same time in harmonizing pitches when another pounced on one nearby. She winced and threw up her hands to cover her mouth as the bulkiest of the bunch hugged a creature physically resembling a human woman from behind then tore open its throat using its huge fangs. It released its hold after, letting the body sink to the ground for the smallest to start devouring. She had memories of fistfights, but nothing compared to the group in front of her mercilessly ripping off limbs, biting and shredding flesh using pointed teeth or claws, and tackling bodies all over the place while either shrieking in pain or cackling with glee. It devolved into utter madness.

The presence haunting Coura grew until her body became paralyzed from her distress. Her eyes remained forward, watching the insanity, even when she noticed a shadow stretched along the ground in front of her. A warm breath gave her goosebumps before something tickled the right side of her neck. In response, she whirled around with an arm raised to swipe at the source only to find herself on the surface once again, as if she had never slipped into the chasm.

The fiery light and demons vanished, leaving her by herself in the silence. Her breathing grew heavy though she didn't exert her energy while in that new place, and it differed from the previous gasping.

It's…just an illusion…

As Coura repeated the words, she began walking in a random direction with the eerie notion that she had never been alone in the first place.

*

There was no telling when she parted from the dream world. One moment she slept, then the next she found her face buried in a soft pillow and her body under a thin sheet.

She first noticed an additional string of energy consistently roaming outward from her center over her shoulder blades. Never before had she experienced such a sensation, which compared to the feeling just before casting a spell and needing to create an exit point. In response, she reached an invisible hand to investigate and prodded it.

At her touch, the energy sprang forth to manifest in the form it prepared for. Coura kept her eyes closed the entire time since she barely woke enough to process the situation, but a weight rested on the spot. As she figured from the familiarity of the magic, a feathery blanket draped over her back, and her wings' tips slipped off the bed to brush along the floor.

Before she could understand what happened, hurried footsteps sounded nearby, then somebody threw open the door. A woman gasped, a man muttered, and the individuals approached her bed.

She didn't remember much, except Byron and Emilea were the people in the room. They spoke in hushed voices about the wings and how they sensed unfamiliar energy. One of them ran a hand along the entire length of her wing, then the pair left.

The spell remained until she flicked it off thoughtlessly before letting herself sleep again. This time, no illusions or demons disturbed her, though she didn't dream.

*

Heavy trudging in the room woke Coura, and this time she became fully aware of her surroundings. Without opening her eyes or moving from her comfortable position, she groaned to let the person know she was up.

"It's about time you came to," Byron's voice joked from next to the bed.

She slowly opened her eyes to blink in the dim light flooding the room. *Where are we?*

As her foggy mind stitched the memories together, she watched him drag a chair over from the opposite side of the room and sit at her bedside.

"How are you feeling?" he asked in a more serious tone.

Her body remained weak from the strain on her muscles and her head pounded, but the hole in her stomach made the other issues seem miniscule. The energy stretching along her back and shoulders didn't disappear either. Coura closed her eyes again, then rolled onto her stomach to bury her face in the pillow.

"That well, huh?" Byron replied with a hint of humor and shifted in his seat. "Here, take this."

When she turned her head to look, he offered a mug displaying thin streams of steam flowing upward. "Emilea and I figured you would be in this condition. This was the first time you drained your reserves, right?"

They both knew the truth, but she didn't answer since there had been more to it.

Instead, she began pushing herself up from her stomach using both arms. They trembled as she extended them to raise her torso, yet the annoying sensation along her shoulders distracted her. Without considering what took place during the first instance she interacted with that energy, she reached out and activated the spell. The pair of black wings manifested, adding little weight despite their size, yet in her current condition it was enough to cause her arms to give out. Her upper body dropped back onto the bed as she let out a startled squeak.

Byron didn't comment on her triggering the wings or their appearance, but she noted how his eyes read everything.

"Make those go away, and I'll help you," he instructed while setting the mug on the table at her bedside.

Releasing the spell was easy, but the irritation returned in an instant. The energy buzzed like swarm of insects to tickle her flesh, yet swiping at it would only repeat the manifestation. She assumed it was a result of the additional power from the demonic creature and accepted it as she had with every other change.

When Coura took Byron's outstretched hand, he guided her into a sitting position with ease, shoved the mug into her hands, and raised it to her lips to force her to drink the liquid inside. The warm syrup seemed to stick in her throat as she reluctantly gulped it down at once. After, she coughed and set the empty mug aside before lying on her back to settle some of the ache in her stomach, chest, and limbs while she grew drowsy.

"It's bitter medicine, but it gets the job done," he commented. "I'm sure after a nap you'll be ready for dinner."

She drifted off after those words and woke at some point that evening what felt like seconds later. A single, lit candle sat on the table with hardly any wax burned away, telling her someone had been there recently.

Byron spoke the truth about the mug's contents. She found she could move without being hindered by aches, and her center had replenished enough not to bother her; however, the itching along her back and shoulders continued to irritate her. She raised a hand and reached across her chest to rub the spot while contemplating the additional issue.

I need to resist the urge to activate the spell and manifest my wings. Without my attention and control, they'll appear at random and cause trouble if I'm not careful.

She locked away the thought for the moment to rise, grab the candle, and exit into the hallway.

The Traitor's Identity

Figuring out where everybody gathered didn't prove difficult. Since she stayed at Clearshot's home before, Coura felt comfortable wandering toward the staircase and what sounds and light came from below. After placing a hand on the wall to balance herself, she descended at a steady, noiseless pace.

Those on the first floor were involved in a discussion about matters relating to the palace, but the voices abruptly stopped when someone noticed her lingering at the bottom of the stairs. Each of her companions either sat around the dining table, in the sitting room's chairs, or on the floor. The children, who appeared half asleep at Emilea's feet, piped her name. Marcy stood from her spot at the table and wore a concerned expression while Marcus and Will smiled, as if relieved. Despite their attention, nobody went to her.

"What's going on?" she asked into the silence following the greetings.

The master mages shared an unreadable look before Byron gestured for her to join them.

"Emilea was just informing us about what's happening in the palace."

"We were going to wait for you, but I'm afraid we're going to miss our opportunity to act if we waste any more time," the light mage continued while avoiding Coura's eyes.

Why does she seem so timid? In fact, everyone's acting a bit strange.

"It's fine," Coura replied and accepted the invitation to move into the room. Although Byron straightened from his seat in the farthest armchair and prepared to offer his spot, she decided to stand beside the unlit fireplace. After setting the candle on the mantle and leaning against the wall to face the entire group with her arms crossed, she continued the conversation. "Can somebody summarize it for me?"

Clearshot waved a hand in the air before resting it on top of his wife's. "We weren't too far along. Darling, why don't you start over? Let the news be fresh in all our minds."

Annoyance etched across Emilea's face, but she caved in. "I'll go to the beginning then. When most of you left Verona in search of Coura, odd occurrences began taking place in the palace. Grace supposedly left to return to Yeluthia without any explanation. The council concocted their own theories based on what the high priest said since he had been one of the few to see her last, and we figured her absence was due to homesickness. Then, His Highness started to act indifferent to the rising issues. With the increase in demonic creatures, I decided to keep the children at Lady Katrina's home while I continued working. The demonic energy affects them, as well as the mages around the capital."

Coura noticed Mace and Lexie scoot closer to their mother. She understood their opposite energies would create differing stirs of emotion and wondered if the power she carried made them uncomfortable.

"The lack of traveling allowed me to participate in the private dinners on a regular basis. Whenever I talked to King Aaron, he wouldn't speak except through short responses and indirect movements. I wanted to hear his thoughts on recent matters, such as Grace's leave and the Sie-Kie warriors' arrival, yet I couldn't get anything out of him."

At the mention of the people from the Western Woods, Coura's eyes widened with a mixture of astonishment and elation. *Barnelus actually convinced his father to let their hunters go to Verona? As excited as I am, I hope the mages from the capital can protect the Sie-Kie. It's still dangerous, even though the creature we defeated isn't lurking around.*

Emilea went on in a wavering voice, returning her attention to the situation at hand. "I asked Hendal several times that week about His Highness' behavior. He only claimed they were handling multiple problems, so the king's mind has been distant. One day, he reluctantly revealed some important news: General Tont's assistant was assigned to head north and speak with a Nim-Valan leader on the council's behalf."

"Nim-Vala," Byron muttered. His tone suggested plenty of anxiousness. "Last I heard, we were concerned they planned to invade Asteom."

Emilea nodded. "In actuality, they proposed to negotiate an alliance."

"An alliance?"

"That's great news," Marcus interjected. Coura assumed his enthusiasm stemmed from pride in his father's participation. "It would prevent a war to the north at least."

"Why would Hendal try to hide the news from you?" Clearshot asked while raising an eyebrow.

"That's exactly what I thought," his wife replied. "He mentioned how optimistic he felt for the fall season, implying it'll happen soon, so a portion of their army will visit the palace before winter. When I pressed him for more details, Hendal ended the conversation and left with Aaron."

"What did my father say?" Marcus asked next.

"I left to speak with General Tont the following morning, but…" Her eyes lowered, and she stared at the floor as she wrung her hands.

Coura considered what could leave a powerful mage in such a nervous state. The idea had her leaning forward in anticipation.

At last, the woman continued. Though her voice trembled, her face remained an expressionless mask. "The demonic presence lingering around Verona grew especially strong inside the palace. I found the general wandering away from the meeting chamber, and when I attempted to approach him, he acted the same as Aaron. His eyes appeared shaded, and he behaved as though he didn't recognize me."

Marcus began to interrupt, but one of Byron's hands flew up in a gesture for him to be quiet. Emilea seemed like she didn't hear him.

"I hurried to the council's room and found some of the noblemen I'm familiar with, Aaron, and Hendal. The energy became most prominent there. That's when I found out what's been going on. Hendal pretended the others' behavior is normal, but he slipped up. When he attempted to reassure me, I discovered he is responsible for Grace's disappearance and covered it with a fake alibi. I accused him of conspiring against the kingdom and stood against him because I couldn't flee."

She whispered the last words while brushing her fingers along the side of her neck. During the pause, Clearshot wrapped an arm around her shoulders for comfort.

"So, Hendal's behind all this," Byron concluded when nobody else spoke.

To their surprise, Emilea added more. "He is mostly responsible."

"What do you mean?"

The light mage cast an uncertain glance at Coura, causing her to fidget, before addressing Byron directly. "Hendal has been working with the same demon we encountered in Dala."

Coura bounced off the wall as a sudden jolt struck her spine. "What?"

Her physical and verbal reaction hadn't been the only one. While Marcy and Aimes questioned the existence of a demon, Will wondered how the high priest could tolerate its energy when everybody else seemed bothered. Marcus, unable to remain still, stood and paced near the kitchen amid the noise. Lexie let out whimpers, which were ignored, and the space grew warmer despite the lack of a fire.

"What did it do to you?" Clearshot growled, his voice tight with rage.

The question brought their group back to the discussion again. Byron urged them to calm down in his authoritative tone, which had the assistant general returning to his seat and Coura pressing her back against the wall, though her hands clenched into fists to display her silent anger.

She meant to go to the palace after all. What about the rogue angels? Why the high priest? What did she do to Aaron and Marcus' father?

"Did Hendal mention anything else?" Byron continued when a hush fell over the room.

Emilea shook her head. "He ordered the children and I to stay here, supposedly under the demon's watch, until I'm of use to him. Three days ago, just before you arrived, I received a summons. The king is throwing a ball to welcome the Nim-Valan soldiers and announce the alliance. I am to pretend I know nothing and stay at Aaron's side."

Her fellow master mage rubbed his chin as his eyebrows scrunched together. "No doubt it's part of Hendal's grand scheme to make Asteom appear superior."

"You don't seem as shocked as the rest of us," Clearshot noted with some irritation beneath his comment.

"I had a feeling he was plotting something, though I never could have guessed it would be this extreme. He must have waited until I went away to act."

The pair reviewed details during the council sessions to suggest Hendal's questionable loyalty before pausing to consider their encounters. Meanwhile, Coura sensed eyes on her and turned to catch Marcy giving her a dubious stare.

"Is this the demon whose energy you've been collecting?" the woman ventured when everybody else quieted.

Coura sighed since she had been waiting for someone to tie in her connection. When she considered the warning from Soirée in Dala and how her companions had dismissed her, it became impossible to hide the aggravation in her voice. "Yes. In fact, I told most of the people in this room that she started working with a traitor in the palace and a group of rouge angels who tried to kill us."

"I had my suspicions for a while," Byron replied to defend himself when his temper rose after hearing her accusation. "It would have been a fool's mistake to take action against Hendal unless we were certain he's the culprit. Not to mention, this wasn't our only issue. Let's not forget the creatures causing chaos around the country and how you left to deal with them on your own. He was bound to catch us all separated sooner or later."

"Or have the opportunity to separate us," Marcus added.

A dramatic yawn from Mace halted the conversation. He covered his mouth, but the sound had been loud enough to distract the group and remind them of the late hour. Even though she just woke up, Coura hadn't fully recovered and still felt physically tired, causing her to yawn along with half the room in response.

"I explained the situation up to this point. There's no hurry for us to discuss what to do next," Emilea reassured them in a gentler manner as she reached down to nudge her children.

They understood her intentions, rose, and walked over to the stairs while rubbing their eyes.

Byron stood and stretched next. "You're right. Perhaps a full night's rest will give us more ideas."

Coura remained leaning beside the fireplace and looked at the floor to process what she learned while everybody else shuffled upstairs. *Soirée's hiding in the palace, that's for certain. What could she have done to Hendal to convince the priest to trust her? There's also the disgust and antagonistic behavior between angels and demons, which should have pushed those five to fight or flee from her. The palace is out of balance, yet Asteom sounds close to forming a positive relationship with Nim-Vala. If they discover Soirée's control over Aaron, the generals, and the high priest, then-*

"Coming?"

She raised her eyes to where Byron lingered near the kitchen with his hands on his hips and straightened off the wall. "I slept enough."

"This will probably be our last opportunity to build our reserves. You should take advantage of the time."

Coura said nothing as she stared down her former mentor while he did the same to her. They waited for the other to speak for a few seconds, then he caved in.

"Keep watch for the night if you plan on staying up." He turned away and trudged upstairs after issuing the order.

She didn't move for a few minutes. Although her mind went blank, she couldn't remove her eyes from where Byron had been moments ago. The home remained warm and stuffy, like a furniture-filled cage, so she strolled to the front door, unlatched the pair of locks, and stepped outside.

A welcoming breeze caressed her skin and blew through her unbound hair as soon as she passed through to the other side. After inhaling the fresh air and savoring the cooler temperature, she began walking down the first path she came across. Nothing in the woods frightened her after they defeated the previous creature. With the energy she possessed, she believed she became the most powerful being outside Verona, or at least she convinced herself of it.

The sounds of the nightlife stayed active to keep her company, but the creeping insects reminded her of the crawling energy itching her back. After figuring there was no use containing the spell when she wandered alone, she focused on repressing the energy so no one would notice. Without a mage around, it wouldn't be possible to tell if she had been successful or not, though it didn't matter to her. The freedom of manifesting her wings and climbing into the sky became too enjoyable to have her thinking about much else.

Coura identified a few animals below as she soared across the star-filled backdrop without feeling bound to the ground, or those on it. For the rest of the evening, she flew laps over the woods, practicing twists, turns, unexpected inclines and declines against the current, and more maneuvers. All the while, her center never emptied or seemed to weaken.

This power is shared between Soirée and I, so that must be why. No hunger, thirst, or weariness can overwhelm me for days as long as I let her energy flow through my body. At first, the idea of the demon's connection influencing her body's natural needs had been terrifying, but she soon decided she could use it in her favor.

*

The grayness of the approaching dawn appeared sooner than Coura expected, signaling the time for her to descend and return to her companions before they worried where she had gone. She landed in front of the house, released the wings, then cursed when the sensation continued to bother her as it did before.

Once ready, she went to the door but found it locked. Somebody must have heard her shake the knob in an attempt to enter, though, for hurried footsteps came from the opposite side and the latches clicked before the door swung open. Clearshot stood in a wide stance to block the entryway with a serious expression; however, he recognized her and stepped aside while rolling his eyes.

"Get in here," he grumbled.

Coura didn't comment as she entered and took a seat at the dining table. They appeared to be the only two awake.

"Were you outside all night?" he asked while sitting at the other end.

"There's nothing threatening us around here," she said instead of giving a direct response to his question. "At least, nothing I could sense."

"Why do I have a feeling you were too preoccupied to search for potential enemies?"

This time, she didn't respond.

Clearshot rose after a moment to move into the kitchen where she heard him working on breakfast.

Coura tapped her fingers together, curled and relaxed her toes, and stretched her neck in an attempt to relax, but she couldn't sit still. Instead of waiting for more people to wake up, she went back outside to walk through the morning fog.

The night had been peaceful yet active under the cover of darkness; the morning seemed similar, though livelier in a different way. Sunlight poured through openings in the canopy, lighting the area to display an array of greens with wildflowers in various colors highlighted against them. Her steps were quiet enough not to startle the rabbits, deer, and rodents searching for food while she strolled. When she grew bored of sightseeing, she sprinted along a chosen path toward the house without a touch of exhaustion.

"Good morning!" someone called as she appeared in the grassy yard.

Marcus waved from where he and Will stood nearby. Each held a lengthy branch in their hands.

"What are you doing?" she inquired and approached the pair.

Will shot her a nervous smile, then he positioned himself into a fighting stance against the soldier. "What does it look like?"

She observed their brief sparring session where the sticks acted as swords until Marcus paused to correct one of Will's attacking motions. After, they glanced at her awkwardly, as if realizing she seemed interested in their exercise.

"You wouldn't want to practice with us, would you?" the assistant general offered in a hesitant manner.

Although she wondered why they continued to behave so strangely, Coura agreed to join them, figuring the activity would give her something to do. She wandered into the woods for a straight yet hefty branch before returning, and they began again.

Because of her sharpened skills, both due to years of training and the inhuman speed and strength from the demonic power, she resisted the urge to overwhelm them and prevent any development. Even so, she never went easy on Will. He kept up with her and Marcus, to her amazement, yet earned several bruises when he left one side more vulnerable than the other.

"Not bad!" Marcus exclaimed when their friend parried a stab to deliver a strike of his own, though it landed too weakly to leave a mark.

Will blushed at the compliment and nodded his thanks. Meanwhile, Coura circled around him, then placed her makeshift weapon at the side of his throat when he became distracted.

"Don't forget your second opponent," she warned at a quieter volume.

He jumped away from her at the words, spun around without his previous control, and swung at her head in a rushed attempt. She ducked under the branch, chuckled, then retreated a couple steps. The intention had been to draw him into closer combat, and she prepared to lecture him on reacting to an enemy's approach until she saw his face.

Behind the lopsided spectacles, Will's eyes were wide and fearful. His hands trembled while he remained in his stance, so Coura abandoned hers first. At the movement, he adjusted his glasses, avoided looking into her eyes, and kept silent. Marcus didn't intervene, yet he appeared concerned by the spontaneous reaction.

I scared him, she realized after noting the still-shaking hands and avoidance.

"I'm sorry," he apologized. "Sometimes, I remember the fighting I've seen and the creatures we encountered. It puts me on edge, then I stop thinking."

Coura rubbed the back of her neck as she considered how desensitized she had become to the violence. Her chagrin increased when she recalled the instances where the herbalist had been present as well, including when she first discovered her potential to use demonic energy. The memories made her consider if her presence reminded her friends of Soirée.

During the pause, Marcus moved to Will's side and put a reassuring hand on his shoulder. "Why don't you take a break?"

The two were sweaty and breathing heavily from the workout up to that point anyway. In response, Will dropped to sit cross-legged in the grass and set the branch aside.

The soldier turned to Coura next, displaying a crooked smile. "Do you want a break?"

She narrowed her eyes with a smirk in answer. Obviously, she didn't, yet she appreciated how he asked if she wanted, not needed, one.

After a shrug, he resumed the combat by charging at her.

***

Once Will removed himself from the spar, Byron let out a relieved breath from where he watched the informal practice session with Emilea, Clearshot, and Aimes in the shade of the brick home. Marcy volunteered to supervise the children, and the three could be heard splashing around by the pond, oblivious to the entertainment taking place on the opposite side.

"At least Will's not courageous enough to try and keep up now," Clearshot commented while Marcus and Coura fought, their wooden weapons meeting to create echoing whacks.

Byron studied his former pupil's movements closely. Based on what he saw, he believed her capable of more but assumed she preferred to participate in casual exercise alongside the assistant general.

"Would it really have benefited the young man any to stand between two professionals?" Aimes countered from where he sat off to the left.

He never ceases to surprise me with new observations, Byron thought as he considered the question.

Throughout their travels and the passing days at Clearshot and Emilea's home, Aimes remained alert yet didn't comment without thoroughly contemplating his words or act without consideration for their consequences.

"Will's smart," Byron added with a chuckle. "He knows when to simply look on and learn instead of push for a lesson. You should have known him before he picked up a sword. I swear, if he wasn't so enthusiastic about being able to defend himself, I would've made sure he stayed locked inside somewhere safe."

"Doesn't he do that most of the time for his studies anyway?" Emilea asked with a playful wink, sparking grins from the men.

A breeze shook the treetops above, and the resulting rustling had Byron glancing upward at the blue sky. Any thoughts about future confrontations or rescuing those in the palace became hard to imagine when their immediate location appeared so peaceful. The group had yet to decide what they would do when Emilea answered her summons for the ball, but it needed to wait until everybody grew comfortable enough with the news to suggest solutions and not rely on their emotions.

His eyes fell on Marcus and Coura once again. The assistant general's clothing shaded in several spots from sweat, though he continued moving without noticeably decreasing his speed. His former student behaved as calm and collected as ever.

It doesn't seem like anyone mentioned the demon's influence to her yet.

The idea bothered Byron enough that his stomach tightened, and he understood why she remained unaware of the effect the unnatural power had on them. As the energy she possessed increased while their journey continued, so did the malicious intent associated with the being. Whether or not Coura carried the same amount didn't matter; whoever she neared felt as though they were around the demon itself. Her physical appearance didn't vouch for much either. The unattractive bruising proved unnerving, and he hoped she could control her wings' manifestation, which he grew doubtful of when she released them twice while in a weakened state.

Despite the changes, he found solace whenever he spoke to her, as her headstrong personality shined through. Her smile rarely faltered, though he saw it less, and the bright, blue eyes distinguished her from the demon and its creatures' violet gazes.

In the midst of Byron's assessment, Marcus stumbled backward from a push against Coura's branch, and she raised the stick with the intent to tap it on his shoulder. Aimes made a noise in anticipation for the blow while Clearshot muttered a comment to Emilea; however, as Coura lowered her makeshift weapon, the assistant general suddenly sprang to life. He placed both hands on his branch to throw his weight into a horizontal swing aimed at the middle of her stick as it lowered. A crack resulted when hers snapped in half from his maneuver, and she stepped away in alarm.

The assistant general didn't miss a beat. He pulled his branch across again with the same amount of strength while his opponent stood defenseless, knocking her alongside the head. Coura dropped to the ground then brought a hand up to cover her temple, and Marcus towered over her, clutching the weapon as everybody who saw tried to process what took place.

Emilea hurried forward, then Clearshot ran a hand through his hair and released a long whistle before following. Byron moved after the master light mage, but the three stopped when Coura scrambled to her feet and Marcus tossed the branch away.

"Why did you follow through?" Will asked while rising.

"What was that?" Coura demanded immediately after. Fresh blood coated the right side of her face, and her eyes lit up from an inner fire.

Byron remembered her rage being directed at him in Dala and said a silent prayer for her friend.

"I'm sorry," Marcus managed, though he sounded more startled by his strike than sincere about the apology.

In response, Coura threw the remaining half of her stick at him. "You had no other way to beat me than to play dirty?"

Will stepped between the two and told them to stop arguing. Unfortunately, Marcus went on without a hint of regret.

"I thought there's no such thing as cheating or playing dirty in a fight? You were the one who taught me that, remember?"

His nonchalant tone made Byron wonder if the blow hadn't been completely unintentional. In any case, it succeeded in setting Coura off. She stomped forward, shoved Will out of the way when he didn't move, and glared at Marcus while standing toe to toe with him. The young man didn't flinch. It was when Byron noticed her hands clench into fists that he realized she intended to throw a punch and came closer to intervene. Before he could, Emilea's firm voice cut through the tension.

"That's enough! You're both too old for this type of childish quarrelling."

Although the fists disappeared, Coura's narrowed eyes snapped to the master light mage, and she met the stern look with a challenge. Marcus left then, strolling past Will to one of the trails without a word. Despite his absence, Byron grew more concerned when neither woman broke the eye contact.

"Go cool off," Emilea ordered in her no-nonsense manner.

With a huff, Coura turned away and stormed farther into the yard before manifesting the black wings, leaping into the air, and flying above the woods. Those still in the area threw up their hands against the gust she sent in their direction.

I didn't like the look of that at all, Byron thought as Emilea and Will came near him.

"Well, it could've been worse," Clearshot said with a shake of his head.

"Coura wouldn't have done anything," Emilea replied matter-of-factly, though she appeared and sounded exhausted.

"How do you know?"

"Because I see plenty of tantrums from my students when they're bested, fairly or not. Besides, we know those two well enough by now. I'm sure we can put this behind us when they return."

A Plan in Motion

Byron gathered everybody together that evening to finish their conversation regarding what should be done about the high priest and demon controlling figures in the capital. Marcus and Coura hadn't spoken to each other after the incident, but there were no more standoffs to worry him. Emilea served dinner as they settled into their seats.

"Let's start where we left off," he began once he'd been handed a bowl of soup loaded with vegetables. "Hendal's in charge and controlling Aaron, General Tont, some of the noblemen, and probably others while working with the angels from Dala and the demon. There's a plausible chance he's planning something for this ball tomorrow evening since the Nim-Valan guests will arrive to announce an alliance. Also, Grace is missing, which means we won't be able to contact each other if we separate. With that in mind, does anyone have an idea where to start?"

Immediately, Coura answered from where she sat at the dining table. "I already told you I'll be going after Soirée."

"Do you think it's important enough to leave the group? What if there are guards too?"

She huffed a laugh and pushed her untouched bowl away. "Soirée wouldn't let anybody protect her, especially not humans. She can defend herself. It's not like she can blend in with the guests at the ball either."

"The demon will stay hidden then," Byron concluded, silently commending Coura's plotting.

"We're assuming the high priest would be separated from the demon and angels too," Will added. "If I were him, I'd make sure they're near me or I'm around enough people to avoid accusations. If we caused a scene, he could shift the blame so we appear to be the villains."

"With so many under his control, Hendal would feel safe anywhere in the palace," Emilea muttered.

They turned over the facts for a moment before Marcy spoke. Her shy demeanor remained at first as she formed the start of a plan.

"From what you mentioned about this man, it seems like splitting up is the best idea."

"What do you mean?" Byron asked. He urged her to elaborate when she hesitated.

"If he has nothing to fear and desires control over the guests, he *will* be present at the event. If the angels you mentioned won't tolerate the demon either, they will leave or blend in to guard the high priest. That means…"

"Soirée will be alone," Coura finished with a slight smile.

Byron was a bit startled to hear Marcus address her afterward based on the conflict earlier in the day.

"You shouldn't go by yourself. We risk too much by sending one of our mages into a deathmatch, assuming the demon is in the palace."

He expected Coura to protest Marcus' words. Instead, she contemplated what he said before responding in a neutral manner. "I can keep her distracted while the rest of you deal with Hendal. Otherwise, I can try luring her out of Verona. Either way, I plan to search for her, and Grace too."

"Your priority should be the demon," Emilea stated.

"You don't want to save Grace?"

The master light mage winced at the accusation. "Of course I do, but we can't make mistakes when restraining Hendal is our goal. He claimed she went missing, so I would wager he has her locked up somewhere only he has access to. She's brave and knows the basic spells. There is no doubt in my mind she will be fine until we can rescue her."

Coura, Will, and Marcus shared a downcast expression but didn't argue.

They're friends with Grace, and Aaron too, Byron recalled. *I never had anybody I cared about much growing up other than Cintra. I can't possibly imagine the pain they're experiencing by putting aside the ambassador and king's safety.*

Despite his pity, he cleared his throat and set his empty bowl aside. "So far, Coura will search the palace for the demon under the cover of the ball and keep it occupied. What about the rest of us?"

"Why not pull the high priest aside and settle the matter?" Aimes suggested while passionately pounding a fist into his open palm.

Emilea answered right away. "There are still those under his influence and the angels who may be wandering about."

"Does the man know of your return?" he asked next while raising an eyebrow at Byron.

"No, and I don't believe he heard we found Coura either."

"Which means he won't be expecting her to stalk through the palace or us to know about his relationship with the demon and rogue angels," Will concluded.

Aimes grunted in confirmation, leaned back in his chair, and crossed his arms in a proud fashion.

At the same time, Marcy tapped a finger to her lip before adding an additional thought and pointing a thumb at the older man. "Nobody recognizes us. We can gather information or spy on him!"

Aimes' eyes went wide upon hearing the idea, and he bent forward to knit his fingers and brow together. "Well, we don't need to get ourselves involved in this mess unless we have to…"

The woman gaped at her partner. "Come on, Aimes! We would be excellent scouts. How else are we going to contribute?"

"I'm not willing to throw you two in danger," Byron started before their personal argument could escalate.

While the older man released a sigh to show his relief, Marcy appeared offended and opened her mouth to protest, though Byron went on before she could.

"I do prefer our chances when the entire situation stays unknown to Hendal. Unless anyone else wishes to share more, I think I'm beginning to figure out what we should do."

The rest of the group leaned closer and shared a hopeful gaze. Clearshot was the only person to verbally respond.

"It's about time you came up with a strategy. That's your specialty!"

Byron ignored his instinct to grin at the compliment and cleared his throat again to cover his vanity. As he prepared to organize the information in his mind, another notion arose. "Emilea, were the children required to accompany you to the ball?"

His fellow master mage stirred at the mention of her children, who were upstairs studying under their parents' orders. "He didn't mention them in his letter."

"In that case, we'll assume they're out of his way. Will they be all right on their own here tomorrow evening?"

This time, Emilea glanced at her husband, and they exchanged a concerned look. "I would think so, but Hendal mentioned somebody would be watching us, most likely the demon."

"I haven't sensed any other sources of energy besides us since we've been here," Coura mentioned to Byron before he continued.

"Me neither. I'm assuming he lied to scare you into behaving or assumed you wouldn't act alone if you called his bluff. Our move against them might provoke him into targeting your home, though, and we wouldn't get a chance to return."

His heart ached at the mention of their children being in danger. *I wouldn't put it past Hendal or the demon to harm them if it means hurting us.*

In the next moment, to Byron's surprise, Aimes offered to stay behind. "I wouldn't be much use in a fight," the older man explained. "If Marcy goes along, you'll have your undercover guest."

"We can send them to Katrina," Emilea suggested instead while facing her husband.

Clearshot instantly shook his head. "I doubt she would miss the opportunity to be present at a grand event in the palace. I don't trust anyone else in her home to care for them if their lives depended on it. It's better to keep them here."

"No," Aimes added, startling everybody with the firmness of the word. "I'll lead them farther away and camp out. According to Coura, these woods are safe from any more creatures. We can find an opening nearby and stay until someone comes for us. I doubt they would explore the area if they don't find them at this place first."

Marcy set a hand on Aimes' shoulder. "Are you sure about this?"

Byron smiled when her partner patted her hand and nodded. Clearshot turned to him after.

"That ties up the loose end. What about the rest of your plan?"

"With Coura handling the demon, we'll send Marcy and Emilea to scope out the hall. The rogue angels *could* join in the festivities, but something tells me Hendal would prefer to hide them and their relationship when he's in public. If anybody were to recognize them after the event, it could make the situation messy. Emilea is bound by his orders; however, that doesn't prevent her from chatting with the other guests." Byron nodded to Marcy, who caught on to his idea.

"I get it. She can tell me if she senses magic related to the demon or the angels. I'm able to leave freely, so I can repeat what she says to the rest of you."

"What should we be doing in the meantime?" Marcus asked next.

Byron had been considering the best answer to that question as they worked their way through the discussion. *An attack of any sort without a legitimate threat would only make us look like the enemy, especially if Hendal plays along. It's too difficult to lure him away or wait for him to be by himself, and with Aaron behaving thoughtlessly, I doubt Hendal will leave the hall at all. We're left with one course of action then...*

"I'm going to confront him during the event."

Some in the room voiced their concern and issues with the idea because it involved revealing their arrival without leverage. He listened patiently until an opportunity to elaborate became available.

"Hendal doesn't know Emilea spoke with us or who Marcy is, meaning they won't be associated with our return. Those of us left won't enter the palace unless we receive confirmation from them that there's no protection around Hendal. Also, the soldiers and mages at the event *will* recognize us and support what news we bring. At least, I believe I earned that sort of reputation."

Nobody argued with him, which he expected.

"What happens when everyone sees us?" Will picked up.

"You, Marcus, and Clearshot are free to find familiar faces and inquire about the energy in the palace. Gather what information you can while spreading the word to those who haven't figured out there's a demon involved. In the meantime, I'll approach Hendal. I'm curious to see how he behaves during my accusations considering he normally shies away from having his decisions and motives challenged." He recalled the day when Aaron argued for the queen's garden to be open to the public and how the high priest's resolve crumbled when their superior questioned the reasoning.

If they were lucky, the man would be cornered and captured before the end of the night.

As he wrapped up the plan, he turned to Coura. "By the time everybody retires for the evening, I expect you to return here, no matter what happens."

She met his eyes and dipped her head in a slow nod.

*

They worked out a few details regarding timing, outfits, and positioning before Byron felt satisfied. Emilea collected the discarded bowls once the conversation died down, and he assisted her when the topic shifted so no one spoke to him. The only person who didn't eat had been Coura, which bothered him. When their host confronted her about the untouched meal, she denied being hungry.

"Are you ready?" he asked his fellow master mage as she began washing the dishes. He took it upon himself to prepare some tea to settle everybody's stomachs.

"To be honest, I'm not sure how Coura will fare," she answered at a lower volume in order to avoid the others overhearing. "I didn't even see the demon when it appeared in the council chamber. Next thing I knew, it pressed a blade to my throat."

Byron couldn't think of anything to say besides reassuring Emilea of Coura's abilities and determination as she reached for the final dish, which happened to be the untouched bowl. He noticed her hand hesitate above it while he poured several mugs and began bringing them into the other room to distribute two at a time. When he returned to the kitchen after the second round, the woman thrust one of the remaining cups into his open hand.

363

"Give this to Coura and make sure she drinks it."

He glanced at the steaming liquid, then up into her face with a knowing look. "What did you do to it?"

"She hasn't eaten since she's been awake," Emilea answered while scanning the wall off to her right. "I spoke to Cornelius about it this morning when she went outside, and he admitted how little she ate, drank, or slept during your travels. It's because of the demonic energy she's collecting, which I believe will cause more damage to her in the end. Maybe I'm too concerned about nothing, but a proper rest will benefit her before tomorrow."

Although going behind his former student's back instead of addressing the issue didn't sit well with him, he obeyed the request.

***

Throughout the entire evening of plotting, Coura's stomach twisted and her chest tightened during periods of anxiousness, shortening her breaths. She feigned confidence in order to avoid acknowledging her own emotions until the strategy had been sorted out. The mood adjusted to reflect the group's weariness and anticipation.

I'm afraid, angry, and responsible for what Soirée has done, and is doing. Aaron and Grace, as well as countless others, are suffering because of her, Hendal, and the rogue angels. I just need to focus on finding her and trust Byron can handle the high priest.

On the outside, she hid her insecurities behind a mask of indifference. She longed to fly ahead and scan the surrounding area or practice her aerial skills; sitting around doing nothing seemed like a waste of precious time. Before she could make up her mind, Byron set a mug of steaming tea in front of her. When she didn't grab for the cup right away, he nudged it closer while setting another down for Aimes, who had moved to sit beside her.

"Drink it," he ordered before returning to the kitchen.

"You heard him," Aimes added before gulping his despite the temperature.

Coura reached for the mug and wrapped both hands around its sides to savor its warmth. The disapproving stares from her companions when she avoided meals and rest hadn't escaped her notice as the days passed. Still, her only excuse had been the truth.

I'm not hungry, thirsty, or tired because the demonic energy sustains me. I feel I would make myself sick by trying, and I'm more productive with the extra time.

While she pondered the same notions again, Byron and Emilea returned from the kitchen with their own mugs in hand. Marcus and Will chatted in the sitting room while Marcy listened, the light mage returned to the armchair across from her husband, and her former mentor sat across from Aimes. The two didn't feel the need to spark a conversation, so the table kept quiet.

Coura caught Byron frowning at her and decided to sip at her tea in order to make him stop. A bitter, almost familiar aftertaste lingered, but she ignored it.

He prepared the tea, not Emilea, she remembered, and that seemed to explain the poor flavor.

It did succeed in settling her nerves, which became enough reason to continue drinking until the mug emptied. With an unexpected yawn, she pushed it aside as Emilea and Clearshot collected the dishes and everybody began shuffling upstairs. She intended to remain awake for the evening; however, her eyelids grew too heavy to keep open without effort. Aimes offered his arm when he noticed her sluggish state, which proved to be unfortunate for him because she found herself leaning against the frail, older man for support as they climbed the stairs.

*

Bright light entering from the nearest window brought Coura out of the sleep she never desired. With a groan, she sat up, stretched both arms, and found herself alone in one of the bedrooms.

What time is it? How did I get here?

Her mind felt foggy and eyes itchy, yet she dragged herself to her feet to get dressed and move downstairs at the reminder of what was to come that day. The clothes she wore during their travels had been cleaned and mended at some point when she fell unconscious thanks to Emilea, and she donned them while appreciating the woman's thoughtfulness.

I wonder how I managed to earn a place on her good side. Ever since she healed me in Dala, we've grown closer through the moments we spent together.

365

Coura's tongue became dry enough to distract her for the first time in weeks, and the unpleasant bitterness from the previous night's tea sat in her mouth. As she considered the plan and their discussion, she abruptly remembered why the drink tasted familiar.

It's similar to the sleeping potions they forced me to take when I was recovering in Dala. Did Byron mix one in with my tea? Her temper flared when she acknowledged the answer.

When she finished dressing, Coura descended the stairs and found she had been the only person still in bed by that point. Will greeted her while munching on a piece of fruit at the table along with Marcus and Marcy, who sat on either side of him. The two smiled but didn't say anything.

"Where's Byron?" she asked, hoping to skin him verbally before her anger quelled.

"He's outside with Emilea and Clearshot. They helped Aimes, Mace, and Lexie pack for their trip and were leading them to where they're supposed to camp."

"We already said goodbye," Marcus added. "It's just before noon, and they wanted to go as soon as possible."

At the mention of Aimes and the children, Coura forgot her grudge and hurried out the front door. She raised a hand above her eyes to block the sun, scanned the area, and found herself alone. Instead of sinking into regret for missing their exit, she flicked the energy tickling her shoulder blades to manifest her wings before pulling herself into the sky. It took a minute to distinguish the group trekking away from the house, and though she would have rather skimmed the trees above to reach them right away, she dropped back to the ground. Her wings disappeared as she released the spell while sprinting along their trail.

She aimed to catch up until realizing they were in no real rush and instead slowed to a jog. The natural environment allowed her to enjoy the freedom and clear her mind against the pressure stemming from the rest of the day.

The location where Aimes, Mace, and Lexie would stay happened to be near a pond to the south. Astonishingly, the path Coura currently followed matched the one their group used to escape the previous demonic creature, though they had been too preoccupied to observe their surroundings. A hill overlooked the pool of water surrounded by grass as trees circled like a wooden wall, leaving the trail she followed as the only clear way in or out.

She forgot how quiet her footsteps had grown as she entered without alerting anybody. Clearshot, Emilea, and Byron dropped the bundles they brought along while the children ran ahead and Aimes strolled near the water.

"This is a neat hideout," she commented and crossed her arms. A mischievous grin stretched across her face when everyone wheeled around in alarm before realizing who joined them.

Clearshot laughed in response. "Give us a warning next time!"

On the other hand, Byron didn't sound too pleased. "You forget we're worried about being watched. Don't act so recklessly."

Coura prepared to reprimand him then and there until Emilea interrupted with a comment for Aimes. "We often bring the children here for picnics or to practice magic, so they know the way home in case you need to return."

"Just don't forget about us here," he joked before pointing at the children. "I don't want to be shoved into my grave so soon. These bones can't handle too much activity!"

"If you're settled, I suppose we should head back and prepare ourselves," Byron said with a seriousness that shifted the mood.

Clearshot and Emilea looked at each other before the latter called Mace and Lexie over. While the children hugged their parents, who held their emotions in check by lecturing them on taking care of their sibling and Aimes, Coura went to their older companion.

"Are you sure you won't run out of energy?" she teased. "They're pretty demanding, even for their age."

Aimes chuckled and startled her by opening his arms to pull her into a friendly hug. "I'll manage. Take care of yourself."

She returned the embrace, then the two broke apart. When she turned around, Mace and Lexie were there to wrap their arms around her waist with their own goodbyes.

"Be careful," the eldest child mumbled as he stared at his feet.

Lexie sniffed from the tears shed earlier and repeated her brother's words.

Coura appreciated their concern and felt motivated enough to place a hand on their heads. With a reassuring smile, she met each set of eyes. "You're worried about *me*? I'm not the one stuck here with that crazy man."

From behind, Aimes let out a "Hey!" at her jab; his reaction spurred matching smiles from the children.

"I'll be here as soon as I can," she offered. "You should show me what you've been working on then. Does that sound fair?"

At the thought of displaying their magic, both sets of eyes widened. They nodded before Aimes gestured for them to help unpack the bags, and Coura, Byron, Emilea, and Clearshot departed along the trail with a final wave.

"You sure have a way with children," the soldier commented once they were on their way.

Coura shrugged. "I just know how to talk to them."

Speaking of talking to people…

"Byron, when did you plan on telling me about the sleeping potion in my drink last night?" she asked after a pause, letting her irritation seep into the question.

He scratched his chin from where he walked ahead of her as Emilea led at the front and Clearshot held up the rear. Although he looked back to respond, the light mage's words came first.

"He didn't do that. I did."

The confession caught Coura off guard. "Why?" she countered, unsure whether or not to be upset or wary.

"Clearshot told me you haven't been eating or sleeping. Byron's been willing to let it slide, but I understand how dangerous that is, especially when you possess the demon's power. My duty is to heal, including more than just physical wounds."

Emilea's voice didn't sound as hostile as Coura expected based on yesterday's fight with Marcus. A tiny voice in her mind agreed with the light mage, yet the distrust already bloomed.

"I don't care," she snapped. "For all I know, you could've slipped poison in instead, and I wouldn't have suspected it either. I'll stick to my instincts and the energy I can rely on."

The others' displeasure was palpable, but no one responded since they saw the house ahead.

*

Because it would take until sundown to reach Verona at a rushed speed, Emilea and Marcy expected to head out immediately, and Byron, Clearshot, Marcus, and Will planned to leave an hour later. The women wouldn't associate with the second group, who could wait outside Lady Katrina's home on the southern side of the city. Coura focused on her own part instead of paying attention to the details of theirs. Like Aimes, Marcy gave her a hug as Emilea and Clearshot embraced before the pair wished them all well and departed. Nobody felt up to conversing after.

When the time came, the remaining master mage broke the silence by deeming it safe for their group to go to the capital. They had prepared their packs earlier, and Coura followed them outside. There, Will nearly knocked her over while wrapping his arms around her.

"Stay safe," he muttered before releasing her, adjusting his glasses, and shouldering his bag.

She tried her best to smile, yet it was obvious they all felt anxious about the next few hours. Marcus held her briefly in a similar manner while saying the same, then Clearshot put a hand on her head like she had done to the children and wished her luck. She repeated the sentiment. Lastly, Byron stood in front of her to look her over, as if she were the one heading off at the moment.

"Remember, we'll be in the palace too. If you need help or something unexpected happens, send us a signal."

"I will."

"You should return here when the ball concludes. We're supposed to act as though we didn't find you. Keep that in mind with Emilea and Marcy too."

She rolled her eyes. "We covered this already. I know what I'm doing."

He sighed, seemingly relieved to hear her confirm that, then he smiled as his way of saying goodbye. "Let's be off," he said louder for the others.

Coura's gaze never strayed from the four until they disappeared into the woods, and she stood completely alone.

Throughout the remainder of the day, she couldn't sit still. She double checked each lock on the doors and windows in the house since nobody would be around before Clearshot or Emilea, and without a reason to bring a pack, she needed nothing more than the clothes on her back. The empty house grew haunting and suffocating, so she moved outside to escape the brick walls.

It became both a blessing and a curse to see thicker clouds crowding the sky as rain would hide her, yet it could impact her flight. She wandered across the yard until the sun began to set along the edge of the treetops, which had been her signal to go.

Stay hidden. Find Soirée.

She repeated the words in her mind to stay focused and counter the rising apprehension as she manifested her wings and stretched them in what remained of the sunlight. Once she felt ready, Coura leapt into the air, pumped herself higher until she floated among the clouds, and set off toward the palace.

The Grand Ball

The western road in Verona appeared clear, as Byron figured it would be when they entered the city. Night and the overcast it brought shrouded the estates in darkness except where their owners had lanterns lit inside and out. Though less elaborate, more lights were in place along the streets to make it visible for travelers.

At the moment, the four waited beyond the gate in Lady Katrina's front garden, keeping to the shadows. Emilea and Marcy stopped beforehand to don their formal dresses and inform the woman of the second group's arrival. For the sake of her reputation, the lady vowed to never speak a word, not that Emilea would mention enough to risk her friend's safety.

Byron expected Katrina to be aware of them lingering near her home, yet she went out of her way by ordering her butler, Leo, to open the gate so they could remain as unnoticeable to the public as possible. During his time stationed at the palace, the two enjoyed flirting with each other but stopped once she became engaged to a wealthy merchant many years her elder. Still, he recalled their fling fondly.

Nothing had ever been serious, which was why it seemed so fun. Katrina was raised to be a lady and desired nothing more than the life she has now. I wouldn't mind catching up with her sometime, if we get the opportunity.

"We're waiting here longer than I expected," Clearshot whispered from Byron's side to draw him out of his thoughts.

Will paced behind them while Marcus kept watch closer to the gate.

"You don't suppose anything happened to her, do you?" the herbalist asked while staring at the sky.

"I doubt it," Clearshot answered. "If she slipped in and out right away, it would be too noticeable. Besides, she's pretending to be a relative of Katrina's. Marcy wouldn't be able to easily escape anyway."

Byron remembered Will had met the lady before and assumed the young man understood her clinginess when he didn't question the comment. Not long after, Marcus gestured to them.

"Someone's coming!"

They heard the faint clicking of heeled shoes above a quiet conversation then a woman's laugh. The steps ended in front of the gate, and Byron recognized Marcy's voice.

"I can't thank you enough for the escort."

"Not a problem," a man replied. "It's a shame you're not feeling well tonight. I hear there's big news His Highness will be sharing."

"Yes, but my head is just throbbing. I'm sure my cousin will be kind enough to inform me of it upon her return."

As the two parted, Byron marveled at Marcy's acting and said as much when she came through the open gate to where they waited. She brushed off the compliment, claiming she knew how to behave around men. He sensed more beneath her explanation yet kept his mind on what she reported.

"The situation is normal, according to Emilea," she said first. "I was able to speak with her when Lady Katrina called her over to diagnose my feigned headache. When she took me aside, she told me to say there is no angelic energy and nobody present who matched their descriptions. Hendal positioned her by the king's side before I left. I noticed he kept disappearing and reappearing, and the rumor is they won't announce the alliance until after dinner is finished. The servants were starting to enter with trays of food when I chose to exit."

"We need to move," Marcus added with a glance at Byron.

Clearshot patted Marcy's back while offering a sincere smile. "We can't thank you enough. You did an exceptional job!"

Even though the garden lacked proper lighting, Byron pictured the woman's blush as she mumbled a response, then she stepped away from the gate. With her task complete, she would remain at the estate in order to avoid suspicion until it became safe for her to return to Clearshot and Emilea's home.

Marcus waved them onto the empty road where they began hurrying to the palace after.

*

The king and his council hosted all palace events in the grand hall, as Grace's arrival ceremony and Aaron's coronation had demonstrated. Dinner was served in individual portions on trays by the kitchen's servants, allowing guests to continue mingling without being limited to tables and chairs. Still, the space indoors meant anybody interested in freedom from the crowds had to go outside to line the bridge or wander across the main road. Even the training ground contained pairs or trios of soldiers and mages drinking to themselves on most occasions.

It didn't take longer than a few seconds for someone at the ball to recognize Byron, and he felt grateful the individual ranked as a more experienced dark mage. According to the plan, Marcus, Will, and Clearshot spread out and socialized with those who knew them while he pulled the dark mage aside to inquire about the questionable energy in the area.

He learned nothing besides how the man grew physically uncomfortable at being exposed to such power, which Byron revealed stemmed from a demon. The man's square face didn't expose as much shock as there would have been if he hadn't suspected the source first, and they wished each other well after Byron encouraged him to spread the word.

He aimed to reach the grand staircase where he could see Hendal beside the throne, even at a distance. Along the way, several people, some he recognized and some he didn't, stopped him to chat about various topics. He did his best to answer what he could while warning them about the presence in the palace. Those with magical capabilities understood instantly and promised to be careful while everyone else seemed to pay no mind to his words.

Between the conversations, he also picked up on how few of his fellow mages heard accurate details about his reassignment. They questioned him about the southern base and its general as much as he had been asked about Fester, reminding him of the crumpled note supposedly from Aaron. In order to avoid misunderstandings down the road, he clarified their assignment to Dala and the purpose during each encounter.

Soon, Byron wound up at the bottom of the staircase where Clearshot waited despite their idea to avoid grouping together. He figured the soldier hoped to be near his wife, presumably in case Hendal put her life in danger during the confrontation.

His friend showed no indication of his concern and waved an arm at the stairs in a regal manner. "Shall we?"

He avoided the urge to remind the soldier of the seriousness of their situation and glanced at those on the upper floor. The king sat on a throne brought out for the necessary events and remained surrounded by six, armored guards. One look at the young man and Byron noticed what Emilea had described when she claimed something seemed wrong. No emotion graced his features, though he wore a slight smile, his eyes were dull, and he stared at a single point across the hall.

Meanwhile, Hendal had disappeared from the section above.

The troops blocking the bottom of the stairs nodded to Byron and Clearshot when they approached, yet the two needed to state their business before being permitted to pass. After, the latter climbed the steps to reach his wife and embrace her, as if the two hadn't spoken hours earlier. Byron prepared to follow when a hand dropped on his shoulder, keeping him in place just beyond the line of soldiers.

"What a time to meet you again, Master Byron," came a greeting from a familiar voice.

He turned to face General Casner, who waited at his side, and the two clasped hands once he noted no sign of Hendal's influence on the man.

"General, you're looking well. How fares Verona in my absence?"

"It hasn't burned to the ground, yet."

Casner cracked a grin after his words, and Byron mirrored it. The man had never been one to share information unless prompted, so he revealed few details about matters within the council until Byron mentioned the news of an alliance.

"Trust the gossiping hens to let it slip," the general commented while scratching his beard with an annoyed glare. "In any case, we were expecting their arrival this afternoon before the ball."

"I wonder if they had trouble on the road."

Casner grunted. "Whatever's slowing them, I don't like it. Life's been eerie enough as it is around here ever since I returned from the north."

Byron prepared to ask what the general meant, but Clearshot appeared to tug at his arm.

"General," his friend said with a nod. "I need to borrow our master mage for a moment. My wife would like a word."

I'm not supposed to interact with Emilea, Byron recalled as Casner waved in a dismissive motion. *Hendal might become suspicious if we're around her for more than a few minute.*

Against his wishes, Clearshot led him to where Emilea stood alone. She pretended they hadn't seen each other with such genuine emotion that he believed it to be true for a moment. Their small talk stayed simple and lasted long enough to bore him, something he associated with regular conversations between noblemen and ladies. Then, she introduced a new, interesting subject.

"Have you seen the high priest yet?" she asked.

Byron caught her eyes dart to Aaron and his guards, then back again. *They must be listening to report on us.*

"No," he answered while continuing to play dumb. "Shouldn't he be here?"

"He's nervous because our guests from Nim-Vala aren't in Verona yet. I'm sure General Casner informed you of the news."

Byron dipped his head slightly to acknowledge the message. *Hendal is hiding. Without the guests, this grand setup was for nothing, and he must figure out how to deal with their disappearance. I just hope they're not in danger. Otherwise, we may have another, major problem on our hands.*

"Why don't we wait for him?" he suggested while offering a smile. Although Clearshot and Emilea returned it, he sensed they were all anticipating the high priest's next move.

***

375

Loud laughter and chattering could be heard even from the southern side of the palace where Coura snuck in through the outdoor balcony. The rotating soldiers guarding the area mentioned their intentions to join the festivities after their shifts as she avoided them to perch onto a windowsill. Part of her wished to dance, watch and listen to the performances, and eat and drink with the friends she made over the years, but her immediate concerns tore her away from the distractions.

I don't have much time to find Soirée. Not to mention, the angels could be lurking around here too. Where should I even begin?

After releasing the spell on her wings, she slipped inside the building without being detected. She landed on the top floor to scout the upper areas before venturing where people would be more likely to notice her. Every hallway contained at least one or two people wandering around, which made sense since the rooms were for the soldiers and mages. She avoided creeping around because those she saw wouldn't have a reason for her to act abnormal, and she didn't allow anybody close enough to notice the stray markings.

Coura winded through the halls for hints of the demon until she stopped herself in front of Grace's room. When she tested the knob, she wasn't surprised to find it locked. Although she considered breaking the door down, the action would only serve to create noise.

If she's being kept inside, which I doubt, she's safer here than by me.

Reluctantly, she proceeded through the rest of the floor. A section near the southeastern corner caught her attention since she had never been in that direction, but she understood why when she explored. The hallways were empty and rooms noiseless, which meant they either remained unoccupied or held people participating in the event. In any case, Coura listened for voices or footsteps as she forced herself to walk forward instead of pressing against the walls.

She came upon a space at the corner where the door had been cracked and hesitated to enter. Without any traceable energy, she would be trespassing at her own risk, whether it ended up as a trap or not. As she retreated from the area, a tendril of demonic power brushed by, like a light breeze, causing her to spin around.

No one appeared in the hallway.

Soirée?

A second wisp of energy passed in answer.

Although brief, Coura was able to track its source farther below and hurried down the hallways toward the nearest staircase. Her heart beat faster, both from her concern at how close it felt to the grand hall and from descending the stairs two at a time while skipping the third floor entirely. Once she landed on the second, the trail became a straight path into the center of the palace. Only then did her steps slow into a cautious walk. It became impossible to stay out of sight from the palace servants and guests who mingled in more private spaces, though they ignored her.

A thought occurred to her as she considered their lack of interest and the demonic presence thick in the air. *Soirée's stringing me along. There's no use in attempting to cower when she already knows I'm here to meet with her.*

The notion provided an extra burst of courage, pushing her through the hallways until she recognized what led to the council's meeting chamber. Even if she hadn't been aware of its location, the trail continued in that direction.

So, she intends to stay away from the event and trap me at the center. I suppose this is one of the better outcomes of my search, even though I won't be able to lure her somewhere else.

Coura expected to find several guards in the area, yet none waited at the entrance to the chamber. The lack of additional soldiers amazed her despite what she knew about the demon's preference for working alone. The door was also unlocked, so she shoved it open and went inside.

A single candelabra had been kept lit on the circular table, shrouding all except the wooden surface in darkness. She didn't want to take any chances. With her right hand, she summoned her blade and prepared to cast a fire spell to brighten the space with her left until Soirée's voice sounded from farther ahead.

"I wouldn't do that."

She froze. Before she could speak, there came a soft groan, which didn't belong to the demon, revealing they were not the only two present. "Who's there with you?" she demanded.

{*Shh…*}

The room fell silent as Soirée stepped out of the shadows on the opposite side of the table from Coura. The demon pressed a finger against her lips while they curved upward into a smirk.

{*You wouldn't want to wake the little Yeluthian, would you?*}

Despite her resolve, Coura gasped at the mention of Grace. She didn't tell her companions, but she planned to find and free her friend during her time in the palace. Now, as she listened to the continued grunting from across the chamber, she squeezed the hilt of her sword tight enough to make her fingers ache.

"You always play tricks, but this is beneath you," she spat. "Using the ambassador as a hostage is pathetic."

"I completely agree," Soirée replied with a scary amount of enthusiasm. "I told the high priest it was tacky, but he insisted I keep her under my watch. To be honest, I'm not certain why he left her alive at all. She's more than worn out her usefulness."

"Shut up!" Coura pointed the tip of her sword at the demon, then she considered her friend. "Grace? Can you hear me?"

A weary moan followed and some shuffling along the floor.

Meanwhile, Soirée wore an unamused expression before retreating into the shadows once more. Coura lunged forward to stop whatever the demon planned and flinched at the sight of a bright fireball summoned in Soirée's open palm. In the other hand, the demon held Grace by the back of her neck.

"If you hurt her," Coura began, growling the threat through her teeth.

"I don't care what happens to this Yeluthian. In fact, at the moment she's in our way."

With inhuman strength, Soirée tossed Grace onto the table where her body rolled across and off its wooden surface to land on the floor in front of Coura.

"Grace!" she cried and threw herself to her knees at the girl's side. "Are you hurt? Come on, answer me!"

"This is also in our way," the demon added nonchalantly while approaching the table again.

Coura threw herself on top of her friend when Soirée held both palms outward to release waves of flames and lightning bolts powerful enough to destroy the furniture with deafening booms. Their remains crackled as new firewood and cast a red glow around the room.

When the sound died down, Coura sat up to desperately shake the Yeluthian's shoulders in an attempt to wake her. Smoke filled the enclosed chamber, but she forgot any irritation it caused when her friend opened both eyes and began coughing.

"Grace!" Coura ignored the demon, who acted surprisingly patient, and hugged the girl with a weak chuckle.

"Coura? Is…that really…you?"

She nodded and noticed how blurred the sapphire eyes appeared, revealing her friend's sedation while in captivity. As her anger welled, she glared at Soirée to wordlessly demand an explanation. The two stared at each other until Coura grew uncomfortable from the increasing heat and smoke.

She hasn't come after me. Was this just to bring us together or deal with me alone? The question sparked a strange sensation that quelled her emotions and steadied her racing heart. She believed it was a sort of acceptance between them, as if they were meant to settle their past.

Her gaze dropped to Grace again. This time, the Yeluthian's tear-filled eyes showed some recognition.

"Y-You saved m-me," her friend stuttered.

"Can you move out of here on your own?" Coura asked quietly while ignoring her own feelings.

It took Grace a moment to process the request, but she bobbed her head and attempted to push herself away. Coura let her shift onto her hands and knees where she started crawling toward the door. Once she passed through, Coura stood to face Soirée.

"Back to business," the demon chimed, flashed a smile, then licked her lips.

"What are you doing in the palace?" Coura asked and avoided the urge to rub her eyes or cough as she remained in the cloud of smoke.

The demon didn't answer. Instead, she released an excited cry and charged, manifesting her black blade in the process.

With no other choice except to fight, Coura matched Soirée's movements to block the offensive blows using nearly the same speed and strength. The fire crackled beneath the ringing metal echoing loudly enough to reach the hallway beyond.

It became apparent to Coura as she held her own that Soirée didn't intend to kill her. Every strike came from the weapon and followed a routine based on her training sessions. She became confused by the demon's behavior before deciding to attack. When her opponent brought the matching blade down, aiming for her skull, she slipped to the side instead of meeting it with her sword. Soirée recovered instinctively, yet the dodge allowed Coura to swing at the demon's exposed chest. Her blade made contact, though along the arm instead as the creature twisted away.

Soirée had used wide but powerful swings when they began, so Coura decided to stab and focus on precision next. Her sword poked her opponent a couple times, but it hadn't been anything serious enough to incapacitate or hinder further progress. At last, the demon returned to the offensive side, initiating a dance around the tongues of flame and embers. The increased temperature made Coura sweat while Soirée appeared unaffected and kept a wicked smile, reminding her how this seemed to be just a game for the creature.

Suddenly, an irritated, male voice interrupted the rhythm of their fight. "What is going on in here?"

The additional noise distracted Coura, giving Soirée the opportunity to raise a leg and kick the right side of her ribs before retreating. The first physical blow broke bones, and she wrapped her left arm around her torso in response, though the damage already began healing thanks to her opponent's own energy.

Soirée made no attempt to strike again, so she chanced a glance behind to where the high priest stood gaping in the doorway. On the floor at his feet with her eyes squeezed shut and tears leaking down her cheeks sat Grace. The man held the Yeluthian in place by her hair, though she had both hands on top of his in an effort to free herself.

Hendal glared at Coura. "When did *you* get in here?"

She could only stare and blink in confusion before looking back to Soirée, who wore an impassive expression. *Did she not speak with him about meeting me during the ball?*

Despite her lack of an answer, the high priest began yelling at Soirée about Coura's appearance, Grace's attempt to escape, and the damage to the chamber. All the while, the demon remained quiet and even seemed bored. His behavior helped Coura understand that Soirée orchestrated their interaction on her own.

"Don't you have anything to say for yourself?" he barked when the demon didn't respond to his ranting.

A chilling pause followed, punctuated by the popping embers. Most of the flames had died down, leaving a crimson glow as the lone source of light in the space. Soirée's response sounded smooth and menacing to reflect the atmosphere.

"I told you not to interfere with my work."

Hendal's jaw dropped. For the first time in Coura's memory, the high priest recoiled. His personality switched from a figure in a position of authority to somebody possessing a need to be included in whatever was happening without him. The man looked down at Grace, then he dragged her into the room.

"Use the Yeluthian! If we control her like the others, we can use her power for ourselves."

The desperation in his voice horrified Coura almost as much as the idea of losing Grace. She raised her sword at the high priest in a challenge. "I won't let you!"

He ignored her.

The demon released an impatient-sounding sigh. "I thought I made it clear I have no use for that one."

"She can help us reach Yeluthia. We don't know much about their people, so combining our powers could result in something better. Light and dark magic come from angels and demons, and humans inherited it for generations. What if we connect the two sources? What if we merge her energy and yours? Asteom could be the strongest nation on the planet! Angels, demons, and humans together... Isn't that what we want?"

Hendal continued to raise his voice, as though he were preaching, until he shouted nonsense at Soirée. Based on what he said and the demon's lack of interest, Coura got the impression the two ran through the same conversation before. Once the high priest's argument ended, the space remained quiet. She felt disgusted by the man's desires and sensed how insulting the comments must be to both Soirée and Grace.

The demon pinned Hendal under the mercy of her gaze, causing him to squirm. Then, she threw her head back and laughed. The clear, uncontrolled cackling baffled Coura, and the high priest released Grace's hair to rub his hands together in an embarrassed manner while blushing.

"Oh, Hendal," the demon responded and grinned. "Your suggestions must be the most ridiculous ideas I have ever heard in my life."

Coura caught him beginning to bumble a reply, but Soirée continued.

"I suppose your imagination was what intrigued me about you in the first place. You have such hilarious fantasies of the three races, believing we could live to transform this pitiful country into some remarkable place." The demon stopped to chuckle again.

The high priest appeared utterly deflated. Soirée's patronizing words made Coura nervous, as though the demon didn't reveal her true thoughts on Hendal's intentions; however, her blade moved upward to catch Coura's attention. She shifted into a defensive stance in preparation for another charge when Hendal spoke again while clutching the top of Grace's head.

"At least use her to get rid of that abomination," he begged while gesturing to Coura, who frowned at his feeble attempt to manipulate Grace for his own purpose.

This time, for the first time she could remember, Soirée was the one hesitating to speak.

I've never seen her uncertain of herself...

When the demon chose not to respond, Hendal blurted more and inched his way forward until he moved as far into the room as Coura. "Consider the power a Yeluthian wields! You should want to learn more, to have their abilities for yourself. With this girl, the light energy and her goddess gift are available!"

Soirée lowered her sword and lifted her other hand in a gesture for him to stop talking. The man pressed his lips shut, as if he were under a spell, and she spoke in a disquieting tone. Although her face stayed expressionless, some inner mischief flickered behind her eyes.

"Don't you understand? I already have a Yeluthian in my possession."

Before Coura could process the demon's words, Soirée's eyes slid like knives to meet hers.

***

A heavy silence resulted from what the creature admitted, which proved to be for the best since Grace's mind hadn't cleared enough for her to think without a delay. Before Hendal left his quarters in the afternoon, he made sure she drank another dose of the vile potion muddling her head. That had been hours ago, so she became more alert than she'd been in weeks.

Did it say…another Yeluthian?

Hendal released Grace's hair, leaving her to drop to the floor. She stared across the space to where the demon watched Coura with an unwavering gaze. From her position, she couldn't see her friend's face, but she heard Coura's voice.

"What did you say?"

Hendal mirrored her disbelief. "You don't mean *she's* a… Look at her! She's nothing like this one."

Coura didn't wait for an answer. She charged ahead to slash at the demon before the two engaged in combat. The wild movements looked like blurs to Grace since her mind wasn't able to keep up with such actions, and a lot became lost in the surrounding darkness. The pair ended up across the embers and farther away before the creature moved next to the throne, which remained the only piece of furniture left. Coura leapt over the single step raising the chair and stabbed forward. Grace heard Hendal exclaim the demon's name when the blade pierced through its shoulder.

For half a breath, she grew hopeful. Her friend removed the sword by stepping away, but Grace noticed the demon's weapon had vanished. It ignored the wound and lashed out to seize Coura's wrists. With a spin that hurt Grace's head, the creature ended up behind Coura to bend her arms backward in an uncomfortable-looking position, forcing her to release her grip in the process. The sword clanged when it hit the floor, and they went still, though Grace could see Coura shaking as she struggled to free herself.

It brought its mouth close to her friend's exposed throat and grinned, baring pointed canines. Grace held her breath once she understood the dangerous position Coura wound up in.

"Let me tell you a story," the demon said over the frustrated grunts. "It's been fifty-three years since I found my way to the surface in search of a goal to further my research. I experimented on my own kind for so long, and I needed a new project. After all, you saw what I dealt with."

Grace noticed Coura stop fighting against her captor.

"You didn't figure it out yet?" the creature teased. "When you absorbed my energy and fell unconscious, our bond strengthened. I shared a handful of my memories as your reward. They're nothing special, just beings I worked with, or rather on, in the past. I wandered into Asteom and played with the humans and animals, but they proved tiresome to care for. It wasn't until I stumbled upon your precious town that something alluring caught my eye. You might think this was when I met you, Dear One; however, this happened nearly twenty-five years ago. A young man possessing similar energy to your friend over there arrived with a human woman. At the sight of a Yeluthian, I became furious."

The grasp on Coura's wrists tightened, and the fingernails punctured her skin, causing fresh blood to drip down her arms.

"As I was saying, my primal instincts kicked in," the demon continued as though she hadn't just relived the aforementioned moment. "I plotted how to destroy him, his partner, and their wretched home in the most entertaining fashion. When I considered the options, it reminded me of my purpose as a being born to discover and learn, so I decided to postpone murdering them. For years, I waited, and my patience was rewarded when they welcomed a beautiful, baby girl!"

Grace could only look on helplessly as the creature giggled and nuzzled her friend's cheek, like an animal, while Coura yanked her face away.

"Although I wanted *so* badly to steal the child, I controlled myself. Unfortunately, the light-blooded must have caught on to my presence because he fled. I followed him as far east as I dared go, but something in the sky was apparently more important than his family on the ground." The demon laughed again at Coura's expense. "I created new projects to stay occupied, spreading my power throughout the country. It's quite astonishing how many demonic creatures the royal family ignores. When I remembered you, you gave me the perfect opportunity to snatch you up. All I had to do was mention killing those you considered important."

When Coura attempted to free herself again, the creature released her, and she whirled around.

"To think, I've known you since before you were born. I had plenty of time to figure out what to do too. Don't worry, I believe I made the best decisions. My demonic energy suppressed any natural power without possessing your mind, though in order to repress your memory, I needed to delve deeper. The bonding was accidental, but it proved a unique test of my control without manipulation. You were able to grow into the demonic energy while our connection let me play with what was left."

"You're lying." To Grace's amazement, Coura's response didn't sound as hurt or aggressive as she expected.

The creature tilted its head. "When have I ever lied to you? Did you truly believe those wings of yours were my doing? Thank you, but I prefer to remain on the ground."

Grace sensed more beneath the questions reliant on the bond they shared. She couldn't hold back her tears once she understood the truth. *Coura's parents had been stalked before and during her early life. Once they were out of the way, she was forced into acting as a host just to save her home. She is half-Yeluthian, and not one of my people deserves the fate she lived through!*

The demon turned to Hendal then, abandoning the charisma from her explanation. "That is why I don't need the ambassador. An impure Yeluthian has the capacity to balance demonic energy while remaining sane. Coura carries barely less than equal to my power now, yet only a fraction caused her to seal her natural energy away. It's interesting, really. I had been using humans lacking magical power and those housing dark energy, but their bodies were unsuitable."

I cannot believe what I am hearing. Demons have always been monsters who attack and kill for sport, but this one can execute plans and research on its own. How many lives were lost because of its experimenting?

Grace longed to grow upset and let anger give her strength, yet she could only cower on the floor when she realized how vulnerable she was in the presence of such a terrifying creature. It mumbled indifferent comments about the beings under its control while Coura stood unmoving. Meanwhile, Hendal took a step backward, then another. She glanced up to see an uncertain expression on his face, as though he were weighing whether or not to stay or flee, and she recognized her chance to escape.

"High Priest," the demon called in a flirtatious manner before Grace could begin crawling away. "You've been gone from the ball for quite a while. Your guests will begin searching for you soon."

"What about-"

"Leave these two to me. I'll make sure they stay like obedient, Yeluthian girls and-"

The rest of her sentence cut off when a flash of lighting shot from Coura's hands in a surge of demonic energy. Grace threw her arms over her face and winced as sparks stung her exposed skin like dozens of pins before the feeling abruptly ended. When she looked again, a violet shield had been placed in front of her and Hendal. On its other side, Coura sent blast after blast of magic at the opposite end of the chamber. Grace couldn't see the demon, but she did notice blood dripping down her friend's arms, legs, and chest to pool at her feet. Dark-colored designs decorated the exposed limbs as well, which she somehow believed were the creature's doing.

Coura! Against the thunderous ruckus, Grace threw the name out with her mind, hoping for it to reach across the barrier. A response came immediately.

{Get out of here now!}

Her friend's inner voice didn't hint at any emotion except impatience, as though they needed to hurry. The notion made her wonder how long Coura would be able to maintain the shielding spell.

By that point, her mind cleared enough to where she understood the urgency. Hendal had abandoned the scene once the lightening started flying, so nothing restrained her from crawling out the door and into the hallway. She expected he would wind up wherever the ball took place, which she just learned of thanks to the demon's remark; however, her physical condition would allow him to overpower her if she chased after him.

If he catches me, I will be locked away again.

The weeks of being held captive and drugged took a toll on her mentally. Grace's body involuntarily trembled at the thought of being crammed into a closet with rope tied around her neck. Still, she needed to find help, and at the moment, the best way to do so was by staying out of Coura's way.

Fleeing the Palace

As the event continued, Byron's eyelids grew heavy while he waited for the high priest's return. He wanted nothing more than to have the confrontation over with, so he kept by Emilea even when Clearshot returned to the lower level to continue mingling. The initial nerves and thrill wore off once dessert had been served, and the guests started taking their leave with visible disappointment.

Where could he possibly be hiding? It's well after dinner. There are no strangers who could take the place of the Nim-Valans.

His frustration, in addition to his concern for Coura acting on her own, left him with no choice except to locate the man himself. As he shifted to face the nearest set of doors leading farther into the second floor, Emilea set a hand on his arm.

"Not yet," she cautioned at a lower volume.

Byron figured she worried about those under Hendal's control warning the high priest, but he became too worked up to care. *I'll risk my own life if no one else will volunteer.*

In response to her concern, he shook his head. "Good evening, Emilea."

"To you as well," she replied and opened her arms for an embrace. When he accepted it, she whispered a message. "I'll leave shortly to join Marcy and return home tomorrow for Aimes and the children. Have Clearshot bring Marcus and Will, and we can regroup at another time."

Against his wishes to deal with Hendal together that night, Byron understood the risk they would all face when the ball ended and those under the high priest's control were aware of their return.

The pair broke apart, and he moved to exit when there came a sudden series of booming sounds, like thunder rumbling in the distance. Those below quieted to listen before murmuring their unperturbed assumptions with each other; however, Byron, Emilea, and any mage in range of the palace went rigid at the pressure from the accompanying demonic energy practically calling out.

It has to be Coura... She's signaling to us! One look at Emilea told him she reached the same conclusion.

"Let's go," she ordered, but they turned to find the soldiers who were guarding Aaron now blocking the set of doors.

Before they could decide what to do, the young king rose to approach the staircase for the first time. His voice rang above the hushed conversations, drawing all eyes to the royal figure.

"My guests, I have been informed by our master mages of a disturbance deeper inside the palace. Those of you with magical abilities might sense it as well."

When he paused, Byron began to sweat as he considered what Aaron, or rather Hendal, planned to do.

"They confirmed the presence of demonic energy."

Chaos started below. Those with less self-control became hysteric, gasping, crying out, or scrambling toward an exit. Soldiers and mages possessing leadership skills began issuing orders to guard the doors and main gate. In the midst of it, Aaron continued without appearing or sounding phased.

"Do not panic. Upon discovering this threat, I alerted our honored guests, the Nim-Valan soldiers, who were on their way to Verona, and we agreed they should remain outside the city for the time being. For everybody's safety, I insist you return to your homes until more information is available."

Some of the noise died down at the king's direction, and Byron spotted Clearshot leaping up the staircase to join them. His confusion reflected their own.

What trickery is Hendal plotting by stirring up the palace and admitting the existence of demonic energy here? Byron wondered before moving to stand nearer to the throne. Emilea and Clearshot did the same.

Their king didn't seem to notice the trio. "To my loyal soldiers and diligent mages, I order you to find and eliminate the source of such treacherous power. The energy emanates from a young woman with black hair, blue eyes, and the ability to conjure dark wings similar to an angel's."

Byron felt the blood leave his face and acted when Aaron prepared to reveal Coura's name. He placed a hand over the king's mouth before grabbing the young man's arm and yanking backward. Aaron's legs gave out, and he dropped to the ground at the foot of the throne. With his mind flustered, he wasn't certain what he should do and stepped closer to the mindless figure. Emilea's movement stayed his own as she put herself between him and their king.

"It's not Aaron we're after," she stated firmly yet with a wavering voice.

Clearshot went to the young man while his wife spoke and helped Aaron to sit on the throne. The dull gaze never shifted from the wall across the hall after, and the joyless smile returned, though he didn't rise to address the guests again.

On both floors, people rushed in and out of doors bearing weapons. The guards protecting the throne returned to their positions with swords drawn.

Byron covered his mouth and glanced away. "They're going to kill her," he muttered in disbelief.

"She'll be fine," Clearshot replied and shook his shoulder. "Our job is to find and capture Hendal. Otherwise, this madness will continue."

After a moment, Byron nodded. He wouldn't forget Coura and the predicament she was in, yet he vowed to see their task through to the end.

Emilea gestured for them to enter the double doors and head farther across the second floor. "Those blasts came from closer to the center," she explained as they hurried in the direction of the council's meeting chamber.

Mages, soldiers, and servants unlucky enough to be caught in the search filled the halls to locate the enemy identified by their king. The sounds of constant shouting increased while the trio went along, and they had to halt or push people aside at several points. While they waited to slide around a pair of female mages standing still in the middle of the corridor, Byron heard Clearshot yell before his friend disappeared down another hallway. Emilea kept close behind as they changed directions to follow. When they caught up to Clearshot, the soldier shoved somebody into the wall while three guards unsheathed their swords.

It startled Byron to find Hendal was the one pinned by the throat with General Tont and two men pointing their blades at his friend. Emilea called to her husband and lunged for him, but Byron extended an arm, preventing her from becoming caught in the scuffle. The high priest sneered at them, hinting that he didn't seem altogether sane.

"What's going on?" Byron asked, raising his voice while gesturing to the space behind where people frantically continued their search. "Explain yourself!"

Hendal's eyes widened, then his face fell as he started laughing, which became a gurgling noise due to the forearm pressed against his throat.

Clearshot's glare narrowed. After a few seconds, he hit the high priest's chest with a fist. "Answer him!"

In response, General Tont and the other soldiers raised their swords so the tips of their blades touched Clearshot's back. Emilea begged them to stop, reminding Byron of her own experience with Hendal and the demon and how her family's lives were already in danger. The high priest's chortling died down, though he didn't respond, so Clearshot removed his arms with an irritated grunt. He returned to his wife while raising both hands in the air as the swords lowered.

Hendal coughed, rubbed his neck, then brushed down his robe to collect some illusion of composure. "Now then, what's this about?"

"Don't play dumb with us," Clearshot growled but didn't attempt to go after him again.

Even so, Byron reached an arm in front of his friend before answering. "We know you're affiliated with the demon and manipulating King Aaron, General Tont, and others in the palace."

Hendal's eyes darted from Byron to Emilea. "It seems honest confidants are a rare commodity."

Byron took a step forward to draw the high priest's attention once more. "What good will it do you to lead a demon and rogue angels against the kingdom? What are you trying to accomplish?"

"I don't answer to you, no matter how much superiority or power you claim to have." He turned to leave through the opposite corridor.

"Wait," Byron began and hoped to keep the high priest occupied until he could consider a way to restrain him.

Hendal scoffed at his attempt. "Let me make this clear. If any of you wish to live, or for the general, His Highness, and the others serving me to remain unharmed, I advise you to mind your own business and leave me to continue with mine."

To emphasize the threat, he dipped his head. At the cue, Tont and the two guards adjusted their swords until the blades rested along their own throats. Their expressions never changed from the blank stares as they did so.

Byron shuddered, realizing they could do nothing without risking the lives of those under Hendal's hold. Unless they broke the spell, people would die.

Now isn't the time to shed blood, not when the palace is up in arms already. We're aware Hendal is the culprit and can deal with him at another time, hopefully in front of witnesses. There are also the rogue angels and demon to worry about.

"Answer me one question," he found himself asking. "Will the victims under your control be safe?"

His friend shot him an incredulous look, as if appalled by the idea of retreating.

Hendal's expression softened before the man nodded, then his lips curled into a pompous smile. As he walked away, his three guards lingered with their weapons poised until the high priest merged with the crowd beyond, reaffirming what was at stake.

***

Coura continued launching her spells even after she believed Grace had escaped from the chamber. She refused to do so until she couldn't continue any longer, her energy reached its limit, or the magic killed Soirée, whichever came first. The power remained unrestrained, though not strong enough to destroy the walls, floor, or ceiling, and allowed those in the palace, specifically Byron and Emilea, to locate them.

If anything, they can rescue Grace, she thought against the repeated wave of emotion threatening to sweep her away. In order to prevent herself from collapsing under Soirée's words, she unleashed what she could manage while shielding her Yeluthian friend.

Over the spells' noise vibrating the room, she heard the demon scream for her to stop. Coura hesitated before cutting off the spells as she spotted the shadowy figure standing unharmed behind a shimmering wall. She cursed under her breath while Soirée dismissed the shield before snarling.

"What has he done?" she hissed and grinded her teeth.

Coura was clueless as to why the demon grew so furious and decided to wait for her to share her reasoning. As expected, Soirée's rage melted, and she offered a bittersweet smile.

"I'm sorry, Dear One. That fool of a priest went and spoiled our time together. I wish we could have more fun, but that must wait until our next meeting. Just make sure you don't die."

After her mysterious explanation, the demon retreated to lean against the farthest wall, blending in with the darkness like she had done earlier. Coura, though perplexed by Soirée's behavior and comment about Hendal, reached into her center to resume launching spells until she heard shouting from behind.

"She's in here!"

"Block the doorway, then we'll surround her!"

It took Coura a second to understand they were referring to her, and the sound of stomping feet filled the enclosed space. Her head swung around to see a handful of troops entering with lamps in hand and others staying in the hallway. At first, she became concerned for their safety because Soirée lingered across the space, so she raised her hands for them to leave. The soldiers flinched at her gesture. One in the middle carried a shield, so the rest huddled behind.

Their fear shocked her, but she couldn't warn them since two of the people in the doorway shot fireballs and icicles at her. The unexpected attack had her dropping to her knees in order to duck under the projectiles. When she rose to her feet, those inside had moved closer.

They don't think I'm an enemy, do they?

The mages threw more spells in succession, forcing her to retreat farther into the room. This allowed those in the hallway to enter with spears, clubs, and knifes in hand. Coura chanced a glance to where Soirée had been moments ago only to find the demon had slipped away. She scoured the chamber for any sign of the creature as her breathing sped up against a lump in her throat.

She got away!

"Come quietly," one of the men beckoned as they all crept closer. "We won't hurt you if you do."

"I'm a soldier too!" she retorted while clenching her hands into fists.

He repeated the words, prompting his companions to do the same while Coura remained at a loss for what else to say. When defending herself verbally didn't work, she recalled Byron's order to retreat and resorted to fleeing. She attempted to sidestep along the nearest wall, but the soldiers met her with weapons stabbing for her legs and torso. The strikes that landed healed as she returned to her original spot.

Their pigheadedness pushed her to try bowling them over with magic. She called upon her blade, sent explosive fireballs at their feet, and succeeded in knocking down those in front; however, at least a dozen soldiers and mages shoved each other to fit into the chamber.

They just keep coming, she realized. *If I can't get out of here, they'll exhaust me until there's an opportunity for a killing blow.*

In an effort to escape the claustrophobic chamber, Coura manifested her wings, surprising those in front enough to extend their arms and push the growing crowd backward. Those who couldn't see protested the movement while she analyzed what room was available above.

There's enough to glide at the top, but I'll need to land in order to pass through the door.

It would be impossible to leap upward given the space, so she ran and jumped to soar above the first row of heads, though those who noticed her maneuver raised their weapons to slice at her legs and stomach.

{Coura! Can you hear me?}

Grace's voice distracted her as she released the spell on her wings to tumble in front of three swordsmen, who didn't hesitate to slash at her. Though she became surrounded, she faced them with her demonic blade and kept an eye on the exit. Weapons and spells from every direction hit various parts of her body no matter how much effort she put into blocking and dodging. Initially, she ignored the pain until the wounds steadily healed more slowly while her center stirred.

Did I expend too much energy against Soirée? she wondered as she ducked under a spear aiming for her head. *No, that's not it. The power is there, but something else is preventing me from reaching it. Could this be Soirée's doing?*

{You have to leave!}

From behind, a sword cut across her right calf, sending her down to one knee until she grit her teeth to stand as it healed. There were too many people to avoid, and she refused to injure anybody on purpose, limiting her options.

Grace, where are you? Coura threw out the question with concern for her friend's safety. The response sounded just as worried.

{I am in another hallway around the corner. No one recognizes me or will listen. It seems like they have been given orders to come after you.}

Can you reach Byron?

In the resulting pause, she tripped up a soldier only to back right into a spear. She had no doubt those in the chamber intended to kill her, and she grew dizzy following their movements without attacking. She pushed the weapon aside and swung to scratch the man's arm. Although shallow, the movement had him grabbing for the wound while stepping away, providing an opening for her to pass by. She took advantage of the moment to shove him with all her weight. It didn't make him fall over, yet those behind either shuffled out of the way or adjusted their weapons to avoid harming their comrade. Their lack of focus proved to be enough for her to sprint through the mass and toward the doorway where the pair of mages waited. Fortunately, her running start allowed her to reach them before they could release another spell, so they shrank away from what they expected to be an attack.

More people stood outside, but it became apparent they hadn't been able to watch what went on inside when she burst through and down the corridor to frightened and alarmed cries. Those who noticed her after attempted to stand in her way, so she released the spell on her sword and favored fleeing instead of challenging them. The crowd from the chamber struggled to keep up, and their shouts and footsteps grew fainter as Coura located one of the staircases. Still, others continued searching for her, so she dodged their strikes, sometimes winding up worse off for it.

During the hectic situation, she remembered her Yeluthian friend. *Grace? Are you there?*

{Yes. Byron said he is looking for you with those in his group. I am not sure who they are, but he told me they were not able to capture Hendal.}

The sudden despair at hearing their failure against her own halted Coura's steps in the middle of an intersecting hallway. She tilted her head back as tears stemming from her guilt stung her eyes. The added weight seemed to amplify her body's pain from still-healing cuts and bruises and hinder her breathing.

Soirée's gone too, she projected without repressing her gloom. *Tell them I plan to-*

She caught a flicker of movement out of the corner of her eye before something struck her in the back of the head, knocking her to the floor. A burley figure donning all-black clothing emerged from where he had been pressed against the wall. In his hands was a wooden club splotched with blood. Coura's vision grew hazy from the blow, making her lose her balance twice when she tried to stand while scrambling away from the figure, who stalked forward in an imposing manner.

Soirée's story, losing the demon and Hendal, and knowing everybody in the palace was trying to kill her became too much to keep her thinking straight. When the man came closer, she threw up a hand to release a blast of fire into his face, then she jumped up to scurry away. The spell had been as minimal as she could control, which caused him to drop the club and cover his head with a scream.

She flew by more people attracted to the yelling until she reached an area she recognized near one of the outdoor hallways. The door was closed, but instead of storming through, she paused, leaned over, and cracked it open. Two voices belonging to a man and woman joked without mentioning the search or details relating to the evening's events.

While she had a minute alone, Coura called to Grace for a final time. The Yeluthian acknowledged her, though the inner voice sounded fatigued, reflecting the nightmarish evening they went through.

Please, tell Byron everything the demon and Hendal said as soon as you're safe, she instructed while a wave of sympathy washed over her.

{*Where are you? What is happening? Why are the soldiers trying to find you?*}

Even without seeing or hearing her friend in person, Coura sensed the Yeluthian had started crying, and her heart ached to reunite with Grace and reassure the girl they would be all right.

I have to hide until the palace calms down. I don't know if I'll be able to talk to anybody, so I need your help.

{*Do not go! Please, I-I am scared...*}

Numerous sets of footsteps echoed down the corridor.

You must be brave, Coura replied while glancing at the noise, irritating her throbbing head in the process. *Find someone you know to help, and they'll never trap you like that again. I promise.*

Grace continued begging her to stay, but she already threw the door open. If the two in the hallway were aware of the search or planned to restrain her, Coura didn't find out. She manifested her wings, hopped onto the window sill, and jumped into the air. While she remained near the palace, stinging in her left wing told her an archer embedded an arrow into its target. Even with the distractions, threats, and pain, she refused to slow her pace as she aimed for the forest across the southern clearing.

***

Grace's mind was broken, Byron felt certain of that. He split up from Emilea and Clearshot once Hendal disappeared with the intention of locating Coura; however, the young Yeluthian found him before he moved far. The second floor became heavily populated, so it grew bothersome to decipher her hysterics against the outer sounds. He understood she escaped the meeting room where Hendal dragged her to the demon. Coura had been present as well, but the girl left to seek assistance once the spellcasting began. She remained somewhere in the vicinity, wandering the halls while weeping and repeating her friend's name in her mind.

In order to avoid panicking, he narrowed his focus to finding Grace amid those cluttering the halls by starting his search near the meeting chamber. He ignored the room, mainly because there were too many people arguing or peeking inside, and combed his way around the area. All the while, he projected sympathetic thoughts.

On his route to the rear end of the palace, he noticed the Yeluthian huddled on the ground, hugging her knees and burying her face in them. He let out a sigh of relief, carefully approached, and knelt while placing a hand on her shoulder. The girl jumped at the touch and raised her head to study him. Once she recognized him, she began sobbing while wrapping her arms around his waist. Byron continued to speak comforting words until she settled down and could listen.

"Can you walk?" he asked while offering a hand. When she shook her head, he pulled her into a standing position then scooped her up in his arms. Together, they moved into the grand hall.

It had grown late, much later than Byron would have guessed, but soldiers, mages, servants, and even some curious guests from the ball wandered through with mixed expressions. Aaron and his guards were gone, so he set the Yeluthian on the top stair, dropped beside her, and covered his eyes to ease his headache.

"M-Master B-Byron?"

He glanced down into Grace's red-rimmed eyes and felt grateful she calmed enough not to cry more. "What is it?"

"I-I h-have t-to t-tell you ab-bout C-Coura..."

Nearly every word was said with a stutter until he hushed her despite his attempt to be kind, mentioning she could tell him what she needed to when she relaxed. In reality, he became uncomfortable gathering unfiltered information from a victim obviously under the influence of a mind-numbing potion.

I would venture to guess Hendal obtained a sedative from the healers and used it to keep her from contacting us with her goddess gift. What a despicable thing to do to one so young and innocent.

Enough time passed for Byron to grow weary of waiting. He prepared to ask Grace to locate the rest of his original group when Emilea and Clearshot returned below with Will and Marcus in tow. They rushed over and expressed warm greetings to their Yeluthian ambassador and friend.

"We found these two in here a while ago and decided to look for you," Clearshot explained as they all sat on the staircase.

"According to Grace, the demon got away," Byron admitted, his tone mirroring the defeat displayed on each of their faces. "With everybody hunting Coura because of Aaron's announcement, I'm assuming she'll return to the woods and wait for us. There's nothing else we can do with Hendal threatening others' lives right in front of us."

"Coura," Grace mumbled, drawing their attention and pity.

"I'm sure she's safe," Emilea added with a reassuring smile.

The girl shook her head while growing emotional again. "You do not understand. The demon, it told us about Coura!"

Byron raised an eyebrow at Emilea, though the light mage seemed just as bewildered by the outburst. Neither of them interrupted her after as she proceeded to elaborate as best as she could through her grief. That was when he heard the truth regarding his former student. Once Grace finished, no one could think of anything to say.

Coura is…half-Yeluthian? In all the years I've known her, I never would have guessed. The demon's ploy to manipulate her as much as it did made him sick to his stomach.

"She is gone. I was too distracted to help," Grace concluded before weeping into her hands.

Byron couldn't come up with the words to comfort her or motivate his companions, who continued to helplessly stare at each other.

***

Although flying became dangerous in her condition, Coura soared through the night under the clouds. Her body didn't feel right. The healed areas where she had been wounded were tender, as if they bruised, and the energy in her center fluttered. What arrows dug into her wings wiggled to burn and itch, though the spots wouldn't mend until the shafts had been removed. Shooting pain lanced through her head with every wingbeat, and her sight shifted in and out of focus. The main goal started with reaching Clearshot and Emilea's home; now, it was to land as far into the trees as she could.

Nothing pursued her as far as she could tell, which she considered a blessing given the activity in the capital, and the land below steadily neared as she descended against her will. Inside, she sensed the demonic energy at a standstill with an unknown force.

Coura grazed the treetops while bracing herself for the inevitable impact. When she couldn't stay above any longer, she dropped through the canopy feetfirst, squeezing her eyes shut, pulling her wings against her back, and putting both hands over her face. Branches scratched against her skin and feathers, sending shots of stinging pain everywhere as she slammed into thicker limbs, and her right foot caught on one part before tearing away. Her instincts had her waving both arms and legs in a wild attempt to position herself upright, but it proved a useless effort that lost precious energy. If anything, the trees assisted in preparing her for the imminent landing.

First, her feet connected with the ground, then her back. The crumpled wings beneath her prevented her head from taking as hard of a blow. Only when she stopped moving and heard no other sounds besides her labored breathing did she force her eyes open.

Coura lied between a pair of wide tree trunks in an area full of them without a trail she could make out or an area suitable for her to crawl to and extend her limbs and wings. Because she couldn't assess her physical injuries, she remained where she was, staring up at the hole she made in the canopy. Beyond, the stars twinkled, and soon the nightlife resumed its chatter.

What should I do?

Her mind grew foggy against the pain already beginning to numb her body. At the thought of being alone and immobile, Coura recalled Soirée's confession. The mention of her parents, her lineage, and the life that had been stolen from her brought tears to her eyes, and she didn't stop herself from crying. Beneath the physical and mental damage, the demon's words, and her recent failure to fulfill her assignment, a faint, familiar warmth rose to swaddle her like a blanket.

Glossary

CHARACTERS

Aimes Occaily – an older, former seaman from Clearwater who joins Coura during her venture to defeat the demonic creatures roaming Asteom

Aaron Vanstriann – heir to the kingdom of Asteom and son of King Hernan and Queen Freia

Assistant General Calin – leader of the Dalan base under General Tio

Asteom generals – Tont, Casner, Dillon, Preston, and Tio

Barnelus Dagger-Diver – son of the Sie-Kie's *shimla* and their people's lead hunter

Byron Rinod – a master mage who wields dark magic and acts as Coura's mentor, an instructor at the Magical Arts Academy, and eventually the academy's representative in the palace

Cintra Amaldi – Byron's childhood friend who lives in Fester and works as a seer

Cornelius "Clearshot" Bayporter – a distinguished soldier who specializes in archery and Byron's close friend and comrade

Coura (core-ah) Galdwin – a dark mage and soldier with the ability to wield demonic energy and manifest black wings

Drake Telkanar – a rouge Yeluthian working with the traitor in Verona

Emilea Bayporter – a master mage who wields light energy and acts as the palace's lead healer; she is married to Cornelius and has two children: Mace and Lexie

General Tio – leader of the Dalan base

Grace Zelnar – Yeluthia's ambassador sent to Asteom's capital; possesses a goddess gift that allows her to speak mind to mind with others

Hector Lauple – a rouge Yeluthian working with the traitor in Verona

Hendal Duers – Asteom's high priest

Jaspire Uskinor – leader of the rogue Yeluthian group assisting the traitor in the palace; possesses a goddess gift that allows him to heal from a distance

Lady Katrina Neneme – wife of Lord Donovan Neneme and friend of Emilea

Marcus Tont – an assistant general in Asteom's army and Prince Aaron's closest friend

Marcy Kilguire – a woman from Dala who joins Coura during her venture to defeat the demonic creatures roaming Asteom

Soirée (sw-our-ae) – a demon who appears like an adult woman who forms a soul-bonding with Coura

Thelma Boncarl – a rouge Yeluthian working with the traitor in Verona

Urvin Tsansa – a rouge Yeluthian working with the traitor in Verona

William "Will" Shairp – an herbalist from Clearwater who focuses on medicinal potions

LOCATIONS

Clearwater – the southernmost city in Asteom primarily known for fishing

Dala – a city in southern Asteom housing a military base led by General Tio

East Hoover – northern town housing the Magical Arts Academy

Magical Arts Academy – often referred to as the MAA, this school houses primarily light and dark mage trainees and is located in East Hoover

Medina – a town located in the southwestern section of Asteom and the site of a demonic creature's massacre

Neston – Coura's hometown located in the forest south of East Hoover

Nim-Vala – country north of Asteom

The Valley Beyond – open area between a series of tunnels connecting Dala, Clearwater, and Fester

Verona – Asteom's capital city

Western Woods – an extensive forest covering most of Asteom's western coast and home of the Sie-Kie people

Yeluthia – also referred to as the City of Angels, this kingdom consists of a people who are closely connected with light energy, allowing some to manifest wings and thus giving them the nickname angels

MISCELLANEOUS

Ancestral weapons – items gifted to Asteom's royal family consisting of two, golden swords, daggers, and bows; crafted with a sealing spell to protect against demonic energy

Chi-alve (key-al-ve) – term for soul space or center of power

Goddess gifts – special abilities used by certain Yeluthians involving telepathic communication, long-range healing, portal manifestation, and other spells

Mintelians – a secluded people who live in the Ghurun mountains and value artistic trades

Shalma – Sie-Kie's term for witch, or one who uses magic

Shimla – Sie-Kie's term for chief

Sie-Kie (sih-kai-e) – a tribe living in the Western Woods who value tradition over magic

About the Author

Courtney Lillard was born and raised in Appleton, Wisconsin as the middle of five children. Growing up, she loved music and theater, and participating in both allowed her to develop a deeper interest in the arts. She graduated from Quincy University in 2015 with a B.A. degree in Broadcasting and Public Relations Communications and from Western Illinois University in 2018 with a M.A. degree in Communication Studies.

Aside from writing, Lillard is a fan of reading fantasy stories and the classics. Her other hobbies include cooking, playing video games, and doing puzzles, at least until her cats knock the pieces off the table.